THE FALLEN ALPHA

C.L. LEDFORD

CONTENTS

Copyrights   VI

Dedication   VII

Content Warning   VIII

1. Chapter One   1

2. Chapter Two   7

3. Chapter Three   13

4. Chapter Four   20

5. Chapter Five   27

6. Chapter Six   32

7. Chapter Seven   38

8. Chapter Eight   44

9. Chapter Nine   50

10. Chapter Ten   56

11. Chapter Eleven   62

12. Chapter Twelve   68

13. Chapter Thirteen   75

14.	Chapter Fourteen	81
15.	Chapter Fifteen	88
16.	Chapter Sixteen	94
17.	Chapter Seventeen	100
18.	Chapter Eighteen	106
19.	Chapter Nineteen	111
20.	Chapter Twenty	117
21.	Chapter Twenty-one	122
22.	Chapter Twenty-Two	127
23.	Chapter Twenty-Three	132
24.	Chapter Twenty-Four	137
25.	Chapter Twenty-Five	142
26.	Chapter Twenty-Six	148
27.	Chapter Twenty-Seven	154
28.	Chapter Twenty-Eight	160
29.	Chapter Twenty-Nine	166
30.	Chapter Thirty	171
31.	Chapter Thirty-One	176
32.	Chapter Thirty-Two	181
33.	Chapter Thirty-Three	186
34.	Chapter Thirty-Four	191
35.	Chapter Thirty-Five	196
36.	Chapter Thirty-Six	201

37.	Chapter Thirty-Seven	206
38.	Chapter Thirty-Eight	211
39.	Chapter Thirty-Nine	216
40.	Chapter Forty	221
41.	Chapter Forty-One	226
42.	Chapter Forty-Two	231
43.	Chapter Forty-Three	236
44.	Chapter Forty-Four	241
45.	Chapter Forty-five	246
46.	Chapter Forty-Six	251
47.	Chapter Forty-Seven	256
	Did You Love The Fallen Alpha?	261
	Also By C.L. Ledford	262
	About C. L. Ledford	263

DEDICATION

For all the readers who love an older man in their life.
One that would lay down his life even when he knows you can take care of yourself.
This book is for you.

CONTENT WARNING

This book is an Age Gap Paranormal Romance. The following warnings are inside:
Death of spouse and unborn child, mention of death of unborn child, mention of stillborn, mention of memory of child death, Death, Alcohol consumption, Battle Scenes, Knotting, Breeding, miscarriage, mentions of bullying, poison.

CHAPTER ONE

The night was young as I strolled through the crowd of werewolves. Each of them bowed their head as I passed. The sky was clear, showing off the stars and golden moon. Every year, our pack had this week-long party to bring all the packs in the surrounding area together. It had always been my favorite time, especially since I had come of age to find my mate. This year, however, was the first time I had been Alpha.

My father and mother had stepped down reluctantly to allow me to step in. You may wonder why they were reluctant, right? I was the heir, so what was the problem? Well, I had yet to meet my fated mate, and I had just turned twenty-five. No one had ever heard of an Alpha taking over without a Luna. Yet here I am.

Harlen continued as my Beta since his daughter was only seven. I was hopeful that I would meet my mate at this party since I was getting older. Glancing up, I noticed that Sydnie was in her father's arms as he talked with the Beta from the Obsidian pack. Beside the Beta stood a woman.

At first, I thought she was his mate. Until I realized she shared his same features. Pixie-cut blond hair with a dash of purple color hidden underneath. She hid her face from everyone, and I could tell she wasn't happy to be where she was. The night was warm, but she shivered every so often.

She intrigued me as I made my way up to my beta. Sydnie spotted me and squealed as she threw herself into my arms. The girl glanced up, and I locked eyes with her. She tore her beautiful hazel eyes from mine as I stopped beside Harlen. When we had locked eyes, I had hoped she was my fated, but there was no pull. "Beta Mark, this is Alpha Fin of Dolostone. Alpha, this is Beta Mark. I was just about to come find you to introduce you."

"Alpha, thank you for inviting our small pack to enjoy these festivities. Apologies that our Alpha couldn't make it. His Luna is due any day to have their pup. This is my daughter, Kalila. Kalila?" Beta Mark glanced at his daughter, who kept her head bowed and away from the group. Kalila trembled before she swept her gaze over me. The lights that had been hung shined down on her beautiful face.

"Alpha, it's a pleasure to meet you. If you will excuse me?" Her voice was soft as she bowed her head and left our group before I could respond. Beta Mark sighed before he turned back to me, his face pale.

"I'm very sorry, Alpha, for her behavior. Please do not be angry with her." He looked scared now that his daughter had left him there to deal with what he thought would be an angry alpha. I wasn't angry, just intrigued by this female that didn't want to be here.

"Don't be. She is fine to leave when she wants. Does Alpha Cain know what the pup is?" I told him with a grin to try to settle the tension she had caused. Sydnie squirmed in my arms, and I sat her down on her feet. As soon as they hit the ground, she was off into the crowd, and I laughed. The girl couldn't handle being in one place for very long. She was going to make a great beta someday.

"Thank you, Alpha. She is not herself today. No, they wanted this one to be a surprise since they had lost their first heir fifteen years ago." The sadness in his voice didn't go unnoticed. It had to be hard to lose a pup.

I nodded and excused myself from the group. The Obsidian pack had it rough over the years. It had taken their Luna and Alpha years to conceive, only to lose the child. I had often wondered why my parents didn't try for another. Was I that bad of a pup?

Kalila didn't talk to anyone as she made her way through the crowd of wolves. I stayed just far enough back to watch her. She wasn't my mate, but the misery that poured off her hurt my heart. What could have happened to her? I stayed in the crowd staring at her standing at one of the multiple food tables on the patio. Kalila's arms wrapped around herself as she waited for the red-headed wolf to finish cooking the vegetables in front of her.

Another male approached her, and she shied away from him just as she did with me and Harlen. I didn't know this wolf, so he had to be from another pack. He continued to push himself onto her until I couldn't help but intervene. I pushed through the crowd and went up to them. Grabbing the black-haired wolf by his t-shirt collar, I pulled him away from her and stepped in between them as I shoved him backward. "Is there a reason you're hounding her?"

"Sorry, Alpha. I just wanted to get to know her." The male bowed his head as he waited for me to dismiss him. Others around us stopped what they had been doing and the wolves from my pack looked on with hopeful eyes. They thought that she was my fated, and that I was protecting her from another male.

"You shouldn't be apologizing to me. Kalila should be that recipient." Crossing my arms over my chest as I waited for him to look up. I could be imposing at times even though I didn't like to use my alpha abilities on others. But it pissed me off when male wolves wouldn't leave a female alone. That wasn't how it was in my pack and while the others were here, that's how they would act in my territory.

He nodded and then stood straight as he glanced around me to Kalila. "I am very sorry. It won't happen again."

The whimper behind me spurred me to nod to the male, and he left quickly. Turning to Kalila, I realized she was silently crying. I lifted her chin, bringing her gaze to mine. "Is everything okay?"

"Yes. Thank you for the help." Her hazel eyes swam with tears as she held my gaze. Something was tearing her apart as she tried to put on a brave face. Glancing behind her, I took the plate the wolf had finished for her. I nodded to him in thanks and ushered her with me. Through the tables in the grass, away from all the others.

"I know you don't know me. But I can't help but notice you're hurting. Is there anything anyone can do to help?" I placed her plate of food on the table and urged her to sit. Plopping down beside her, I watched her pick up her fork and play with the food before her.

"It's my mate. He rejected me before we came here." She never met my gaze as she spoke to me. Her soft tone was just barely audible with my wolf hearing. "My father doesn't know."

"Why wouldn't you tell your father? How old are you?" I was curious. It had been years since I stopped searching for mine. All I could take from that is that she was either dead or not born yet. Which wasn't uncommon for wolves since we could potentially live for a long time. I couldn't understand why a mate would reject their fated. A fated was a blessing from the Moon Goddess herself. A blessing that I had been waiting for for seven years.

"Because if I told him, I would be weak in his eyes. I'm twenty-two and mateless." Kalila finally glanced over at me with her hazel eyes. I grinned at her before I took her hand with my large one. She didn't pull away.

"The male that rejected you is weak. No one should think you're the weak one." I told her. I still couldn't wrap my mind around why someone would reject her. She was gorgeous.

"Not in my little pack. I'm not next in line to take over for my father. He wanted power," she answered as she took a small bite of her food.

"Well, try to enjoy yourself while you are here." I stood and kissed the back of her hand. The rush of color that went to her cheeks made me smile. I turned and walked away from her to continue to mingle with the other packs and talk with the other alphas that had come.

After that first night, Kalila and I hit it off. I discovered she was intelligent and fierce as I came to know her. She had everything I wanted in a mate and more. It felt right to be near her. So when the last night of the party arrived, I had to ensure she would stay with me to lead my pack.

When I told my parents what I was doing, they were upset. They were fated and didn't like that I was choosing my mate. Yes, I was throwing away my chance at true happiness with my mate, but I felt like I would never find her, and Kalila was right here. So why not?

Because you could anger the Moon Goddess with this. Aloysius was always trying to lead me in the right direction. But I was lonely, and I wanted to be with someone. And not just any person. I wanted Kalila. Aloysius rolled his eyes while I strolled down the pack house steps.

I searched for Beta Mark, Kalila's father, through the crowd of wolves preparing to leave back to their own territory. For this to work, I needed him to be on board with this. But I didn't know if she had finally told him that her mate had rejected her. Spotting him conversing with my Beta, I hurried over to them. Harlen turned to me, a grin on his face, "Hey, Alpha, what's wrong?"

"Nothing. Beta Mark, do you have a moment?" Grinning from one Beta to the other, I motioned for him to follow. Beta Mark nodded, stepping away from Harlen to come with me. We walked in silence, the nerves threatening to bubble over.

"Alpha Fin, is there something that I can help you with?" He glanced over at me as he cleared his throat and rubbed the back of his neck. The nervousness coming from him was not unnoticed by me.

"I'd like to talk to you about your daughter." I told him as I stopped in my tracks beside the dark river which reflected the stars on its surface. It was one of the natural waterways that ran through my territory.

"What has she done now, Alpha Fin?" The tremble in his voice brought my attention back to him. The man had sweat racing down his face. His pupils were dilated as he stared at me. He thought she had upset me.

"She's not in any trouble. I want to make her my chosen mate," I told him as I held his gaze. His jaw slackened and his blue eyes widened. He wasn't expecting that answer.

"Why would you want my daughter to be Luna? Don't you want to wait for your mate?"

"I've been to every pack around here, and she was not at any of those. So, I'd like to take your daughter as a chosen since her mate rejected her." Beta Mark turned his back on me before he paced in front of me.

"I thought something like that had happened. She was fine one moment and then sulking the next. Does she want to be your chosen?" He faced me, his arms crossed over his chest. The fierceness in his eyes reminded me of hers.

"I haven't asked her. But I wanted to ask you first. I guess to get your blessing."

"If she accepts, I would be fine with you choosing her, Alpha Fin." Beta Mark nodded.

We made our way back to the crowd of wolves that were saying their goodbyes. Kalila had made friends with a few mated females from my pack while she was here. I spotted her talking to Jade and a few other she-wolves from my pack. The dress that she wore hugged her in all the right places as she held her suitcase. I chuckled since hopefully that bag and her would be staying here with me.

Making my way up to her, I place a hand on her shoulder. Kalila glanced up at me and smiled before she turned to face me. "Can I borrow you for a moment?"

"Of course, Alpha." She sat the suitcase down and turned with me.

I led her away from the crowd and down a path through the woods to my favorite spot on my territory. Kalila strolled beside me, glancing around at the different flowers and trees that lined our route to our destination. I had never brought anyone to this spot, as I wanted to wait to bring my mate. In a way, I still was, only I was bringing my chosen instead of my fated. Aloysius whimpered in my head, but I ignored him.

When we arrived at the waterfall, a soft gasp sounded beside me, and I glanced over. Kalila's hand hovered over her mouth as she stared at the thundering water racing to the silent lake below. I had the same reaction when I first found this spot as a teen. Knowing that one day I would share this beautiful sight with the one I would spend my life with.

I took her hand and steered her further around the lake. Our footsteps echoed off the rocks on the mountainside. To say I was a little nervous about this conversation was moot. She could reject being my chosen. It wouldn't kill me if she did. Not like if a fated rejected you. Kalila didn't die, so it might not kill too many of us.

We continued around the lake until we reached the other side of the waterfall. The crashing of the falling water sprayed us with rainbow droplets as the moon reflected off the clear liquid. She was such a beautiful woman. I couldn't figure out why her mate would reject her.

Kalila spun to face me, her eyes wide with wonder. "What is this place?"

"This is my favorite place on my territory. I stumbled upon it when I was younger and vowed to only bring the special person in my life to see it with me." I told her. The realization that swept over her features made me chuckle.

"But I'm not your fated mate. She could still be out there. Fin, what are you trying to tell me?" Her eyes searching mine as I tried to think of what to say.

"I know my fated could still be out there, but she could also be dead. Kalila, I'd like for you to be my chosen mate. I'd love for you to stand by my side and be my Luna of Dolostone pack." I stood there in front of her as she stared at me. Tears formed in her eyes as her hands covered her mouth and nose.

"Do you really mean this? Fin, we have only known each other for a week. What about my father?" She dropped her hands and stepped forward, resting her head on my chest. I pulled her close as I wrapped my arms around her small, delicate frame.

"I really do mean this, and I've already spoken to your father. He is fine with me choosing you if you accept. Besides, why does it matter that we have only known each other for a week? I have my whole life to spend with you, learning more about you each and every day."

Kalila pulled away from me to stare up into my eyes. All she was going to find was the truth because she was the one I wanted, and I knew she would be good for the pack. She smiled at me and then nodded. "Okay, I'll be your chosen."

CHAPTER TWO

I sat in my office going through the pack expenses when a knock came upon the door. Kalila was out shopping with Jade and Harmony, so I knew the person behind them wasn't my mate. It had been two months since I announced that Kalila would be my Luna and had her ceremony. She made me happy every day.

"Come in."

The door opened, and my uncle strolled in. Uncle Wade came back to live with our pack after his mate died. Setting down my pen, I shut the books as he approached my desk. My uncle liked to put his nose in matters that he had no business being in. His hard eyes latched onto mine, and he tried to smile. Which he didn't pull off. He was one of the people in my pack that didn't like that I took Kalila as my chosen instead of waiting for my fated.

"What brings you to see me, uncle?"

Uncle Wade plopped down in one of my high-backed leather chairs and crossed his leg over his knee. The black pants tightened around his legs and thighs as he got comfortable. He stared at me for the longest before he grinned at me. My uncle never really liked that I had taken over without a mate at my side.

"Well, nephew, I've noticed an influx of rogues at our borders. Something that hasn't happened in some time. Do you have a plan in place to handle them?" he pulled his gaze from mine to look at his hand and nails.

Inwardly, I growled. My wolf Alloysius didn't like what he was implying. I sat up straighter in my leather chair, regarding him with a glare. "The pack warriors know their orders. I know this isn't the reason you are here. What do you want, uncle?"

"Always one to know a bullshitter. That's your father's side in you." Uncle Wade shifted in his chair, swapping his crossed leg with the other. "What were you thinking, taking a chosen mate? You could've been stronger with a fated."

"Uncle, I don't have to explain why I did what I did. The pack is fine with her, and she is a strong wolf. If this is all you want of me, you can leave my office." I told him as I leaned back in my chair. My uncle stood from his seat and bowed his head before turning on his heel and heading out the door.

Sometimes I believed that he was after my pack. Especially now that I had chosen my mate. Most of the pack loved her, and that is all that mattered. She was everything that I could've needed in a mate.

Quartzite's Alpha had called me, wanting to arrange a meeting with me, him, and the Rhyolite's pack alpha. This was nothing new since they tried to form an alliance when my father was Alpha, and he refused to meet with them. I thought it was stupid not to. Why not have the support of the other two large packs in the region?

This was another thing that I felt like my uncle had sway over my father. As much as he told me I was like my father in spotting a bullshitter, my father couldn't from a mile away. Uncle Wade seemed to want to alienate us from the others. But with me leading this pack, he would never be in my ear whispering his lies. I picked up the phone on my desk and called the Quartzite pack. Someone picked up on the other end. "Hello?"

The soft voice of a little girl came through the receiver. At first, I thought I might have called the wrong number. "Is Alpha Roman there?"

"Oh, you have a very big voice! Just like my daddy! Are you an Alpha too!" The little girl giggled as she breathed in the speaker. Some part of me wanted that someday. To have a little mini-me running around or a mini Kalila.

"Yes, I am. Do you know where your daddy is?" I asked her again, a little more gently. She giggled again just as a door opened on the other side of the phone. The sound of footsteps resonated through the phone.

"Amora! I'm expecting an important phone call! Why are you in my office?" I heard a stern male voice on the other side. The little pup giggled again as the footsteps came closer to their destination.

"I was just talking to the other Alpha. He said he needed to talk to you." She said sweetly. I had a feeling that little pup could get away with murder. A sigh and another giggle sounded out as the phone was exchanged.

"Hello? This is Alpha Roman." The gruff voice of the Alpha came on the phone.

"Hello, Alpha Roman. This is Alpha Fin from Dolostone. You had wanted to arrange a meeting between my pack, yours, and Rhyolite. I would be more than willing to come to this meeting. When would you like to set this up?" I asked him as I stood to stare out the window. Kalila and Jade had just made it to the packhouse and unloaded the stuff along with some warriors. I swear the woman bought things for the rest of the pack before herself.

"Ah, Alpha Fin! Yes, we can meet in two days if that is okay with you. I'm sure Alpha Nero would be delighted to meet with you. Hopefully, we can come to an alliance."

"Of course, that will be fine. Where would this meeting take place?" The smile on Kalila's face brought a grin to my lips. She was so beautiful standing there under the brightly lit sky.

"We will have it here in my pack." The groan of a chair on the other side reverberated through the receiver.

"That's fine. I will see you in two days." We said our goodbyes, and I returned the receiver to its holder. Hopefully, with an alliance with the next two largest packs, we can build a better comradeship with other packs in the region.

I walked into the brightly lit dining room, where Kalila and the omegas were standing around the table, making up the following weeks' dinner plans for the pack. She always wanted to make sure that we tried something different each night. The omegas bowed their heads as I approached them, and Kalila turned to me.

With her sudden movement, I noticed the subtle change in her scent. I grinned as I tried to figure it out. As soon as I reached her, I pulled her in and kissed her. She never seemed to mind my public displays of affection. If I didn't know any better, I would bet that she loved it just as much as I did. Kalila softly pushed me away as she giggled. "Fin! There are young eyes in the room!"

"Don't worry, love. I won't do much more than kiss you. How was shopping? Did you get anything for yourself?" I let her step back from me, and she took a deep breath. As she fixed her hair that I had ruffled.

"Yes, and no. More like for the both of us. But mostly for the pack. I got the nursery some new blankets and onesies. And I got some new training mats for the training wolves." Like I said, she only really thinks about the pack.

"Kalila."

She smiled at me and then continued her discussion with the omegas. The doors opened, and I saw Harlen coming in. He didn't look too happy. Actually, he looked pissed. He bowed his head to Kalila and me before he straightened up. "Harlen what's the matter?"

"That damn uncle of yours is trying to change your orders to the border patrol. He thinks that your plan isn't good enough." Harlen snarled, his face red as an apple. I had only seen him this mad before when I was a teen.

I took a deep breath before turning to Kalila and kissing her on the temple. Motioning for him to lead the way. My uncle really didn't get the concept that he wasn't the Alpha. Harlen led me through the doors and out to where the leaders of the patrols were at. The sun was still high in the sky and the weather was warm enough to still allow the younger wolves to swim. A soft breeze brought with it the smell of peony and cedar while it ruffled my hair and clothes. The scent had always been a favorite of mine.

Each of the leaders shook their heads as I made my way toward them on the dirt walkway. I could tell my uncle was getting mad at them for refusing to obey him. His hand gestures were getting more and more erratic. But they would never obey him unless he took over, which wouldn't happen unless he challenged or killed me.

"Uncle!" I bellowed, bringing everyone's attention to me. The leaders of the patrols dropped to one knee, both fists on the ground, as my uncle spun on his heel. I shook my head. I hated this salute.

"Ah. Nephew! I was just telling these incompetent leaders that you wanted to change the plan." I swear that he had to have something wrong with his brain. Like he was getting dementia in his older age, which was unlikely since we were wolves.

"Uncle, I didn't tell you to come to them and change the plan. My plan is solid. Please stop harassing them. They aren't going to deviate from their orders." I was being nicer to him than he deserved, that was for sure. Once I was stable in my pack, he would be gone. One way or the other and my father would have no say.

"Of course, nephew. I thought that was what you would've wanted. I will see you at dinner." He bowed a little too dramatically for my tastes as he left. Rolling my eyes, I turned to the leaders, still on their knees with their heads down.

"Rise, you don't need to do that. I'm not my father. If my uncle tries to do that again, let me know as soon as possible. Luckily Beta Harlen was able to get to me in time." I motioned for them to get up. It always unnerved me the way my father wanted them to bow to him. Some of it made me think it was my uncle feeding it to my dad in his ear.

"Yes, Alpha." They spoke in unison as they stood. Each one had been with my father for as long as I could remember, and each one was good at their job.

"You're dismissed. Thank you." I turned with Harlen at my flank and headed back to the packhouse.

The walk was silent as we headed back. It was always nice to walk with my Beta. His knowledge and years helped me this past year, and I knew it would in the future as well. I never had to worry about him making decisions on his own without letting me know first.

When we arrived back in the dining room, Kalila and the beta female Bella were sitting there talking with each other at one of the tables. I was glad that they got along. "She's with pup."

I spun to stare at him, trying to find out which one he was talking about. He laughed and then slapped my back. "My Bella, she's with pup. I'm hoping it's a boy this time."

"That would be fun. A mini you running around?" I laughed as I returned my gaze back to Kalila. What would she look like round with pup? Maybe one day I would find out.

Kalila turned to me with a smile. I could live with that smile for the rest of my life. Choosing her was the right thing to do. I could feel it in my soul. Sitting beside her, I leaned over and kissed her temple before grabbing her hand in mine. "Were you able to handle the problem?"

"Sort of. There will have to be something done before it gets better. But let's eat. We will talk about this later." I kissed her hand before grabbing my glass to take a drink of the dark liquid.

Kalila nodded as we waited for the food to come out from the kitchens. I had a strict rule that the kitchen staff ate first and then the patrols since they were just coming in and going out. Everyone seemed to like that arrangement, other than my uncle, of course. He thought that since he was of the Alpha bloodline he should eat first.

After dinner and a shower, I stepped into our room and spotted Kalila sitting on the bed, her hands in her lap and her head down. Going up to her, I pulled her into my arms and took a deep whiff of her scent. It had slightly changed. I didn't imagine it. There could be two different times when a female's scent changed. When she was in heat or when she was with pup.

Kalila hadn't gone into heat since we had mated; with her going into heat, it would be easier to get pregnant. But that was something we hadn't talked about yet. Kalila nuzzled into my bare chest as I sat on the bed with her straddled on my lap. Her silk nightie riding up to her hips as my hands played with her thighs. The towel keeping us apart. "Kalila, are you going into heat?"

She jerked from me, her hazel eyes wide as she stared at me. Kalila pulled her lower lip between her teeth and softly chewed on it. I had noticed that it was a nervous tick with her. Chuckling, I caressed her cheek and ran my hands through her blonde hair. It had gotten longer since she had been here. Almost touching her shoulders.

Kalila used her fingers to trace the lines of my muscles. I loved her touch and how it made me feel as she slipped her hand beneath the towel. She gripped my cock, using her other hand to undo the towel. Her mouth mere centimeters from mine as she nuzzled my nose. The silk nightie grazed my chest.

Slipping my hands up to her ass, I realized that she wasn't wearing any panties with it. Kalila knew this was what turned me on. That and her sleeping on her stomach with her leg cocked up. Mhmm. I flipped her underneath me on the bed and the towel fell to the floor in my haste to change position. "Love, you didn't answer me. I need to know. Because we haven't talked about pups. And I don't want to assume you are ready."

"Well, that worry would be a little too late, Fin. You're going to be a daddy."

I stopped mid-kiss to her neck and jerked up to see her face. My heart racing in its cage. Kalila's brows furrowed, and she chewed her bottom lip again. Did I just hear her correctly? Did she just tell me that I was going to be a dad? "Say that again."

"You're going to be a daddy?" She shrugged as she started to chew the inside of her cheek.

"You're not joking? You're carrying my pup inside you?" She nodded, a small grin forming on her lips as she stared at me. I pulled her flush to me and hugged her. This was the happiest moment of my life. "Kalila, you've just made me the happiest wolf in this pack!"

CHAPTER THREE

I woke up just as the sun started to rise above the mountains. Kalila was snuggled against my side. Her soft breaths fanned over my chest as I lay there thinking back to last night. The thought of being a dad was amazing. It made me feel lighter than I had ever been in my life.

What I wanted to do was get up from this bed. Go to the balcony and shout it out to the pack that an heir is coming! That's what I wanted to do. But I was content to wait until Kalila told me to announce it. I pulled her in closer as I took in her scent. It was changing even more as time went on.

Planting a kiss on her forehead, I got up from the king bed. The silence in the packhouse was pleasant as I stared at myself in the bathroom mirror. I didn't look any different, but today was. It was the beginning of something new and would change my life as I knew it.

Kalila's arms snaked around my waist as I stood there. I smiled, covering her hand with mine as she nuzzled into my back. "Are you okay, Fin?"

"Of course. Why wouldn't I be?" I glanced up as she came into the mirror with me. Her bright hazel eyes shining back at me. Turning to her, I picked her up and sat her on the counter. Wedging myself between her legs. Our naked skin touching, making me want her before we went about our day.

"Because, like you said last night when you thought I was in heat. We hadn't talked about pups, and then I told you I was pregnant." The worry in her hazel eyes flowed through me as I stared at her.

"No, love. You've made me the happiest wolf in this pack. I don't care what anyone says. We were fated to be together. If we weren't then why bless us with a pup? We will have to tell my parents though. Your scent is changing quickly." I nuzzled her nose and then kissed the tip. Making her giggle. I loved the way she giggled.

"When are you wanting to tell them?" Kalila nuzzled me back, her hands roaming my arms. Sending goosebumps following her hands.

"I was thinking today at lunch since I have a meeting with Rhyolite and Quartzite Alphas tomorrow. You think that would be okay?" Kalila nodded and smiled. I kissed her lips, pulling her ass to the counter's edge.

"I'll have to tell my father too."

"Go ahead, call your dad. I'll let my dad and mom know to meet us in my office." She nodded again and slid off the counter, heading into the bedroom. I watched as she left, that beautiful ass sashaying in front of me. Before searching for my dad in our mind link.

Dad, I need you and mom in my office at lunch. You and her only.

Sure, son. Is everything okay? The worry in his link pressed to mine.

Yes, dad. Just need to talk to you and mom. I chuckled as I replaced the towel on the bar.

As you wish. It was unnerving when he said things like this but that was what he wanted so I didn't worry too much about it.

I cut the link and began my morning routine. Heading back out of the bathroom, I went into the closet and pulled out some jeans and a T-shirt. Slipping on my shoes, I exited the bedroom I shared with Kalila. Descending the mahogany wood stairs, I felt even lighter as I reached the bottom. Wolves were heading to their jobs within the pack and bowed their head as I passed.

Entering the large kitchen, I followed the delicious scent of banana pancakes. A stack of them sat on the large marble island, waiting for the incoming patrols. No one would notice if one was gone, right? I grabbed one quickly and headed back out to the front of the packhouse. A giggle sounded out behind me. Which brought a smile to my lips. Everyone was having a wonderful day.

Rolling up the cooked batter before taking a bite out of the sweet dough, I strolled down to the training fields. Pups in training were wrestling and fighting, trying to over-match their opponents. Starting them a little young was my dad's doing, and I felt that it was a good thing for pups to get their energy out. At least it gave them something to do other than sitting in front of a screen fighting with fictional characters. Besides, I was one of the first to start young like these pups here. There's no reason why they couldn't do the same.

When I became Alpha, I allowed the girls to join in the training if they wanted. Some of the girls did, and they didn't back down from the boys. They fought tooth and nail to be just like their male peers. A couple of the girls were even better than some of the boys, and I chuckled at that. No one would be able to tell me that girls couldn't protect themselves if they really wanted to.

I continued to watch them as Sydnie came from behind me and ran down the steps to her little friend from school. She was always excited to be able to play with others, and I could tell that she would be one little girl to watch in the training ring. Harlen didn't baby her much. He taught her to be independent, but she was his baby girl, and he would kill someone if they hurt her. I would too for that matter, I would give my life for anyone in this pack.

Making my way down to the patrol house, I noticed that some of last night's patrols were coming in. I spotted Zac as he bumped fists with another warrior around his size. He and I used to be friends in school, but when he found his mate, he never really had time for our other friends or me. Zac had a full house with all the pups he and his mate had. I would really like that one day. In a way I envied him.

"Alpha, you're up early." One of the deltas, named Grant, approached me as the morning patrol wolves headed out. These wolves were in top form as they raced to the territory line. They ran most of the day keeping an eye on the territory lines.

"Yeah, just came down to check up. My uncle hasn't been making a nuisance of himself anymore, has he?" I glanced around to see if any of the other leaders were here today.

"No, sir. He hasn't been back down yet. I do have to report that we did sight a rogue last night. He barely got away. But he is fast." The flicker of the wolf's eyes told me that he was upset that the rogue was able to get away from him and his team.

"Thanks. Keep a heads up and report anything else that might be worrisome."

"Yes, Alpha." Grant turned and headed into the packhouse to grab some breakfast. Everything was like it should be. Beautiful sunny day, the breeze blowing, keeping it at just the right temperature.

Once Kalila was further along, we would tell the entire pack. Granted, the ones near her the most would notice the change in her scent. But right now, only our parents need to know. I continued down into our little town. I used to run through this place as a child with my friends, and one day, so would my little one. The stone roadway under its feet as it raced to the ice cream shop or the candy store and then he or she would be in training.

Female she-wolves were talking to each other, holding newly born pups against them. Some feeding them, others showing them off to the others. Everywhere I looked, I saw females either with pup or recently born pups.

I spotted Bella lugging some bags up the sidewalk and went to help her. She didn't need to be carrying that much.

"Alpha! You don't have to do that." Her breathlessness told me that yes, I needed to. She was starting to show.

"Don't worry, Bella. How are you feeling?" I chuckled as I threw them over my shoulder.

"I'm doing fine, Alpha, thank you. It's been a long time since I saw you in the streets at this time of day." She giggled as she glanced up at me. Bella was one she-wolf besides Kalila, who I allowed them to make eye contact with me.

"Good. Yes it has, I have been away from the town for far too long." We walked back up to the pack house in silence. The sun was high in the sky, meaning lunch was getting nearer and that meant that I would be telling my parents that they would be grandparents.

"Alpha, are you okay?" I glanced down at Bella. She gave me her 'there's something you're hiding and aren't telling me' looks. I chuckled as I opened the door to the packhouse.

"Yes, Bella. Just have to talk to the parents today."

Bella placed her hand on my forearm and smiled. "You will do fine. Whatever you have to tell them, everything will be okay."

I nodded, and she took the bags I had in my hands and headed for her and Harlen's room. Harlen was lucky to find this woman. She was definitely his other half.

Continuing my way down the recently painted hallway to my office, I noticed the doors were cracked, and my mother's voice floated out to me. Pushing my way into the room, they became quiet when they spotted me.

Kalila was sitting on the couch, and my mother sat with her. Holding her hands on her knees. My dad stood by the window, which had also become my habit when I became Alpha. The only thing I could think of why we did it was because we spent so much time here and not with the pack.

I closed the door behind me and walked up to the front of the desk. Leaning up against the furniture, I reached out my hand to Kalila. Untangling her hands from my mother. She came up to me and stood by my side. A worried smile on her face. "Can you come sit down, father?"

My father rounded the desk and sat in one of the chairs in front of me. I glanced between them both before I pulled Kalila closer to me. Her hand wrapped around my waist as her heart raced. "So I brought you both in here because we have something exciting to tell you."

"Well, spit it out, Fin. Don't keep us in suspense." My mother chuckled as she leaned forward on the couch. She had come to respect my decision about making Kalila my mate. I had never seen my mother lay her elbows on her knees. That wasn't how she was brought up.

"You will soon have a little grandpup running around," I told them just as the doors opened and my uncle entered the room. The gleam in his eyes told me he had overheard what I said. He was the last person in the pack that I wanted to learn that I had a pup coming.

My mother jumped up and hugged Kalila, and my father came up and shook my hand. He still wasn't too keen on my decision but he was civil about it. Uncle Wade stood by the door with a sneer. I didn't like how he acted over the last couple of months. "Congrats, nephew! A pup is wonderful news for the pack."

"Isn't it, brother! How about a cigar to celebrate?" My father turned to the bookshelves and pulled a decorative box down. I didn't expect him to be excited about it. Opening the lid, he held it out to me and then his brother. Uncle Wade took one and held it in his hand as he stared at Kalila. I didn't miss the evil glint in his eyes.

"Why don't we get some lunch. When I get back, I will announce the pregnancy to the rest of the pack," I told them as I pulled Kalila to the front door. She glanced up to me with a confused look and I shook my head at her.

I really needed to learn to lock that stupid door. No, I shouldn't have to. I was Alpha, people should knock to be able to enter that door. Whether they were family or not. Aloysius snarled in my head with agreement. He had never liked my uncle either.

"What do you mean when you get back? Where are you going, son?" My mother caught up with us as we exited the room. Her hand landing lightly on my forearm.

"I'm going to Quartzite pack to ally with them and Rhyolite tomorrow." I told her as I headed down the hall. I made sure to say it loud enough that my uncle would hear me.

"That is a bad idea, nephew. They just want to take the neutral land, and the only way to do that is to make you believe you are allied with them." My uncle chuckled behind me.

"Well, I think it would be a good thing to be allied with the other two larger packs," I growled as we headed into the dining hall. My good mood from this morning was slowly dissipating as my uncle continued to butt his nose in.

Lunch was a protracted affair as I sat there with my mate and parents. Uncle Wade had left after one plate, but I didn't like that he knew about the pregnancy. Bella was on the other side of Kalila, talking with her. Harlen kept glancing over at me from the corner of his eye. I had half a mind to send one of my best trackers to follow Uncle Wade.

It didn't help that he knew I was leaving early in the morning to meet up with the other two packs. The lightness that I felt this morning was no longer there. A drowning feeling kept pulling me down, like something terrible was going to happen.

All the wolves in this room were laughing and having a good time. But I felt out of place in their joy. I felt like it was dimmer than it really was. Kalila's hand slipped into mine under the table, and I glanced over at her hazel eyes. She smiled and went back to talking to Bella. The pit in my stomach only grew more prominent.

⋅◆○◆⋅

Alpha! Rogues at the border!

I sat up in bed at the urgent mind link. My heart racing as the mind link had woken me from a deep sleep. Turning to Kalila, I shook her awake, and she woke suddenly, her eyes bulging as she glanced around the dark room. Jumping from the bed, I pulled on some shorts and threw Kalila one of my shirts. "Hurry, love, I need you to get to the shelter."

Kalila scrambled to her feet, tugging the shirt on and coming to me. We hurried down to the first-floor, omegas were rushing to and fro as they helped she-wolves and pups to the shelter behind the kitchen. A dark-haired wolf came up to us and reached for Kalila. "Alpha, let me take her to the shelter."

I nodded and then placed a crushing kiss on my mate's lips before letting her go. Harlen and my dad were on the porch. More warriors were amassing in front of the packhouse. I stepped up in front of my father and Beta. "Dolostone pack! Rogues are coming onto our land! What are we going to do about that?"

"Protect what's ours!" They shouted in unison, some allowing their wolf to the surface. Howls rose in the distance.

"Good, now let's show them why they shouldn't be at our borders!" I shifted, and the warriors followed suit. Running full speed to the sounds of fighting, I mind-linked sections of my group. *Left flank, head to the south. Right flank, head to the north. The rest of you follow me!*

Wolves veered to their destinations as I continued to the heat of the battle. When I got to the fighting, I didn't even stop to look at how many were attacking. I went headfirst into the action. Tearing into wolves that weren't part of my pack. Blood and fur littering the ground in my wake.

My teeth sunk deep into a wolf's neck, and I shook him until he was limp. Another wolf jumped onto my back, slashing my shoulders and back to pieces. Rolling, I threw him and jumped to my feet, ready for his next attack. My fur was matted with blood from all the wolves I had killed. But there were still white patches through the red. The wolf before me licked his lips and swished his tail as he stared at me. That deep feeling of dread swelling in my stomach. I lunged at him because to me he was part of the reason my mate was in danger right now.

FIN! Kalila's voice screamed in my head. Fear rushed into me as I felt her panic. The brown wolf snapped his jaws as I turned and ran from the battle back to the undefended packhouse. My heart racing with my thundering paws. Pushing myself to get back to her quicker than when I left her.

Fin hurry! He's going to kill me! Her inner voice begged me. I could hear the tears in her tone.

I dug my paws into the ground, sprinting faster than I ever thought I could run. As I rounded the corner of the house, I spotted her. She was being held by her blonde hair. Blood on her skin and clothes. I couldn't tell if it was hers or someone else's. Tears ran down her face as she struggled to get away. My gaze went behind her, and I snarled.

My uncle was the one holding her. A sadistic grin appeared on his face as his eyes flashed his wolf's. I skidded to a stop; the pebbles flying around me and digging into my paws.

"Just in time, nephew! I don't think you will need this little thing where I'm sending you." His hands went on either side of Kalila's face. Her hazel eyes were full of tears and sorrow.

I love you, Fin!

And just like that, he twisted. Breaking her neck right in front of me.

CHAPTER FOUR

Kalila's body crumpled onto the stone steps, rolling to a stop in front of me. I nudged her shoulder with my muzzle, a whimper escaping from my throat. Kalila's hazel eyes were still open as they stared at me. Accusing me that I didn't protect her and our pup.

The knowing she was no longer on this earth with me came when the snap of our bond broke along with her neck. While my heart shattered inside my chest. Anger like I had never felt surged through my body. I wanted blood, but not just anyone's, I wanted his blood.

My eyes snapped up at my uncle, and my lips pulled back off my fangs as I stalked forward. He was going to die for taking my family from me. The family that I had chosen for myself. Not a mythical goddess. Not some bond that was waiting for me. She and the little pup growing inside her were my chosen family.

Uncle Wade knew what he was doing when he brought me to this point. The sadistic smirk on his face brought me closer. I wanted his blood on this stone porch just like hers, and that was what I intended to do. Lunging, Wade shifted and met me in the air. We fought, tearing chunks of flesh and fur from each other's bodies. Blood spilled over the once pristine river stones as teeth sunk into bodies.

I didn't know if I would make it out alive, but at the moment, I didn't care. All that was on my mind was his death. My uncle ceasing to live was the goal because he took them away from me. Everything around me went quiet as our battle continued. The only thing I could hear in my head was her panicked voice as I stood there. Doing nothing to get to her before he had made his move.

Not only was I mad at him, but I was also mad at myself because I couldn't protect her. The one person that I was supposed to have given my life. Instead, she gave her life for mine. At least for now, I allowed the fury to take over me. I wanted his blood for taking them from me.

Aloysius demanded retribution now since Wade had taken his own pup from him. A life for a life, and I was all too willing to surrender to Aloysius, letting him take the life of my uncle. A small cry brought me out of my blood lust. Turning my massive head blood and saliva slung from my jaws, I spotted Sydnie on her knees beside Kalila. Her small face was full of tears.

Sharp claws swiped up along my belly, and I snarled as Harlen came up and grabbed her. Taking her away from the scene and the battle between my uncle and me. Wade rammed into me and sent me through the air before crashing onto the ground. My gaze snapped up just before Uncle Wade pulled back his large paw. Everything went black.

My surroundings were blurry as I sat up. Aloysius sat deep in my mind. Things started to become clearer the longer I blinked. The air was damp and musty, which informed me of exactly where I was at. How long I was in the dungeons under my territory, I didn't know. But the memory of Wade snapping Kalila's neck tortured my mind. I was too late. I should've known he had something to do with the rogue attack.

I kept my head low as the squeal of the door echoed off the empty brick walls. Steady footsteps made their way to my bars. His familiar scent made me lift my head and Harlen came into view, his face haggard as he stood there staring at me. "Did you know this was going to happen?"

"No, Alpha. But I need to get you out of here. He is planning on killing you tomorrow. You have to live." Harlen's statement brought my thoughts to how long I was out. I ran my hands over my face as he continued to stare.

"How long have I been out?" I stood, realizing that I was completely naked. Not like he hadn't seen me. Hell, the man was there when I was born.

"Three days, Alpha."

"Why do you keep calling me alpha. I'm no longer your alpha Harlen." I grumbled as I paced the cell. Would it be so bad for me to die and join Kalila and our unborn pup? I didn't think so. It wasn't like my mate was out there.

"Because you will always be my alpha. Wade was never in line for the title and will never be alpha. You have too many loyal pack members. Now come on, I have a pair of shorts and a shirt for you. You need to get out of here." The door to my cell opened, and Harlen came up to me with clothes. Staring between him and the garments in his hands, I backed away. I didn't want to run, I wanted to die and be again with my mate and child.

"I don't run, Harlen." I crossed my arms and stood there waiting for him to turn around and leave me to my fate. The glare that he sent my way was something I had never seen him do before in my life. It would have scared me into submission if I were a lesser wolf.

"Listen here, boy! I know you think Kalila's death was your fault, but it wasn't. You have other lives that need to be saved from this tyrant, and if not you, then who? So, get your ass in these clothes, and you get out of here until we can get you back in power." Harlen had stalked up to me, making himself look bigger than he was while he stuck his finger in my face and he shoved the clothes in my hands, "If you make it to where my daughter, mate, and unborn pup have to stay in her family's pack, I swear I will never forgive you."

Harlen must've thought fast at the decision. I personally was glad that Sydnie would be fine, and so would his mate. *Would it be too bad to run? So that we can regroup?* Aloysius asked me as I mulled things over. If I ran, would the loyal wolves think I was a coward? Or would they wait until I came back to take back my title? My eyes locked with his, and I nodded. "Fine, I'll leave. But you must stay so the loyal wolves know they haven't been abandoned."

"You know I would never go against a command," Harlen answered as I pulled the shirt over my head. He grabbed my upper arm and ushered me through the bars while he picked up a blanket and threw it over me. We headed up the cool stairs and through the door that led to topside. Not one guard was by the door as we exited the dungeons, the stars in the sky were dim as I took them in. The full blue moon hung in the sky with the stars.

Scanning my surroundings, I glanced over to Harlen, who nodded, and I took off to the east as Harlen made his way back to the packhouse. I turned at the tree line and looked back at my home before stripping out of the clothes that Harlen had given me. This would be the last time I would be here.

I shifted in one deft motion, grabbed the clothes and blanket in my teeth before sprinting away into the night.

Aloysius was a beautiful wolf with solid white fur and ocean-blue eyes. A complete opposite to me in human form with my black hair and brown eyes. We are polar opposites, he and I. It had been a few weeks since I had escaped from Dolostone pack with the help of Harlen. I had thought about hiding out at his mate's family's pack but then thought better of it. So the past few weeks, I roamed the wilderness, trying to figure out what I needed to do next.

Tonight, I sat at a bar in the middle of nowhere, drinking bourbon. It needed to be renovated, but it was fine under the circumstances. The owner allowed me to take a shower and chill for a few hours. Which was nice of him because I was starting to stink and bathing in the river was becoming a chore. Being on the run wasn't all it was cracked up to be. That was for sure.

A cute little blonde kept eyeing me from across the room. She sort of looked like Kalila if only her eyes weren't brown. She came up to me, running her long slender fingers across my shoulder blades. "I've not seen you around here before."

I stared at her as she sat down to my right, her hand playing on my thigh. It had been so long since I had been with anyone. Not like it mattered anymore who I was with. My chosen mate was gone. The fated mate that the Moon Goddess promised all wolves was nowhere to be seen. Why not have some fun? "No, I'm not from around here."

She giggled, in a high-pitched attention seeking sound, another thing that wasn't Kalila. It was all wrong the sound. I allowed my eyes to roam her body. Taking in her outfit. Its blue fabric was skintight, insinuating her curves as she sat there. I took a deep breath. Breathing in her scent. She was rogue like me now. Her brow tweaked up along with the corner of her red stained mouth. "Then why don't we go upstairs and have some fun. I've not felt an aura like yours in a long time."

Downing the rest of my bourbon, I left the empty glass and the last of my cash on the counter. The blonde she-wolf took me by the hand and led me up the rickety stairs. Down a hall that needed its wallpaper redone as spots of it were torn and sagging. I brought my attention back to the rogue she-wolf who had my hand. If I didn't look her in the eyes, I could pretend that she was Kalila. I followed her into the room and shut the door behind me.

The room was small with a single full-size bed in the middle of it. Curtains that could use a wash hung in the window. The smells from this room told me that I wasn't the only male that this she-wolf had brought up here. She glanced over her shoulder and winked as she peeled off her outfit.

Pulling my shirt over my head, I stalked over to the full-size bed she crawled onto, undoing my jeans and I dropped them to the outdated carpet. She lay there on her back, her small frame on display as she started to play with herself. Cocking my head I watched her for a few moments as her fingers slipped inside of her cunt. I flipped her over onto her stomach and brought her to her knees.

I didn't say anything to her as I filled her from behind, my hand pressing her head into the mattress. Her moans sounded out as I assaulted her pussy. She tightened around me as her muffled whimpers made their way to my ears. The friction built up as I hit her cervix with each thrust.

Wrapping my hand in her blonde hair, I jerked her head back. Her shriek with each thrust brought a smirk to my features. She didn't mind that I was rough with her. Just as I was on the brink, I pulled out of her unleashing my load onto her back. I plunged three fingers into her to allow her to get hers. I had never been deemed a cruel lover. Her content sigh and the rigidness of her body told me I had obtained my goal just a few minutes after I did.

I removed myself from behind her and made my way to the bathroom to clean up. Her arms wrapped around me, making me stiffen at her touch. No one had held me like this since Kalila did the morning after she had told me that she was with pup. "Lover, you're not finished, right? There's more left of the night."

My eyes stared back at me in the spiderweb broken mirror as I tried not to shrug her off. That's one reason I always fucked them doggy-style or tied their hands. I didn't like to be touched anymore. "I have to leave."

Twisting out of her arms, I returned to the bedroom and redressed. She came out of the bathroom still naked, her arms crossed under her breasts. She wasn't bad to look at, but she just wasn't her. "When could we do this again?"

"Never. I won't be back here." It was cruel the way I said it, but at the moment, I didn't care. I opened the door and shut it just as something crashed against it. Heading down the stairs and out of the bar, I made my way along the sidewalk.

The night was young, and cool as the wind picked up. I probably could've had a warm place to sleep if I had stayed with the blonde. I skidded to a stop as a silver-haired woman stepped in front of me. She glanced up at me, and her eyes made me shiver. She had the brightest grey eyes that I had ever seen. "Excuse me?"

"You're excused," She motioned for me to go around her. The grin on her lips pissed me off. Like what the fuck did she do that on purpose? Grumbling under my breath, I rounded her and started to walk away before her willowy voice spun my attention back to face her. "Fin."

"How do you know my name?" I stared at her as she came back up to me. Standing face to face with her as she smirked at me. Aloysius whimpered in my head as she held my gaze. This woman made me want to kneel in front of her until she told me to stand.

"Oh, I'm sure you can figure that out, Fin." She threaded her small arm through mine and led me to a concrete bench overlooking the lush green grass of a park. It swirled and danced as the wind picked up. I tried to pull away from this female, but I couldn't get away from her. She sat me on the bench and nuzzled into my side. Who the fuck was this chick? Aloysius whimpered again, his paws over his head as he lay down in my mind.

I glanced around, noticing that most people averted their attention elsewhere as we sat here. She was a little different from what I was used to. It had gotten so quiet that I thought she had gone to sleep. "So, Fin, I have a job for you."

"I don't know who you are, lady, but you can't just come up to me and tell me this." I stood up finally and stared at her, crossing my arms over my chest. She stared at me with a curious expression before she giggled. What was with these females tonight?

"Well, Fin, since it's taking you longer than your wolf to realize who I am, I guess I will just tell you. Fin, my name is Selene, the Goddess of the moon. The one you worship." It took me a moment to realize exactly what she was talking about. The burning in my chest started to spread through my body. I could feel the anger building in my nervous system.

She decided now to show up! When she could've kept Kalila alive with my unborn pup! The deep growl that escaped my mouth did nothing to affect her. I stalked up to her, caging her with my arms. As I leaned over her. "No. I will not help you! You allowed my mate to be taken away and now ask me for help? No!"

"Ah, but that is where you are wrong, Fin. She was never your mate, and if you would've waited, you wouldn't feel like this right now." She gave me a look of concern even though I was in her face and could crush the life out of her. "Your actions changed your destiny. So, this was your fault."

I snarled at her. Moon Goddess or not, she wasn't going to tell me what happened to Kalila, and my pup was my fault! "No. It's yours! You could've kept her alive! You destroyed two lives. Don't come to me again! I will not help you! I will not be your fucking lap dog!"

"Fin." She started to place her hand on my cheek, but I pulled away before she touched me. A growl again rose from my chest at her and I walked away into the night. I didn't need her. And she wasn't going to get any help from me! *I wouldn't think that Fin. I'll be seeing you again. We have time.*

CHAPTER FIVE

One year later.

The one thing I didn't like about being rogue was that I had no one to actually talk to. Sure, I interacted with a few of the other pack-less wolves but not like when I was part of my pack. One that I would never get back.

News about the new Alpha of Dolostone traveled. He was a vengeful tyrant, along with his predatory warriors. Rumors circulated that he had killed his brother, his brother's mate, and their heir. Taking up the mantle of alpha of the pack. Others said the heir was out there, biding his time to take the pack over. How wrong they were. On both accounts. I chuckled as I steered the machine around to grab the product beside me.

In the year that I had been rogue, I realized that there were two types. One was that some didn't mind being rogue and worked among humans, while the other set took it out on packs like the ones that helped Wade. I kept to myself most of the time unless I needed to get laid. Then I'd find someone to spend the night with. Leaving the next morning before they were up. I had learned my lesson the first time not to leave in the middle of the night. Since the Moon Goddess had caught me at that time.

Aloysius had pretty much stayed quiet since I went off on the Moon Goddess. She hadn't returned to me, which was good because I meant what I said. I wasn't going to help her. No matter how much she asked. She could beg me on her knees, and I'd still tell her no. She was nothing to me anymore. I had no faith in her and never would.

Sirens went off, and I stopped the machine I was using to move pallets to listen. Aloysius was alert as we sat there. People around me had stopped too. Emergency vehicles sped past the open flimsy metal door of the factory. Their lights flashing inside of the building as they went.

The smoke filled my nose. I jumped from the machine and went to the entrance, staring at the burning building across the street. The heat from the flames made me back away before I stepped out of the door into the cold day. People were down below as the emergency crews tried to set up a barricade to keep people from the fire.

The buildings in front of me held not only people's livelihood but also their homes above. A scream from the top sounded through the air. My attention went to the window to the top left. Someone was hanging out, trying to hand off a young child to the firefighter on the ladder. Without thinking, I ran across the street. Aloysius gave me some of his strength to get to the building quicker.

Entering the other brick building, I made my way to the roof. Something about the little girl reminded me of Sydnie. I rushed over the tops of the buildings, getting to the fire-entrapped mother and daughter. I stood there trying to figure out how to help as the flames lapped at my clothes. The woman tried to toss the child and didn't make it. My heart dropped as the child screamed along with the mom. So, I leapt from my position on the roof.

Free-falling until I had the little girl. I pulled her close and twisted my body. Using my other hand to grab hold of anything that I could. Finally, connecting to the metal fire escape, I dropped us down onto the landing. Metal creaking and groaning underneath me and the child. The little girl had tears in her eyes as I gazed into her green orbs. She shook as the adrenaline from the fall started to leave her. I turned my attention to the woman in the window, but she was now in the arms of the firefighter. Tears flowing down her burnt and blackened face.

I made my way down to the alleyway, and when the girl's mother was on the ground, she ran over to me. Her arms wrapped around her daughter and me as she sobbed. Soot and the smell of burnt hair and flesh filled my nostrils. The woman pulled away from us, and I handed her the child. Smiling, I turned and ran right into the one woman I never wanted to see again in my life. "You did a wonderful deed here, Fin. Just like an alpha. How about you do this job for me?"

"I told you no last year. The answer is still no this year. Now go on your merry way and stay away from me." I growled as I walked past her. Leaving the silvery-haired woman in the alleyway. A coolness blew through me, even though the fire still blazed behind me.

"You've left me no choice, Fin. Next time we meet, you will heed my call." I turned just as she disappeared, a smile on her face. Why couldn't she just leave me alone? She had done enough harm in my life. First, not allowing me to find my fated mate. Then destroying the life that I had built with my chosen.

No matter how many times she came to me. There would be no way that I would do what she asked. Heading back to the factory, people stared at me as I pressed past them. Their skin coming in contact with the holes that the fire had made in my shirt. Some congratulated me. That wasn't why I did it. For the life of me, I didn't know why I did. Other than that, the little girl didn't have to die like that. Her mother didn't need to live the rest of her life, knowing she couldn't save her daughter. She didn't have to be like me.

No one had to live with the pain that I had to live with on a daily basis. Ever since that day, I could feel myself sliding into a darkness that I couldn't quite climb out of at the moment. My whole life since her death has been in darkness. There wasn't a person here that I could call my friend; it was the way I wanted it. I had to get out of this place. Start over just like I did a year ago, but this time it would have to be different. Aloysius whimpered in my head at my thoughts of leaving another town.

It wasn't hard to pack up what little I had and move to another city. The hardest part was finding another job. But where I was going, I didn't need one. Living off the land would be a little hard, but being a wolf would make it easier. With my rucksack over my shoulder, I took one more glance around the simple studio apartment and then shut the door.

Why do you always leave when the Moon Goddess shows up? Aloysius questioned me as I began my descent from my floor. He was still one hundred percent loyal to that bitch. He didn't mind that I had taken a chosen mate, but he wasn't completely on board with it, either. The loss of his pup, though, made him different. But didn't blame the moon goddess.

Because, if she is in this town, I don't want to be in this town with her. I growled at him as I made my way through the door. Readjusting the rucksack on my shoulder, I headed down the sidewalk to the forest. This time there would be no cushion beds or a heating and air unit. It would be the elements from here forward.

You do realize that you will never be able to keep away from her, right? Aloysius snapped at me as I moved to the tree line. He was right, but I would try my hardest to keep from interacting with that she-devil. Aloysius snorted before shaking his massive white head.

Getting further into the woods, I dropped my rucksack and shed my clothes, shoving them in the bag. My shift was quick, and I grabbed the bag from the ground with my mouth as I took off away from the town. I felt free in my wolf form even when Aloysius was being a prick. The pounding of my paws on the soft forest floor drummed with my heartbeat.

I traveled along the raging river for a few hours before I stopped to rest. Leaving my rucksack by a tree and making my way down to drink from the river. A sound caught my attention on the other bank and I stilled as the brush rustled. The bunny's scent came to me and my stomach rolled with hunger. It had been awhile since I had eaten anything.

Crouching in the tall reeds, I watched as the brown and grey rabbit made its way to the edge of the water. Just as I was about to pounce, a hawk swooped down and grabbed my prey with his ugly clawed feet. Damn bird! I growled as the bird flew away with the rabbit.

I lay in the reeds as my stomach rumbled. This whole foraging for food made me second guess my decision to live off grid. But I needed to, because I had to stay two steps in front of Selene. *That will be difficult, Fin. You know she is everywhere. Or did going rogue go to your head?*

Listen Aloysius, she could've saved Kalila and our pup. But she allowed Wade to kill them and take over my pack. It's not something I'm going to let her get away with. I growled back at him. I shook my massive head before getting up and grabbing my rucksack from the base of the tree.

Tramping through the tall grass, I caught the scent of a beaver. I slowed my steps to a crawl as I watched the reeds move with the mammal's body. It poked its head through the tall grass and came face to face with me. The animal stilled and I could hear its heart rate speed up. I pounced, grabbing it with my jaws and cutting off its airway. Putting the beaver to rest quickly.

I devoured the animal in my wolf form, knowing I wouldn't be able to take it and my rucksack with me. Finishing the last of the beaver, I licked my jowls and stood to my feet. Blood still stained my muzzle as I grabbed my bag and took off further down the river.

The sun felt amazing as I sat on the boulder I had found a few days ago. After I figured out a way to hunt for food. I found a cave to keep out of the weather. The view from this rock let me see as far as I could. It reminded me of the waterfall at home and then of Kalila. Why couldn't I have just been left to be happy with the family that I chose?

Aloysius lay in my mind, curled up. He didn't talk to me much about Kalila and the pup. That's what I missed the most. Being able to talk to Harlen. He was my biggest confidant. Someone that would be able to help me through this darkness that continued to darken. I often wondered how he and his family were doing under the rule of my uncle. It still pissed me off that my uncle had taken my pack from me. But what was I going to do?

The wind picked up, bringing with it the scent of another wolf, a scent of peony and cedar. Aloysius swiveled an ear but didn't move another muscle. It was another shifter, female to be exact. Granted, she had yet to shift. But I knew she was a wolf. I didn't move, since the scent was far away from my position. A hawk flew overhead, skimming the taller trees as it circled. Damn bird. It had taken more of my prey than I care to admit. Aloysius snorted. *What was that for? Huh?*

If you would stop taking your time, that bird wouldn't get what you are hunting. Every time you let me take over, I get the food. Aloysius raised his head and looked at me over his shoulder. I rolled my eyes as I stood from my spot and stretched.

I jumped from the boulder and made my way back to the cave. Even though I had been out here for a few days, the clothes I had brought with me were torn. So, most of the time, I stayed in my wolf form or just stayed naked. The wind changed position once more, taking the other wolf's scent with it. As I entered the cave, I glanced up and saw her again. "You just can't leave a wolf alone. Can you?"

"Fin. You have a destiny that Kalila and the pup didn't play a part in. Other wolves are searching for the prophesied alpha. I need you to find the ones that search for him." Selene cocked her head, a smile playing on her face as she gazed behind me. There was nothing normal about this she-devil.

"And you know I want nothing to do with this. Find someone else to do your bidding. I'm through with you." I growled at her as I stalked past her to my bag, pulling out the handmade water sack.

"I know you're mad at me. But if you do this, then you are back on track with your destiny. I don't enjoy splitting up loved ones." I threw the water bag down and stalked up to her through the water that spilled from the sack. She didn't flinch as she glanced up at me.

"I told you no. So, stop asking me this."

"You don't scare me, Fin. This is your destiny. Four other wolves are on the same path as you. The first one will find you within the next year. They are going to be there for you as much as you are going to be there for them. And you all will be there for the prophesied alpha." She smiled once more and patted me on the face before she vanished with a pop.

CHAPTER SIX

One more year later

I t had been a long day and right now I sat by my fire cooking the rabbit I had caught a few minutes ago. The sun was setting in the east, throwing oranges, pinks, and soft yellows in the sky. Today had an unusual feeling about it. Like something was going to happen, but I didn't know what at the moment.

I had been moving constantly since my encounter with Selene again. There was no way I was searching for some other alpha. Fuck that. Why the hell did I have to find him? And why did there have to be four others with me? No, she could go fuck herself. She did me dirty and so I would never trust her again.

My head snapped up as a bush rustled in front of me. I was so deep in thought; I didn't realize another wolf had come so close. A male one at that. Extending my claws longer, I waited for him to exit the brush. I had no intention of letting someone get the best of me.

"Hello, mind if I sit and warm myself by your fire?" The stranger asked as he approached me. He was like me, wearing only shorts. He was darker than me, like he had been in the sun for years. I guess I probably looked the same since I had been out here for the past two years in nothing or just shorts.

"Sure," I told him, and he plopped down. His dark green eyes held curiosity in them, and he messed with his blond hair before he brought them to the flame. Something about this male put me on edge. Not a single rogue wolf had come up to me since I lived in town. His eyes darted to my right hand before a smile lifted his lips.

"So, how long have you been out here?" Here it was, the questions. This is why I enjoy being alone. No getting to know people.

"Why do you want to know? It's not like we are going to be friends. Get warm and leave." I growled as I pulled my rabbit from the flames and stood heading to the cave. I didn't want anything to do with this wolf. I just wanted to live my days alone.

"Has she come to you yet?" His question stopped me in my tracks. No, this is not happening! I turned slowly, my eyes locking with his. He cocked his head and raised an eyebrow with his question.

"What did you say to me?" My eyes narrowed and my breathing became heavy as my heart started to race. You have got to be shitting me.

"By the way you are glaring at me, I'm going to assume that she did." The male wolf stood and brushed off the dust on his shorts before sticking out his large, calloused hand. "I'm Markus and you are?"

"No, I'm not doing this for her. She fucked me and now I have nothing to do with her." I snarled at him and stepped back. Shaking my head, I stepped further back. I wasn't going to do this for her. I refuse!

"Well, I don't think you have much of a choice. I was told to come find you and then we would find three others." He stared at me as if what he just told me was going to convince me to find whoever these people were. But I did have a choice and I had made it the night she killed my Kalila.

"I've told her. No. And I'm telling you no now. Leave me or I'll be beating your ass all over this rock face." I lowered the tone in my voice and yet this wolf didn't make a sound nor move to leave. He had balls.

"Well, I'm here and there's nothing we can do about that but go forward. Do you want to live in a land that is ruled by a tyrant?" So, my uncle had been making a name for himself. Still, I didn't care. The things that made life worth living were gone.

"He doesn't affect me. I live on the land, no pack to tell me what to do. Nothing he does will have anything with the way I live."

"That's where you're wrong. I've grown up with an alpha like him. They are a plague on the land. Each generation is worse than the other until someone changes." The way his green eyes glowed with that statement made me wonder. What was so different about this prophesied alpha than any other? How was he different from me?

"Yeah? Well, sometimes a plague is needed to cleanse the world." I told him and turned back to go to the cave. I didn't want anything to do with this. He had my pack so there was no way for me to take it back now.

"That is true. But if you want to find that fated mate of yours, then helping to defeat that tyrant will bring you that much closer." His statement stopped me again for the second time. How did he know I didn't have my fated mate? Did she tell him? To get under my skin?

"Yeah? Well, I'm pretty sure I don't have one. I'm twenty-seven years old and haven't found her." A heaviness in my chest made me short of breath as I glanced down at my feet. I shook my head and turned my gaze back to the male wolf. "Leave! You and her can go fuck yourselves! There's no mate for me!"

"Fin, you're still a young wolf. Have you thought she might not be of age? It's not uncommon."

I had told myself this exact line back when I had met Kalila. Could she still be out there? If she didn't have her wolf that would be the reason, I couldn't find her. I growled to myself at how stupid I had been. Shaking my head, I continued into the cave and sat down. The rabbit cooling on the wooden stick I had been carrying around.

The male wolf followed me into my rock home and stood at the entrance. He was quiet as he stared at me. The sun finally letting go of its hold on the sky. I glanced up at the wolf that was sent to me from the Moon Goddess. As much as I didn't want to help her since she took my chosen and pup away from me. I still wanted to find my fated and if getting to this prophesied alpha would bring me closer to her then fine. "Take a load off. Looks like we'll be together for a while."

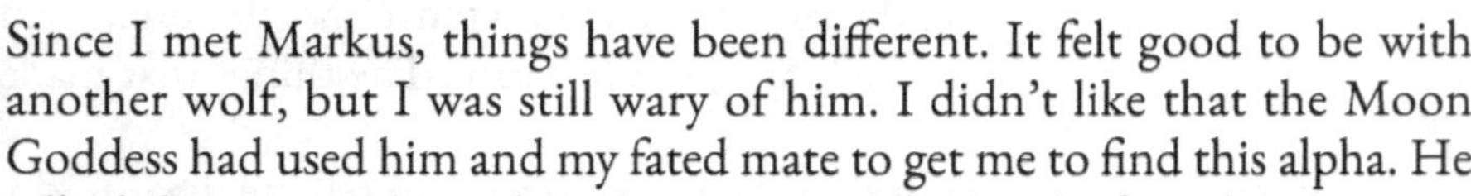

Since I met Markus, things have been different. It felt good to be with another wolf, but I was still wary of him. I didn't like that the Moon Goddess had used him and my fated mate to get me to find this alpha. He talked about everything, from his past to now when he found me.

Aloysius liked when we traveled in wolf form. His favorite thing to do was playing with Naik, Markus' wolf. He acted like a pup. One of the good things about having another wolf was that we could take down bigger game. No more rabbits for this wolf.

In the two years that we had been together, we had yet to find the other three wolves that the Moon Goddess had wanted us to find. Which was pissing me off. It made me feel as if she was pulling my paw. I wouldn't put it past her.

We had run into members of my old pack. Luckily, they had never met me while I was alpha, so I didn't think anything about them escaping after Markus and I kicked their asses. They had turned tail and booked it away from us. If I wanted, I could track them with as much blood as they were spilling. I didn't tell Markus that I knew their smell. There was no reason, really. It was no longer my pack.

"You've been quieter than normal Fin." Markus' voice made me turn to face him, the leg of the deer being rotated on the spit to cook it evenly. The deer was what had led to the attack by the other wolves.

"Nothing, just ready to get this whole "quest" over with." I told him as I air quoted the word quest. My stomach growled as I sat there staring at the meat spinning on the stick. The sizzle of the fat dropping into the fire made it worse, causing my stomach to roll.

"Yeah, well, we still have to find the other three of our group. So it might be a while before we find them and then this alpha." Markus answered me. He was older than me by five years and had a lot more patience than I had. I felt like a much younger pup with him. Markus was easy to talk to once I allowed myself to open up to him. He reminded me of Harlen.

Sighing, I stood and went to get more firewood. This wasn't how I thought this was going to go. I mean, hell, we were wolves. Why couldn't we just be able to sniff them out? And if it was so pertinent to find these wolves, why didn't the moon goddess give us their scent?

A splash brought my attention to my left. The ripples in the lake stopped me in my tracks. When the red head crested the surface, my jaw dropped. I stood there with the wood in my arms and when she turned, my jaw dropped even further at the cute face staring back at me.

"Stalker much? Can you not turn so I can get out?" The mousey little voice that shouted back at me didn't have the effect I was hoping for.

"Sorry, maybe you should make sure there isn't anyone around before jumping naked in a lake in the middle of the woods." I snapped back at her. A twig snapped to my right, and a grey wolf pushed through the brush on my right. His lips pulled back off his fangs showing the pinks of his gums.

Dropping the wood, I shifted just as the other wolf lunged at me. Another rushed through the brush as we fought. I didn't understand why they would be attacking me. The grey wolf was fast and part of me thought maybe he was an alpha, but he wasn't as big as I was.

Three sets of claws fought in the scuffle, two to my one not unlike when I would train in my pack. I jumped back away from the two wolves. The other wolf that had joined him was brown with splashes of black in his fur. They were rogues, too. My white coat was splattered with their blood as I stood there snarling at them. Brown, grey and white fur littered the ground. Aloysius snarled ears to the back of his head.

My ears swiveled just as Markus' wolf crashed through the woods behind me. Naik's golden yellow-brown fur stood on end as he took his place beside me. The brown wolf shifted back to his human form. He was older, but I didn't take my eyes off the grey wolf beside him. Who still bared his teeth at me.

"We didn't mean to start a fight. We are looking for two wolves. Selene has sent us."

My eyes went to the older man, and I felt Markus move beside me. Were these the wolves that we needed to find? Was I that much closer to finding this alpha? That much closer to finding my fated? The man's eyes flickered between me and Markus beside me.

Shifting back to my human form, I went up to the older man. He sort of reminded me of Harlen. With his greying hair and the deep set of his eyes. His eyes held so much knowledge in them it was unreal. I reached out my hand to the man and he clasped his with mine. "My name is Fin. This wolf behind me is Markus. Are you here to help find the prophesied alpha?"

"Yes. My name is Olli. This young pup is Harley, and you met Hannah already. She was the female in the lake." Olli laughed as Harley snorted before he shifted to his human form. The likeness of them told me they were twins.

No wonder he attacked me. He was protecting his sister.

"Well, we just took down a deer. Are you hungry?" I asked them. Hannah, the female that was in the water, came up the bank in shorts and a cami. Damn, these wolves were young.

"I'm starving. These two wouldn't stop to hunt." Her mousey voice reached my ears. I hope that my fated wasn't like this. I don't think I could handle her being this young. Her eyes roamed my body and she smirked as she winked at me. Fuck, I forgot that I was naked.

"Then follow us." I turned and shifted as Aloysius, landing on all four paws with Naik behind me. The others behind him.

We all sat around the campfire cooking more of the deer so that everyone had plenty to eat. I had part of the deer's thigh while the torso of the animal rotated on the stick. It felt a little weird having other wolves around other than Markus. Being on my own for two years really changed me. I often wondered how Harlen and the pack were doing since I left. There were days when I thought that I should've gone back and claimed what was mine a while ago.

Were there any wolves left that had known me and my parents? I shook my head and stood. All the wolves in the circle glanced up at me but didn't make a move to follow me into the cave. Soon we would find this alpha and then maybe I would find my fated. I mean, hell, I was twenty-seven in human years. It was a good thing that being a werewolf kept us young as a human.

I leaned up against the cool, hard cave wall and fell asleep with a full stomach.

CHAPTER SEVEN

Six years later.

We had been following a scent for days in the woods, since we had caught it in our camp. Olli was sure that it was the alpha that we needed to find. I was tired since I was on guard duty last night. Markus ran beside me while the twins, Hannah and Harley, ran in front of us, and then Olli was in front. Just like a pack formation, granted, I should have been first. But this wasn't my pack to lead.

We were passing by some moon flowers along the trail when I caught the familiar scent of the other wolf. I stopped and stalked into the brush. The others were right behind me. He looked like a wolf I had seen before, but I couldn't place him. A snarl came from beside me. Harley had his ears to his head. The kid needed to learn when to keep his trap shut. There really wasn't a reason for him to act like this. When we came to the other side of the brush, the young wolf glanced up with his blue eyes at the five of us.

It startled him at first, and then he stood, stripping his clothes off as he glared at us. The way he carried himself spoke to me about this wolf. He seemed like me. Defeated in his mind before his body. I spotted the yin yang wolf on his chest with the moon and compass. The wolf shifted into a huge black and grey wolf with golden eyes. Our growls ceased as the singular wolf stood in front of the five of us, ready to attack.

Olli crawled forward on the grass, his belly rubbing against the green blades as he made his way to the wolf. I had never seen him act like this. Turning my gaze to Harley and then to Markus when he shook his head. I didn't get this either. Olli shifted back to his human form and knelt in front of the wolf before him while baring his neck. "We have been waiting for you, Alpha Nolen."

We all shifted other than Hannah, who stayed in her wolf form. The wolf before us glanced around at us as if what Olli had said was somehow a joke.

He shifted back to his human form and Olli looked up. He was young, even younger than the twins now that I was closer to him.

Nolen's blue eyes stared at each of us as we pulled on clothes. Hannah came out of the brush dressed in her shorts and cami. Markus sat down beside the small stones on the ground making himself at home like always. I continued to stay near the brush. While I tried to figure out who this young wolf was because I knew I had seen him before. I just couldn't place where.

"What do you mean you were waiting for me? Hell, you came up to me about to tear me apart." Nolen glanced around at all of us. I finally sat toward the back of everyone, watching as this young alpha fidgeted in place.

Olli turned to him before glancing over at our group. Markus nodded to him and he returned his gaze to Nolen. "We didn't realize who you were till you shifted. The Goddess didn't inform us what you looked like in human form. We're sorry about the almost attack."

"What do you mean, the Goddess?" What were they teaching these young pups nowadays? I mean, he grew up in a pack. Right? Did he not worship her? I mean, I didn't like her at the moment either, so maybe she did something to him as well.

Olli shook his head as he turned to face the boy in front of us. "Boy, do you have some kind of condition? Or are you just plain stupid?"

"I'm not stupid, and I don't know who you are, but I will not be spoken to like that!" I could tell that his wolf had risen to the surface, his eyes had changed to a golden color. Olli visibly submitted before he brought his head back up to face him.

"You could've fooled me. Want to fill me in on why you are here and not with your pack?" Olli's counter even took me aback. He had never spoken to me or the other four like that in the last six years we had traveled together.

I knew that pain in his eyes. The pain of losing what you had worked so hard to obtain. Only to have someone rip it from your hands.

"I lost an alpha challenge. Now I have to figure out how to get it back, if they still want me." The dullness in his voice wasn't lost on me, and I was sure that it wasn't lost on Olli.

Nodding his head, Olli began to busy himself with building a fire. Nolen fiddled with a stick that he had picked up at the edge of the firewood. Once again glancing around at us as if he was trying to memorize us. "So, will I learn your names anytime soon?"

Olli had been waiting for him to get curious to want to know our names. He was the same way with us. I figured it wouldn't have taken him so long. But what did I know?

"My name's Olli." He turned to us, a huge smile on his face. Motioning to each one of us. "The others are Hannah, Fin, Markus, and Harley. We've all been summoned to help you."

"Help me what? There's no way the six of us can defeat the Dolostone pack." This young alpha must have gone through a lot. He held so much doubt in his voice I felt sorry for him. Hell, I had been the same way. Besides he wasn't wrong there was no way the six of us could take out an entire pack.

Olli burst out laughing and Nolen stood and walked away from us. I watched him for a moment before standing and heading after him. We both lost our packs, so the only person that would be able to get through to him would be me.

As we continued in the forest, Nolen finally rounded on me. His wolf was almost to the surface. He had the makings of a powerful wolf. So, how did he lose his alpha challenge? My uncle wasn't that strong. "What do you want? You come to laugh at me, too?"

I crossed my arms while I stood there inspecting him. He held my eyes the true making of an alpha. After sizing him up, I took a deep breath before answering him. "Listen, I understand what you are going through. I lost my pack a long time ago, and then a few years ago, I was guided here to the wolves back there in the clearing. I don't know what the Goddess has in store for you, but I do know I'm here to make a difference for you, and so are they. You need help, and we are here to do that."

"And what are you and they going to teach me that I haven't already been taught?" He asked, as he glared back at me. His arms crossed over his chest.

"We can teach you a lot and guide you to be able to obtain your pack back." I came up to him, face to face. I was just as big as he was. A few more years and he might even be bigger than me. "You have too much strength to be letting this old alpha take what is yours. It's time Alpha Wade is taken out before he decides he wants to be king over all of the werewolves."

No one in this rogue pack knew that Alpha Wade was my uncle and I wanted to keep it like that.

"So, what are you all wanting me to do? Why would the Goddess care if I lost my pack? Alphas lose their packs all the time. What makes me special?"

"Have you heard the prophecy?" The prophecy wasn't something that I believed in, but if it would help get this young alpha in the right frame of mind, then I would use whatever I needed.

"I've heard rumors of a prophecy. But I'm not unmated. I have a mate; she's just not old enough to feel the bond."

"Still unmated, my friend. You've not consummated the bond with her. So, she and you are still unmated. This prophecy may not be world-changing, or it might be. No one knows but the Moon Goddess herself. But I was instructed to come to this band of wolves to find you and help you along in your journey. If you are too proud to take help or want to wallow in self-pity, then I will take my leave right here." I glared at him and noticed the recognition take over his features.

I waited there as he gazed at the ground. He seemed to mull things over in his mind as he stood in front of me. I had been in his position before I met Markus and the others. Holding onto my self-pity and anger. Now I wanted to take my uncle down so that I could live in peace.

Nolen glanced back up at me and nodded, determination gracing his face and stance. "Fine, let's get started."

One night, we had all been sitting around the fire. Olli was cooking and everyone shared how they came to be rogue, I left out a few details. I sat against the wall of the cave we had found a few days prior, watching and listening as each one shared their story with Nolen. The thing about me and Nolen was, we were just alike in some ways. My uncle had taken his pack from him just like he had taken my pack from me.

There wasn't a fiber in my body that didn't want to rip that son of a bitch apart. If I got the chance, I would. Just because he was family wouldn't hold me back from taking his life with my fangs sunk in his throat. As his blood gushed down my throat. Ever since we found Nolen I had thought of nothing more than finding my uncle and ending his reign.

Nolen was a quick study. He took to training like his life depended on it. Which, in a sense it did. He had his issues at first and I didn't take any pity on him. Nolen was an alpha, and I was going to treat him and train him as such. Just like I would do to my pup if I had one. The other wolves in this rogue pack were warrior wolves that could teach him what he needed to know about those aspects, but fighting like an alpha that was all on me.

Before this whole thing happened, I was going to make sure he was the best there was to be. He had to be if he was the prophesied alpha. If what the Moon Goddess had told each of us was true, then this territory relied on him to make things right.

I watched as Nolen, and Hannah trained. Hannah and Harley were the ones that were teaching Nolen patience and speed. If I didn't know any better, I would have thought they both had alpha blood in their line somewhere back in their family tree. Nolen had almost caught Hannah multiple times, but she would always dance away from him just out of reach.

For as young as Nolen was, he was wise beyond his years. There was talk among the packs before I'd been exiled, that our wolves were reincarnated from previous ancestors. If so, that could be why some of us were wiser than others. Aloysius remained quiet as we watched the training. He couldn't wait to have a go at his wolf. My wolf could sniff out alpha blood in his sleep. I glanced up at the sun and sky. There were stars already trying to take over the sky from the day.

"You are learning fast, Nolen!" Hannah's voice drifted over to me, bringing my gaze back to her as she flipped out of Nolen's grasp. Hannah was putting him through his paces.

"Apparently not, since I still cannot catch you." Nolen groaned as he turned, keeping her in his sight. I had taught him that, and boy, did I teach it well. He couldn't stand straight for a couple of days after that training exercise. I might have been a little rougher than what was needed.

"No one has ever caught me but my brother." Hannah laughed at him as she finally came to a stop. "Anyway, I guess we can quit. It's about time for dinner."

I watched them as they made their way back to the cave before heading into the rocky structure myself and sitting down by Markus. Harley was doling out the food into the wooden bowls that Olli had made. Hannah and Nolen came in and we each nodded to them before Nolen made his way to the side of the cave. I had noticed that he was coming away with less and less marks on him than before.

Hannah sat beside me and gave me a nudge with a grin. I flirted back with her even though she was a friend to me and I didn't think of her in any sexual way. But it was fun to have Harley sending me evil glares as I did. When she found her mate, he would have to deal with his overprotectiveness differently.

Olli had taken to the young alpha and made sure to sit with him after each training session. I was sure that he had been a delta wolf or someone who trained the younger wolves. I watched as Nolen left the cave to wash his bowl after he had finished it. It didn't take him long to come back in and head to the back of the cave to shift. He was going to be a great alpha once we got his pack back.

His wolf was something to be amazed with. They always laid by the entrance. It was an alpha thing to do. To protect those in your pack. I guess I had lost some of that instinct. You haven't lost that part of you, Fin. You just haven't been in that position for quite some time.

Yeah, I will never be an alpha again.

You don't know that. I believe the Goddess has a plan for all of us that she is using to help this alpha. We just need to stay on the right path.

Movement at the front of the cave woke me. I was always a light sleeper. My eyes adjusted to the darkness and landed on the silvery wisp that led Nolen away from us. So, the Moon Goddess decided that she was going to meet with him.

Since Nolen had left I sat up in my sleeping bag to keep watch. It was still too early to wake everyone and it would be awhile before Nolen would be back. That I was certain.

CHAPTER EIGHT

The sun had yet to rise when I heard something in the woods. It was a wolf, the scent told me as much, but it wasn't Nolen. I quickly pulled off my clothes and shifted to Aloysius just as the brown wolf emerged from the thick foliage. My growl echoed in the cave, waking the others behind me. The wolf in front of me instantly went to his stomach before shifting into his human form.

He was a platinum blonde man and on the smaller side as he kneeled and bowed his head before he glanced into my now blue eyes. "I'm looking for Nolen. I followed his scent to this cave."

Olli came up beside me and placed his calming hand on my shoulders. Keeping me from lunging at the male. "Who are you, and why are you looking for this wolf?"

Olli had always been wary of people, and this wolf was no different. The man stood and glanced around our group as if looking for Nolen. "I'm from the Quartzite pack under Alpha Sawyer. My name is Trent. I hold the gamma position in the pack. I need to see Nolen right this minute."

His urgency made me wonder if something was about to get bad. I relaxed my stance and turned my massive head to Olli. That was a name that Nolen had mentioned before when we were all talking about our pasts. Olli motioned for the wolf to come up. "He is out right now, but he will be back. Come sit."

Turning to the group, I realized I was the only one to shift. Hannah came up and gave the gamma some shorts. While running her eyes up and down his body. I rolled my eyes. She always had to check out each naked male. I snatched up my clothes and went to the back of the cave to redress.

When I reached the group, Harley was giving the gamma his signature hateful look that he always threw my way when Hannah was sitting next to me. Plopping down beside Harley, I nudged him in the arm. Bringing his attention to me as I shook my head at him.

"Do you know when Nolen will be back? We need to leave soon. We need him at Quartzite to help with the coming battle. Alpha Wade is on his way. By the amount of wolves he's bringing, it's going to be bad." His eyes were wide as he continued to glance around the cave.

"What do you mean?" I questioned the gamma.

"Alpha Wade not only has his pack, but he now has control of the Rhyolite pack. I figure that if they see Nolen, then they may switch sides. Otherwise, I think the whole of Quartzite will be demolished." Trent's eyes locked with mine and I could feel the pleading that was in them. He was afraid for his pack, and rightfully so.

I had trained those wolves, and had been with them since I was a boy. Unless the wolves that I had been with were gone. There was no telling if he kept them or killed them, since they were loyal to me. Once this was all over, I hoped that this Alpha Sawyer and Nolen would allow the Dolostone pack to join their packs. I was no longer alpha material.

As the sun rose over the mountains, the sound of Nolen's paws hitting the ground came to my attention. He was on his way back from talking with the Moon Goddess. When he entered the cave, he was in his human form and naked as the day he was born.

The gamma turned and then jumped up from his seat, running up to Nolen. "I'm so glad I found you! We need to go now. The Dolostone Alpha wants to fight our pack. We need you and anyone else willing to fight."

Nolen glanced over at our group, and from the corner of my eye, Olli nodded. We all stood from our seats and nodded to him. It looked like I would be fighting my pack members. But I would have a chance to kill my uncle and that was my main concern. I wanted revenge on that motherfucker. I wanted to feel his warm blood rush into my mouth as I tore into his throat.

"Okay, let's go. How far are we from the pack?" Nolen's tone changed to an alpha tone and I smirked. There was no taking an alpha from someone. *You should be the one to talk, Fin. Maybe you should practice what you preach sometimes?*

"A day if we don't stop. Hopefully, the Dolostone pack hasn't started the attack yet." The Gamma's voice was shaky as he turned his gaze from Nolen to the rest of us. My gamma had never been this skittish but he never had something like this riding on his shoulders with me.

"When did he say he would attack?"

"It took me a day to get here. Which was the day he threatened to attack. If we leave now, we could sneak in under darkness where the safe house is." He was getting more confident that we would be coming along. So he would not only be bringing with him the previous alpha of Rhyolite but five others as well.

"Then we need to hurry, because I guarantee that he attacked early." How right Nolen was about my uncle. But then again he could be stupid and not go early.

The gamma nodded, then shifted Nolen right behind him. We all followed suit, leaving everything in the cave as we took off after the gamma to make our way to the Quartzite pack.

We arrived at the back to the gamma's pack around dark, like he had said. The smell of moon flowers permeated the air. I could hear the sounds of a battle raging and echoing against the trees. Nolen was right; my uncle attacked early. Which didn't surprise me in the least. Scanning the open field, I noticed a silhouette of a body on the ground a few yards ahead of us, and then Nolen took off after it. Trent tried to grab hold of his tail but he was too fast.

I hung back with the others as they whined for him to stop. He was stronger now. I didn't have any reason to hold him back. Nolen seemed to be worried about something and when he got to the dead wolf on the ground, he turned his gaze back to us. Motioning for us to follow him.

We stalked through the back of the territory and rounded a building I could only assume was the packhouse. The commotion from the battle was deafening as it rang in my ears and the stench of the dead bodies and blood assaulted our noses. Snarls and yelps came from the east, which spurred us on faster. Bodies littered the ground as we sprinted to the battle, now in progress. I spotted a few wolves that I had trained laying in a pool of their own blood. My heart constricted at the loss of their lives. They were too good to die like this. For a tyrant that didn't care about one single wolf on this battlefield. The rage from the unnecessary loss of life fueled me onward to find and kill my uncle.

He is going to die! I couldn't agree more with Aloysius as I raced with the rogue pack.

I joined the fray with the group tearing into wolves that I didn't recognize and trying to make the ones I knew to stop fighting. But I was no longer their alpha, and it had been ten years since I had seen these young pups.

Trying my best to keep from killing the ones I knew. I broke legs and rammed them to hopefully keep them out of the battle. They didn't deserve this. They had too much life yet to live. I spotted a grey wolf with black on her underbelly tearing into wolves with such ferociousness that I definitely wasn't going near her. She looked like she could even best me and I wasn't going to chance that.

I made my way through the battlefield, breaking the bones of the wolves that I knew and then killing the ones I didn't know. That's when I noticed that some of the wolves that were attacking the Quartzite wolves turned and started attacking the Dolostone wolves. I guess the gamma was right about Nolen's pack. They saw him and their allegiance changed.

Nolen and a grey and white wolf were battling together. That had to be the other alpha that Nolen had trained with as a pup. I spotted my uncle fighting with some wolves; I went to start toward them when another wolf rammed into me. Knocking the breath out of me, along with getting me off my feet. I got back up to my paws, about to rush the wolf, when I noticed it was Naik.

I cocked my head, and the golden wolf shook his at me. Since we weren't pack mates, we weren't able to mindlink. But I knew what he was telling me. It wasn't time yet. Nolen and the other alpha ran to my uncle as he was fighting the small pack of wolves. My uncle threw a wolf, and they jumped in unison over him. Before they could get to him, a band of Dolostone wolves cut them off.

By the way Nolen was acting, I could tell that he was fighting with his wolf to go after my uncle. I feel the same way, Nolen. I thought to myself as more wolves circled the small band of Dolostone wolves. They all shifted back and laid on the ground in submission. A couple of them I recognized, the others I didn't.

They knew they had lost. The grey and white wolf raised his head and howled. Others joined him and the sound of victory rang through the land as wolves shifted back to their human forms. The victory was bittersweet as I saw some of the pack that I had helped train lay on the ground in a pool of their own blood. This was going to happen and there was no telling how many had been lost before this battle.

I lopped over to one of the young wolves. I had broken a leg and shifted back to my human form. The shock on his face as he shifted back to his human form told me he knew who I was. Helping him up with his good arm, I walked with him to where they were treating the wounded.

Making my way back over to the rogue wolves I had been with for six years, I noticed that Nolen was heading our way. They both stopped in front of us and we all bowed our heads before Nolen introduced us.

"Sawyer, this is Olli, Fin, Markus, Hannah, and Harley. Guys, this is Sawyer, the Alpha of Quartzite pack and my best friend."

More wolves came up and surrounded us, all of them on one knee. It seemed like this was the Rhyolite wolves. They were a skinny bunch of wolves. I was surprised that they could even fight in the condition that they were in. If these wolves looked like this, then there was no telling what the wolves from Dolostone looked like.

I watched as Nolen knelt down in front of a red-headed male and raised his head. The shock on his face must have meant that he knew the wolf. "Lucas! Where's Daylen and Axel?"

"Daylen is here somewhere." It wasn't lost on me that he didn't mention the other wolf that Nolen had asked about. His voice was raspy, telling me he hadn't used it much.

"Axel?" Nolen's wary voice was answered by the shaking of the wolf's shoulders. He didn't make it and by the way he acted it was a while ago.

"He's dead. Wade killed him after he refused to be his beta. Left him on the ground for scavengers to pick at him while he rotted in front of the packhouse as a warning to anyone who went against him. I want to avenge his death."

I could see my uncle doing that. I wonder whatever happened to Kalila? Did he leave her where she dropped? Did she get a funeral? I only hoped that Harlen had laid her to rest peacefully.

"We will. We will avenge all our brothers and sisters that he has taken from us. I promise you that." Nolen grasped his hand and pulled him to stand. Glancing over the wolves that were his pack, I could see the defeat in his eyes. I felt that way right now at all the Dolostone lives slaughtered for nothing other than greed. "If you will take me back, Rhyolite pack, I promise you will never know hunger again; I will go hungry before you will."

The Rhyolite wolves glanced over at the wolf named Lucas. He squared his shoulders and straightened his back. "There's no better leader than you, Nolen. It might have been short, but we all appreciated that you tried to save us from battle with the Alpha challenge. Each and every one of us wants you back."

Nolen nodded and clapped him on the shoulder. Another wolf ran up to him and the relief that washed over Nolen's face told me that this was a wolf from his pack. But this one seemed to have a little more meat on his bones than the others. "What about my parents? Are they still alive?"

"Yes, they were still alive when we left. I don't know if they will spare them if we attack them." The way this wolf answered him had me thinking something was wrong. I was going to keep an eye on this wolf. My instincts were never wrong.

"Nolen, I have your back, man. We will take back the Rhyolite pack together like we always do. We are allies, and you're practically my brother. I would do anything for you and your pack." The Alpha named Sawyer spoke up, his hand landing on Nolen's shoulder.

"Thank you, Sawyer. That means a lot to me."

"No question, brother! You mean a lot to us, and we will always be your allies."

Nolen's head whipped up and his eyes began to glow with his wolf's as he searched over the group of wolves that had circled around him. I could smell the scent of moon flowers again. When he finally spotted whoever he was looking for, the word that came from his mouth squeezed my heart.

"Mate!"

Blood covered the light brown-haired woman that ran to Nolen. She threw herself in his arms as he wrapped his around her. He had lived to be reunited with his mate. Nolen had told me about her, that she was younger than him. But now it looked like she was of age to know that he was her mate. I turned to leave. There were other places I could be of use instead of watching mates being reunited.

CHAPTER NINE

Markus and Hannah followed me over to the wolves that needed medical attention. A nurse brought us clothes over along with bandages and antiseptics to help clean wounds that would need time to heal. I went over to a pup that I knew back when I was in the Dolostone pack. The young wolf laid on his back; trying to hold back the pain that he was in from the bite in his side.

"You'll be okay. I'm going to clean this up and bandage it." Pouring the liquid on the bandage, I placed it over the wound. His wail was like nails on a chalkboard. He glanced over to me, his eyes welled with tears as I wrapped tape around the bandage to cover his wound.

"You look familiar."

"Yeah? And who do I look like?" I asked him as I cleaned up the mess around him and me.

"Like the previous Dolostone Alpha. Only older. Are you him?" His eyes fluttered as he tried to keep them open. He had fight and that was a good thing. That meant he was going to survive this.

"No, I'm not. Rest and don't think about the past, young wolf." I stood and turned from him. That alpha was no longer me and he would never be me again.

"We really wish he would come back. Beta Harlen believes he will be back." I turned to see him finally succumb to the fatigue from the wound and the battle. Sleep kid, one day you will have an alpha that actually knows your worth.

I glanced around to see if I could spot Harlen. Was he here in this battle? Did he make it? I hope he did, for the sake of Bella and his pups. They needed him. Hell, if he was game for it, he could be the next alpha of Dolostone and let his line continue the pack. Because I wasn't in the right frame of mind to take over and rebuild. Aloysius whimpered in my head, he didn't like when I talked about not returning. He wanted me to go back because that was what I had promised Harlen all those years ago.

Nolen and Sawyer walked to the packhouse along with the other wolves. The wolf that Nolen had called Daylen stayed behind, watching as the warriors took the wolves that had surrendered to the dungeons.

"What's up, Fin?"

I turned to Markus' voice and then nodded to the wolf in front of me.

"I'm not too sure about that Rhyolite wolf. He's acting differently. We need to keep an eye on him. He's up to something." He turned and spotted me watching him. The wolf quickly turned and headed for the packhouse. Yes, run you slimy bastard. Because I have my eye on you.

Looks like we will be sleeping outside tonight, Aloysius.

Yep. He isn't going to get by us. The snarl from my wolf brought a smile to my lips. He was always up for a battle.

I shifted to Aloysius and laid at the edge of the woods. It was a little harder to hide since we were white. Where we were, I could see the front of the dungeons. I had learned that there was no backdoor so if he wanted to get to the wolves inside, he would have to go through the front door. The night was quiet other than the cicadas chirping and an owl hooted from somewhere further in the woods. Luckily, there was no wind right now to let anyone know that I was here. Guarding the dungeon from the outside.

The guards were inside the door so he would have to overpower them to get to the cells below, but I was here to make sure he didn't even get in the door. As much as I was tired from running to get here and then fighting the rest of the night and most of the day, I forced myself to stay awake.

Laying there for hours, I continued my watch, waiting for him to come. I normally had a good sense of people and he seemed like bad news.

"What are we waiting for, Fin?"

My eyes snapped to my left side and landed on the Moon Goddess sitting there with me. Being in wolf form, I didn't know if I could actually communicate with her. She softly laughed, bringing my gaze completely to her.

"I can talk with you either way, Fin. Now tell me, what are we waiting for?"

You want me to believe that the all-knowing Moon Goddess doesn't know? I quipped as I rolled my eyes.

"I do know. But I thought it would be fun to see if you would tell me. So? Why are you so keen on stopping this wolf?" She asked me with a giggle. She acted like she hadn't even fucked my life up.

Because he is up to something and we are trying to keep this from being as bloody as possible.

"Ah yes. What are you going to do about your uncle?" Selene's silver eyes held my blues as I stared back at her. That was a loaded question.

"I'm going to destroy him. That's what I'm going to do. Limb from limb." I snarled, showing my fangs. Selene nodded as she stared at the front doors to the dungeons.

"You would want to do that. But that isn't your task in this upcoming battle. That falls to Nolen."

I cocked my head at her answer. No, he took Kalila away from me. She couldn't take this away from me.

"I know you want to be the one to end him. But that isn't your task. You need to help sway the young alphas to allow Dolostone to join them. Because you know that all of them are not as bad as some of the others." Her hand glided through my white fur as I stared at her. "Look, it seems that you were right about this one. Farewell."

The Rhyolite wolf made his way to the door. Before I stood, I needed to make sure that he was going to the dungeons. He reached for the knob and opened it. I didn't want to burst in there and make them think I was the one attempting to do anything to help him.

Sounds of fighting came from inside of the building and I sprang into action. As soon as I reached the door, it burst open as a guard was thrown out. Leaping over him, I crashed into the Rhyolite wolf, pinning him to the ground as I sunk my teeth into his arm and drug him out of the small room.

More wolves ran up to us and the two guards came up to me. The sun was starting to climb in the sky when I released him. Turning my head, I spotted Sawyer in the circle with me. I shifted just before he reached me.

"Why are you out here? Did you have anything to do with this?" For someone as young as he was, he had the Alpha voice down pat.

"No, Alpha Sawyer. I had noticed that he was acting strange after the battle. Plus, he wasn't as skinny as the other wolves in Alpha Nolen's pack." I lowered my head in respect before bringing my eyes back to him. He had offered me a room so I knew the reason why he was suspicious of me being out here. So I offered an explanation and hoped that he would understand. "I've been living the past ten years as a rogue. The bed was just too soft. But I thank you for your hospitality."

I could tell he was mulling what I told him over. He nodded and relaxed his stance. "I found that to be suspect, too. Come with me. We'll tell Nolen together."

"All due respect, Alpha Sawyer. I think it would be wise to tell him that your guards caught him. Which they did. I just made sure that they got him." I answered him. I didn't know how much Nolen actually trusted me.

"Okay. Thank you for protecting mine and Nolen's pack. This could've turned bad." Sawyer inclined his head and turned. The guards dragged the bleeding wolf to the packhouse behind their alpha and nodded to me.

The other wolves dispersed, leaving me naked for the rest of the pack to see me. Shifting back, I lopped in through the woods back to the spot I had chosen to sleep. I wasn't lying when I told Sawyer that it felt wrong sleeping in a bed. Being rogue for so long has its disadvantages. But it was better than losing your life, right?

"Fin! Fin. Wake up, we have to get to the front of the packhouse." Opening my eyes, Hannah came into view. I stretched and stood as I shook out my fur. Hannah held out some shorts to me and her eyebrow curved. I shifted quickly and turned to pull up my shorts.

"Okay, okay I'm up. What's all the fuss?"

"The guards caught the Rhyolite delta trying to free the prisoners. Now we are going to take back Nolen's pack." Hannah took a few steps ahead of me before motioning for me to follow her.

By the time Hannah and I got to the front of the pack house, Nolen and Sawyer were placing wolves in regiments. Markus, Olli and Harley were standing over to the side.

"So, what's the plan?" I asked Olli as I settled in beside him.

"We are going with Nolen, Sawyer, Lucas, and Amora. Hannah and Harley are going to see if they can find his parents. Since they are the fastest of us. We are going to be the ones heading onto the pack grounds." Olli pointed to all of us and then the four on the top of the stairs.

I nodded. I was going to make sure Nolen killed my uncle.

Running with this pack of wolves brought back memories of when I would go on hunts with my father and the sense of belonging while I was with them. As we got closer to the Rhyolite pack lands, I could smell the death on the territory. That was my uncle's calling card to warn other wolves away from the land. The right and left side of this band split off, skirting the edge of the territory to flank the Dolostone wolves on the other side of the land.

Nolen nodded, and Hannah and Harley took off ahead of us. For as fast as they were, they were also eerily silent as they crashed though the underbrush. The rest of us continued on as we slowed and made our way stealthily over the pack border. Something didn't sit right with me.

By the time we had gotten all the wolves at Quartzite placed in regiments and then the run to the lost pack, it was starting to turn dark. Which was good for us. That would mean that we should be able to sneak up to the pack house and not have too much blood lost.

As we padded further into the pack land, the smell of blood and decaying flesh became stronger. A soft growl came from Nolen and his mate went up to him. They were just like his tattoo. Yin and Yang. They were definitely made for each other. The Moon Goddess didn't mess up when she fated mates together.

We continued forward through the bloodstained ground and dead bodies in the woods. It was eerily silent, even with it being almost nighttime. There should've been patrols running, but there was nothing. Nolen's gamma stopped and shifted back to his human form and kneeled beside the big black and grey wolf. "The pack is there but are unsure if Dolostone is still here since they told the others to get in their home and not come back out."

Nolen and Sawyer shifted, and I went on the defensive. Keeping my eyes and ears peeled for anything that would jump out while they were vulnerable. "Sawyer, ask the wolves that went to the rear if they have seen anything. I don't see Wade running back here and not trying to fight to keep the territory."

Waiting used to not be one of my stronger traits as an Alpha. But being rogue had taught me to be patient.

"They haven't seen anything on their end either. We need to take a few wolves with us and scout the inner part of the pack territory."

Nolen nodded and glanced behind him searching for something. He motioned for me, Markus and Olli to come up to him. "Alright, you guys. I need you all to come with Sawyer and me. Lucas stays here with Amora, and I'll signal when everyone needs to attack."

Lucas nodded and Nolen turned to Sawyer and gave him a quick nod before they shifted back to their wolves. The five of us snuck out of the wood line and into the clearing where it looked like a training field used to be. More decaying bodies and bones littered the ground. I didn't know if there were even enough wolves in this pack to be considered a large pack anymore.

The odor masked our scent as we stalked further inward, but each rustle of sound stalled our progress through the territory. The pack's stores were closed. They looked like they were starting to fall apart. Wolves were normally clean and so this made me wonder what Dolostone looked like. And it turned my stomach of what could be at the pack that I had to leave all those years ago.

My uncle had this pack scared of him. Being an Alpha was more than this. Anger was seeping into my soul the further I walked in this pack. Nolen hesitated a moment before he continued around the last building. The smell of urine and feces wafted to our group. My eyes snapped to the top of the stairs in front of the packhouse.

A woman was on her knees with a warrior holding her by her knotted hair and my uncle at their side. The cruel sneer on my uncle's face told me that this woman meant something to Nolen. This must be his mother, not like I could tell, because he looked nothing like her. I know Nolen. He is one cruel motherfucker. But he won't live to do this to anyone else. That I promise you.

Nolen nudged Sawyer, and he slunk back, and I took his place. My lips lifted from my teeth the pink of my gums showing as slobber made its way to the ground. But I didn't make a sound. If he recognized me, he didn't let on as he stared at Nolen.

"So, you thought you would sneak up on me? Too bad one of your little omegas saw you in town and is mated to one of my warriors."

Depending on the warrior, this could be a good thing for Nolen or a bad thing. Sawyer came to my peripherals and he nipped Nolen's tail. Nolen shifted back to his human form and I could feel the anger coming off him. "I can't help what a mate does for their other half. But if you think that I will just sit back and let you take packs, you are wrong."

My uncle laughed and went over to the warrior holding his mother, a sinister smirk on his lips. Déjà vu took over me as he grabbed hold of his mother's arm and forced her to stand. The other wolf stepped back, away from his alpha. "Tell me, Nolen, what do you think will happen to your mother if you try to take back these weak wolves? As we speak, your dad is hanging by his wrists in silver chains."

The woman whimpered. All I could think about was standing like this in my own pack with my mate in his arms all those years ago. Sawyer pressed his nose into Nolen's palm, making him glance back. He nodded to him before bringing his gaze back to my uncle and his mother. "Wade, you're going to wish that you had never come across our packs. Because today you will cease to exist."

CHAPTER TEN

Nolen shifted and leapt forward, making his way to my uncle and his mother. From the corner of my eye, I spotted Hannah racing toward us from our right side. She was going to make it to them before Nolen. My uncle was so focused on Nolen that he didn't see Hannah until it was too late and Nolen's mother had climbed upon her back.

As soon as Nolen landed on top of my uncle, other wolves rushed us. I worried our wolves wouldn't get here soon enough. A wolf grabbed hold of my fur around my neck and I turned and grabbed hold of his snout. Crushing his muzzle with my jaws, he fell to the ground at my feet and I went to take down another that had Markus pinned to the ground.

I crashed into the wolf that was on top of my rogue pack mate. Aloysius was enjoying the battle as we went from wolf to wolf, taking them down. Blood and fur in our mouth and matting our fur. I barreled into a horde of nine, as they had one wolf on the ground trying to defend itself. Standing over the wolf, I continued to dispatch each one that was in the group. It was exonerating being able to protect others.

Blood was everywhere after I finished and I glanced under me and my heart sunk at the sight. I didn't get to him quick enough, but I had avenged him. Turning to head to my next fight, I saw my uncle running into the woods.

My first thought was to run after him until I saw the black and grey wolf speeding to catch up with him. Every instinct in me wanted to follow him and take him down together. But the Moon Goddess told me not to, and since I was on the right track now, I didn't want to screw that up. I had to learn to delegate things. I had to let destiny run its course.

Nolen will take him down, Fin. And then the pup and Kalila will rest in peace.

I know Aloysius. But it will be bittersweet.

Aloysius shook our massive head as I searched for my next target. When this was all said and done, my goal was to be red rather than white.

I was muzzle deep in another wolf's throat when howls erupted from the open area. Glancing up from the wolf, the others from Dolostone shifted back and surrendered. Another howl rose from the forest, and I knew my uncle was no longer on this earth. I searched the vicinity for any of the wolves I had spent the last six years with.

Olli was helping an injured wolf back to the packhouse. Hannah and Harley were talking with Nolen's mother, and I could only assume his father because they looked identical. Markus was tongue deep in a she-wolf's mouth, and the only thing I could think was that he had found his mate. Good for him. He needed someone to ground him.

The surrendered Dolostone wolves were rounded up and placed at the bottom of the stairs, with Quartzite and Rhyolite wolves circling them. A familiar scent floated over to me and I began to search the dead. I didn't find him there and so the only other option was that he was in the surrendered wolves. There were a lot more dead bodies on the ground as the Rhyolite wolves came out of the houses above the stores.

A few of the younger wolves shied away from me, which was fine, but then it also hurt me. I had never hurt pups in my pack, but my uncle had ruined these pups. But it could also be from all the blood that was staining my fur. I was red now instead of white. My goal had been completed.

Another howl rose from the woods. But this one was mournful as it slowly faded. I lifted my head and answered him. Others did as well, making it a chorus of sorrow.

I spotted Nolen leaving the wood line. Blood covered his entire body, soaking into his fur. He held his head high as he made his way to the packhouse. Nolen was a true alpha and as much as I fought to not go on this journey, I'm glad that I had.

Olli came up beside me with some shorts. I shifted back and put them on.

"You're a mess." The old man commented as he ran his hand through his hair.

"Yeah, that was the goal." I laughed as we made our way up to the packhouse.

Nolen had already instructed the warriors to take the surrendered wolves to the dungeons, but was going to be sending food down to them. He was better than me. If that was me, I wouldn't have done that until I knew they were going to be worthy of being in my pack.

The familiar smell receded as Olli and I made our way up the stairs behind Nolen and his pack. Hannah and Harley came up to us. They were covered in blood as well; I glanced around for Markus but didn't find him. The dining hall was crowded with all the wolves that were in the room.

Grabbing a sandwich, I went up to an omega. She was a small thing with brown hair and dark eyes. Standing with other omegas as they passed out drinks and directing the battle wary wolves to beds or to the shower.

"Is there a shower I can use?"

"Of course... It's down the hall last door to the left. It's a community shower." The she-wolf stammered before getting herself together. I didn't miss the flicker of her eyes as they roamed my body. Every female did this when I didn't have a shirt on or was completely naked.

I nodded and shoved the rest of the sandwich in my mouth. The need to get the blood off my skin had become my next goal and then I was going to find somewhere quiet to sleep. When I stepped into the room, it immediately enamored me.

The room had at least twenty showers and then on one side of the room there were cabinets I could only assume held towels and possibly extra clothes. I found the soap and went to one of the showers and turned it on. The warm water loosened my tight muscles as I scrubbed the blood from me. The water ran red as it drained into the floor.

I found multiple wounds from the fight, but luckily, they were minor and were healing quickly. After all the blood was gone, I stepped out and toweled off. Feeling better after the warm shower. The shorts I had been wearing had blood on them, so I wrapped my towel around my waist to find more. If I didn't find some, I was going to crash here in my towel.

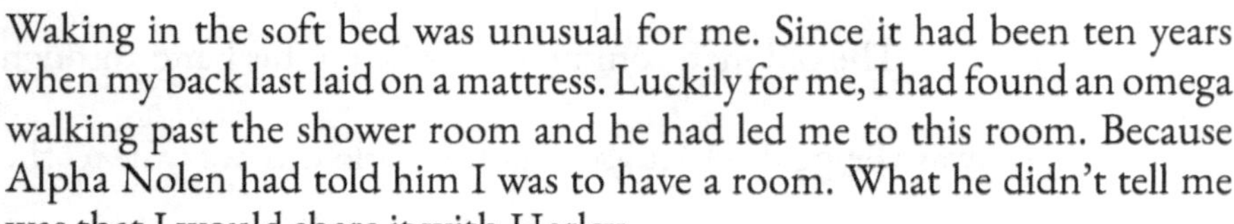

Waking in the soft bed was unusual for me. Since it had been ten years when my back last laid on a mattress. Luckily for me, I had found an omega walking past the shower room and he had led me to this room. Because Alpha Nolen had told him I was to have a room. What he didn't tell me was that I would share it with Harley.

Harley wasn't poor company, but his snoring got under my skin. Stretching, I threw my legs over the side of the full-size bed and went into the bathroom to take a piss since it was a longer of a walk to the woods.

Harley still slept in his own bed. If what you called the way he was laying sleeping. Instead of sleeping from head to foot, he was sleeping across the mattress. His head hanging off the bed along with his arms and then his feet off the other side. There was no way that he didn't have the blood rushing to his brain. I shook my head and then headed out of the room to go get whatever that amazing smell was.

As I neared the kitchen, I spotted the amazing smell and went to take a closer look at it. It looked like it was some sort of casserole and it was definitely causing my stomach to scream at me. I hadn't had a home cooked meal in the past seven years and anyone could tell if they were near me.

"Would you like some, Fin?"

I turned and spotted the omega that showed me to the shower rooms.

"If I can?" I inquired as she came up to me and handed me a plate to hold before scooping out a sizeable portion of the dish. She turned and handed me a fork with a smile.

"Thank you." I groaned as the food hit my tongue. Whoever made this was someone like my grandmother. Damn, it was good!

"You're welcome." She giggled as she went to the other side of the kitchen and started unloading food items from the boxes that littered the kitchen.

Scarfing down the rest of the food, I placed the plate and fork in the sink and went outside to see what I could do to help. I spotted Nolen, Sawyer and Lucas heading to the dungeons and part of me wanted to know what they would do with some of the Dolostone wolves.

I decided to follow them, but not let them know I was going with them. When they entered the building, I paced in front of the door. Trying to come to a decision on whether or not I wanted to go down there to see the wolves that my uncle had put through so much. *Stop being such a pussy and go down there.*

Did I ever mention that I sometimes hated having another entity in my head? Well, I did. Sometimes. Opening the door, I made my way to the bottom floor. The sounds of my feet echoing off the walls should have told them I was coming down. But it seemed they were too engrossed in the conversation to even notice. That's when I heard his voice. It had been so long since I had heard that old man's voice.

"That is what you alphas always say to get prisoners to comply with you. What is it that you want with us?"

I leaned against the doorway as Nolen had raised his hand to his gamma and then crossed his arms over his chest and went forward to stand face to face with my old beta. I could see the expression on his face even though Nolen was in front of him. Because he had given me that look so many times in my years. I couldn't help my smirk. He still had it in him.

"Listen, I'm not here to harm anyone of you. That is not my style and never will be. Your alpha has passed on, and I've come; well, we both have come to see if any of you would like to join our packs. If not, you will be rogue unless someone from another pack will take you in. What is your name, sir?"

Mumbling came from the other wolves in the cells and when Harlen stepped back, his gaze went to both Sawyer and Lucas. Pushing away from the wall, I came up beside Nolen and stared at the old man who had taught me so much while I was at my pack, crossing my arms for good measure. "Harlen, is there a reason you're looking a gift horse in the mouth?"

"Fin! What are you doing here? I thought you had been put to death!" Harlen came back up to the bars, reaching his hand out to me. Taking hold of Harlen's hand, I shook it. He knew I hadn't been put to death. What was he saying? Harlen had saved me from death.

"Harlen, you realize these young pups need to go with one of these alphas. There's no reason why you should go rogue after everything you and they have been through. Rogue is not for the faint of heart." I encouraged Harlen. He glanced behind me to the younger alphas before bringing his gaze back to mine. I could only hope that he would do as I said. Like he had told me a long time ago he would always do as I commanded.

"Why don't you return as Alpha of Dolostone? You understand we would be better as three packs instead of two," Harlen answered me. I knew he would do this. He wanted me to return to my position as alpha, but could I? After everything that had happened? Could the pack trust me and would the memories of her haunt me?

"That would not be a good idea. I've been rogue way too long to be an alpha now." I cocked an eyebrow at Harlen when he scoffed at me and then started to pace in his cell. The air in the room grew tense as I watched my previous Beta. I turned to leave and was halfway to the stairs when the rattle of the cell bars grabbed my attention. Turning back to him, I stared at him.

"You know you are the rightful alpha of that pack! Your uncle was never meant to have it!"

I didn't think he would out me like that in front of Nolen and Sawyer. Because I hadn't told them that he was my uncle. I didn't want them to think I could be in league with him. They stared at me as I came back to him. The other wolves behind him had turned their attention to me now.

"Can you please give me the room, Nolen?" I asked. The three of them left out of the dungeons as I held his gaze. Harlen's face was red, but his eyes were cool. This was when he was most dangerous. "Harlen, what do you want from me? I've changed. There's no way I could go back and be the alpha that you think I am."

"But you can. I've told the entire pack that you would be back. Because it's your destiny. I kept the wolves here in this dungeon away from the fighting because they didn't deserve to lose their lives to that bastard's agenda." Harlen pointed to wolves behind him. He was always a father figure to the pack. "The ones that fought were the ones I couldn't convince that they wouldn't be in trouble. But there are others on Dolostone territory that are waiting for your return!"

"I still don't have a Luna and this was all because I chose someone. Rather than wait for my fated. How can they trust me?"

"They have prayed for your return, Fin. They are worse off than the Rhyolite wolves. We need a true alpha." Harlen reached out and grabbed my shirt. I cocked my head and Harlen retracted his hand like I had burned him.

"Why did you say that you thought they had put me to death?"

"Because they said that they had found you in the woods and killed you."

"And yet you still thought I was going to come back?" I crossed my arms and stared at the man in front of me.

"Yes, because the Moon Goddess came to me and told me, you would be returning. As much as I should have believed her. I couldn't understand how she was going to bring you back to life."

CHAPTER ELEVEN

Coming back to the Dolostone territory was nerve-wracking and a relief. I was finally coming home, and I didn't know what I was going to find when I got there. The alliance between my pack, now that I had agreed to become alpha, and Rhyolite and Quartzite packs were tight. They had allowed me to take everyone from the dungeon with me back to my territory. Along with the ones in the dungeons at Quartzite.

Harlen sat beside me as we headed back to the pack. He had told Bella about us returning, but the rest of the pack didn't know that I was. Bella had cried upon hearing that I wasn't dead and that things would be almost back to normal. All that was left was to go before the pack and see if they would want me.

The SUVs entered the territory, and I spotted a few wolves at the border. I couldn't tell if I knew them or not as we went up through the pack lands. As we reached the small town, my heart sank when the disarray of buildings came into view. Some of the wolves were on the sidewalks and stared at the shiny black SUVs that passed with disdain.

When we made it to the pack house, I thought I was going to throw up. He made sure that the place that he lived was immaculate but didn't care about the wolves in the town. We stopped, and I spotted wolves on the top of the steps; they were all in rags that hung off them like they were two sizes too big for them. My heart sunk even further. If my uncle wasn't already dead I would kill him again slowly.

Harlen nodded and stepped out of the SUV before I did. I noticed their expressions lighted at the sight of him. "Dolostone wolves! I have a surprise for you!"

That's when I noticed that the wolves in the town had followed the vehicles to the pack house. I took a deep breath when Harlen motioned for me to exit the back seat. The murmurs from the wolves made my heart quicken. Would they accept me?

"I give you the rightful Alpha of Dolostone!" Harlen exclaimed with joy as I stood from the vehicle.

Gasps came from the crowd and a few of the older women wept as I scanned the pack before me. It was going to take me years to get them back to how they were and even then I didn't think that I would be able to gain the trust of some of them.

"Alpha Fin! Harlen has told us you would come back! Praise the Moon Goddess for your return!" I knew this woman, she was the one who would always give me a candy from her store. I smiled at her and nodded. They would never get this way ever again. It surprised me that they had been able to fight.

The way all of them looked happy that I was back gave me hope I had made the right decision to come back. To become the Alpha that they needed me to be. I allowed my gaze to roam over the crowd once more before stepping forward and shutting the door.

"Dolostone, I'm sorry that this has happened to you. I should've come back sooner. But I'm here now and we have an alliance with the other two bigger packs. Give me some time to get this pack to all its glory because that is my goal."

Cheers erupted from the crowd, along with some sobs. I turned to the wolves on the steps and to Harlen.

"Is there any food in the packhouse?" I questioned Harlen as I passed him.

"Very little. We will have to go over the accounts and see what we can do." My Beta answered me as he stepped in beside me.

I nodded and headed into the house that I never would have thought I would enter again. Compared to the buildings in town, this was almost well kept. But there were signs that the house was crumbling in on itself. They covered watermarks on the celling with recent paint and the floors were cracked in places.

Making my way to the office that had been handed down to my father and then to me. Told me just how much the place was being neglected. As I opened the doors, he had changed the room from the soft tones of paint to dark and gloomy. I opened the curtains to allow the light into the room. The view from this office used to calm me, but the burnt and destroyed land hurt my soul.

The computer on the desk sat waiting to be started up, so I sat down in the new chair and set to work. I wasn't prepared for the battle of trying to get back into the computers that my uncle had changed. When I finally got in, my stomach sank. My pack was broke. He had literally spent so much from the accounts that we wouldn't last the winter. Harlen came in and I glanced up at him.

"I don't know what to do. There's no money in the accounts."

"Alpha Nolen and Alpha Sawyer told you they would help you. Maybe you should contact them?"

I shook my head and stood glancing out over the buildings that needed to be rebuilt and the lands that needed to be helped. There was no way that I could ask them for help. Even though we had an alliance. If I borrowed from them, how was I going to pay them back?

"Look, I know that you just got back. But I think you need to ask them for help." Harlen came up to me and patted me on the shoulder.

Taking a deep breath, I turned to the phone on the desk. Could I ask them for help? I mean, I had to do something, otherwise there would be no Dolostone pack come spring.

I sat down and picked up the phone, dialing Nolen's number.

Nolen had come through for me and my pack. He came to my pack with food and an advance that I didn't know how I was going to pay back. But I was grateful. He and his Luna and Alpha Sawyer and his Luna had come for the alpha ceremony.

This would be no different from my previous one, other than my parents wouldn't be here. Harlen had sent for Bella, Sydnie and his son, Tobey. It was good seeing Bella again and Sydnie had grown since I last saw her. She was almost a full-grown wolf, since she would be eighteen next month. There was never any doubt that the boy was his. They looked almost alike.

I stood on the stage with the elder and Harlen. Alpha Nolen and Sawyer stood behind me as I became the Alpha of Dolostone again. The pack cheered as soon as our mindlink connected once more. It had been quiet in my head other than Aloysius. I felt like I was finally back where I belonged. *Because you are, Fin. Now we need to get this pack right and then find our mate.*

The party after wasn't as grand as my previous one, but I wasn't going to use up too much of the food that I had received from Alpha Nolen. They were happy to be there with me, and it was nice to have Hannah and Harley there, along with Olli and Markus.

Hannah and Harley had become Nolen's gammas, and they were doing a great job. I never doubted that they would be the best for Nolen. Markus was in Sawyer's pack since he had found his mate in that pack and was giving a few of the warriors a run for their money.

Olli had continued to be a rogue since he was the oldest of us. It felt like everything in my life was coming back together. The only thing I still didn't have was my fated mate and Luna. Once I got the pack settled, I would go to find her, like Aloysius had mentioned. Selene had said that I had a fated, and I was holding her to it.

"So, how are you doing?" Markus' voice brought my attention to him as he stood beside me as I stared out over the barren land I was trying to get back to flourishing. It was taking everything in my power to work the lands and help the wolves rebuild the town.

"Doing good. I'm going to have to figure out how to pay Alpha Nolen back."

"You'll figure it out. So anyone here, that mate of yours?"

I chuckled and shook my head. "No, but I can't really worry about finding her right now. Do you really think that she would want to be Luna of my pack with it looking like this?"

"Mates are weird. They do some crazy things." He chuckled with me. A few of the pups still stayed very close to their mothers while the wolf pups from Rhyolite and Quartzite played. I was hoping that with them here, they would know how to be children.

"This is true. How are you doing at Quartzite?" I asked him as a little boy from Rhyolite went up to Tobey and asked him to play.

Once he went to play, the others followed him. Tobey had it in him to be a leader and I was glad that he was able to flourish in his mother's birth pack.

<hr>

Three months later

I sat at the head of the table in what was once our war room. The remodeling of the pack house had come along relatively quickly. I had made sure that the pack's houses were rebuilt first. Because they had been through the worst since I had been gone and it was only fair to have them done first. A lot of the pack wanted to get the pack house done but I refused. I could manage as we did the town.

Harlen was to my left and two of my previous deltas were on the right. The gamma position was open since Wade had killed him and then the one he appointed to the position lost his life during the battle. I hadn't found the right wolf to take his place. But I wasn't in a hurry to fill the position.

"Now that we have the school going up. I hope that packs will utilize it to build relationships with the other packs." I glanced around the table. The omegas had been putting forth more of an effort to keep things clean and polished. The table shone in the sun that came through the open windows. "Furthermore, we need to get more alliances with the other packs."

"Yes, but we also need to find your Luna, Alpha Fin." One of the deltas answered me, bringing my gaze to the red-headed male.

There it was again, finding my mate. Don't get me wrong I would love to find her as well, but I needed to get my pack in order. We had found Dolomite crystals by accident when Harlen and I, along with a few other wolves, had been hunting. A younger wolf had fallen into a crack in the cave and once we got him out, his fur glistened in the light.

I then went back down in my human form into the crevice and what I saw washed me with relief. We now had a form of money and the stress of getting all the homes rebuilt before it got really cold left me. I was able to find an entrance to the underground cavern and let the others know what we had found. Once we started to mine the Dolomite crystals, I was able to pay back Nolen for his help. They had helped bring the pack back in a good financial way and the only packs that knew about them were mine and Rhyolite and Quartzite.

"I know, Hunter. But we still have a lot of things to do to get the pack to normal. Yes, we found the crystals, but we are not strong enough to protect ourselves even from a smaller pack." I stared at the young delta to my side. He was an excellent strategist, but he needed more training and that would take time. Because we still had pups that had yet to shift so they wouldn't be able to defend themselves from a wolf. If their enemy kept to their human form they would have a chance but that would be wishful thinking.

"I think we should go next to the Shonkinite pack. They have a younger Alpha and I think that we will be able to convince him to alliance with us. Besides, they are the closest one to us." Harlen spoke up before the other wolf could begin his sentence. He knew when not to press the luna subject.

I like this idea. When are we going? Aloysius answered in my head, his tail going a mile a minute, as I sat there looking at the map. Bella's birth pack had come back to an alliance with us once my uncle was killed. And then we had gone to another. I had to say that not only was I looking to alliance with other packs, but to find my mate as well. But the one Harlen was talking about we had never been allied with. If I remembered correctly, it was a smaller pack. But it could've grown in the last ten years for all I knew.

I nodded to Harlen and got up from the table. "I'll make the call and see if we can meet with him this week. Thank you all."

The two deltas stood, bowed, and left from the room. I had been to this pack before with my father in search of my mate. She wasn't there then. Would she be there this time if I went? Could she have been one of the younger females there? I didn't want to get my hopes up. As much as I wanted to find her, I didn't want to rush it. What if she hated that I hadn't waited on her?

"I can see the wheels turning in your head, Fin. What is causing the worry?" Harlen continued to sit as I stood there looking down at the map, studying it. Not like I knew where every single thing was on this map.

"What am I going to offer him? There isn't much that I could offer." I stared at the older wolf, trying to find out what I could offer this young alpha. My pack could no longer offer protection. It was still getting back in shape from what my uncle had done to it for those ten years.

"You could always give him a share of the crystals." Harlen suggested as he tapped his fingers on the wooden table. This was true, but I didn't want to let everyone know we had found that on our land. It could cause a war that my pack couldn't handle at the moment.

"Yeah, we could. But do you think that would cause a war?" I leaned over the table, my knuckles resting on the paper map as I stared at my beta.

"Well, if it's something that we can't offer, then we will use this as a last resort."

I nodded. There were so many packs that had been destroyed when my uncle took over. The first one he took was Kalila's birth pack. That land was now neutral territory since there were no wolves left of that pack. I had gone over one day just to see what it looked like and when I saw it; I wandered through the burnt down buildings and the barely standing ones before I couldn't take it any longer.

"Let's see if he would like to meet up and talk. This is our first step."

Harlen bowed his head and stood from his chair. Leaving me in the room by myself.

CHAPTER TWELVE

Fin

Harlen and I pulled up to our neighboring pack in the black SUV. I thought it was a little excessive since we could have run in our wolf forms. But my beta told me that it would be more professional if we took it and if I did find my mate, I didn't want to push her away with my stench. Harlen put the vehicle in park and killed the engine. Taking a deep breath, and letting it out, I opened the door and stepped out.

I had never been to this pack as Alpha but had come plenty of times with my father and then to try to find my fated. The wind softly caressed my face, bringing with it the most amazing smell of peonies and cedar. Taking another deep breath, I glanced around at the pack lands and spotted the alpha and his beta heading our way. They were about the same height, but the beta hung back just a little bit.

"Well, here they come and that's definitely not Alpha Christian." Harlen's voice came from behind me. He was still my beta until his son came of age. His daughter had found her mate in another pack, a beta no less, and I had made sure that the Alpha knew to make sure she was happy. If he didn't I'd hear about it for sure. So another pack was allied with us through fate.

"This Alpha looks young. I feel like an old man with all these young leaders around me." I said as we walked to meet them. The smell came back on the wind and I was tempted to ask the Alpha where the peonies were on his land that produced such a scent! But I held back, we had business to talk about, not flowers.

"Of course he's young, Alpha Fin. He came into power after your uncle took your pack from you." That will always leave a bad taste in my mouth. That and him killing my chosen along with my pup. If Nolen hadn't tore him apart, I would've done it myself! Moon Goddess telling me not to be damned. He wasn't going to live if my chosen family couldn't.

As we came closer to the Alpha and Beta, I pulled out my best smile and held out my hand. The other Alpha did the same. His grip was sure and confident. Just like any Alpha would be. "Alpha Rory, how are you? I haven't seen you in a long time."

"Same Alpha Fin. You are looking good after being rogue for a while." I didn't like the grin he shot over his shoulder at his Beta, but I ignored it. Because the Beta had rolled his eyes after his Alpha turned back around. I was here to make another alliance. To help bring the surrounding packs closer, like Dolostone, Rhyolite, and Quartzite packs.

"Yea, well, I think it made me stronger. So, why don't we talk about that alliance?" I wanted to get this over with quickly. There were other matters in my pack that I needed to deal with.

"Sure! Let me give you a tour of my land first! My father would tell me off if I didn't. You know courtesy and all that jazz." Alpha Rory chuckled as he motioned to his right. We fell into step with each other as he guided us to the training fields. His stride was confident and sure as he walked beside me.

The scent that lingered in the air seemed to be getting more potent as we reached the training fields. That's when I saw her. Dark chocolate hair and the girl had legs for days. The training shorts she had on barely covered her ass and let's not talk about that sports bra. Fuck! If it was any smaller there wouldn't be a reason for her to wear it. The muscles under her skin shifted each time she moved and the way her eyes stayed on her target. Had my heart racing in my chest. She had her long dark chocolate hair pulled up into a ponytail and her fists were up in front of her face. Like any good fighter would.

I glanced over to her opponent and nearly snarled because of his size, the male that she was up against made her look miniscule. He was huge. Why would she even be going up against anyone like that. I had never been one to tell a female who they should fight against but this was ridiculous. *We need to protect her! That's her Fin! Mate!* Aloysius snapped. I wanted to go to her, but she wasn't responding to my scent. So, I stood there beside her Alpha. Watching as this monster of a man strolled up to my mate, cracking his knuckles. She never batted an eye at him. If I was seeing things right, she had given him a smirk.

"She's a little small for that wolf, don't you think?" I tried to sound unaffected, but when Harlen nudged me, I knew I hadn't pulled it off. It was hard to watch my mate stand up against someone twice her size and do nothing.

"Naw man! Just watch! This she-wolf is a force to be reckoned with. She's one of my top warriors," Alpha Rory said excitedly as he crossed his arms and widened his stance. The smile on his face unnerved me.

"So she's a Delta?" I questioned him, glancing at the young Alpha from the corner of my eye.

"No, not yet anyway."

I brought my gaze back to my mate. They circled each other a few times before the male lunged. The she-wolf twirled away, her ponytail swinging up and away from her shoulders, before she landed an elbow to the back of his head. The loud crack as it made contact reverberated off the trees. Damn, she packed a punch.

Turning, the male swung a massive hand, as he went down, striking her ten feet away. I had to ground myself to keep from interfering. Aloysius was howling in my head as I gripped my arms tighter. My knuckles white as I clenched my teeth. If she wasn't confirming the mate bond, I couldn't interfere with what an Alpha allowed his pack to do.

She stood, an eye already swelling, but she grinned as she wiped away a small amount of blood from her lip. This woman just wouldn't go down. When she lunged at him, he stiffened. Her eyes held a wild, blood-crazed emotion. He was down in an instant and she was on top of him, beating him to a pulp. And I wasn't even turned off by it. Hell, if I was being honest, I was turned on by it. The way her body moved as each punch bloodied his face.

My little mate could handle herself in a battle, that was for sure. I couldn't help the smile that spread on my face and the cock of my eyebrow as the wind blew toward her. Her arm hesitated, but her head never snapped up to me. She had her eyes on her prize. *Fin, she's your mate, isn't she? We need to be careful. This could go either way with this Alpha.*

I know Harlen, but isn't she beautiful? The awe even in my mind's voice made me grin. I had never seen a female like her before. She was graceful and full of fire, just what a Luna needed to be. I was love struck and we hadn't even locked eyes.

I noticed Harlen shake his head with it in his hand. Yes, I was excited to be finally meeting my fated and that if she really wanted, she could beat my ass.

Nikita

When the wind brought his scent of forest rain and birchwood over to me, I knew he was my mate. I hesitated for a moment; my fist pulled back to punch the male wolf below me. My wolf howled in my head to acknowledge him. To look up at the opposing figure beside my Alpha. But I didn't. Why did he take this long to come to my pack? Was he not looking for me?

I had noticed him as he stood there watching me. Something deep inside me wanted him to see what I could do to the massive man that had stood before me. My eyes would wander over to the top of the hill where he stood. His dark hair floated on the wind as it wove its way between him and my Alpha.

There had been talk about an Alpha coming from another pack to talk about an alliance. I never would've thought that he would be my mate. As I stood from my defeated opponent, blood dripping from my hands, I finally looked at him. His dark eyes met mine, and that was all it took for me to know he was mine. The way his lips were turned up in a grin and that raised brow. Fuck, and that chiseled jaw with a little stubble in it. I'm pretty sure I might have seen some grey in it. Damn, he was fine! And he was all mine if I allowed him to get close to me.

Yes, he is! I can't wait to meet his wolf. Enyo's tongue lolled as she rolled to her back, her tail beating the ground in my head. I rolled my eyes as I stepped away from my opponent's body. Turning away from the gorgeous alpha in his skintight shirt, my heart hammered in my chest the further I walked away from him.

"Great fight Nikita!"

"You really put a wailing on him!"

"He didn't stand a chance!"

I smiled at the females that hovered around me and the males that thought that they could get into my pants with their smile. It wasn't that I was saving myself. I did that till I was eighteen and then when I didn't find my mate. I was like, fuck it! But now he was here and what would he do when he found out I hadn't waited? Glancing over my shoulder, I saw him turn as if nothing happened and walk away with his Beta and my Alpha. His ass looked just as good as his front did.

Freshly showered, I made my way into the Dining Hall. Tonight, it was mandatory to eat in the pack house. Which a lot of the mateless females didn't mind since they could meet the Alpha from Dolostone. The rumors about him spread like wildfire in this pack. And boy were they things of the imagination!

As I entered the massive room, it was decorated to the gills with streamers and other décor. Its once beautiful arches covered with fake ivy. I noticed that Alpha Rory and his mate were up at the top, along with the Alpha from Dolostone and his beta. He looked bored, but when I stepped further in, his eyes connected with my grey eyes, and he smiled. I froze before nodding. I knew I had to be respectful. Otherwise, I would embarrass my alpha if I didn't.

"Nikita, have you seen the Alpha from Dolostone?" I turned to Crystal. She was standing with her little pack of bitches, a smirk on her thin lips. If she didn't have such a bitchy attitude she might just be someone you could be friends with.

"Yeah, I think he was at the training fields this morning." I came back at her. She would never fight me fair. She knew I'd kick her ass all over this territory and then some. She always hid behind her brother and his rank.

"No wonder he was so upset. It looked like he was going to puke. What male's ego could handle your brutality?" She and her friends laughed as I stalked up to her, bringing her shrill voice to an end.

"Then it's a good thing that I don't need a man to protect me when there's a fight." I whispered in her ear and tweaked her nose. She hated when I did that but she never made a move to me in this crowded dining room.

I made my way to the table that held all the food and grabbed a plate. She didn't bother me and it didn't bother me that I might have bruised his male ego. I stacked my plate full of different foods and made a beeline to the upper levels. The alpha's eyes burned holes in the side of my face as I walked up the red carpeted stairs.

Males and their egos. How easily they can be broken at the drop of a paw. I sat down at one of the empty wooden tables overlooking the hall and realized he wasn't at the table with his Beta. The older wolf glanced up at me and smiled before he began to speak with my Beta. Something was up and I didn't like that his Beta was in on it.

"Mind if I sit here?" I turned at the deep voice and stared into his dark eyes. They flickered between that and a deep blue.

Just the way his voice sounded to my ears made me wet and let's not talk about his scent! He cocked an eyebrow before he took the seat across from me. I didn't even know this wolf's name, but he brought out everything that I shouldn't be thinking about. *Nikita, talk to him! He is our mate! Why are you not opening your damn mouth!*

Shut up, Enyo. I reprimand my wolf. I grabbed a few pieces of watermelon and shoved them into my mouth. Which gave me an excuse to not speak to him. Removing my gaze from the handsome alpha in front of me, I glanced down. Alpha Rory was staring at me, giving me a sickening gaze. He never paid much attention to me unless he could exploit my abilities. But at this moment, he had his hardened gaze on me.

"What's your name? My feisty girl?" He reached over and plucked a grape and cheese wedge from my plate. A soft growl festered deep in my throat. I didn't like to share my food even if it was my mate that was taking it.

"Why do you want to know?" I questioned him. Moving my hand from the table that he was trying to touch. He chuckled as I grabbed more watermelon and popped it into my mouth with my other hand. The juice ran down my chin and before I could stop him, his mouth was at the corner of mine. Suckling the juice from my skin.

The sparks that shot through me caused me to jump out of my seat. Knocking it to the ground. The sound had brought everyone's attention to us. He never moved from his seat as his eyes suddenly turned the deep blue they had been flickering between. While his tongue ran across his lips. It took everything in me from moaning as I tightened my legs together. I ran out to the balcony, and he followed me. My heart raced as if I had been sparing. The night had just taken over the day and its stars and moon shone brightly in the sky.

I turned on him as he shut the doors and stalked to me, his nostrils flaring. No one had ever been able to make me submit to them, but the heat growing between my thighs was ruining my panties. "What do you want from me?"

"Just your name, feisty wolf." The rumble in his chest made it hard to keep my focus. His hands landed on the railing beside me, gripping them so tightly that his knuckles turned white. He was barely near me, but it felt like his hands and his lips were caressing my body. The way he made me feel brought me back to my first time. But this time was a thousand times better.

"Nikita." His breath teased along my skin and prickled the spot where my mate mark would sit. "Yours?"

I didn't want to ask. The less I knew about him, the better, but I wasn't strong enough. He went down the other side, making me so aroused it was torture. "Alpha Fin. But you can call me, Fin."

So, he was an alpha! So many of those rumors were of him pretending to be an alpha, that he was actually rogue. And that the real alpha of Dolostone was locked up in their dungeons.

He still hadn't even touched me, but his nearness had me so wet I'm sure everyone could smell me. It was like he was waiting for me to initiate the contact. *I don't know why you haven't!*

Why hasn't he been searching for me? It's been seven years, Enyo! I snapped at her in my head. I'm sure that was the reason I hadn't touched him yet. Because I knew those sparks would race down and make me even wetter.

"What are you thinking?" Fin whispered in my ear and I shivered as my eyes fluttered close.

"That you are in my bubble and that if you don't get out, we might have a problem." I told him, trying to put some sternness in my tone. He stopped and backed away, his hands in the air, a grin on his lips as his eyebrow quirked up.

"Are you afraid?" His tone was teasing as he crossed his arms. I didn't miss the dip of his eyes or the flare of his nostrils. He knew what he was doing to me.

"I'm never afraid." I told him the grin and his tone now getting under my skin.

"I don't think you could take me." He laughed as he shrugged his shoulders. What did he think he was doing? I know he was watching me beat the shit out of that wolf today.

"I think I could." I snapped at him, crossing my own arms. His eyes went to my breasts before coming back to my face. Fin's eyes had stayed his wolf's the entire time.

"Fine, tomorrow. I'll talk to your Alpha. We will see who comes out on top." With a full-blown smile, he winked and went back into the Dining Hall.

I took a deep breath and then uncrossed my arms. Fighting an alpha could cause a problem. But he was the one that wanted to fight me and a fight he would get.

CHAPTER THIRTEEN

NIKITA

After dinner I went to my room. I had to stay away from Alpha Fin if I was going to be able to make it through his visit and the fight. The way he made me feel when I was near him wasn't something I was used to. I couldn't think straight when he was near.

Nikita! My office now! Alpha Rory mind linked me, and I knew Alpha Fin had said something about tomorrow.

Rolling my eyes, I left my room and headed to the office. Before I could even knock, the door flew open and there stood Alpha Rory. He pulled me in and I knew the other alpha couldn't have been in here, otherwise he wouldn't have treated me this way. Alpha Rory pushed me into the office and slammed the door. I stumbled for a moment before getting my feet back under me to keep myself upright.

I knew not to ever challenge my Alpha, but the way he manhandled me made me want to beat his ass. Keeping my eyes down, I waited for him to tell me what I had done wrong.

"Is that alpha your mate?" He growled in my face. I lifted my gaze to look at Alpha Rory in the eyes. The color had changed to his wolf's. What could I have done to make him this mad at me? Was being mated to this alpha an issue?

"Yes, Alpha." I muttered, and he snarled before walking over to his desk and flinging it at the wall. Things went flying off the desk and wall. He took a few deep breaths before he turned back to me and stalked over his finger in my face.

"This is what you are going to do. He wants to train with you in the morning. After that he and his beta will go home in five days with you. You are not to let him mark you."

"Why? If I need to reject him, I'll do it here and stay..." I stumbled over my words. Enyo whimpered in my head. She didn't want me to reject him but I didn't understand why my Alpha wanted me to go with him if he didn't want me to complete the mate bond.

"NO! You will go to his pack! He is the alpha that chose my cousin as his mate and she died because of him. He didn't even want to wait for you! Once you get to his pack, you are to kill him, otherwise I'll kill you." Alpha Rory's eyes held the most manic emotion in them I had ever seen from any wolf. He used his finger to jab it into my chest.

My mate had taken a chosen? What would he have done if she had lived? Would he have left her or stayed with her? So that means he wasn't a virgin, either. *You can't say much! You weren't faithful either!* Enyo snorted as my stomach clenched.

"Do you understand me?" I glanced up into his eyes and nodded.

"Yes, Alpha."

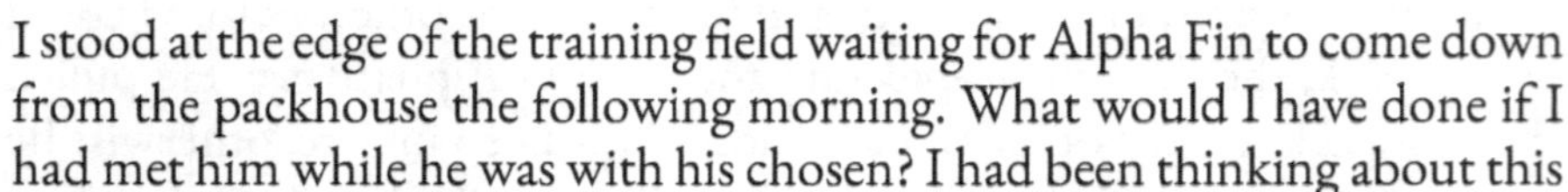

I stood at the edge of the training field waiting for Alpha Fin to come down from the packhouse the following morning. What would I have done if I had met him while he was with his chosen? I had been thinking about this all night. It had kept me up all night and I hoped that I would be able to fight him to the best of my ability.

Why would he not wait for me? I mean, I didn't care that he had fucked others. Hell, I did the same after I couldn't find him. But I never allowed a male to mark me and he had marked another female. Each time I thought of this made me sick.

His scent brought my gaze up, and the sight I saw made my jaw drop. Damn! This male was fine! He wore nothing but grey sweats. His chest and abs on display. Alpha Fin was bare foot too as he strolled down to the pitch.

Alpha Fin's beta walked beside him. Speaking with him. The grin on Alpha Fin's lips made me melt even more. As much as I wanted to be mad at him for marking someone else, I couldn't because I had to believe Selene, the Moon Goddess, had a reason.

"Nikita, this will be a different fight. Alphas are stronger. You're going to have to use your size to your advantage." The Delta I was under spoke to me as I watched Alpha Fin come down the hill to the training fields. I pulled my eyes from him and found Alpha Rory's. The hatred in them as he looked upon my mate stirred something in my being. I had to figure out how to protect my mate from me.

"I know, Delta Kyle." I was getting annoyed with his nagging. It wasn't making me feel any better about any of this. Delta Kyle began to wrap my hands. Not like it mattered. I'd heal quickly enough. But hopefully it would keep me from actually hurting him.

Alpha Fin strolled up to me and nodded to my delta. Delta Kyle bowed and then left my side. I brought my gaze up to his. Every time I held his dark stare, desire rushed through me. He was nothing like the other males I had been with. The way his hair caught the sun just right to make it shine and that chiseled jaw with a tiny bit of scruff. I could only hope that this training didn't make my desire worse. "Are you scared, my feisty girl?"

"I'm never scared of a fight." I told him with a false sense of fearlessness. Resting my hands on my hips to keep from touching him because damn did I want to touch those washboard abs of his. Truth be told, I wasn't afraid of the fight between me and Alpha Fin. I was wary of what Alpha Rory would do to me if I didn't complete the mission that he forced me to do.

I had concluded that if I didn't complete this mission, I'd die, but if I did and got caught, I'd die. There wasn't a way I was getting out of this alive. Alpha Fin ran one of his knuckles down my cheek and I had to keep myself from leaning into his caress. "Alpha Fin, this is a fight. You won't be able to win this with being nice to me."

"I never intended to win, Nikita." He chuckled as he made his way to the middle of the arena. What alpha wouldn't want to win? Why would he want to show my pack how weak he was by letting me a lower ranked female win?

I jogged into the arena with him. This male was something else, and I wondered what had made him the way he was. The crowd had grown around the enclosure. There had always been an audience with my fights. Hell, a lot of the males placed bets. I wondered who they had bet on today? Him or me?

"This is a fight to submission. Or knock out. Fighters, are you ready?" I nodded and so did he. Alpha Fin's eyes never left my gaze. Those eyes of his sent butterflies into my stomach and made my heart race. I took a fighting stance and waited for him to do the same.

But he just stood there with his arms at his side. I took a chance to glance at the delta as he dropped his hands and his muffled "Fight!" barely made it to my ears as I began to circle my mate.

Alpha Fin never moved a muscle unless you count his eyes. Even when I went around his back. Nothing. I finally lunged at him and I swung. My fist made contact with his chest, throwing him into the dirt of the arena. He didn't even try to avoid it. What the fuck was he playing at?

He stood, brushing off the dust as if he wasn't even in a fight. *Cocky alpha!* Enyo wagged her tail in excitement. I lunged again, throwing punch after punch, which he now evaded. So I swept his legs out from under him and that's when the sparks raced up my leg. It shocked me so much that I became off balance.

Before I landed on my ass, more sparks raced up my arms as Alpha Fin crushed me to his chest. My gaze roamed over the crowd in front of me. They all knew he was my mate. I felt his breath on the shell of my ear. "My feisty girl. Do you see all the males that know you are mine? They won't ever look at you or touch you the same ever again."

So he knew! And my current conquest wouldn't even look at me. This was the reason he said he wasn't interested in winning the fight. This was to show all the males and the females that I was his and he was mine! It was never about the fight. I had never felt more defeated in my life.

Fin

The way Nikita slumped in my arms told me she had figured out what I was doing. Her sweet scent drove me and Aloysius crazy. The mate sparks snapped between us as I held her back to my chest. Our sweat merged as we stood there in the middle of the training pitch.

My eyes swept the crowd, and I noticed that one male kept his eyes averted more than the rest. He must have been the one she was currently messing around with. I couldn't blame him. She was gorgeous. There would be none of that now. Everyone knew she was mine.

I told you the Moon Goddess would have us a mate! But no, you wanted to wallow. Aloysius scoffed at me as he wagged his tail. Nikita elbowed me in the kidney, allowing her to leave my arms. Her eyes flickered between her wolf's and hers. She took a deep breath before she glanced over to the left side and then walked away from me through the crowd.

I let her go so as not to cause a scene. Nikita's hunter green eyes held something other than the joy of finding me. Was there hurt in them? Sadness? Harlen came up to me and clapped me on the shoulder, bringing my attention back to the now.

"You did great. I'm glad you didn't actually fight her." Harlen's smile reached his eyes. I knew he hoped I would find my mate. He didn't mind when I chose Kalila, but he wanted me to be strong.

"I told you I wasn't going to fight her. I know how tough she is, and I know that she could take me if she really wanted to." I told him as I spotted Alpha Roy coming up to me. His face was stoic as he stopped in front of me. Nothing like it was when I arrived yesterday.

"I hope you figured out what you wanted to know. How about we meet in an hour to discuss this alliance? That will give you plenty of time to shower and make it to my office." Something was off with Alpha Roy now. Did he have something against me?

"That's fine. Thank you for your hospitality." I nodded to him as he turned and left with his mate. Something was definitely wrong, and I was going to have to watch what I said and did while I was here.

"Well, I don't see why he wouldn't give you the alliance. I mean, you are the mate to one of his pack members." Harlen walked with me to the packhouse. What he said was true, but once Nikita left this pack, they would lose one of their better warriors. And I didn't think that he liked that too well.

Nikita stood on the steps with her Delta as she unwrapped her hands. I couldn't get over the way her body moved. As much as I loved seeing her in the clothes she was in, I didn't like that other males could see her like this as well. Her eyes flickered over to mine, and I grinned at her before she brought her gaze back to her superior. Since the male was mated, I didn't mind her being so close to him.

I knew where her room was and I planned on going to her, or maybe I'd have her come to me in my room. I wanted to know more about her. What was her life like? Was she disappointed when she didn't find me? I'm sure she would be upset I had marked another she-wolf. Hell, what would've happened if I was still mated with Kalila? Would I know Nikita was my fated? Or would we pass by each other like I did any other wolf?

"Your mind is going a mile a minute, Alpha Fin. What's got you so deep in thought?" Harlen's voice cut through those thoughts as I glanced over to him. I swear he knew me like the back of his hand. He should, since he was my dad's best friend and had become like a father to me since I came back to lead the Dolostone pack.

"Just thinking about what would've happened if Kalila was still alive. Would I know Nikita was my fated? Or would I pass by her like I do any other wolf?"

The sad smile on Harlen's face made me think that I would have just passed her by without a second thought. As much as I missed her and my unborn pup, I now knew this was supposed to happen since I had changed the Moon Goddess's plans. "I wouldn't know Alpha. I had never known of a person choosing a mate and then finding their fated."

We made our way up to our suite. Harlen went to the kitchen, and I went to the shower in my room. Stripping from the sweat and dirt covered grey sweats, I stepped under the running water. Nikita packed a punch. Which was why I evaded the others that she threw at me. I scrubbed my body, making sure to clean my hair as well.

She was all that I could think about. I wanted to take her in the shower, on the bed, up against the wall. Hell, even on the forest floor. Just thinking about the ways I wanted her was making me hard. Could she feel my wanting? I hope she could because maybe it would bring her to my room.

Aloysius wasn't much help as he pushed thoughts in my mind of what we could do to our mate. I was never one to think of things like this, but they were intriguing. Would she like not being able to use her hands? *Stop, we don't know if she would even like that.*

My wolf shook his head and then cocked his head to the side. I'm sure that if he would have had eyebrows, one of them would have been raised.

CHAPTER FOURTEEN

Fin

I knocked on Alpha Roy's office door and waited. Alpha Roy answered the door and he stepped back, allowing me inside before shutting the door behind me. The curtains were open showing off the training fields. That rested just below the edge of the hill.

"Have a seat Alpha Fin." Alpha Roy's tone was a little different since yesterday. I doubt he liked I was Nikita's mate. He sat down in front of me on the other couch in his office. "So, how were your first couple of days here in the Shonkinite pack?"

"It has been very enjoyable. You have a beautiful pack and territory." I answered him, trying to gauge what he was really trying to do in this meeting.

He nodded before leaning up and grabbed a glass off the table in front of us. I remembered being in this office plenty of times with my father as he spoke with Roy's father. Alpha Roy had changed a lot of this room to fit him. I noticed the desk was missing and my mate's scent was slowly fading from the room. Why was she in here? Did he already know before the training this morning that we were mates? I mean I didn't technically hide it when I saw her at the dinner yesterday.

"I think it's been horrible that our fathers couldn't ever come to an alliance. So, what do you want from my pack in this alliance?" Alpha Roy smiled as he poured what smelled like wolf whiskey.

I had come here to talk about him trading goods. Since my mate was here, I figured I would offer him something more since she was an asset to him and his pack. "I don't need anything from your pack other than my mate. I have some resources that I can help with, since you will lose one of your top warriors."

Alpha Roy sat back with his glass in his hand, swirling it around. "So, Nikita is your mate. Isn't she a little young for you? You're what? Fifty?"

I knew what he was doing. He was trying to push me into being the aggressor. I used to use this tactic with other wolves myself. I chuckled before reaching over and pouring myself some of his wolf whiskey. A slight growl came from him. If he wanted to be this way I could too. "Well, I'm sure your father was way older than your mother than I am of Nikita. Besides, one doesn't go against the Moon Goddess without consequences."

If I wasn't paying attention, I could've sworn that his eyes changed to his wolf's before he reined in his emotion with a smile. His smile widened and then raised his glass. "This is true. The Moon Goddess is known to strike down wolves that mess with her plans."

"This is true and I'm not fifty. I'm thirty-five in human years." I threw back the drink and sat the glass back down on the table before leaning back in my seat. He wanted to play hard ball about something like he was trying to get me to admit to something.

"Then I guess you're not that much older than she is. What do you have in mind about sending me in her place?"

"On a protected part of my territory, we have found some dolomite crystals. I can send you two percent of the crystals to do as you wish." Two percent of the crystals were worth ten of Nikita. Before I came out here, I had an estimator come out and look at them. Which was why I made sure to mention that it was protected and on my territory.

"Okay, when would I expect the first shipment?"

That was easy. I expected him to negotiate a little more, but I could handle that. There was something going on and I couldn't quite put my finger on it. "Once I leave here with Nikita and get back to my pack."

He nodded and placed his now empty glass on the table next to mine. "Well, let's get out of here and have some dinner."

We both stood and left his office. Something about this was too easy. *Harlen, can you find out more about this pack? I figured Alpha Roy and I would've been in this meeting a lot longer. There's something fishy going on.*

Yes, Alpha. I'll see what I can find out.

I sat in the Dining Hall on edge each time the door opened. But Nikita never came. I was a bit disappointed. Glancing over to Harlen, I nodded and stood. He nodded back to me, but continued to sit as I left the room. He was still trying to find out more about this pack.

Where was my feisty wolf? I turned down one of the corners and saw her. Standing where I was, I watched her and the pack of girls that had confronted her. My first instinct was to go to her and use my status as Alpha to make the she-wolves leave. But I knew Nikita wouldn't like that at all. She was proud to say the least.

"Warrior Nikita looks like she's scaling the ranks. How'd you get him to pick you? Huh?" The red-headed she-wolf snipped with a smirk on her face. I could tell that this she-wolf thought she was the best looking female here.

Being this close to Nikita, I could feel her growing anger and I wondered if she would fight all of them. She had yet to make a move to the she-wolf. So I wondered if she was of a higher rank than Nikita but she didn't look like a warrior and she was too old to be the beta's daughter. She could be the beta's sister. I noticed the others didn't seem too keen on being there.

"I didn't make him pick me. If anyone did, that would be the Moon Goddess herself. And as far as scaling the ranks. I couldn't give a damn about being Luna. Besides, I don't need to be Luna to put you in your place." Nikita's voice held so much venom it made me shiver.

She was right. Nikita didn't need a title to put anyone in their place. Hell, the Moon Goddess would've done herself a disservice if she hadn't mated Nikita to someone with a rank. If needed, she didn't need someone to protect her, but that wouldn't stop me from doing my job. I would protect her with my life.

Are you not going to go to your mate? Aloysius' thoughts came through and I made my way to her. He didn't have to prompt me twice. The other she-wolves noticed me as I came down the hall and they lowered their eyes. Nikita spun around just as I got near her. The surprise in her green eyes made me grin. Nikita was gorgeous.

"If you would excuse us, ladies." The other she-wolves scattered like mice as I held Nikita's gaze. I could get lost in her eyes forever. What I wouldn't give to pick her up and take her to my room.

Nikita crossed her arms and cocked her hip as she stared back at me. I waited until I couldn't hear or smell the other females at all. After we were alone, I didn't know what to actually say to her. I felt like a pup meeting my first crush. That had been a disaster in its own form.

"Take a walk with me?" I finally asked her. The sheepish smile on my lips was nothing like what I felt. Just her smell was making me want to hold her closer to me. I wanted my scent to cling to her so that the males that weren't at the training field this morning would know she was mine.

"A walk? Really? You came over to me just to ask me to walk with you?" She cocked her eyebrow, this time with a roll of her eyes. "I'm not in the mood right now. I still need to shower and get ready for bed. I have patrol tonight."

"Then I'll come with you," Nikita tilted her head to the side when it dawned on me that I didn't finish my sentence. "I mean that I can come patrol with you."

Dumbass, Aloysius groaned in my head as he covered his head with his paws.

"I'm good. I don't need any help with patrol. Bye, Alpha Fin."

I caught her arm and spun her back to me. Pressing her against the wall. A soft moan exited her lips. I hated that she continued to use my title. "Why do you insist on calling me by my title?"

Nikita shivered against me, and her arousal assaulted my nostrils. I wanted to pick her up and take her back to my room to devour her more than ever. But the way she acted toward me had me thinking she didn't really want to be my mate. "Tell me, feisty wolf. Why do you insist on calling me by my title?"

"Because that is a sign of respect, is it not? Now let me go. I need to get ready for my patrol." She pushed at me but didn't use as much of her strength as I knew she had. But the way her palms landed on my pecs made me wonder again if she didn't want me to go.

"It's not a respect thing when it's your mate." I growled as I ran my nose up her neck. She sighed as she leaned her head to the side, giving me more access to her neck. Damn, I wanted her right here and now.

"Fin, please..." The small sigh that rushed out from her lips took me to a whole other level. Nikita didn't know what she did to me. Or maybe she did, but was using it to her advantage. The way she said my name and then begged. Hell, I wanted to know what she would be like in bed.

"Yes, feisty wolf?" I was leaking so badly that I'm sure she could smell it and if I moved from my position, there would be a wet spot. I had never been like this before with a woman.

"I really need to get to my room to shower." Nikita's eyes locked with mine. They were flickering between her hunter greens and her wolf's deep golden color. There wasn't much for me to do other than let her go. That would be the right thing to do anyway.

She reacted to me like any normal fated female. The only thing that got me was the unsureness in her eyes. Did she not want to be with me? I watched as she jogged up the stairs. Her hair bouncing with each step and fuck if that ass of hers was calling to me. Nikita's room was on the second floor with the deltas and other top warrior wolves. Tonight I was going to be there with her on her patrol. She just didn't know it yet.

I stood on the steps of the pack house waiting for Nikita to exit the doors. She finally came out and stopped when she spotted me. Shaking her head, she walked past me, causing me to smile. I followed her to the edge of the woods before she rounded on me.

"What are you doing? I told you I don't need you here!" Nikita's hunter green eyes shone from the darkness of the woods.

"I can't run? Aloysius has been wanting to stretch his legs ever since we got here." I shrugged at her. The corner of my lip tugged upward. Nikita was unsure about what I really wanted. I came out of my shorts and I didn't miss her green eyes traveling down. Which made my smile even bigger.

"Fine, but stay away from me." She told me as she brought her eyes back up to my face. I could hear her heart racing in her chest. Yeah, she wanted me and she wanted what I had hanging.

"Okay, feisty wolf. But I bet you wouldn't even be able to catch me." I challenged her as I walked around her and did a backflip in the air as I shifted into my solid white wolf. I glanced over my now massive shoulder and tilted my head. Yes, I was goofing off and trying to impress her.

Nikita's mouth hung open as Aloysius and I took off into the woods. The pounding of another set of paws caused my left ear to swivel. Turning my head, I spotted her. She was closing in on me as we ran the trail. I sped up, losing her around a corner.

Nikita's wolf was a beautiful red with black and brown mixed in. But it was her face that got me. The white made it look like she had eyeliner on. Her eyes were the deep golden color I had seen them flickering between in the hall earlier. It was nothing I had ever seen on a wolf before but had heard of a pack that was full of them.

I slowed when a scent caught my attention. Nikita came up to my left side. Her hackles up, a growl low in her throat. She hadn't been protective around me, but her wolf could be taking over. Aloysius pressed me to allow him to take over and shifted closer to her. Her tail wagged before the female came out of the bushes. I could tell that the she-wolf was egging Nikita on, so Aloysius nuzzled into her neck before running his tongue along her muzzle.

The she-wolf dropped her head and then trotted away, leaving us on the trail. Nikita snorted and then ran. I took off after her, keeping pace with her as we rounded the bend. The way we flowed with each other just proved that we were meant to be. Nikita turned on me and shifted. I shifted with her and she shoved me into the rocky face of the hill we were next to. Her naked body pressed against mine. "Listen, I don't need you as a mate. I can take care of myself. Why don't you just reject me?"

"I'd never reject you, and I know you can take care of yourself. I've been searching for you for years."

Nikita shoved me again, harder this time, on the unforgiving surface behind me. There would be a cut on my back that was for sure. "You're a liar! You didn't show your face for seven years! I waited for you and you never came!"

"Nikita, I did look for you when I turned of age. I was a rogue for ten years so I didn't have a way of looking for you then." The hurt and anger in her eyes made me wonder what she was thinking.

She stepped back, letting me off the rock wall. Her brows furrowed as she stared at me. "What do you mean? You were a rogue. Were you not always an alpha?"

"I was. But my pack was overtaken by my uncle who then put me in a dungeon. I escaped and was a rogue for ten years." *Tell her about Kalila. You need to be honest with her.* Aloysius was right, but how do I tell her I had stopped looking for her?

"I've heard rumors about you taking a chosen. Is that true?" Nikita's hands went to her mouth after that. Like she didn't mean to ask or even talk about it. Someone in this pack must know that I had taken Kalila.

I sighed and ran my hands over my face before I locked my gaze back to hers. "Yes, I took a chosen. Because I was already the Alpha of my pack and I needed a mate. I looked for you for years before I took her."

"How long exactly?"

"Seven."

"I'm confused. How have you looked for me for seven years? When you were rogue for ten?" Nikita crossed her arms over her very naked chest. I hadn't even looked at her since we started talking. She didn't even have tan lines.

Harlen had found out from the Shonkinite beta that Nikita was twenty-five. Which was the reason I couldn't find her when I started my search at eighteen. She was just a pup. If I had just kept looking for her, and waited I would have found her. But that would also mean that my uncle would probably still be alive.

"Why are you confused? I'm ten years older than you."

CHAPTER FIFTEEN

Nikita

That's the reason he couldn't find me when he shifted for the first time. I was just a pup when he started looking for me. If I had been looking for my mate for seven years and didn't find them, I'd probably have done the same. So, how could I feel like this for what he had done?

"Nikita, if I had just been stronger and waited a little longer. None of this would've happened. I was weak." His voice wasn't his confident tone and when he caressed my face, I couldn't help but lean into those sparks.

"If she was still alive. Would you know I was yours?" my voice cracked because I thought I already knew the answer.

"No, and that's why the Moon Goddess punished me. She allowed my chosen and unborn pup to be taken from me by my uncle. Because she knew you'd go through this life without me." Fin pulled me close to him and my body ignited with sparks and desire. I wanted him just as much as Enyo did. The sadness in his aura and touch made me wonder. Was he sad for me or for her?

"I'm sorry Nikita. But I promise to be the best mate for you. To take care of you even when you don't need it. That and because I won't screw up twice is why I won't reject you." With one hand on my face and the other on my lower back, Fin pulled me flush against him. Even though I needed to keep my distance from him to be able to carry out my mission. There was nothing wrong with sharing a kiss with your mate. Right?

When Fin's lips met mine, I felt like I was in heaven. All the kisses from the other males that I had been with were nothing compared to his. My hands rested on his chest as he asked me for access to my mouth. Which I greedily allowed. Our tongues fought against each other, and the desire that I felt for him was like no other. Damn if I wasn't in the middle of my patrol I'd I have my way with him.

You should tell him about Alpha Roy's plan. He can help you. Enyo popped into my head. As much as I wanted to tell him, the order from my Alpha wouldn't let me. *Then let him mark you! Then you can work together and end this. You don't want to hurt him.*

As much as it pained me, I broke our kiss. The sparks still numbed my lips as I backed away from him. My heart raced in my chest and Fin's dark eyes were smoldering as they scanned my body. A hint of blue started to take over his eyes. "I need to patrol. I'm going to get into trouble if I don't get going."

"Then run, feisty wolf. I'll be right behind you." Fin's eyes flashed to his wolf's and at that moment I knew that kiss wouldn't be enough for him.

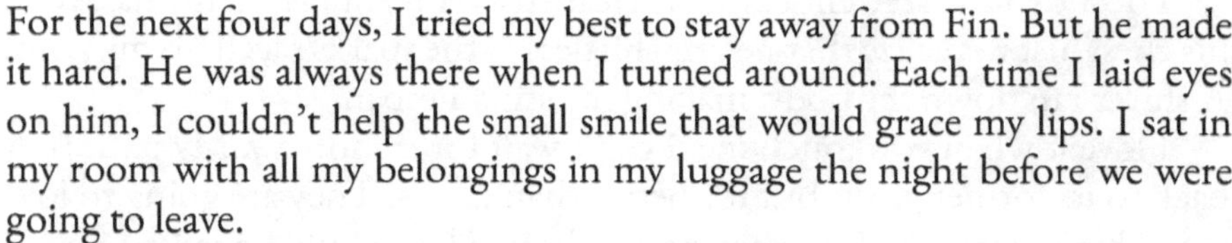

For the next four days, I tried my best to stay away from Fin. But he made it hard. He was always there when I turned around. Each time I laid eyes on him, I couldn't help the small smile that would grace my lips. I sat in my room with all my belongings in my luggage the night before we were going to leave.

Enyo I don't know if I can do this. I sighed as I tossed myself onto the mattress. Part of me wanted to go to him and tell him to mark me so that I could tell him what was going on. But then the submissive part of me told me I couldn't because my Alpha gave me an order to not let him mark me.

What do you mean? Enyo's head cocked to the side in my mind. She always acted like she didn't know what I was thinking. I think she did that so that I would have to talk it out.

If I leave with him and his Beta. It will mean that is when my mission starts. I'm not strong enough. I sat back up and stripped out of my clothes. It was hot in here and this would be the last time I would be in a bed alone and I doubt he would allow me a bed of my own.

Enyo curled up as I lay back on the bed. What was I going to do? Either way, I would lose my life. That's what I would deserve for killing my mate. *But you don't have to kill him, Nikita. There is another way to go about this. It's not fair that Alpha Roy has made us do this. I understand she was his cousin, but I doubt Fin would have been careless about her.*

You know that if she didn't die that we wouldn't have a mate. I snapped at my wolf. My body and mind were tired. I just needed some sleep.

Sparks raced up my arm, making me turn to my side with a moan. I wasn't ready to wake up yet. Fin's scent filled my nose, and I jerked fully awake. His dark blue eyes glowing in the dark.

"Fin!" I pulled the cover up where it had bunched around my waist. I didn't know why since he had seen me on the trail naked and I had seen him.

"Sorry, I didn't mean to wake you." His eyes glowed brighter in the darkness before he blinked.

"I doubt you mean that. If you didn't want to wake me, you wouldn't have been this close and touching me." My heart was returning to normal, but the fire that was beginning in my lower region was making me hot. And Fin didn't miss it either. His nostrils flared, but he didn't make a move.

"I mean every word. Why have you been avoiding me?" Every word out of his mouth made me even hotter. I wanted to reach down and touch myself as he watched me.

"I don't know." He chuckled and leaned over me. I placed my hands on his chest just to realize that he was shirtless as the sparks raced up my arms. A shiver ran down my body, making me stifle a moan.

"I love it when you touch me. I can't wait for tomorrow. My pack isn't back to its former glory, but it's better than it was. They are going to love you." Fin's words made my heart skip a beat. They would be calling for my death when they found out I was going to kill their alpha. "I want to kiss you again. Can I?"

I nodded. What was I going to tell him? No? Hell, I wanted to kiss him again, too. I had been thinking about him and his lips each night since that night on the trail. Fin leaned over me, his chest on mine as his lips locked with my lips.

The sparks exploded, and my desire to have him ignited. Why did I do this to myself? This was pure torture to know what this felt like and then take it away from me. I would be the one taking him away from me.

My fingers wove into his hair, pulling him closer to me. Fin's arms wrapped around my body and he brought me into his lap, pulling me away from the sheet. The groan from Fin as I seated myself above his cock made me smile. What I wouldn't do to feel him inside of me?

Fin broke our kiss this time and the soft whimper that came from me surprised even myself. "Nikita, I want you. But I don't want all these other males to hear you or smell you."

I knew he wanted me. Not only could I feel it through our bond, but underneath me as well. Fin was rock hard underneath me. If I didn't take him now I didn't know if I would be able to sit beside him to his pack.

He was everywhere right now, and I had to keep myself from saying what I wanted to say. "Then why are you here?"

"Because I needed to be near you. I don't know why you have been avoiding me, but I needed to see you. To feel you before we are stuck in a car for almost a day." His hands ran up and down my sides, sending more sparks down my body. So he was in the same boat as me. Maybe getting him to fuck me wouldn't be so bad. Fin's eyes were blue, telling me that his wolf was right at the surface.

"The room is soundproof." I blurted out. Enyo was enjoying my torture as she laid on her back, exposing herself. The little slut.

"I know, but not smell proof, my feisty wolf." Fin chuckled as he ran his tongue up my neck. Sending goosebumps along my skin. I normally didn't like being licked, but Fin was different.

"Take me Fin." The way he was making me feel made me say things I shouldn't. I shouldn't fuck him, but I needed the release that only he could now give me. But I had to keep him from marking me. I was in a dilemma, for fucking sure.

Fin's eyes glowed as he slipped off his shorts underneath me. His cock springing to attention as I straddled his lap. I took hold of him and he groaned as I covered him with my dripping wet pussy. He felt amazing as I rocked my hips. The feeling of being full was something I wasn't entirely used to. Fin's fingers dug into my hips while mine stayed on his shoulders. I thought I heard my door open, but didn't realize it until it was too late.

"Nikita, I think we need to..." The familiar male wolf's voice died off as the deep warning growl from Fin surged from his throat. The desire that it brought out in me made me wetter as I continued sliding up and down his girthy cock.

"Get out!" Fin's snarl excited me. I could feel his anger and desire through our bond.

"Oh! I...I'm... I'm sorry Alpha Fin." The door snapped shut just as quickly as it had opened. The fact that the other male had gotten an eye full of me riding Fin didn't bother me at all. I wanted to have this orgasm. I needed his cock to make me come and the pressure at my core was coming faster and if I lost it, I'd not be able to get it back.

"Why are you in such a hurry to end this?" Fin groaned as I bucked my hips. His hands running up my back to my shoulder blades. His voice in my ear made it that much hotter.

I didn't want to have this end, but I was chasing this desire like I hadn't ever done before. He fit just right inside of me and his hands being all over my body allowed me to feel the sparks wherever Fin decided to run them.

Fin was amazing, but it could also be the bond that we shared that made me feel like this.

Fin ran open-mouthed kisses along my jaw and down each side of my neck. When his lips came to where my mark would be, I stiffened. If he marked me, I would be dead before I left here with him. I pushed him away and got off his lap. The growl from him wasn't what I was expecting. "What's wrong, feisty wolf? Do you not want to be marked yet?"

I noticed that his canines had lengthened and it made his voice even more animalistic. Gulping, I glanced down. I had never been one to submit to anyone. What was I going to tell him? He stood coming up to me. I couldn't help but move my gaze to his hard cock at attention that dripped with my wetness. Fin was every mate's dream to have. Hell, the unmated she-wolves had their sights on him since he came to the training pitch.

Fin lifted my head to lock his gaze with mine. He cocked his head as I bit my bottom lip. I was never nervous around a male before. But Fin made my whole body act strange. "Nikita? Talk to me."

"I'm not ready." My voice came out timidly as I stared at him. It wasn't that I wasn't ready, it was that my Alpha had commanded me not to let him mark me. Hell, if I knew I would be able to get in the SUV without starting a war on my pack land between my mate and my Alpha, I would've let him sink those gorgeous white fangs into my mate mark.

"Okay. I won't mark you till you tell me to." I nodded and Fin crashed his lips to mine as he pulled me into his arms. He took me back to my bed and laid me on the mattress while he covered me. The moan from him as he slipped inside of me excited me and I wrapped my legs around his waist.

Fin grabbed hold of my wrists and pulled them above my head. His thrusts were slow and precise as he continued to hit the spot that none of my other partners could ever find. If there was a way to keep from dying on this mission, I wouldn't mind fucking him every day of my life.

My climax hit me all at once, just as he emptied inside of me. For as cold as I kept my room, it was sweltering in here. Fin dropped his forehead to mine as he held me close. The puffs of steam from our breath lingered between us.

"You are amazing." His husky voice whispered in my ear while his tongue lapped at the shell of my ear. I was finding I loved to be licked now and not just on my pussy.

"You're not that bad yourself." I chuckled at his expression when he rose to his hands.

"You wound me. Are you saying that I will have to kill the wolf that is better than me?" Fin's eyes seemed to shine in amusement, but I couldn't yet tell if he was being serious or funny.

"That's not what I said." I smirked at him.

CHAPTER SIXTEEN

Nikita

I woke up in Fin's arms. His scent of forest rain and Birchwood calmed me. I could lie in his arms forever. Fin started to stir beside me and I wiggled out of his embrace. The sun was starting to rise over the hilltops. It was time to get ready and leave.

"Feisty wolf, come back to bed." Fin's sleep filled voice urged me from my bed. My gaze went to him lying on the bed, a playful smile on his lips. I shimmied into my panties before pulling on the tank top that I had put out the night before.

"That would be a negative. It's about time to leave." I answered him as I searched for my leggings that I loved. Where the fuck did they go?

"Well, if that's true, then you should definitely put some pants on. Otherwise, I'm going to shred those panties and take you before we leave." The huskiness in his tone stopped my search for my leggings and brought my eyes back to him. Fin sat on the side of the bed, his right hand stroking his cock as his eyes stared back at me. The morning sun caressed his skin and brought out the definition of his shoulders and arms.

Turning to face him, I crossed my arms and cocked my hip to the side. While I gave him a defiant look. "Really? Did that work with all the other females you had been with?"

"Yeah. But none of them had made me feel the way you have." He smirked as he continued to stare at me and stroking himself. His eyes went to the door just before the knock sounded on the wooden barrier.

"Alpha Fin. The cars are being pulled around."

I didn't recognize the wolf's voice through the door. He must have been Fin's beta. Fin sighed and stood, his cock standing at attention as he made his way to me. I couldn't for the life of me figure out this male before me.

Fin's hand came to my face, and he ran a knuckle down my cheek and then to where my mark would sit. His eyes resting on the unmarked flesh.

"When you are ready. It will excite me to have my mark right here." Fin's breath fanned over near the barren place in the crook of my neck.

I stared up at him. If there were any chance that he would be able to mark me. I would welcome it. Of course, if he didn't find out the intentions of my Alpha to use me to kill him, I would allow him to mark me. *About time you think like that! I know we are supposed to obey the Alpha, but Fin is our mate. And I never liked being told what to do by that asshole.* Enyo piped up as she ran her long tongue over her fangs.

Yes, that was true, but would he believe me if I told him what my Alpha wanted from me? Or would he think I was lying and kill me? Would he kill me? The mate that he had been searching for? Because he had already told me that he wouldn't reject me. Knowing that the Moon Goddess would punish him again. So would he kill me?

Giving him a small smile, I went back to looking for my pants. By the time I found them, because they weren't where I had placed them the night before, Fin was already dressed and holding my bags. There wasn't much for me to take with me. I wasn't a material type of she-wolf who had to have things to make her happy. Unlike another certain she-wolf.

Training made me happy. Staying to myself made me happy. Running patrol made me happy. So, there wasn't much of anything to pack other than my clothes. I wondered since I was Luna if Fin would still allow me to train. If he didn't, there would be no other way than to sneak and train.

"Are you ready to meet your pack, my feisty wolf?"

Fin's voice brought me out of my thoughts as he handed my bag to his beta with the door wide open. A few wolves were trying hard not to stare as I came out of my room with Fin. I have never been embarrassed because I know the wolves that stared at me couldn't ever bring me down.

I passed Crystal and her posse of she-wolves. Each of them openly eyed me and Fin as we made our way down the hall and to the vehicles. Alpha Roy and Luna Adia stood on the porch steps and Delta Kyle stood near the door of the cars. Luna Adia wrapped me in a hug. I had become close to her when she came to the pack.

"Nikita, you are going to be an amazing Luna! I'm going to miss you though! You will have to call me." She had tears in her eyes as we pulled apart. She was probably the only one that I would miss from here.

"I will, Luna. You take care of yourself."

Alpha Roy was trying to hold his features in check, but wasn't doing such a good job at it. He was going to give us away before I even left the pack. Fin was shaking his hand, and the betas were saying their goodbyes. I spun around and couldn't help the overwhelming feeling sinking in my stomach. I would never return to this place. Either because I was the Luna of Dolostone or Fin's pack had killed me for killing their alpha.

"Nikita?" Fin's voice came from behind me and he had his hand out to me for me to take. I slipped my hand in his and walked past my Alpha. He was snarling in my head because I didn't acknowledge him. But if I did, he was going to ruin everything.

Fin let me in the vehicle first and then slid in with me. His beta climbed in the front seat and started the SUV. Fin took hold of my hand and brought it up to his lips. The shiver that raced along my skin with the sparks was nothing more than erotic. I didn't know how I was going to kill him if he continued to be like this to me.

Blushing, I pulled my hand from his and turned to the scene outside of my window. Fin scooted closer to me and turned my face. He was gentle with his thumb caressing my bottom lip. I wanted to pull it into my mouth and suck on it.

"Are you missing your pack this soon?" The way those dark eyes bore into mine was anything but torture. How wrong he was. I was just trying to keep from falling even further down this mountain with him.

"No, I don't miss it. I'm nervous and I've never been away from my pack before by myself." I told him. Hoping against hope that he would leave it at that.

"It's okay to be nervous. But my pack is going to love you." His thumb continued to lightly rub against my lips as he stared at me.

"Yeah, unless you have some ex-girlfriend that still wants you." I chuckled until I spotted his raised eyebrow. "You don't have some she-wolf that you've been with after your chosen?"

"No, and yes. But not from my pack. That just makes bad blood. I've seen what happens to packs when that happens. So I made sure I never slept with a female from my pack." Fin's features crushed my soul. He wasn't anything like Alpha Roy. He had slept with so many of the unmated she-wolves in the pack, it was unreal. And when I came of age and didn't find my mate, he had tried to get me to get in bed with him.

"While you were a rogue?" I pressed as he turned his gaze back to me.

"Yes. I was in a rough spot when I went rogue. There wasn't a day in my life back then that I thought this would happen. But it did and I'll be here for you for the rest of our lives." Fin kissed my temple before sliding back to his seat.

My heart hammered in my chest. What was I going to do? I knew that he meant every word he told me.

I arrived in the Dolostone pack just before dinner with Beta Harlen and Fin. Harlen had begun to talk about his mate Bella and their two children, Tobey and Sydnie. His son was still too young to take over, but he had started to show him a few things. He was easy to talk to. I was amazed that Fin didn't get jealous. From what I had noticed at my pack he didn't get jealous when I talked with a mated male.

There were two wolves at the gates to let us in. Fin was silent as we pulled through the pack lands. New grass grew from the ground as wolves stood up to watch the SUV pass. Beside them were new trees. Pups ran around parents who were planting flowers in gardens.

New buildings went up beside what looked like just built ones that were ready for occupants. I heard a chuckle beside me and turned my gaze on my mate. I saw the smile in his eyes as he stared back at me. The way he made me feel like a pup was unreal.

"Have you not seen things being built before?"

"No, we haven't built anything in a long time. Was all of this because of your uncle?"

"Yes, he destroyed a lot of the territory. Like I told you at your pack, mine has a long way to go to get back to where it was. With the help of the Rhyolite and Quartzite pack, we have gotten this far." Fin answered me just as Harlen pulled up to the pack house.

I noticed that some of it was being rebuilt as well. Some of the windows had been boarded up, and the sides were being restored with new rock. I was sure that before what had happened, this place was gorgeous.

"Was that the pack with the prophesied alpha? The brother?" I was curious because I had heard about this prophecy before and I wondered what he was like. Because anyone that said anything about the prophecy was never seen again, when Alpha Christian was still in power.

Fin chuckled. I didn't think he would ever get jealous. Well, unless some male came in while he was fucking me. I had to stop thinking of things like that, because just the thought of him inside me made me wet. "Yes, Alpha Nolen and his Luna Amora. They are close friends of mine. Along with Alpha Sawyer, I only met his Luna once at my second Alpha ceremony."

"I've never seen another pack. Unless they came to ours. Like you did. A few tried to buy me off of Alpha Roy."

A growl rose from Fin, bringing my attention back to him. Harlen had turned just as Fin exited the vehicle and shifted. I turned back to Harlen, and he shook his head while getting out of his side and opening my door.

"Did I say something wrong?" I didn't mean to make him mad. Alpha Roy had declined their offers and if Fin would've stayed, I could've told him that.

"He will be fine. Fin, as much as he has matured, is still learning to rein in his emotions. He will be back before dinner. Let me show you to his... I mean both of your room." Harlen grabbed my bag from the back of the SUV and led me up the steps and into the packhouse.

It was beautiful inside. Fresh paint stained the walls and the glass in the windows that weren't boarded, allowed so much sun in that the lights in the ceiling weren't really needed. It was definitely bigger than my previous packhouse. Fin really did know how to run a pack.

Since Fin was the only leader of the pack, I figured it would be more bachelor than neutral. This had a woman's touch if I ever saw one. Omegas were cleaning and placing new flowers in the vases. While other wolves were coming in from the back with vegetables. Damn, they grew their own food?

As I walked by, they all stared at me before going back to work. I could hear some of them talking about me when they thought I was out of earshot. They could gossip, I didn't care. I was used to that type of thing back in my old pack. It wouldn't be any different here.

"Once they know who you are, they won't be like that. They are very nice wolves. They are not too sure about new people anymore." It was like Harlen was reading my mind. Maybe that's why he was so good at his job.

"I'm not worried about them, Beta Harlen."

A beautiful older woman came up to us with a boy at her side. She kissed Harlen and then turned to me. Before I knew what she was doing, she enveloped me in a hug I never saw coming. No one had ever given me a hug even as a child.

"Bella, let her breathe." Harlen chuckled as the woman named Bella stepped back, giving me my space back. "Nikita, this is my wife Bella and my son Tobey."

"She is our future Luna." Bella looked at her son with a smile and the boy had a look of awe in his eyes as he stared up at me.

"How do you know Beta Bella?" I asked her. The curiosity in my voice made her giggle.

"Because I can smell Alpha Fin on you hun, and I'm not meaning the bedroom scent. That man has made sure that no other male will even look at you the same." Bella answered me. I thought the mate mark could only transfer that scent. Bella leaned over to me and whispered. "I taught his mother that little trick. It seems that his father taught him."

I nodded, not knowing what else to do other than that. Harlen shook his head and motioned for me to follow him. He and Bella led me up another flight of stairs. I made sure to memorize where I was going. Each floor looked like it was being renovated as well. When we reached the last floor, I noticed that this one only had a door on the landing.

Harlen opened the door and let me go first. Bella followed me in as I looked around. Harlen walked to one side and down a hall. I assumed it was the hall to the rooms. He came back and held out his hand to his wife.

"Alpha Fin said to make yourself at home. He will be back in a few minutes. Dinner will be served at six." Harlen bowed his head and Bella smiled at me as they left me in the room.

CHAPTER SEVENTEEN

Fin

I walked up the hill to the packhouse, completely nude. Since all the clothes had been taken off the line. Luckily for me, I knew just the way to get to my room without going through the house.

Climbing up the tree near my balcony, I jumped from the limb and onto the Dolostone crystal railing. I went through the open doors and followed my mate's scent of peonies and cedar to the bathroom and leaned against the doorjamb. Nikita was drying her hair when she finally noticed me in the doorway. Her eyes flickered between her wolf's and her hunter green.

Her lithe body trembled, and I caught her rubbing her thighs together. I chuckled and made my way to her. It excited me that she didn't try to cover herself up in front of me. "It's my turn."

"By all means. It's all yours, Alpha Fin."

I cocked my head at her answer. There she was, using my title again. I shook my head and leaned against her and turned on the water once more. Stepping under the warm water, I allowed the warm liquid to run down my mud caked body. I knew I shouldn't have acted that way in the SUV, but the thought of that young alpha selling my mate to another pack pissed me off. It made me wonder why he didn't. Did they not offer enough money?

Hell, he shouldn't have even thought about the idea of selling his best fighter to someone else. Especially someone who was needing someone to help build their warriors. They would be able to use her to take over the pack.

As I cleaned my body, she was brushing out her hair in a pair of panties and a bra. I wanted to keep her in this room as long as I could, but I had heard about the talk about the new woman in the packhouse from the other wolves through the mind link. They were worried about her and intrigued by her at the same time. I didn't blame them.

Besides, they deserved to know that their Alpha now had his fated mate and that everything would be okay. They needed a hope that I couldn't give them myself. They needed her, and I was glad that she was as strong as she was.

I didn't think about training Kalila because we were in an era of peace, so why should my Luna know? But Nikita, she was the polar opposite and I couldn't help but love her for it. She was the breath of air I needed.

There was just one thing that unnerved me. Most females wanted to be marked and mated as soon as possible. Why didn't Nikita? Did she still have feelings for a male in her pack? I mean, it wasn't my fault that I was older than her. It was, however, my fault that it took me so long to find her because I had taken a chosen.

I hopped out of the shower, and Nikita had made her way to the bedroom. She was bent over the bed, digging in her suitcase that she had brought with her. The panties showing off the bulge of her pussy. "I think if you keep bending over that bag like that, then you might not make it to dinner."

She straightened up and glanced over her shoulder. Nikita's eyes flickered between her and her wolf's. "You would be disappointing your pack, would you not? Besides, I think your Beta's female likes me and I don't want to mess that up."

"Bella likes almost everyone."

Nikita giggled before shimming into her pants that she had found. I had never been one for staring at someone as they dressed, but she was a vision I never could have imagined for myself. *She needs to be marked and mated. Nikita would be even more beautiful if she was swollen with our pup.*

She isn't ready to be marked yet and if I learned anything from Selene, then being patient is a virtue. I answered Aloysius as I went into my closet and grabbed some casual clothes to wear to the dinner. Tonight wouldn't be too much of a celebration but it would be where I would announce her as my fated.

Aloysious snorted and turned his back on me. Heading out into the living room area, Nikita stared out the balcony doors at the mountains. If she would allow me to mark her, I'd be able to mindlink her like the other pack members. But I was going to respect her wishes for right now and allow her to get comfortable here at the pack.

"You ready to head down?"

Nikita turned and nodded. I didn't miss the way her eyes roamed my body as she made her way to me. Placing my hand on the small of her back, I steered her to the door and down the steps. The muscles in her lower back twitched and rolled as she walked with me. They reminded me of last night when she was on my lap riding me. I couldn't wait to have her again in my bed screaming my name.

I traced slow circles where my hand rested and she glanced at me from the side of her eye. A few of the younger wolves snickered while others sighed as we walked by. They had never seen me with a she-wolf and nothing like Nikita. The older ones had been there with Kalila, and I hoped they didn't make Nikita's life too hard. Jade and Harmony were sending her glares as I brought her up to the Alpha table. They would just have to deal with this change because Nikita would be here for the rest of her life.

Bella was sitting beside Harlen, their son sitting with his friends. Bella smiled at Nikita as she sat in the seat beside me. I had yet to name a gamma, so the seat beside Nikita was empty. Wolves filed in and took their seats. Tables to the back didn't fill as there were still wolves out in the fields and some patrolling. It had been packed before my uncle took over.

The wolves that were left did what they needed to survive. I didn't blame them for that because I had run when Harlen told me to. So that I could return to them. But I didn't return and a few of them blamed me for what happened to them while my uncle was in charge. Which had often made me wonder if being Alpha again was what was needed.

Jade and Harmony sat at their normal tables but continued to glare at Nikita. Other than them hating her because of Kalila, I couldn't think of another reason they would hate another wolf they hadn't met before. When the rest of the wolves came in, I stood and quieted the murmurings that were moving around the room.

"Dolostone pack. I have some great news for you all." I paused to look over at Nikita and held out my hand for her to take. She slowly took my hand and stood. "Dolostone, this is Nikita, and she is my fated mate."

The silence from them hurt a little as I glanced over at them. Bella stood first and came up to Nikita and hugged her. "I'm glad that Alpha Fin has finally found his fated. I personally am happy that you are here!"

Harlen stood and bowed his head to her, acknowledging her as his Luna. I could feel her anxiety through the bond but she didn't show it on her face. Nikita held her head high as she nodded back to Harlen and Bella.

"If she is your fated, then why is she not marked? And exactly how old is she? Eighteen?" Jade's voice cut through the silence, and a few gasps came from a few of the surrounding wolves. No one would have dared challenge me and I couldn't believe that Jade would in front of everyone.

"For your information, I'm not eighteen. I'm twenty-five." Nikita's voice rose from beside me with authority. If I didn't know any better, I thought I had heard a little bit of an alpha tone to her voice. And since I didn't mark her yet, it wasn't coming from our bond. I was proud of her for standing up for herself, not like she wouldn't.

"Well, you will be no Luna of mine. The real Luna lost her life. There will be no other Luna for me." Jade stood and crossed her arms over her chest. She was one of the strongest females here. That was until Nikita stepped onto the territory.

"That's fine. I'm not here to replace anyone. I'm here because your Alpha found me and I'm his fated. As far as him not marking me, I asked him to give me some time. Not like you really needed to know any of that. And if you still have a problem with me, we can meet at the training pitch." The way she talked to her let Jade know that she was ranked higher than her.

"I'd meet you at the training pitch anytime and day."

I glanced at Nikita before bringing them back to Jade. She definitely had a death wish challenging her Luna. The look in Nikita's eyes told me that she was trying to rein in her wolf. I got in front of them both and I didn't know if that was the best idea, since Nikita and Jade growled at me.

Let them fight, Fin. It will put Jade in her place. Besides, she shouldn't challenge a superior like this. Harlen mindlinked me, bringing my attention to him and Bella. Bella was holding her wolf back as well. She had taken a liking to Nikita as soon as she saw her. That was for sure.

"If you two want to fight. It will happen tonight. Submission only, not to death." I told them, glancing between the two angry she-wolves. I couldn't afford to lose Jade but I also couldn't allow her to disrespect her Luna.

"I'm down with that and I'm ready to kick our new Luna's ass," Jade smirked. She was digging herself in a bigger hole than I thought she would be able to get out of.

Nikita was quiet, but that was when she was the most dangerous. She turned on her heel and left the dining hall. Aloysius whimpered, but I stayed where I was. Nikita knew where to go to get changed.

Jade left as well with Harmony. I didn't know what I had just done, but I hoped it didn't kick me in the ass later.

Nikita

I made my way down to the training field after I changed into my training clothes. This bitch was going to get her ass beat. She thought because I was small that I was going to be a pushover. She didn't know what I was capable of because if she did, she wouldn't have challenged me.

She and her little friend were already in the field. When I walked up, Fin came up to me. I figured he would tell me to not hurt her. But if I was going to be Luna of this pack, then I needed to show them that I wasn't a pushover. At least I would have to pretend to until I completed my mission and then I would allow this bitch to kill me.

"Give her hell." I was shocked when he told me that. But I nodded and stepped away from Fin. He was confident in me and I knew why he was because I had taken down a wolf almost as big as him. When he had showed up at my pack.

The she-wolf smirked again at me as she took a fighting stance. I didn't take my stance; I wanted to figure out her fighting style. She lunged at me and I dodged it. The next punch I allowed to hit me. Making her believe that she could actually win was one of my strategies. It made taking down big male wolves even more fun.

I kept dodging some of her attacks until she shifted to her brown wolf. The corner of my lip tugged up as she attacked me again, this time in her wolf form. Taking a page out of Fin's book, I flipped backward and shifted in mid-air into my wolf. Shredding the workout clothes in the process.

Gasps from the crowd that had gathered around intrigued me. My red color wasn't too common, but what set me apart from the ones that I had met was the black and brown mixed in with my coat. And let's not forget about the white that rimmed my eyes.

Enyo was a force to be reckoned with and I was ready to show this bitch that I was the top bitch here. I was taller than her in my wolf form, which slowed her a moment for me to get my jaws around to the nape of her neck and we threw her.

She landed on her side near a group of males on the sideline. She rose to her feet, lunging back at me, using her teeth and claws to grab me by my front leg. Jade tried to pull me off my feet as she threw me into the air. Coming back down, I landed on my paws and snarled. She wasn't a pushover, that was for sure. If she hadn't tried me, I was sure that she and I could have been friends.

Jade ran at me again and I waited for her to get near me when I jumped her and grabbed hold of her tail. Throwing her again, but this time she landed in front of her friend. The sound of something breaking told me she wouldn't be getting up. So, I ran up to her and growled, showing my teeth at her. She submitted with a little whimper as she turned to her back, exposing her stomach to me. I glanced up from her and over the crowd they were quiet besides the clapping from Bella and Beta Harlen. Fin was smiling beside them, his arms over his chest.

Enyo wagged her tail at him. *Enyo, we can't be fucking him again. The next time we might get marked.*

That is a good thing. Then we can tell Fin about what our Alpha wanted from us.

I sighed and shook our head. The she-wolf shifted back and kneeled before me. She was already bruising from the hits that I made and then when I threw her across the field twice. Everyone here now knew that I wouldn't be some pushover as much as they thought I would.

CHAPTER EIGHTEEN

Nikita

I had been here at the Dolostone pack for a couple of months. Fin had been an absolute gentleman, which made my mission of killing him all the worse. I mean, killing your mate was a disgrace, and the Moon Goddess would probably strike me down, but what could I do?

The sun had set, and I stood on the balcony of his room and watched as the pack had started preparations to go to bed. I couldn't believe a few months ago this pack had been in turmoil over his uncle. A few of them still looked a little skinny, but they were proud of their alpha. Even without the mindlink, I could tell that they respected him and would do anything for him.

"Hey, my feisty girl. Are you missing home?" I turned as he came out onto the balcony. He wore only shorts, his chest bare and glistened with droplets of water, and I couldn't help but gulp. His eyes were flickering from his dark brown to the deep blue of his wolf's. I had never been one to turn down sex, but I was trying to keep him from marking me and fucking him was one good way to get marked.

"No. This is my home, is it not?" I asked as I stared at him. My gaze traveled his body and stopped where he bulged. I wet my lips and he stalked forward, encasing me between his arms like he had when we were at my pack. My hands went to his biceps and the sparks that raced through my body made the desire even worse.

"You smell so good." His growl made a shiver race down my body. It was getting harder and harder to tell him no.

"Yeah?"

"Yeah." Fin grabbed me up, making sparks race across my skin where his hands touched my bare skin. He sat me down and my heart crashed in its cage as I watched him stroll a couple of feet away from me. The lust in his eyes made me wet. "On your knees, princess."

I was panting at those words, but I held my ground and crossed my arms. As much as I wanted to do as he commanded, I couldn't let him think he had that much control over me. Cocking my head as I allowed my eyes to travel his body once more. He was hard and his shorts were tented. I ran my hand down my body and closed my eyes as I caressed my breast. I knew he was watching me. There was no doubt about that. "Mmm, why don't you come over here and make me?"

He chuckled, snapping my eyes back at him. "Don't worry, my feisty girl. I will."

Fin stalked forward, ripping my shirt from my body and crashed his lips to mine. His hands roamed my skin as he nipped my bottom lip, making me open to allow his tongue to fight with mine. I moaned into his mouth as he grabbed me up by my ass and carried me over to the bed. Fin dropped me on the soft mattress and tore my shorts off. The tearing of the material making my heart pick up.

He covered me, and his cock pressed to my entrance. Everything about him made me wetter than any of the males I had been with. Fin placed open mouth kisses to my neck and nipped down to where my mate mark would be. I wrapped my legs around his waist and flipped us where he was on the bottom and I was on top.

The grin on his face and the quirk of his eyebrow told me he wasn't mad about it. One hand went to my hip while his other went into my hair. Pulling it back and making me arch as I sheathed him. "I told you I'd get you on your knees."

I moaned as I slid up and down him. My hands on his firm chest as I rode him and meeting each of his powerful thrusts with my own. Fin unwound his hand from my hair and placed both hands on my hips, digging his fingers into my flesh as he tried to keep from coming undone.

This feeling of power with him excited me. I loved that I was the only one who could make him like this. As he struggled to keep from coming inside of me. This was the first time in a long time that I had allowed him to touch me because I was afraid that if we were more intimate than I would allow him to mark me. And I couldn't do that right now.

"Fin, right there." The breathless moan of his name and the words that had followed wasn't me. I never was vocal in bed it just wasn't something I did.

"My feisty wolf wants to come? I need her to beg me to let her come." Fin's husky tone hit just as hard as he did inside me.

I had never been one to beg. But he was keeping me from getting my orgasm. "Fin! Please!"

Fin sat up and then stood, bringing me with him and up against a wall. He thrusts inside me, hitting just the right spot as he kissed my jaw and neck. I wrapped my hands around the back of his head, pressing him further in as my core tightened.

Let him mark you, Nikita. Then you can tell him what happened. Enyo urged me as she laid her head on her front paws.

I can't. I moaned in my head as Fin's thrusts brought me ever closer to the euphoria I was chasing.

This would be a lot easier if you'd let him mark you. Enyo quipped.

"Nikita, are you okay?" Fin's voice brought me away from the conversation between me and my wolf.

"Yes, I'm sorry. Enyo was distracting me." Stupid bitch. Enyo snorted before turning her back on me.

Fin chuckled before he nipped my shoulder. Sending sparks down my body like an electric current. The moan that escaped from me was nothing if not euphoric.

"Looks like I can bring you back with just a little nip. Can you imagine what it would feel like if I mate marked you? The orgasm you'd have..." Fin's sexy baritone contracted my pussy and when he nipped my bottom lip with his canines. Damn!

I wanted him to mate mark me but what would I say to Alpha Roy when he came to pick up the Dolostone crystals? He'd start a war if I went against him. I couldn't put the pack in that situation. They were starting to grow on me. Even Jade and Harmony. I now needed to protect the pack, because my old pack was just a little bit bigger than Dolostone right now.

Fin's head went to the spot where my mark would sit and I felt his lips clamp down on the spot. But I didn't fight him. Fuck it if he wanted to mark me, then damn it mark me! The suckling at the spot brought me to climax as my hand went into his hair.

"Fuck, Nikita!" Fin's growl almost brought me to another orgasm as he came inside of me. I wasn't too worried about getting pregnant. My heat wasn't for a few more months and hopefully by then I wouldn't be near Fin.

Alpha Roy and his Luna came up the steps of the pack house. Fin greeted them as I stood at the top. As much as this was becoming a thing, I didn't want to be here anymore. I wanted to run, so that I didn't have to be in the same room as him. Because the only thing that he is going to want to do was ask why Fin wasn't dead yet.

I wouldn't be able to answer that. One, Enyo was keeping me from doing it and then the thought of the soul-crushing depression that would come after he was gone would be my downfall. The only thing that I could think to do was allow either the pack to end me or kill myself. I wouldn't be able to live without him now.

Even though we had yet to mark each other, Fin had been so good to me since I had been here. So there was my dilemma. I hated that my Alpha had put me in this position. Why did I have to be the one to do this? He could've very well had him killed on our pack lands.

When Alpha Roy approached me, his eyes fell to the hickey that rested at the place my mark would sit. Before his glaring eyes locked with mine. I bowed my head before bringing it back up. Luna Adia came up to me and hugged me.

"Oh Nikita! It's been so long since I saw you. Why haven't you had your Luna ceremony and you haven't marked each other?" She took my arm, and we headed into the packhouse before Alpha Roy could say anything.

"Luna Adia, it's so nice to see you this time." I smiled at her as she patted my arm. He hadn't brought her the last couple of times he had picked up the crystals.

"Nikita, you don't have to call me Luna anymore. We are of equal rank now. Besides, we are friends first, right?" She giggled before the large ceiling of the pack house caught her attention. "Oh my Goddess! This is a beautiful place!"

When I had come here, the pack house had been being remodeled and Fin had wanted to know what I would like to see in the house. I had always dreamed of a vaulted ceiling and of a nice place for the pack wolves to be able to sit and take a load off.

This pack was completely different than my previous pack. Here, a lot of the wolves helped with everything. The only ranks that weren't blurred were Fin's and Beta Harlen's and his wife's. I had caught him helping out with a few omegas with the garden. I didn't know if this was just how he was or if this was the new him when he came back to be the Alpha of his pack.

"Thank you Adia. It has come a long way."

"I heard! Poor Alpha Fin. He had been kicked out by his Uncle and then had to rebuild his pack back! But this is amazing. You both have done so well with this place." Adia was so enthralled with the place she hadn't noticed that Fin and her mate had walked up to us.

"Adia, baby, we shouldn't talk about the past. So Nikita, how has your stay been here?" Alpha Roy came up to us and wrapped his arm around her waist. She nuzzled into him with a smile.

Fin came up to me as I stood there. His fingers threading into mine. I glanced over at him and his brows were knitted before he smiled at me. Fin had become someone I could lean on and I could only hope that he could do the same with me.

"It's been great. Alpha Fin and the Dolostone pack have been amazing." I answered him, the growl from him told me he didn't like my answer. He hated when I called him by his title.

"Next month on the full moon we will have her Luna ceremony. I thought it would be fitting to have it during the blue moon." Fin's voice carried over the sounds from outside. My heart was racing. What!

I hadn't been told that I would have my Luna ceremony then and having it on the blue moon was something that rarely happens. That was when the Moon Goddess was said to have given us our wolves. A long time ago.

"That is an honor for any rising Luna. We will definitely have to be present for this," Alpha Roy answered with a little too much emotion. He glanced down at his mate and she was the only one to have a genuine smile on her face.

I tried to keep my emotions to myself, but I knew I wasn't doing a very good job when Fin stiffened beside me. At that moment, Beta Harlen came from the other side of the foyer. He bowed his head and then continued forward.

"Alpha Roy, Luna Adia, if you would come this way we are serving lunch and would like for you to let us know how the cooks have prepared it." Harlen bowed his head again and led both my former pack members to the dining room.

Fin turned to me, and I sighed. I just wanted them to leave and never come back. But according to Fin, he had come to terms with Alpha Roy about giving him a percentage of the Dolostone crystals in exchange for an alliance. But what Fin didn't know was that Alpha Roy didn't want to be allied with him since he had basically killed his cousin. He just wanted revenge on the alpha.

"Nikita, is everything okay? Every time Alpha Roy comes here, you are on edge."

CHAPTER NINETEEN

FIN

Nikita shuffled her feet before looking up at me. She had been acting off since I brought her here. But after she showed Jade just a little bit of her strength, the entire pack knew she was every bit of the Luna that they needed. A bunch of them were excited about the upcoming ceremony.

"Nikita? Talk to me." I pulled her closer and brought her gaze back up with my fingers under her chin. The pad of my thumb ran across her bottom lip.

"It's nothing..."

"Nikita, I can feel the stress coming through our bond. What can I do to help you?" Caressing her face made her lean her head into my palm. "You know I love you. You can tell me anything."

Enyo has been telling her to tell us something, but she says she's scared. Aloysius commented in my head. He whimpered before he laid his head on his front paws.

I could tell that she was. Next month I'll meet Alpha Roy with the crystals. I hated she was like this around him. But since she wouldn't let me mark her, I couldn't mindlink with her.

"I just need to be with you. I'll be okay." Nikita grinned up at me, but it didn't reach her eyes. I decided not to push it for now. I didn't want to stress her even more.

"Okay, well, let's get something to eat and send them on their way. Shall we?"

Nikita nodded and walked with me at my side. As we entered the Dining room Alpha Roy glared at Nikita. He must not have let her reject the pack. But why would he still want her under his control?

Harlen. I think Alpha Roy still has control of Nikita. Can you do some digging? I really don't understand why he would.

Of course, Alpha Fin.

I cut the link between us as we settled in our seats at the table. Alpha Roy sat beside Nikita and I could feel the unsteadiness through our bond. He was definitely doing something to her. But I couldn't figure out why she was letting him do what he was doing.

Grabbing her hand, I brought it up to my lips. The shiver that raced down her arm caused goosebumps to follow. Nikita glanced over at me and smiled. A light little blush rushed across her cheeks. I never thought she would let herself blush.

"Alpha Fin, you mentioned that Nikita will have her Luna ceremony next month. Why don't we come then to pick up the crystals?" Alpha Roy leaned over to talk with me and Nikita stiffened as she moved her arm away from him.

"That is fine. I hope that you will be able to make it. I'm sure Nikita would love to have her pack come." I answered him to see if he would give anything up.

Luna Adia grabbed Nikita's hand and smiled at her, but Alpha Roy just scowled at their hands. Something was up with him and I intended to find out what. If not tonight, then soon. Because Harlen was still looking into how Kalila and Alpha Roy were related.

After we had finished our lunch, Alpha Roy and his Luna went on a walk and Nikita went up to our room. I motioned for Harlen to follow me and we went to my office. Standing at the window, I watched as the wolves worked on the inner town of the pack. One of these days, this place would be better than it was.

"Fin, Nikita has been acting strange since he has been coming to collect the crystals. She has always been very confident. But when he comes, it's like she changes."

Harlen came up to me by the window. Bella had gone out of the pack-house with their son. Tobey was now almost a teenager and had been studying to become Beta. He was a hardworking wolf and was coming into his own very well. It was going to be fun when he became beta.

"Some part of me thinks he is keeping her from letting me mark her."

"What do you mean, Fin? Her being your mate should give her a choice."

I ran my hand through my hair and then down my face. "I know, but if he threatened her, I'm sure she would side with him."

"Well, I'll keep looking into him. He's young. He has to have some family somewhere else."

Turning, I laid my hand on his shoulder and sighed. "Thank you Harlen. I just wish that she would talk to me. I can feel that she wants to, but she is always holding herself back."

"Don't worry, Fin. She's strong. I know she will handle whatever is going on."

"I hope you are right."

Nikita

Why would he allow them to come to the Luna ceremony? I just wanted him to go away so I could talk to Fin. But with him, coming to the pack every month was taking its toll on me.

Alpha Roy was pushing me to end Fin. But I couldn't. This pack had become home to me and Fin was a mate any female would ever want. I couldn't do it. Why did this have to be so fucking hard? After pacing the bedroom for a pack,while,I went down to the garden to get some fresh air.

"Nikita!"

I stiffened at his voice. Glancing around at my surroundings, I noticed I had walked straight into the part of the garden he was in. Fuck!

"Yes, Alpha Roy."

He grabbed me by my elbow and forced me further into the garden, before pushing me up against the rock wall. Enyo was snarling and growling in my head. If I was Luna of this pack, he wouldn't have been treating me like this.

"Why isn't he dead yet? It's been two months! What are you waiting for?"

"Alpha, these things take time. I have to make sure that no will suspect me." The way he his eyes flickered between his wolf's and his human ones unnerved me. Like why couldn't he just fight him and kill him?

Because he is weaker than our mate. That's why he is trying to use you to get this done. Enyo answered me as she bared her teeth in my head.

"Not this long! Besides, at some point, he is going to mark you! He is already trying to with that hickey. Kill him and be done with it!" Alpha Roy shoved me harder into the wall.

Enyo was itching to get out to fuck this male up. Alpha or not, she hated he was bullying us into hurting our mate. It took everything in me to keep her from making me shift and attacking him on Fin's territory.

"I will, Alpha. But I need time."

"I expect you to have him lying at my feet before that Luna ceremony."

Enyo was growling and snarling in my head. This was getting harder to do as the days went by. But what was I supposed to do? Alpha Roy shoved me once more before he walked away from me. I slid down the wall as all the adrenaline started to leave my body. Why didn't I reject him and then go rogue?

It would be so much easier if I would do that. Hell, I was ready to kill myself to keep him from leaving this world. I needed some advice but I didn't know who I could go to talk about this. Why was I so weak?

"You know, it would be easy to kill yourself. But then what would Fin do if you were no longer in this world? He went through hell trying to find you."

The silvery voice brought my head up. I hadn't even noticed someone coming up to me. Struggling to my feet, I took in the woman's appearance.

Her silver hair and eyes caused me to shiver, but she smiled and then patted the bench she was sitting on.

"Are you the Moon Goddess?" I stammered as the soft, willowy giggle came from her. Fuck, she was here to punish me for what I was planning on doing.

"Yes, you are definitely quicker than your male counterpart. I had to tell him who I was, and no, I'm not here to punish you."

"You've spoken to Fin?" I asked her as I sat down beside her.

"Yes, but it has been many years ago. What is the problem, child?"

"Alpha Roy wants me to kill Fin. Because he killed his chosen. Well, he allowed her to die and Fin's chosen was Alpha Roy's cousin. I don't know what to do." I laid my hands in my lap as I stared at the ground. A flower poked through the crack beside the bench.

"I know that his chosen died. But you shouldn't have to do Alpha Roy's dirty work. This pack has started to grow and they have two powerful allies if anything was to happen. Alpha Roy should know that death is inevitable. It happens to all of us."

"What should I do?" My voice sounded small compared to what it normally was as I spoke to the woman who gave us all life.

The Moon Goddess placed her palm on my face and smiled.

"You know what you have to do. You've known it ever since he ordered you to do what he wanted. Be the strong Luna that I know you are. That

I made you to be. Because I wouldn't have given Fin you if I knew he wouldn't be able to match your energy."

She kissed my forehead like my mother used to on rare occasions before she died. She was right. I couldn't allow Alpha Roy to push me to do this. I wanted to be with my mate and that is what I was going to do.

Running into the packhouse, I ran into Harlen. For him, being an older wolf, he was still very much a force to be reckoned with. "Oh! Harlen, do you know where Fin is?"

"Yes, he went to the Dolostone crystal mines with Alpha Roy. He should be back shortly."

"Okay, do you think you could tell him to come see me?"

"Of course, Luna... uh I mean Nikita." Harlen bowed his head and then left out the doors I had just came through.

If he had gone to the mines, then that meant they were fixing to leave. Then I could be alone in my pack with Fin. I needed to talk to him and let him know what Alpha Roy was going to do. This shouldn't have gone on for as long as it had, but now I was going to fix that.

Heading to the kitchen, I was already hungry and then thought about bringing up food for the both of us. I spotted Andrea at the counter and went up to her. She was a sweet girl and had been very nice to me when I would come and get food for the both of us.

"Hey Andrea, what's on the menu for tonight?" Whatever she had in the oven was appetizing.

"Oh, hi Luna! I'm making some soup for the sick kids and then I'm baking bread for dinner tonight. Do you want me to have dinner sent to you and Alpha Fin's room?" Her smile was bright.

The other omegas that worked in the kitchen had started working on what they would make for dinner. I hoped it was the first dish that they had made when I first came. It was delicious.

"That would be great. Thank you, Andrea!" I turned and ran into Jade.

Her eyes flashed between her human's and her wolf's. I crossed my arms over my chest as I stared back at her.

"What is your problem this time, Jade?"

"You're my problem, Nikita. You don't even love him, do you?" The snarl in her voice would've been terrifying if I were any other wolf. But I had taken on bigger, stronger wolves than her.

"And why's that?"

The kitchen had gone silent as we stared at each other. This she-wolf was getting on my nerves. All because I wasn't the chosen luna that Fin had taken years before.

"Because I heard what you are planning for the Alpha. But you won't be able to get near him to do anything. I will end you even if I die trying." I could see her wolf rising to the surface as she stood in front of me. Enyo wanted to put her in her place again.

"I don't know what you think you heard, but..." For the third time heard,today, I was shoved into something. My back was going to be bruised if this continued to happen. , but

"Don't tell me what I heard and what I didn't. I know, and I will tell Alpha Fin as soon as he gets back from the mines."

I growled at her, Enyo coming so close to the surface that I could feel the fear from the other wolves in the room. Grabbing her by the neck, I took us out of the kitchen and then into the foyer.

"What you heard was just me getting my old alpha off my back. If you continue to go against me, I will make you pay. I'm not going to be disrespected because you can't get over the fact that I'm now going to be the rightful Luna of this pack." I threw her to the floor and stalked up to her. As Harmony came around the corner. "You can either get on board with this or we will continue to have bad blood between us. You both can choose."

Jade's eyes flitted over behind me and before I could turn, she had blurted out.

"Why should I have to choose when I know that you and that Alpha that just left is planning on killing my Alpha?" The smirk on her face told me that the person was Fin.

CHAPTER TWENTY

FIN

The sight before me stopped me in my tracks. Nikita was again fighting with Jade and Harmony stood behind Jade, ready to jump in when needed. Jade's eyes came to me just as Nikita started to turn.

"Why should I have to choose when I know that you and that Alpha that just left is planning on killing my Alpha?" The smirk on Jade's face as she laid there and the nervousness coming through my bond with Nikita made this whole ordeal that much worse.

"Everyone leave other than Nikita." A group of wolves had gathered in the foyer at the commotion. *Don't be too hard on her, Fin. We know that Alpha Roy kept her linked to him for something.* Aloysius spoke up in my head.

I was hurt, but I knew there was something going on. Every time he came, she tried to stay away from him. But this time, he had been sitting with us at our table.

"But Alpha! I know what I spoke is the truth! I heard her and him talking about it." Jade was frantic as she stepped closer to me. Nikita stayed silent but held her head high as Jade continued to speak. She didn't even try to defend herself.

"Jade, I told you and everyone else to leave us." I growled at her but my eyes were glued on my mate. Nikita never flinched.

Harmony came over and grabbed Jade, and the others dispersed. Harlen followed Jade and Harmony to make sure that they didn't stick around. Nikita stood as still as a statue, her arms resting beside her.

"Are you going to defend yourself?" I had wanted her to beg for mercy, but I knew that wouldn't happen. Nikita wasn't one to beg, and that was what I loved about her.

"There's nothing to defend. I wasn't going to do what he wanted. I knew coming to your pack that if I didn't do what he wanted, he would kill me. So, I stayed away from him. If he comes back to the Luna ceremony and you aren't already dead. He will kill me. I knew when he told me what he wanted me to do, I would be dead either way." Nikita's voice was strong, but it held sadness in it. "I'd rather die protecting you than kill you and live."

"I won't let you die. No one will take you from me." I stalked up to her. Nikita's eyes never left mine, even as I towered over her. "I refuse to lose my mate."

"How are you going to trust me? Now that you know what Alpha Roy had wanted me to do?" Nikita's eyes began to water as she stared at me. My hand was caressing her face. How was I going to trust her? She had been sent to kill me by her alpha, and I didn't even know why.

Fin you know that the Moon Goddess has her plans. If Nikita wanted to keep her secret, she would've killed Jade. Take her to our room and find out more. Stop acting like you have no sense and ask the hard questions. Aloysius reprimanded me as I stood there staring at her. Part of me was proud of her for finally telling me what was going on with her these past two months.

"Come with me. We have more to talk about."

Nikita nodded and allowed me to step ahead of her. She followed just slightly behind me, which I didn't like. Slowing my pace, I placed my hand at her lower back and steered her up the stairs beside me.

My pack probably thought I was crazy for not putting her in the dungeon like I should have, but Aloysius was right. And I trusted his instincts more than my own sometimes. Wolves that were cleaning bowed their heads, but I could feel their disappointment in the link. They didn't know what I knew about Nikita.

I opened our door and Nikita stepped in. Heading to the couch, I sat down and motioned for Nikita to sit with me. She came up to me and sat in front of me on the opposite settee.

"Tell me, why is Alpha Roy wanting me dead? If I die, he not only will have my pack to worry about but my allies, the Quartzite and Rhyolite packs as well."

Nikita sat straighter and took a deep breath. "It's because of your chosen... She was his cousin. He is angry that you took her as a chosen and then allowed her to die. He now wants you to die just like she did."

I stood and went to the big window. It all came back to Kalila. My decision to take her as my chosen affected not only me but others as well.

Not one person from her pack was alive anymore. I slammed my fist against the glass, and it shook but didn't crack.

"I'm sorry. I won't blame you if you want me gone. Just tell me what you want to do. If you don't want me here, I'll leave and we can reject each other. Or you can take my life after we reject each other. I should've told you as soon as we got to your pack. But..." I turned to face her, tears were pooling in her eyes and threatening to fall. "I was scared. Enyo was begging me to tell you."

"That is why you wanted to reject me in the woods at your pack. Because he had already told you what he wanted you to do. Why didn't you kill me then?"

"Because he didn't want the death to be connected with his pack. Even if it was me doing it. Deep down, I think he would've killed me after I had killed you. So that he could make an example of me." The tears were falling down her beautiful face now as she held my eyes with hers. My heart constricted in my chest at the sorrow in her voice and on her face.

I couldn't let her go. She was my mate, my fated mate at that. I went up to her and brought her to stand in front of me. Taking her face in my hands, I brought it up to mine. Nikita made no move to fight me. I could snap her neck right here and that was probably what she was thinking I was about to do. She was limp in my hands, waiting for death to come.

The kiss I pressed to her lips shocked her. I could feel it in our bond as she relaxed even more and kissed me back.

Mark her. She wants you to,. Don't let her reject us. Aloysius told me in my head as I lifted her in my arms and she wrapped her legs around my hips as I took her to our room.

This was going to be a new start, and I was going to mark her. I placed her on the bed, her hair all around her as I took a moment to take her in. Stripping my shirt over my head, I let it fall to the ground as I covered her.

"I'm going to mark you." I told her as I allowed my hands to wrap in her hair.

"Okay," Enyo's voice laced with Nikita's as she answered me.

My canines ripped so fast through my gums I could feel the blood pooling in my mouth. Enyo had come to the surface as well, her eyes glowing as they stared back at me. Shredding her shirt, I sunk my fangs at the base of her neck where my mark would sit. Nikita's body arched into mine at the connection.

Nikita sunk her canines into me and I had never felt so good in my life than at that moment. Our bond snapped into place, bringing with it all her emotions that had been dampened since the day that we met.

When our mindlink connected, she showed me the day that he had ordered her to not let me mark her. She had told him she would reject me, thinking that it was because she would be lost to him. But he wanted me gone. Alpha Roy didn't want me to be an ally. He wanted me six feet under. Well, he better hope that doesn't make a move on my pack. Because that would be the last thing that he would do on this earth.

"Fin," Nikita's moan in my ear made me more aware of the want from her. I pulled my fangs from her mark and licked it to close the punctures. My scent mixing with hers from our blood mixing.

Standing, I tugged her shorts off and unbuttoned my pants as Nikita laid there, running her hands up and down her body. I was so hard it was painful. Nikita moved further to the middle of the mattress and I covered her again.

I hit her cervix as I bottomed out. She felt so good wrapped around me it took all I had not to bust inside of her. Nikita's nails bit into my shoulders as I rolled my hips in an antagonizing slow pace. She arched under me, her stomach rubbing against mine. Sending more sparks racing through our bodies with each touch.

My mouth went to a peaked nipple while she ran her hands up and down my back. She was close. I could hear her in my mind urging me faster. I smirked because she was about to lose it with my slow, hard pace. The way she begged me in our minds had me hoping that she wasn't broadcasting it to the entire pack. Before I remembered, she wasn't connected to the pack yet.

One hand went to her other nipple as my other held onto her hip to keep her from pulling away with each of my thrusts. I wanted her to feel me everywhere in her body as I fucked her. Her moans surrounded us and resonated inside my head as she came closer to her climax.

"Fin, faster please! I'm almost there!" I picked up my pace while I sat up on my knees and brought her up with me. Nikita's legs wrapped around my waist and her lips crashed to mine. Her lust and desire laced the kiss as I nipped her bottom lip.

She tightened around me, which brought me over the edge with her. I had her so tight against me; I was sure she would have bruises on her hips. Nikita's pants and mine mixed while we came down from the high. Goddess, please don't let this be a mistake.

I woke up and glanced at my side. Nikita wasn't in bed. Sitting up, I spotted her on the balcony of the bedroom.

Did you think I ran?

Fuck! If I had never heard her voice outside of mindlink, I would have thought I had died and went to be with the Goddess Selene.

I'm glad you didn't. Then I'd have to hunt you down. I growled in her mind.

That would be fun. She quipped back.

Nikita never turned from the balcony railings as she mindlinked me. She was gorgeous in the morning sun, standing there in its rays as they hit off her bronze skin. Standing, I went to her, hugging her from behind. She snuggled into me and her scent was my type of drug as I ran my nose up her neck.

The wind rushed past us and with the scent of the woods mixing with hers. The scent brought me back to the day Selene had come to me for the last time. Before she sent Markus to me.

Nikita, have you ever been away from your pack lands?

Yes, I was always being sent out with the other warriors.

This might be weird, but I'm sure I caught your scent when I was rogue. But it wasn't as potent as it was when I met you at your pack.

She turned to me, the sheet between us as she stared up at me.

"Really? That was so long ago. I hadn't even shifted yet." That had been what I had thought when I caught her scent. But I hadn't really thought about it until just now. I guess with the right smells mixed with hers, I was able to remember the scent back then. Or maybe Selene was letting me know I was close to her without even knowing it.

"Yes, it seems like the Moon Goddess wanted to see if I could detect you or not back then."

"She is a wonderful person. She was the one to finally convince me to tell you about Alpha Roy."

Why wasn't I surprised by this? Why wouldn't the Moon Goddess try to keep us together? Other than her making it our destiny to be fated mates?

"Well, I'm glad that she did. Because I don't know what I would do if something was to happen to you. I just found you, and I promise I would give my life for yours. No matter what you said." I caressed her face as we stood on the balcony together. If anyone saw us, it would be fine since they needed to see us as a united front.

CHAPTER TWENTY-ONE

Nikita

When Fin marked me, I was suddenly crushed with so much emotion from him. Being able to talk with him through mindlink was amazing because his voice inside my head was just as tantalizing as the one he spoke with to others. The only thing that was making me nervous was that there had been a crowd of wolves when Jade announced to them I had planned with my previous alpha to kill my mate.

It was going to be hard to convince them it wasn't what I wanted to do. Jade and Harmony kept following me everywhere that I went. Which didn't bother me. Let them because if they couldn't see the mark on my neck that showed me and Fin were now mated and that he knew everything I had been hiding. Then they could follow me to the ends of the earth.

Bella was about the only wolf that didn't detest me. And it was the only time I wasn't being followed by Jade or Harmony. Which surprised me. I guess they thought because Bella was a Beta that she would be able to keep Fin safe.

"What's on your mind today, Nikita?" Today we were sitting in the garden talking about anything and everything. Bella was a wonderful mother figure.

"Not much. I know that I let down a lot of the pack with what Jade had said. But if I had wanted to kill him, it would've already been done." I glanced up from the drink I had in front of me to look at Bella.

"I know how you feel. It was hard for me to adjust when I first came here. Fin's mother didn't like me at all. I didn't blame her. I had come from a pack that was an enemy and she thought I was going to kill her husband.

But all I wanted was to be able to be with Harlen." Bella reached out and held my hand on the table as she smiled at me. "Besides, the Moon Goddess doesn't make mistakes. She knows that you are what this pack needs as a Luna and she knows damn well that Fin needs you."

"Yeah, I'm just glad that you are on my side. Because it would be even harder to deal with all of this if I didn't have anyone but Fin." It was nice to be able to have a friend in the pack to help me through this crazy shit that's happening right now.

"But that is all you truly need. You and him are the pillars that will hold this pack together. The pack just doesn't know it yet." Bella patted my hand and then took a drink from her cup.

I nodded and smiled back at her before frowning.

"What was she like? Fin's chosen?" It hurt to ask about her. But there were no pictures of her in the pack house. Probably because his uncle had come and turned this pack upside down in a matter of months.

"She was a sweetheart. Very timid and sweet. Her mate had rejected her. That is the only reason Fin had made her his chosen. No one had a problem with her besides his uncle and when he found out she was going to have his pup was when he killed her right in front of Fin on the pack steps." The sorrow in her tone made me sad. Fin had made sure that he didn't ruin her life by choosing her when she had been rejected.

She didn't even have a chance to defend herself. That poor pup didn't even get to take a breath for the first time. It wasn't Fin's fault that she had died. It was his uncle's, the person who had taken her life in front of Fin. There was no way that couldn't have fucked with him. Seeing the female that he had chosen murdered in front of him.

"Wow. I'm surprised he is still upright."

"Fin has always been a strong wolf. Ever since he was a pup. He didn't waiver when he was put with older, stronger wolves. But he was such a kind pup. He bullied no one," Bella's smile widened, "so when he turned eighteen and I saw the white wolf, I knew he was special. But the longer he looked for his fated, I could see the light fading from his eyes."

"I was so angry with him for taking a chosen. It hurt me, because no matter how many males I had been with, I never allowed them to mark me. But it seems that Fin had been happy with her." My thoughts started running amuk in my brain as I thought of her still living and never knowing that this beautiful male would never be mine. But if he had been happy, why take that happiness away from him for me?

"He was happy. But he had gone against the Moon Goddess' design, so she had to rectify that. You and him are supposed to be together because you have to help him with his destiny. It wasn't Kalila's destiny."

Kalila, so that was her name. Why did it sound so much better with Fin's name than mine? The Moon Goddess should've just allowed him to be with her. I would have been fine alone if that would have allowed him to keep that happiness.

"Nikita? You know he is happy with you. Right? I haven't seen him like this in a very long time. Fin is happy. You make him that way."

"Bella, you have been part of this pack for a long time. What was it like when Fin's uncle was over the pack?" I had often wondered about the tyrant that had ruled over the Dolostone pack before Fin took back over. He had luckily not made his way to our small little pack.

"I don't know. Harlen sent me to live in my birth pack, so that our pups didn't have to grow up under his rule. So I wouldn't know, but Harlen would know. He stayed on as Beta to help keep some of the morale up until Fin came back." Bella sighed as she sat back. She played with the straw in her drink.

"Oh, I'm sorry. I'm sure that was hard."

Bella nodded before she refocused her eyes on me and smiled. "It was. There was always the moment that Harlen wouldn't be in this world anymore. But I couldn't think about that since I had just given birth to Tobey, and I had Sydnie, who was counting on me. When Harlen came to get me and the kids, I cried because not only did he come. Fin did as well, and he had grown so much since I had last seen him."

"What are you two doing?" Fin's voice came from behind me. His eyes glancing between both me and Bella. Harlen was behind him, a smirk on his lips.

"Nothing, just some gossip between friends." I answered him with a smile. The thought of Kalila standing next to him instead of me twisted my stomach. Just because it was our destiny to be together. Why did she take the person that he cherished?

Fin came up to me and kissed my temple. The sparks from his lips felt so fucking good as they spread from their starting point and over my face. They pulled me out of the depressive mood that I was in.

"Well, I need you to come with me. I have a few things that need your approval." Fin held out his hand to me and I took it.

What would need my approval? Fin led me away from Bella and Harlen and further into the woods. It was a comfortable silence between us as we continued our trek. Fin had never brought me this deep into the woods and I started to think that maybe this was where the dungeons were and he was finally going to put me in there. I wouldn't blame him if he did.

"Why are you nervous?" His voice brought me out of my head and to his face. Fin grinned at me with a wink. "There's nothing to be nervous about."

He stopped and stepped in front of me. Fin's hands held my face as he stared back at me.

"For your Luna ceremony, I'd like to hold it here, just beyond this thicket. You will be able to see the moon that night along with the sky. This was also the place that I had wanted to bring my mate and my mate only. But I ended up bringing my chosen here and I'm sorry about that." Fin's forehead wrinkled as he frowned. The sadness I could feel through our bond made me wrap my arms around him and pull him close. I placed a chaste kiss to his cheek before bringing my gaze back to his eyes.

"It's okay Fin. I know what it's like not knowing if I would ever find my mate. It would honor me for you to show me this place." I felt his arms wrap me up and lift me. On instinct, I wound my legs around his waist.

"Okay, my feisty wolf. I'd love for you to have this place as the setting for your Luna ceremony." The smile on his face brought me joy as he exited the woods.

It was like the edge of the woods was concealing the sound of the most beautiful waterfall I had ever seen. Unwinding my legs, I slid down his body to get a better look at the place. It was gorgeous! The waterfall rushed down the mountain and into a large lake as it bellowed at its surface. Its currents echoing off the rocks of the mountainside.

As I walked up to the water's edge, the cool breeze brought the smells of the water and flowers to my senses. It was like the quiet place that I had found when I was younger. For as long as I could remember, I had been the only one that knew about it.

"Fin, this place is perfect! But I thought that this was your place?" I asked him as I turned with a smile on my face.

Fin strolled up to me and pulled me to his body as he kissed me on the top of my head.

"My place is now and forever by your side. Besides, I'd rather you had your Luna ceremony here than try to hide the place from the rest of the pack. Which I'm sure I'm not the only one who has found it." Fin brushed a strand of hair away from my face. "This place will be the best spot for your ceremony. Especially with the full blue moon."

"Does Alpha Roy have to come?" I didn't like the fact that I sounded afraid of him. But in truth I was a little bit. Just because I had gone against his orders, but I knew it was the right thing to do.

"Yes, because I want him to know that you are my Luna and my mate. That if he tries anything, then my pack, even as it is, will stomp his ass in the ground." The roughness in his voice as he answered me made me wet. I could never get over the sound of his baritone.

"This is true, and I'll be right there beside you." I answered him. Fin was so gorgeous under the waning sun.

"There is no other place that I would want you to be."

I pulled away from him and stripped out of my clothes. His eyes flashed between his wolf's and his human's. Finally pulling my hair down and shaking it out, I glanced over my shoulder and grinned. "Are you going to come and take a swim with me?"

The growl that had erupted from him made me squeal as he enclosed me with his arms and thrust us into the lake. Fin was still clothed but I could feel him growing inside of his pants as we crested the water. Even though it was in the warmer months, the water was still chilly. Making chill bumps erupt along my skin.

"You didn't take off you clothes, now you are going to be cold when we head back." I told him as I hung on his body while he treaded the surface.

"I'll be okay. Besides, I think there will be plenty of time to get warm here in this lake." The devilish grin that graced his lip aroused me. Thankfully, I was in the water and he wouldn't be able to tell until we got out of the water.

"And what do you have in mind, Alpha?" I coyly asked him while I hung from his shoulders, rubbing my pussy against his stomach.

"Feisty wolf, you know better than to try to tease me. It never really goes your way."

CHAPTER TWENTY-TWO

FIN

It had been a bad idea to jump into the lake with my clothes, but she was stark naked and I know that she wasn't paying any attention to the fact that there were wolves heading our way during their patrol.

Ever since I marked her, I could tell that her scent was starting to change. Not only did my scent mix with hers, but I was sure that she would be going into heat soon. And I wanted to make sure before we didn't have the chance to was to talk about the idea of pups. I would love to have pups running around. To watch them grow inside of Nikita and then grow as we raised them in the pack.

I pulled her closer to my body before the two over large wolves came up to the edge of the water. The brown one snorted before nudging his grey companion with his nose. I knew what he was silently saying to the other.

Continue your route. We are okay. I mindlinked them. They bowed their heads and took off leaving dust in their wake. As their thundering paws receded, I turned my attention to Nikita.

Nikita wiggled out of my arms and swam away from me and to the waterfall. The way she swam up to the colossal spray of water and ducked under the spray had me worried that it would push her under. As many times as I had been out here, I never went up to the crushing water. I dove under to follow her and when I broke the surface Nikita was laying back on a rock. Her head hanging off the edge.

The smirk on my lips grew while I watched her play with herself as she watched me come up to her. Nikita was beautifully splayed on top of the Dolostone rock. Her dark brown hair touched the water, keeping the tips of them wet. Wading over to her, I took her face and crashed my lips to hers. The soft moan vibrated my lips as I asked for entrance into her mouth.

"Fin, why are you waiting? Are you not going to take me?" Her breathless question made me harder than what I was. We needed to talk about pups, but I didn't want to ruin the mood.

"Is that what you want? You want me inside you making your pussy and body hum with excitement?" Aloysius' voice joined with mine as I ran my hand over her already heaving breasts.

Nikita's eyes flickered between hers and her wolf's. She was one hundred percent going into heat. I pulled the now skintight shirt off and flung it onto another rock before peeling my pants and boxers off as I lifted myself out of the water. Her eyes never left mine as I climbed on top of her from the other rock.

"Yes, and you're taking too long." Nikita's body arched into mine as I settled between her beautiful legs.

"So impatient, feisty wolf." My fingers slipping into her pussy as she played with her clit. I loved how confident she was while I pumped my fingers in and out of her.

"Fin! I need you inside of me. Like now." Nikita begged as she arched with each thrust of my hand. My other hand went to her neck as she contracted around me.

I smirked at her as she came around me. The way her scent from her cum traveled to my nose. Nikita was in the beginning of her heat. Drops of water from my body dripped onto her toned and tight core as I hovered over her. I took one of her pert nipples into my mouth before shoving my cock into her tight pussy.

"Fuck, Nikita! Are you going into heat?" I groaned as she met me thrust for thrust.

"Yes, right there! Make me come again!" Damn, the way she ordered me around made me want to give her anything and everything she wanted. Starting with making her come again.

"Nikita, I need to know if you are going into heat." I groaned as she let her hand roam my body. As many times as I had been with other females, I had never been with one going into heat. The way she took hold of my base and held it in her small hand sent the sparks racing up my cock and torso.

"I think so. Why?" Nikita moaned loudly as I crashed into her. Making her breasts bounce as I kept her pace.

"Because you know this is when you can get pregnant, and I don't want to make that choice for you." She was going to have to make a decision soon, otherwise I wasn't going to be able to pull out of her.

"I know. But I've never been in a heat like this before." Nikita was panting as she answered me.

Fuck, this was going to be her first time while being in heat. She would probably end up pregnant.

It's because she is marked Fin. Aloysius spoke up inside of my head.

Kalila was marked. She didn't go into heat.

That's because she wasn't our mate. She was a chosen. Pregnancy can happen with chosens but it normally takes longer. You must be potent. My wolf explained as he lolled his tongue from his mouth.

Nikita's lips pressed into mine, and her arms wrapped around the back of my head. Fuck, I loved when she took control.

"I don't care if I get pregnant. If the Moon Goddess wants it that way, then so be it. But please, I need you to make me come." She then wound her legs around my hips, bringing me further into her.

I crashed my mouth onto hers. Thrusting deeper and harder into her and encircling her with my arms. I could feel her tightening around my cock and fuck if it didn't feel fucking amazing. That's when I could tell I was swelling inside of her. My heart was racing as she stilled.

Nikita's wolf was at the surface when the growl erupted from me. She tried to pull away from me, but I unwound my arms and grabbed hold of her hips, holding her in place. Nikita's nails bit into my ribs as I emptied inside her. She arched as I felt her first spasm. This was something I had never experienced with anyone but her.

"Oh. My. Goddess! Fin! Fuck!"

"Was it that good?" I chuckled as I continued to be locked with her. Nikita had stilled and was no longer trying to pull away from me.

"Yes, it was. I never felt as full as I had just now." Nikita loosened her grip from my back, letting her arms fall above her head as I was able to pull from her without hurting her. The sigh that erupted from her as I withdrew from her pussy made me grin.

"My feisty wolf satisfied?" I asked her as I laid down beside her on the rock. My cock slick with the combination of her cum and mine.

"Damn, we need to do that again. I feel like you just ignited something even more." Nikita flipped to her knees and straddled me.

"Feisty wolf, just remember you let this happen again. There's an even greater chance of you getting pregnant." I answered her, my hands resting on her hips as she ground her pussy over the underside of my cock.

"This is true but I want to feel that again." Nikita's voice was laced with her wolf's while she continued to ride me.

Nikita's body was like a furnace under my hands. I had seen a mated pair so into each other that they both had to be taken to the pack hospital for dehydration. There was a lake below us. I could send us below its surface. But the shock to her system could do more harm than good.

"You are giving me an ego boost, my feisty wolf." Lifting her, Nikita wrapped her hand around my girth and positioned me at her entrance.

The gruntle moan that released from Nikita sent my body into overdrive as she rode me. I was already harder now than I was for the first time on this rock. Each of her movements brought me closer to knotting with her again. She was so fucking tight from the last time due to her swelling from when I locked with her. Nikita braced herself with the palms of her hands on my chest.

The sparks that snapped and raced through me at her touch made me tighten my grip on her hips. At this pace she was going to have me locking with her quicker than I had when I was in control. I felt myself engorging inside her and her movements became slower just until she couldn't move up my cock due to the knot.

I didn't think I would have much more to coat her insides with since it had been only a few minutes before I had tied with her. The sharp little yip that came from Nikita told me that she could no longer pull too much away from me.

But that didn't stop her from grinding herself back and forth with me still locked inside of her. Sitting up, I kissed her lips before sinking my teeth into her mate mark on the base of her neck. I grabbed a hand full of her hair just as she spasmed again around me and she clamped on my cock.

"Yes, right there Fin! Fuck yes! Please don't stop!" Nikita moaned as she ground herself deeper against the head of my cock.

"Take whatever you fucking want, my feisty wolf." I groaned as our bodies tired with exhaustion. "I'm yours to use."

Nikita came around me as she sank her canines into my mate mark. I didn't think that I would be able to come any more, but she surprised me. Damn, now I knew why my parents were upset that I wouldn't be able to have what a mate could offer. She pulled out and licked my wound to seal it.

I loved this she-wolf to the moon and back for eternity. Fuck if anyone wanted to try to come and take her from me. I'd die trying to keep them away from her.

"Fuck, I don't want this heat to ever go away. I want to be able to do this all the time, not just when I'm in heat." I chuckled as I slowly removed myself from her. Even though I wanted to stay inside her as long as I could, I collapsed down against the rock as she straddled me.

"If you stayed in heat, we wouldn't get anything done and our pack would demote us for not being good leaders."

Nikita smiled before leaning down and kissing me. The way she kissed me kept me grounded with all of these emotions running through me. At this time I could fuck her again and still not have enough of her. It was a good thing that she had gone into heat this month rather than the month we would have her Luna ceremony.

"So, do you think we need to be getting back to the pack house? I'm surprised your guard isn't here to make sure I don't kill you."

"Yeah, it might be wise to get back to the pack. The only thing is I'm going to need you to get me some clothes. I have a shirt, but my underwear and pants are at the bottom of this lake." I kissed her forehead and sat back up with her in my arms. "You know, no one would know that we are here. No one ever comes this close to the waterfall."

"Then it will still be our little place together. Even with the Luna ceremony being held in the field before the lake."

I nodded to her and smiled. As much as I hated to admit it, I was in debt to the Moon Goddess. She knew who I needed, and that was Nikita. Even though she was ten years younger than me, she completed me.

CHAPTER TWENTY-THREE

Nikita

Being in heat had its wonderful moments, and then it had its terrible moments.

The enjoyable moments was when Fin was near enough to make the ache go away. And damn, could he make them go away. When he knotted inside of me. I thought I was going to pass out with how full and stretched I was. Regular sex was going to be something I would have to get used to when this was all over.

The bad moments were when Fin wasn't near and I had to either wait on him to come back or handle the deed by myself. And that didn't last as long as when he fucked me.

One of the heat moments hit when I was talking with one of the other she-wolves that was around my age and Fin had walked in through the front doors with Harlen. Fin's head snapped to me and his nostrils had flared. Which made me even more wet when his wolf's blue eyes took over Fin's.

Just with that one look, he sent shivers down my body and I had to excuse myself away from the she-wolf. I felt like a teenager trying to get my kick before the adults found out. Fin was so much more in control than I was about this. He had warned me about getting pregnant, but at this point I didn't even care because fuck, it felt so good!

I mean, he had gotten his chosen pregnant and apparently she didn't ever go into heat. So if the Moon Goddess wanted me to be a mother, then that was my destiny. I wanted to run to him and jump him right here in the packhouse's foyer, but there were far too many young eyes.

My feisty wolf wants me? His eyes flashed to his wolf's before going back to his own. It was so exhilarating when I saw the blue color.

Yes, badly. Are you going to do something about this? I coyly smirked as I turned my back to him and pulled my hair to the other side of my neck. Showing off my mate mark to him. He groaned in our mindlink, but I knew that everyone in this room could see that something was up between us.

Harlen nodded to him and I could feel the unease flowing through the mindlink, but it wasn't more than the desire that rode with it. Fin didn't enjoy putting off his duty as Alpha, but Harlen was smiling as Fin made his way over to me.

You are making this entire room smell like you. Fin growled in my mind.

I'm trying to entice my mate to come breed me. I answered back and the growl that came from him stopped everything and everyone in the room.

Fin crashed his lips to mine as soon as he reached me before picking me up and carrying me down the hall to his office. It was the closest place to get to. I needed him now and if he didn't hurry, I just knew I was going to die with need.

You are going to have all these males in this house at my office door if you don't control this. Fin was on edge but continued toward the office door.

Then I guess you need to take care of me. It's your fault that it's this bad. You haven't touched me since this morning. I quipped back at him and nipped his ear lobe.

Fin shouldered the door to the office open and kicked it closed. His lips and nips with his teeth, never leaving my neck and collarbones. The crashing of things from his desk didn't faze us as he placed me on the top of the wooden furniture.

I grabbed his shirt and tore it in half, which allowed my hands to slide over his muscular torso. The sparks chasing my hands as they went to his pant button. Fin continued his assault on my neck and jaw as I fumbled with his pants.

Damn this man's control. Fin's hands went under my ass, bringing my core closer to the bulge in his pants. One that I was trying my hardest to get out and slip inside of me. I wanted to feel that fullness again. Enyo was on her back in my mind, her tail wagging.

You are so needy today. Fin groaned in my mind, the control not quite making it through the bond from his physical calm.

I told you. You haven't touched me since this morning. I moaned, sending him the image of the shower this morning.

"Fuck, Nikita!" The deep timbre of his voice excited me even more than his fingers slipping into the top of my jeans. Fin pulled them from my body and down to my feet.

The warm breath on my wet and aching center caused goosebumps to run up my body while I arched into his lips. Fin's tongue slowly lapped up my excitement, bringing out the loudest moan from me. Fuck, why did this have to be so good?

My hands went to his hair, pushing his mouth closer to my core. When his tongue entered me, I thought I would come right then. "Fin... please..."

I hated begging for anything, but I'd beg for my life for what he could do to my body. Fin stood and unbuttoned the button I had been having trouble getting undone. He grabbed his throbbing cock at the base and I couldn't help but slip my hand down my body to my clit.

"You want this inside you?" Fin's eyes flickered before staying blue.

"Yes..." The breathlessness in my tone tormented me as much as it did him. Fin's grin as he entered me made me wetter. Allowing him to slip in easily because his girth was already thicker than this morning.

"Damn! You are so tight right now." Fin's grip on my hips was bruising as they tightened more. I arched as he finally hit my cervix.

Don't stop!

Don't worry, I'm not. You feel so good wrapped so tight around my cock.

I grabbed hold of his forearms for stability as he rammed into me, making the desk inch further away from him with each thrust. As much as we had been fucking, I wasn't too surprised that I was swollen inside. But fuck, did he feel so damn good inside of me.

Fin pulled me up and grabbed hold of my hair. Yanking my head back as he nipped his way up and down my neck before he crashed us against the wall. My legs wrapped around his waist as he plundered me. His cock was swelling inside of me and his thrusts became deeper, as he couldn't pull out as far as he used to.

"Fuck!" The growl in my ear made me shudder before he sunk his canines back into my mate mark.

He was so fucking thick at the base that I couldn't even move. And the warm cum really had nowhere to go as I felt it hit my cervix each time it shot out.

"You need to take a bath and soak. If we keep this up, I won't be able to enter you without hurting you next time." The soft tone of his voice allowed me to come down from the high that he brought me to each time he fucked me.

"Okay, but I'm going to need you before dinner." I sighed as he pulled out.

"You are going to end up pregnant if we keep at this. Not that I mind, and I don't want to get to the point where it no longer feels good for you." Fin kissed me tenderly as he brought us over to the couch in his office and sat down.

I straddled him as his hands roamed my body. If he continued to do that, I was going to fuck him again. This was a drug that I didn't know if I would be able to wean myself off of.

"I told you I didn't care if I got pregnant." I answered him as I ran my hands over his pecs.

"I know you have. But being in heat can make it so that you don't care." His eyes held so much concern. Did he worry something would happen to me if I got pregnant? Like it did with his chosen?

"Are you worried about something, Fin?"

"Maybe just a little bit. But it's nothing you have to worry about. In the next couple of weeks, you will have your Luna ceremony."

"But you have been on me about the pregnancy thing. Is it about what happened to Kalila?" I knew bringing her up was bringing up his past. But I needed to know what was going on in his head.

"Nikita..."

"Don't Nikita me. I need to know. Are you worried I'll get hurt?"

The sigh and the gentle pull of his hands to bring my face closer to his was my answer. He was worried. I could protect myself and his uncle was no longer here to hurt me. The only other person that could hurt me would be my previous alpha, but I could take him.

"Nikita, when you are pregnant, you know you can't shift. You would be in danger and when Alpha Roy finds out that you are no longer under his control, then he could hurt you. I can't let that happen again. I wouldn't be able to live without you." His kiss was soft as he moved the kisses to the rest of my face.

The fear in his eyes was something that I never thought I would see in them. As much as I wanted him during my heat. I would make sure that I didn't bother him about it. Fin couldn't look like this when he had a pack to run. There was no way that I was going to be the cause of his distraction.

"Okay. I'll stop tempting you."

"That's not what I want you to do, Nikita. I've never felt this before, just like you, and I don't want it to end because you think I don't want you. I just don't want you to hate me if you get pregnant and then can't protect yourself because you can't shift. That's it." He pulled me close to him and I wrapped my arms around his neck.

"Okay, but I think I can still protect myself in my human form. Enyo will give me some of her strength."

"I hope you never have to protect yourself like that. Because then that would mean I'm not doing my job."

I stood from his lap and went to my clothes that he had discarded in front of his desk. Pulling the shirt over my head, Fin was in front of me bringing up his boxers and pants. His shirt lay ruined on the edge of a chair's arm.

"I'm sorry about the shirt."

Fin chuckled and then grabbed it up, tossing it in the trash can beside the slightly moved desk. I glanced around and noticed that everything that was on his desk was now on the floor.

"Looks like I need to help you clean this up." I bent down and grabbed a picture off the ground. It had his parents and him in it, along with another female. She had to be Kalila. "Here. I'll grab the other things."

"Nikita..."

"It doesn't bother me. She was before me, and I'm sure your parents loved her as much as you do." I grabbed another item from his desk and then his laptop from the floor and put them on the top. He walked over to one of the shelves in the room and placed the picture on one of them before coming back to me.

"I know it does, Nikita. But I love you and I can't wait to make you my Luna officially. This was our destiny from the start. I just fucked that up because I didn't wait for you." He pulled me to a standing position and held me close. Being in heat altered my moods so quickly, and I wasn't surprised when the tears fell from my eyes and onto his bare chest. "We are meant to be. You were born for me and I was born for you."

I glanced up to his gaze and noticed the tears that were still in his eyes. In the entire time I had been here and been alive, I had never seen an Alpha cry or even tear up. Using the pad of my thumb, I wiped them away before placing a chaste kiss on his lips. "I love you, Fin. And I will try my best to make you and this pack proud of me."

CHAPTER TWENTY-FOUR

NIKITA

The pack had been preparing for my ceremony for the past two weeks; and during those two weeks, I had their Alpha wrapped up in my desire to jump him each time he was near me. Fin wasn't as worried since our conversation in his office, but I was more worried that my heat was still going on.

No one I had spoken to had their heat last this long. So what was wrong with me? I hadn't brought it up to Fin as he had so much on his plate at the moment with talking with my previous Alpha. He and Harlen were going to be going to get him and his Luna tomorrow. I worried that when he saw the mark on Fin's neck that he would try to kill him.

I had tried to get him to let me go with him so that I could help protect him. Fin had assured me that Harlen and the deltas that he was taking with him would be sufficient. I wanted to protest, but Fin just smiled and kissed me on the forehead. Which sort of pissed me off, but I knew that being in heat made me hormonal and so I let it slide. Fin knew I was a great warrior. So if he needed me he would take me.

Bella had been around me more since it was getting closer to my ceremony. She was showing me what all she had been doing in the absence of a Luna. Most of everything that she showed me was what my previous Luna had done. But then there were some things that Bella showed me that happened behind closed doors.

"Bella, you are a goddess send. If I didn't have you to show me all of this, I would be the worst Luna in all of Cairn." I giggled as she showed me another thing with the financial books.

"You would never be the worst Luna, Nikita. Fin would be able to show you this if I wasn't here. But I'm glad that I'm the one to be able to do this with you." Bella smiled at me before she sat back in the chair and stared at me. "But I do have a question for you."

I turned to her and dropped the pen before stretching out my muscles. It had been a long day and Fin hadn't mindlinked me or spoke to me since he went into the meeting.

"Okay, I might be able to give you an answer."

"I've been told by some of the other she-wolves that you have been in heat a little longer than normal. Is this your very first heat?" She was like my mother in the way that she looked after me and the way she treated me.

"No, I've had heats before and my Alpha would send me and any of the other unmated females away to keep the males from us. Which would be the reason I didn't go into heat when I first met him. The previous month I had been in my heat."

Bella laughed, which caused me to tilt my head in curiosity. What did they do with their unmated females? Didn't they send them away? Why did each pack have to be so different?

"Hon, I don't know what your alpha was doing, but those small heats are nothing but signaling your mate. It's more like a beacon to help find your mate. Since you weren't around Fin, I'm not surprised that you wouldn't have snapped at every male that wasn't your mate."

Thinking back, I remembered the day before my seventeenth birthday. I had been out on a run with a few other female pack members and I thought I had caught the scent of another wolf. Come to think about it, that was the same day that Fin had mentioned smelling my scent. Was my body calling for him like Bella had said?

"Fin did mention smelling my scent before he had met up with the other rogues and then Alpha Nolen. Do you think that my body was signaling him?" I questioned her as she sat back in her chair and contemplated on what I had just told her.

"It could be. Knowing him, he didn't even try to see where the scent was coming from. He had always been a cautious boy. If he wasn't he might have been able to find you sooner. The closer you are to getting your wolf, the more your heat becomes stronger to try to find your mate."

"So since you don't send the unmated females that go into heat away, what happens when the other males are around? Don't they try to fight for them?" I genuinely was curious since I would be taking over the pack in the next day or two.

"Well, if they have a mate in our pack, then him being around her would keep the others away. But if she didn't the female would keep the ones who weren't her mate from her. I've seen a few males get on the wrong side of a female when she was in her heat." Bella laughed again as she stood and went to check on Tobey in the corner of the office that we were working in. This would be my office once I took over. "Besides if the male was raised right, he wouldn't try to bother a female that wasn't his mate."

The young pup in the corner played with his figurines as his mother taught me what would be expected of me. Sydnie had come to like me since I first came to the pack. She had been weary of me and then I had to earn her trust after Jade and Harmony started telling the entire pack about what she had overheard. Sydnie was very fond of Fin. Luckily, she wasn't in the pack but she had been told about what had happened.

Some of the pack still didn't know if I could be trusted and that was okay because I intended to earn that back somehow. Then there were others like Bella and Harlen that knew that I could no longer lie to him or keep secrets since he was inside my head. And when he was inside my head when he was fucking me. Damn!

You're thinking about me again my feisty wolf. I jumped when his voice entered my mind. I must have really been pushing my thoughts to him since he decided to talk to me while he was in a meeting with is Beta and Deltas. He was coming up with a game plan to make sure he nor I would get hurt during my previous alpha's stay.

Shouldn't you be concentrating on what your guard is telling you?

Naw, I've heard everything before. Besides, Aloysius has been begging me to send you some more positions. Fin chuckled in my head as he sent the images that his wolf wanted us to try. A few of those I didn't know if I could even do.

I'm surprised he would want to try the balcony one. There is always a risk of another wolf seeing.

Yeah, we won't be doing that one. I'm not to that point yet to be that bold. But I do like the one with you on your knees with your ass in the air, letting me take you from behind. Apparently, he doesn't remember us doing this position yet.

I laughed out loud, startling Tobey and Bella. Raising my hand, I tried to subdue the laughter that I couldn't quite stop at the moment. Tobey smiled with me as Bella shook her head and continued to try to pick up the toys that he was playing with.

I want to do that with you. But I want to change it up. Meet me in the bedroom once this meeting is over? And we will try it out?

Sure, but you know we won't have much time. Since you have to go and get Alpha Roy.

It won't take me too long to get him and if I wanted to be mean, I could put him in the room below our room and make you scream all night. You think he would like that?

Why are you wanting to egg him on?

Because he wants me dead and he wanted you to kill me. I want to show him just how much control he has over you now that we've marked each other.

Fine, but not too loud. Adia isn't the problem. It's him.

Fin chuckled again before he cut the link. I stood and stretched again before going to the floor to ceiling window in my office. The view from this room was amazing and, depending on the time of the day, it was even more beautiful than other times. A few pups were playing tag in the woods. What would it be like to have pups doing this?

Playing in my office and in the woods when they got older? I mean, I hadn't even thought about having pups until I met Fin and then the heat. But pups needed to be the last thing on my mind until the Luna ceremony was done. Because then hopefully I would be out of this heat.

Then I could worry about earning the pack's trust back. Because I would need to have them behind me if anything was going to happen. Pups didn't need to be brought into this right now. I had too many things to right before that.

⬥◯⬥

I stood on the steps of the packhouse waiting for Fin and his detail to get back with Alpha Roy and Luna Adia. Bella and her son stood beside me. A few more of the Deltas stood behind me, more for Bella's protection than mine.

When the SUVs came up the road, I held my breath. Had Alpha Roy seen the mark I had given to Fin? Or had he not noticed since he wasn't always a person to pay attention to details? Which was why I had put him on his ass more times than I could count when we were younger.

Bella's hand went to my shoulder just as Harlen and Fin exited the vehicles. I had to keep myself from running to Fin in front of my previous alpha. Adia's smile brightened when she spotted me and she came up to me first, giving me a big hug. I wrapped my arms around her.

"You look amazing! You both finally marked each other! This is so exciting." Adia exclaimed as she moved my hair from my mark.

"Thank you. Yeah, it's something I've been getting used to." I glanced over her shoulder and could see the daggers that Alpha Roy was throwing at me. He was pissed but I didn't care.

Fin came up to me and wrapped his arm around my waist and turned to one of the omegas. He motioned for the male wolf to come to him.

"Danny, take Alpha Roy and Luna Adia to their room so that they can freshen up before dinner."

"Yes, Alpha." He bowed his head and then turned to Alpha Roy and Luna Adia. "This way Alpha Roy and Luna Adia."

They both followed the omega into the house while Fin held my attention. I didn't feel as uncomfortable as before with him being here. But I was worried about Fin.

You've got this. I won't let him hurt you.

I know you won't but will the pack back me? They still hate me.

Fin glanced around at the surrounding wolves. I couldn't bear to take my eyes off of Fin. His gaze returned to mine as he grinned. *Not one wolf here will let you get hurt. If they do, then they are not loyal to their leaders.*

Fin, you can't make them do what they don't want to. You will make them hate you.

They will never hate me. And they don't hate you. They just don't understand what was going on. Fin kissed me in front of the rest of the pack. The sound of the wolf whistles from the younger wolves made me blush.

"Come on, feisty wolf, let's get ready for dinner." Fin steered me to the front doors, past the other wolves, and up to our room. He opened the door and allowed me to go before him.

CHAPTER TWENTY-FIVE

Nikita

We had showered and dressed in more classy clothes than what we would normally wear. As we entered the dining room, I noticed that a lot of the wolves were here and already sitting waiting for Fin and me to get there. Alpha Roy and Luna Adia were at our table and Adia was talking to Bella.

Roy looked like he was about to blow a gasket. The good thing this time was that Fin moved me to the chair that he normally sat in and sat beside Alpha Roy. I didn't like that he was that close to Roy, but I knew he wouldn't be so bold to try to kill him in a room full of another pack.

Fin kept his hand on my upper thigh as he talked with Alpha Roy about the Luna ceremony and the Dolostone crystals. I didn't understand why we were still giving him the crystals when I should've been the bridge of our pack's alliance, but it seemed that Alpha Roy had another thing he wanted out of this. Other than Fin dead.

Fin, do we have a guard to keep an eye out? There is something else that just doesn't sit right with me.

What do you mean, Nikita?

Why is it that we are still sending him crystals when I should be the alliance factor?

Because it was the only thing I had to offer. We weren't back to full strength and at the time I felt bad that he would be losing such a badass warrior such as you. Fin chuckled as the omegas started to bring in the food.

When the omega sat down my plate, I glanced over to Fin. My favorite dinner had been made, and I was excited to have it again. The head chef had made the caprese chicken my first night, and I had fallen in love with the dinner. Beside the main dish was a baked potato with sour cream, cheese, butter and bacon bits and corn next to it.

"Thank you, Fin.." I kissed him on the cheek and waited for the rest of the wolves to get their plates.

Fin squeezed my upper thigh, which started the whole need for him again. I finally got control of the need before he slid his hand up my skirt. Which in turn made me wet and the unmated wolves in the room turned to find the scent.

Fin you need to stop. The other wolves are noticing. I sighed in my head as I tried my best to rein in the control that he took from me.

Feisty wolf, you need to learn some control. As good as you are as a warrior, I expected some control.

My heart was racing as the wolves continued to search for my smell. The only reason they hadn't found it was because of Fin's scent right beside me. Damn him and his control. Enyo wasn't much help either, as she rolled over onto her back and wagged her tail.

I bit my lip to hold back the moan that threatened to escape me when his fingers slid against my slit. When his skin brushed against my bare core, I tightened my legs against his hand to try to get him to stop. Fin leaned over and ran his tongue along the shell of my ear before fanning it with his warm breath. Which just made me wetter.

Why are you doing this?

Because Alpha Roy is over here, squirming more than those unmated wolves are at the other end of the room.

You're doing this because of him? I couldn't help the moan inside of my head pushing the thoughts of our most recent escapade into his mind. *What has gotten into you? You don't normally act this way in front of everyone.*

I told you why. And just because I always seem like I'm in control doesn't mean that I am.

Fin pulled his hand out just as one of the deltas bowed his head and stood waiting for acknowledgement. My mate kissed my cheek before turning his attention completely to the wolf in front of us.

"Yes, Dawson?"

If he wanted to play that game, I could too. I slipped my hand into the crotch of his lap and palmed the bulge in his pants. It twitched each time my fingers caressed it and I didn't miss each time he tried to reposition himself.

"Alpha, we have the lake ready for tomorrow. Is there anything else that you would like done before tomorrow?"

Fin cleared his throat and moved again to try to keep my hand from my target. He cleared his throat again before his hand went to his lap and tightened on mine.

"No, Dawson. Thank you for your help. Get some food along with the others."

The wolf in front of us bowed his head before his eyes glanced over at me and his nostrils flared. He then bowed to me and left to get a plate and to get the other wolves that had been with him.

Bella was right. Most of the unmated males didn't act on a female in heat. I didn't think that he would try to mess with his Alpha's mate. But there was always that chance.

"Alpha Fin, maybe you should take Nikita to your room. Every male in this room is uncomfortable with her being in heat." Alpha Roy's voice silenced the entire room as each of the pack looked to their Alpha.

Fin turned to Roy, and I could feel the anger through our bond. This wasn't going to be good. I glanced over to Harlen before placing my hand on Fin's shoulder.

"Are you trying to tell me what to do with my Luna in my own territory?" Fin's wolf was at the surface and if the wolves were uncomfortable before, they were tense now.

"Well, look at them. Is there a reason why the females in heat are not somewhere else?"

Oh, Alpha Roy was ballsy. He was about to get his ass handed to him if he said something else about the Dolostone pack to Fin.

"I don't see why you think they are uncomfortable. If they can't handle females in heat, then they need to leave. We don't treat our females the way you do in your pack. And I would never tell you how to run your pack." Fin was angry, but he was keeping control of himself. The years he had on Alpha Roy becoming more apparent.

Luna Adia was trying her best to make Alpha Roy stop before he ended up losing his life to Fin. A few of the warrior wolves stood from their seats, ready to jump when their Alpha told them to. Harlen came to the other side of Fin to get his attention.

"It's late. I think everyone is tired. It might be a good idea to head to bed. What do you think Alpha Fin?" Harlen's voice was calm and collected as he spoke to Fin. He never raised his voice to his Alpha but held his attention all the same.

"Sure. Tony, take the Shonkinite Alpha and Luna to their room. And if they want another plate, take it with them." I didn't miss the growl in his voice as he spoke to Harlen and the omega that came up to him.

Luna Adia stood and brought Alpha Roy up. She held my gaze and mouthed 'I'm sorry' before ushering Alpha Roy behind Tony. I hated that he made her look like that when he was in one of his moods.

I mean, I wouldn't be surprised if he tried to find a way to kill me before my Luna ceremony tomorrow night. I stood from my seat and took Fin's arm and urged him to get up. He stood and towered over me like he always did.

"You won't be without me or a guard. Do you understand?" the deep blue of his wolf's eyes shone bright as he started back at me. Right now wasn't the time to argue with him.

I nodded before urging him once more to come with me. Fin was way too over stimulated to be down here. He needed to be in bed to chill out. Alpha Roy almost got his way. He wanted Fin to attack him so that he could attack and try to kill him. He never changed in his fighting style. Alpha Roy would try to find something on the table to help him.

If he killed Fin, there was a possibility that I could die with him. And that was probably what he wanted now. Since I had sided with the male that had killed his cousin. If I didn't die, then I would make sure Alpha Roy died slowly. There would be no way I would let him live if Fin was gone.

"That fucking piece of shit. Thinking that he could tell me how to run my back. Why do the females have to be away from their families when the young males can be taught not to be an issue?" Fin swung his arm and the lamp that was on the table hit the wall and shattered.

"Fin, stop worrying about that. He wanted to get a rise out of you. You are more than him and you know it." I stepped in his way as he was pacing and grabbed hold of his face. Fin stared back at me and took a deep breath. His eyes continued to be the deep blue as I stared at him.

"I know, but I wanted to make an example of him. The way I've learned that he has been treating his females. It's like it's their fault that they go into heat." Fin pulled me into him and took a deeper breath at my mate mark.

His scent enveloped me as he held me. There was one thing that I loved about being here and that was the way Fin treated me. He never raised his voice to me and I didn't know if that was because he knew I could take him or if that was just the way he was with me.

"Fin, did you actually put them in the room below us?" With his scent all around me, it was becoming harder to think with him so close.

"Yes, I did you want to show him just how much I can make you scream?"

He knew what I was thinking and when I nodded; he scooped me up by my ass and headed over to the bed. There wasn't going to be any sleep tonight, that was for sure.

Fin used one hand to unzip the dress and tossed me onto the mattress. His hand snaked up my arm sending sparks racing to catch it. Fuck I loved his hands on my skin. I arched into him and he took that as initiative to pull my dress off me.

"You're so beautiful my feisty Luna." Fin groaned on the inside of my leg.

I was so needy for him as he got closer to my core. Fin pulled my panties to the side and slipped two fingers inside of me. His lips wrapped around my clit and lapped it with his tongue. Damn him and his tongue!

Nikita you taste amazing. I think you're going out of heat. Fin's voice in my head made me squirm while he added another finger.

Fin I need you inside of me! I was panting as I was getting closer to my climax. Folding my fingers in his hair I pulled his face closer into my pussy. His lapping stopped and he began to suck on my clit changing the pressure on it.

Feisty wolf you're supposed to be screaming my name. And I can't hear it with my ears. He pulled off my clit with a pop and his eyebrow raised. The smirk on his lips showed off the canine that had elongated.

Then put that massive cock inside me. I reached down and stroked him and Fin sucked in his breath as I continued my assault on his cock. Fin closed his eyes while he allowed me to continue to work him. When he opened them, his wolf was at the surface, his beautiful blues glowing at me.

Fin grabbed me up sitting back on his feet as he sheathed me to the hilt. "Fuck Fin! Harder!"

I wrapped my arms around his neck trying to ground myself against as he pounded me. Each one bringing out a moan from my lips. "Yes! Fin! There! Harder!"

Fin grabbed hold of one of my nipples and nipped it with his canine. He was starting to swell inside of me, he pulled me down as he thrust up and emptied inside me. I could feel him jerking while he held me close to him.

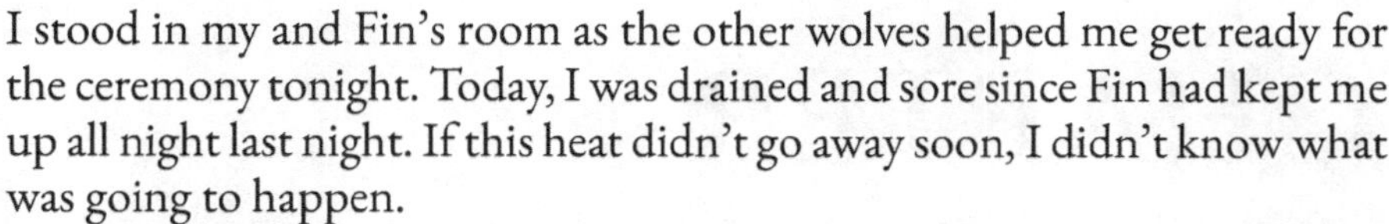

I stood in my and Fin's room as the other wolves helped me get ready for the ceremony tonight. Today, I was drained and sore since Fin had kept me up all night last night. If this heat didn't go away soon, I didn't know what was going to happen.

The only thing that would be okay with it. Was that I wouldn't get pregnant if I continued to be in heat. But that also meant that I would be jumping him every time that I could.

A door behind me opened and I could feel the entire room go still. The only person I could think it would be was Alpha Roy. Turning, I spotted Jade and Harmony in the doorway. I turned back around and motioned for the others to continue their work.

"Is there something I can do for you?" I could see them in the floor-length mirror. They glanced at each other before Harmony nodded to her friend.

Jade took a step forward and took a deep breath. She bowed her head before bringing her gaze back up to mine. "Nikita, I'm sorry about not just coming to you about what I heard and then announcing it to the pack like I did. I hope that after this ceremony and maybe even after this apology that we can be friends?"

"Jade, I have no problems with you. But things will have to change a lot. I won't sit and deal with this bullshit again. I don't normally give people a chance like I am you." I answered her as I stared at her with unblinking eyes.

Jade lowered her eyes from mine and then kneeled. Which surprised me for a moment.

"Get up Jade. You don't have to kneel. I'm no queen. All I want is peace between us and have a nice quiet life."

Jade stood up and then bowed her head before turning and heading out the door with Harmony. I wonder who told her to come in here and do that? It could only be either Fin or Harlen. At this point, I didn't care because I still needed to calm myself.

Tonight I would become Luna of the Dolostone pack.

CHAPTER TWENTY-SIX

NIKITA

The woods had been decorated and lighted up along the sides of the trail. I walked barefoot in my dress to the hidden waterfall. From what I had seen of Luna ceremonies, each she-wolf that took the Luna position had always been barefoot to be closer to our roots. Taking a deep breath, I came into the clearing with the pack and the waterfall.

I glanced up and spotted the most amazing thing I had ever seen in my life. The moon had a blue tint to it, but what got me was the kaleidoscopes of color that encircled the moon. It looked like a circular rainbow. I stared at the scene for so long that I felt a nudge at my side.

Turning my gaze down, I spotted Tobey. He took my hand and led me forward to the makeshift stage. I had seen only one Luna ceremony and most of the time, a mated male of the female's pack takes her down. But since I didn't have a parent or anyone there, I chose Tobey. Fin and one of the elders were standing on the stage. Alpha Roy and Luna Adia were in the front, along with the two Alphas that Fin had become friends with when he was a rogue. I think he put them near him so that if he decided anything, then they would be able to help.

Both of them were big wolves and complete opposites. I had yet to meet them personally but they both looked scary. I mean, I'm pretty sure that I could take them, but I didn't want to find out right now. Fin had said that they were nice, so I would be taking him for his word.

Fin came to the steps and helped me up them and to the middle of the wooden structure. He kissed me before handing me over to the elder. The moon's glow made it look like I had a spotlight on myself for the ceremony. I glanced over the crowd and spotted Bella, who had tears in her eyes.

The elder turned to me with the knife in his hands. I took a deep breath and held out my hand. Fin's body closed me in and his hand came parallel with mine. I glanced up at him and he held my gaze just as the elder slashed into both of our hands. He then began to speak in the old language that wasn't taught to anyone unless they were going to be elders. But the wolves that we connected with knew what he was saying and the shiver that ran down my body was like someone had dumped cold water on me.

My hand stung as Fin clasped his with mine and if Fin hadn't been behind me, then I'd have been on my ass. The snap of the pack mindlink hit me and my head flung back into Fin's chest. All the voices taking precedence in my head. My breathing and heart rate increased as I tried to put my thoughts to the front of my mind.

Nikita, I'm glad that you have chosen to be Luna of the Dolostone pack. Your destiny has just begun and I look forward to seeing you flourish along with the pack. I hope you liked your gift tonight! Speak to you soon.

The voice in my head was nothing like anything I had ever heard before. It drowned out the others from my new pack. But was similar to someone I had met. Could she really be the person in my head? I had never heard of someone seeing or hearing the Moon Goddess.

Nikita, are you ok? Fin's voice came into my head. I tried to remove my hand from his, but it was like my hand was glued to his.

My heart is running out of my chest. I never expected all these voices. Even my inner voice sounded breathless to me. And let's not talk about the desire that seemed to increase as our hands stayed connected.

It will all be over in a minute, feisty wolf. You're such a good girl. Such a strong Luna. Fin's praise sent my desire into overdrive. I needed him now, and this was taking forever.

Just as I thought I was going to die, everything snapped back. It was quiet in my head and Enyo sat in my mind, tilting her head back and forth. The sound of the waterfall came back to me, but everything else was quiet.

Glancing around, I realized I had been lowered to the floor of the stage. Fin was beside me, petting my head as he held me close to him. I reached up to his face as if seeing it for the first time. Was he always so handsome? I mean, hell he was, but damn, it was like the moon rainbow was making him even more gorgeous.

"Fin. What just happened?"

Fin glanced up at the elder, and he stood with me in his arms.

Luna, you have been given a special gift. The Moon Goddess Selene has bestowed on you with a rare sight. There haven't been many Luna ceremonies that have had the Lunar Halo. You and Alpha Fin have a greater destiny in this life. The power that you both share is one that hasn't been seen in years.

Dolostone pack meet your Luna! Luna Nikita!

Their shouts in my head were more subdued than it had been when I became one with them. A lot of them were surprised by the elder's declaration. Because he didn't just speak with me but to the whole pack.

When Fin walked by them, they each kneeled on one knee. Jade and Harmony stayed on both knees as Fin strolled by with me in his arms. I was content with him carrying me because there was no way that I would've been able to walk right now. My legs were jelly, and I felt like I wasn't actually in my body.

Don't faint on me now, my feisty Luna. When we get to the pack house, you can rest, but right now, you need to stay awake.

Fin, it's hard.

I know. But tomorrow will be better. I promise.

I nodded, trying to keep my eyes open as he took me back down the trail with all the lights guiding our way.

⸺◆⸺

Fin

When our blood touched, I could feel the power that she possessed. I knew she was strong, but when our strength collided, I couldn't hold us both up. I went down to my knees with Nikita in my lap. Glancing up, I spotted the Lunar Halo. From what I had heard about them, they were a gift from the Moon goddess. And they were very rare. I had only been told about four Lunas that have been given a gift this rare.

I was proud that Nikita was one of them that was given it. Her body glowed and shimmered under the light. Not only did she have the Lunar Halo, but the blue moon was something that was rare as well. When the Moon Goddess told me that we were destined I didn't know that this was what she was meaning.

The look on Alpha Roy's face was priceless when he noticed that there was a Lunar Halo. He knew right then that he had lost a very special wolf. The entire pack had taken a knee when the elder announced to them she was now their luna. Nikita was special. She had always been, and now she was even more special.

The wind caressed our bodies and played with Nikita's hair as she hung in my arms. At first I thought that something had gone wrong. But Aloysius was adamant that she was fine and when I noticed she was still breathing, I could breathe myself. This hadn't happened with Kalila, but when she joined it didn't connect as powerful as Nikita's.

I carried Nikita into the packhouse and up to our room. Laying her down on the bed, I covered her and left her in the room. As much as I didn't want to leave her in the room by herself like this, I needed to go back to the guests and pack members. She still glowed in her white dress as she laid there. I wanted to lay down with her but I couldn't leave Harlen to deal with the guests himself.

Harlen, send Dawson and Keith up to watch my door. I don't trust that Alpha Roy will stay where he needs to be.

Yes, Alpha.

Taking one last look at my Luna, I closed the door to our room and headed back down to the first floor. Tobey came running up to me and tried to go around me. Hoisting him up in my arms, I carried him back to Harlen and Bella. Dawson and Keith headed up the stairs just as I spotted Alpha Roy starting toward the door.

"But Alpha Fin! I want to see Luna Nikita! She has been blessed!" Tobey whined as he struggled to make me let him go. He was so excited when she chose him to take her up to me.

I chuckled at the young wolf and handed him back to Harlen. "I know she is blessed. We all are to have a Luna like her."

Sydnie came up to me and tapped my arm.

"Yes, Syd?"

"Will she be okay? Kalila didn't do that with her Luna ceremony." Sydnie's eyes welled with tears. Making my chest tighten. When she had called me and told me what Jade had told her I was furious with jade for bringing Syd into this. She was already questioning Nikita and that didn't help when she was trying to get everyone's approval.

"Yes, she will be okay. She is just tired and needs some rest."

Sydnie nodded and then took off to find her mate. Sighing, I turned my attention to the four wolves that had made their way to my pack for this occasion. Nolen had grown into his own as he settled into his alpha status. It looked like Sawyer's Luna was again pregnant.

"Thank you both for coming." I held out my hand and Nolen took my forearm in an Alpha handshake. He was definitely stronger since I had last seen him.

"You know that we wouldn't miss this," Nolen answered me with a smile. For him being so young, he had always been wise beyond his years. His little mate stood beside him. "Fin, who is the other alpha here? I don't think I remember him."

"This is Alpha Roy. He is the Alpha of the Shonkinite pack." I introduced him to the alpha, standing by the door like he was about to bolt. "And this is his Luna."

"Luna Adia. But you can call me Adia. We are a smaller pack than the three of yours." I never could understand how she was always so kind when her mate seemed to always have something stuck up his ass. But that was the way of the Moon Goddess she paired wolves that would complement each other.

Sawyer's and Nolen's Lunas shook hands with her and then led her over to the food table. I noticed that Sawyer was starting to size him up. As much as I had been around the two of them, I had figured out the quirks of each of them. At this point, if Alpha Roy said anything out of the way, Sawyer might just cause a pack war. Not like it would be much of a fight. Shonkinite pack was still smaller than many of the pack in the Cairn territory.

Alpha Roy would be a dumbass if he thought he could fight all three of us. Or even one of the others. He didn't have enough wolves, and he didn't have Nikita anymore. So like I said he was going to ruin his pack if he started anything with us.

"So, when did you come into power, Alpha Roy? I don't remember you being in power when my father and I toured the packs." Sawyer crossed his arms over his chest and looked as if he was peacocking. This would be interesting.

"It has been a while. I took over a few years ago. After I found my Luna." Alpha Roy's eyes flickered between his wolf's and his human's. I didn't like that his wolf was that close to the surface.

"Ah. Well, how have things been? Sawyer and I have been trying to get around to the rest of the packs to see how everyone was doing after the defeat of the tyrant Wade." Nolen stated as he grinned. The kid was too kind for his own good. Sometimes I wondered how he even became the alpha.

"Well. Some packs didn't make it when the former Dolostone alpha came through. We were fortunate that we were so small because he didn't even try to come to my pack." Alpha Roy glanced over to where the girls were at the table. "I think it's about time for me and my Luna to retire. It will be a long journey tomorrow."

"Okay, I can have an omega help you up to your room." I answered him.

He raised his hand with a shake of his head and went to get his Luna. I watched as he grabbed her by her elbow and pulled her away from the other two Lunas. She seemed to not want to leave. I couldn't blame her, it looked like he didn't want her to mingle.

Lynn, follow the Alpha and Luna to their room. But stay far enough back that he doesn't suspect you. I'd hate to have to kill an alpha on my territory.

Yes, Alpha. Lynn's sweet voice answered me as I watched her scurry to the steps.

I didn't trust him as far as I could throw him. Which I'm sure would be pretty far, but we won't go into that right now. I just couldn't understand why he had such a problem with me. He surely couldn't have been that close to her. But how did I know? Kalila never talked about the pack and family that she had left to come and be my Luna.

The only thing I had to make sure of was that he didn't hurt Nikita. I would burn this entire world for her. Starting with him if I needed to. No one would be safe if something happened to my Luna.

CHAPTER TWENTY-SEVEN

NIKITA

I startled awake in the bed. The dream that I had was almost a nightmare. My body trembling and sore as it rested on the soft mattress. Sitting up from my prone position, I sniffed the air to try to find Fin. His scent was barely in the room as I swung my legs over the side of the bed and stood.

The dress I had been wearing for the ceremony was wrinkled and covered in dirt. I headed over to the closet and pulled out another dress. Laying it on the bed, I took off the dress I had on and slipped the other dress over my head.

My brown curls were a little looser than when they were put in. I opened the bedroom door and smelled two wolves at my door. Tilting my head, I sniffed again and stood there. Why were there guards at the door? Did something happen that Fin needed to have me watched?

Fin? I didn't think that he would answer me since he thought I would sleep until the morning. Well, I would have if the dream hadn't woken me.

Yes, my feisty Luna. Why are you not resting? It took everything in me not to shudder at his deep, husky baritone. If he had been in this room with me, he would be mine.

Why are there guards at the door? And where are you? I didn't quite understand why he would station guards at the door. I mean, if there were still people here, I wouldn't think anyone would be so bold and try anything.

I'm downstairs. Just tell them to move out of your way. I shook my head at his brutish way of saying things sometimes. But I wouldn't trade him for anyone else.

I know how to excuse myself, but why are they here?

Because I don't trust Alpha Roy. I won't make the same mistake twice.

I shook my head and opened the door. The two warriors bowed their heads before stepping behind me as I made my way down to the first floor. I was never one to have a guard before, since I was always the one being the guard. So the two of them behind me didn't really put me at ease.

I spotted Alpha Roy and Luna Adia coming up the stairs to their room. Adia looked like she was in pain, with Alpha Roy's hand clutching her elbow. The warriors behind me bristled as I walked past the leaders of my old pack.

Alpha Roy reached out and grabbed hold of my arm, spinning me around as Adia cowered on the landing. One of the warriors took hold of his arm, his claws extending into the other alpha's flesh. Alpha Roy winced as the claws entered further into the muscle and sinew. Enyo tried to rush forward to make me shift to protect myself. But I held her back.

"Take your hands off our Luna." One of the warriors growled. His voice laced with his wolf's. Fuck I'd hate to be alone with this wolf in a dark forest.

"You think you can be Luna here, but all you will be to this pack is an outsider that conspired with me against their alpha. You lost their respect when that female overheard our conversation. This isn't over." Alpha Roy released my arm in turn, ripping his from the warrior beside me. The anger that flowed through me was more than my own. I could tell that Fin was riding this with me in our bond as I glared at the alpha before me.

"Not like I was respected in my own pack. You just liked that I was the strongest warrior of the pack. Yet you never made me a delta." I spat at him just as Fin's scent made its way to me.

Alpha Roy grunted and left before Fin got closer. Adia's face was flushed as the tears ran down her face. I never realized how much Adia was scared of Alpha Roy until now. If there was a way I could save her, then I was going to do that. I just hoped that she would be strong enough to cling to her part of her soul.

I turned just as Fin crested the landing below me. The warrior beside me had retracted his claws and fangs. My arm still stung from Alpha Roy's grip, but I needed to make sure that Fin didn't know. Blood stained the stairs since Alpha Roy tore his arm open to get away. Since that would cause a war between my pack and my old one. And I didn't want to have that on my conscience.

Fin grabbed my hands as I tried to reach for his face. He looked me over, almost with a fine-toothed comb. I winced when his hand touched the already bruised skin of my forearm. The look of fury in his eyes was not lost on me as I struggled to compose myself.

"Did he do this?" I opened my mouth, thinking that he was asking me since his eyes were glued to mine.

"Yes, Alpha. I made sure that he had a souvenir as well." The warrior answered before I could and when the hard blues flickered, I knew this wasn't going to be good if his wolf rose any closer to the surface.

"Fin I'm fine. Let's go down to the party. He will be gone tomorrow and when he leaves in the morning, those crystals will be the last that he gets from us." I touched his face with my other hand to try to get him to see reason. We didn't need a dead alpha on our hands. Besides, if there was a way, I wanted to keep the alliance until we got stronger.

"This is punishable by wolf law. He shouldn't have touched you!" The snarl was more animalistic than before as he stared at me. I knew that he was on his way to being unreasonable the more he got mad. This couldn't get out of hand. I needed to make sure he calmed down.

"No, he shouldn't have, but he did, and you are the better alpha. So, please let's go down to the party. I would love to meet the two alphas that you talk about." I brought my lips to his and started with a soft brush of my lips to his. Fin deepened the kiss and picked me up. Carrying me back down the stairs that he had just come up.

Facing behind Fin, I could see who exactly half shifted to grab his arm. I'm sure that the claw marks on his arm would be there for a while before they were fully healed. The one who had protected me bowed his head and smiled before heading down another hallway with the other wolf. I would have to make sure that I learned his name so that I could thank him for his protection.

Fin stopped and let me on my feet in the foyer. Which had been decorated with streamers and flowers for the occasion. The omegas did an amazing job with everything. Turning my gaze around to face the way Fin was, I realized the two younger wolves were in front of me. The ones that had been in the front row of the ceremony. Both would have any unmated wolf dropping to their knees in front of them. Now that they weren't sitting, I could tell that they weren't that scary like I had thought. One held himself like any other alpha, but the other one clearly didn't like to be the center of attention.

Which brought my gaze to their necks and noticed that they were mated. Whatever females they were mated with could only be their opposite. I could see that a few of the unmated she-wolves here were already upset.

Some were still trying to get their attention, but they didn't even give them the time of day.

"Nolen, Sawyer, this is my Luna, Nikita. Nikita, this is Alpha Nolen and Alpha Sawyer of the Rhyolite and Quartzite packs." Fin pointed to each of the alphas. The dark-haired one named Nolen seemed to blush before a blonde female came up to his side. She had similar features to the alpha from Quartzite. Another dark-haired female came up, and she was most definitely pregnant.

"This is Alpha Nolen's mate and Luna, Amora, and this is Alpha Sawyer's Luna and mate Danika." Fin continued his introductions as they both smiled. Amora had the most beautiful eyes I had ever seen. The amber of them made them dance and glow like fire. I had to do a double take when I glanced over to her.

I shook each of their hands and introduced myself. The other female, who had come to Alpha Sawyer's side, didn't look like Nolen, so I didn't think that they were related. Most mates were found in the same pack that they were born into. While others had to find them in other packs.

"So are you and Alpha Sawyer related?" I asked Luna Amora, my curiosity getting the better of me. I could tell that she was younger than the males and the other Luna but I needed to know.

"Yes, he is my older brother." She giggled as Sawyer shook his head.

"So, you are both alpha blood?" Female alphas were rare. No wonder the Moon Goddess gave her to Nolen. She was one of a kind.

"Yes, I mean that's normally how that works, right?" Amora giggled again. The way that Alpha Nolen looked at her sent my heart to flutter. Did Fin look at me like that?

You know he does. When we are near him, he normally never lets his gaze stray very far. Enyo answered my internal question.

I glanced at him from the corner of my eye, and he was most definitely staring at me. But he was also making sure to keep everyone else in his sight, too.

"I know. But I had never heard of females being born to alphas."

"Well, it happens." Amora chuckled. A smile brightened her face as she looked up at her mate. "I think that the Obsidian pack alphas had a daughter didn't they?"

"You four are welcome to stay and then leave tomorrow morning." Fin's deep voice sent a shiver down my spine. I still noticed that I reacted to him quicker. So I guess that means I was still in heat. This was going to be interesting.

"Thank you, Alpha Fin. We will take you up on that." Alpha Nolen answered as he pulled his gaze from his mate and back to Fin.

"What pack are you from, Nikita?" Luna Amora asked me. I couldn't help noticing the look that she got from Luna Danika.

"I'm from the Shonkinite pack. I was one of the top warriors there." I answered her with pride. My previous alpha was a prick, but I could still be proud of myself. Hell I rose through those warrior ranks with my own gumption.

"Oh! So that is why the other alpha is here? I bet he didn't like that he lost you." Danika commented as she allowed her gaze to look me over. I knew what she was thinking. How could a small she-wolf like me could be a top warrior?

"He was able to make an alliance with my mating to Fin. So I don't think that he was too heartbroken with it." I shrugged and glanced up at Fin. I didn't know how much he had told them and I didn't want to tell them if he hadn't.

"Wow, and how much younger are you than Fin?" Amora asked me. I could tell she was genuinely curious.

"I'm ten years younger than him."

Luna Amora jumped at me and grabbed my hands. I didn't understand why she was so excited about this information. Pulling slightly away, I stepped back away from the group.

"Sorry, I just have so much to ask you! I'm younger than my mate and I could start to feel the bond before I was eighteen. Was it the same for you?" The way her eyes brightened at the thought of me being able to answer her.

"We didn't meet until about a few months ago. But I think I smelled her before I met Markus." Fin answered her, and she slinked back to her mate. I hated the sadness on her face that the information from Fin put there.

"But if you noticed the way he worded that he 'thought' he smelled me." I came back with my statement as I elbowed him in his side.

Fin chuckled as he wrapped his arm around my waist and pulled me close to his side. As much as I didn't need a male to protect me, I liked how Fin made me feel safer. I would never allow him to put my safety over his though because we were a team.

"You know Fin. I never expected you to be this way. But I didn't know you before being rogue." Alpha Nolen's voice brought me out of my thoughts as I turned back to the group before me.

"Yeah, well, young pup, I didn't tell you or teach you everything that I know." Fin chuckled again as he clapped Nolen on the shoulder.

"I can believe that." Nolen laughed. The way he looked at my mate with admiration told me that he respected him.

These Alphas were younger than me, but they didn't act as young as they were. But that was what happened when you became a leader of a pack at a young age. You grew up faster than the rest of us. And most of the time that responsibility made you grow up, while other times it didn't.

CHAPTER TWENTY-EIGHT

Fin

The morning after the Luna ceremony was chaos as some of the pack leaders of the other packs left. I kept an eye on Alpha Roy since he wasn't too happy that Nikita didn't kill me. For the life of me, I couldn't understand why he wanted me dead. Yes, I chose Kalila as my chosen, but I didn't want her dead and the man that killed her was gone. She had gotten her justice along with my unborn pup.

Harlen and Bella were spending time with their daughter and son-in-law. The wolf wouldn't come near me. I think I scared him. *You think?* Aloysius asked me with a wolfish grin. He was happier than he had ever been since we met Nikita. To be honest, so was I.

I watched her as she went from female to female, telling them bye. She stopped in front of Luna Adia and gave her a hug. I didn't know if they had been close before she took the Luna position of the Shonkinite pack. But it pained me that the female had to go back to live with that mate of hers.

My heart was beating fast as I continued to watch Nikita make her rounds. She was everything that I could ask for, as my mate and Luna. There was nothing I wouldn't do for her and my pack.

The sound of footsteps descending the steps brought my attention to the four that I had been hoping wouldn't be leaving just yet. Nolen, Sawyer, Danika and Amora walked down the stairs, a few omegas, helping them with their luggage. Those four were the ultimate power houses. The way their auras cast around them told the others that they were not to be messed with.

You and Nikita are a powerhouse too. As you say. Did you not see what the Moon Goddess blessed your mate with? Aloysius growled in my head.

I know, but we are having to rebuild everything.

I was proud of Nolen. He had taken my training while rogue to heart and he was almost as strong as me. One of these days, I would show my pup that training. The group came up to me as Alpha Roy and his Luna left through the front doors. Which would be the last time they would be in my pack house.

Because according to my Luna, the crystals they were taking with them would be the last of what they would be getting. She was right, because he had gotten enough since technically she was the bridge for the packs. I just hoped that he didn't turn on this alliance because I don't know who in that pack was really loyal to him.

"Well, how's this morning gone?" Nolen came up to me and stood beside me as I continued to survey the foyer. I wasn't too sure if Alpha Roy would leave the pack so there were wolves set out to watch him leave the territory.

"It's been good. I haven't had any issues so far." I chuckled as Nikita headed my way. She was so beautiful and if she wasn't my mate I would be one jealous wolf.

"Alpha Fin, I don't know how you did it, but you got yourself a beautiful mate and Luna." Amora sounded out as she nudged Danika, who nodded with a smile.

"Yeah, I will never know what I had done to deserve her." I smiled at her as she wrapped her arms around my waist. Nikita glanced up at me. She fisted my jacket that I had put on before I left her in the room to get dressed.

"What are you talking about?" I could hear the purr in her voice. She was still in heat and I was loving it. I didn't want to not be covered by her. Hell I was about to tell everyone to see themselves out and take her upstairs to have her sheathing my hardening cock.

"You, my feisty Luna." The smirk that graced her lips as I moved a piece of hair away from her face made my heart speed up.

"I think Alpha Fin and his Luna needs to get a room." Alpha Sawyer's voice said as a giggle escaped one of the Lunas beside me.

I turned my blue gaze from Nikita and on to Sawyer.

"I know what you are thinking, even though you are not part of my pack, Sawyer. And yes, I can keep up with her. Just because I'm older than her doesn't mean I can't."

"Damn, Sawyer, he burned you!" Danika quipped as she laughed out loud. Her hands holding her swollen belly.

Harlen and Bella turned at the sound along with Sydnie. It was weird that she wasn't in my head anymore. I missed the little pup. Sawyer nudged Danika, which just sent her into more fits of laughter.

"Sorry, Fin. I mean Alpha Fin. You know how they are." Nolen quickly changed the way that he addressed me. I didn't mind him just calling me Fin. When we met, I wasn't even an Alpha.

"Your fine Alpha Nolen. I'm not offended." I told him as I pulled Nikita close. She was warm. Warmer than usual. Glancing down, I noticed that her face was red and sweat was pouring off her. "Nikita, are you okay?"

Nikita started to nod before her eyes fluttered and she went limp in my arms. I glanced around and Harlen and Bella got to me before I lowered us to the floor. Nolen knelt down beside me as Amora and Danika backed away.

Doc! Come quick! Luna Nikita is unresponsive! I yelled through the pack mindlink. Which I shouldn't have done. Since panic set in and the wolves in the house flooded the foyer. Warriors were making a barricade and others were moving wolves that weren't part of our pack to the walls.

This had been protocol since before I was born. I didn't even have to tell them what needed to be done. The way they did what was needed told anyone that was in this packhouse just how much training that they had.

My attention came back to my Luna. I couldn't lose her now. She just became Luna, and I found her finally. If the Moon Goddess allowed her to die on me. I would rip her limb from limb. She couldn't allow my fated to die after she had given her a blessing like that.

Bringing her closer to my body, I looked around trying to find the Doc. He needed to get here. If he didn't, there would be no more Dolostone. I would renounce my alpha status and find the person who had done this to my mate and I would torture them slowly. Why did she do this! What was the Moon Goddess' plan for this?

Doc pushed through the crowd of wolves and kneeled beside Nikita as she labored to breathe. Aloysius was pacing in my head as I stared at my mate, struggling. I tried not to hold her as close to me so that Doc could examine her.

Fin. Why is everything so hot? Everything hurts. Even her voice in my mind was weaker. Something was wrong. I needed her to survive!

Don't worry, feisty wolf. You need to stop talking. Doc will figure it out.

"Alpha, we need to get her over to the pack hospital. I believe she has been poisoned." The worry on his face and voice unnerved me. He never acted like this. He was always very calm and poised.

Nodding, I scooped her up in my arms and ran after him to the pack hospital. The whimpers coming from her constricted my heart even more. And made me nauseated as I ran to the building. The sounds of our feet reverberated against the tile floor. Wolves stared at me as I raced down the halls.

Doc ran into a room and other nurses were already in there waiting with bags of what looked like water but smelled like salt. And something else I couldn't quite put my finger on. Laying her down on the bed, they started to work on her and basically pushed me out of the way.

Nikita's skin flamed red as they stuck needles in her arms, connecting her to the bags already hanging on the IV poles. I stood there, not knowing what to do. Doc was doing a more extensive exam on her and it took everything in me to keep from sliding down the wall and crying. Why did this have to happen?

The creaking of the door startled me awake and brought me to my feet. A growl ripped through me before I realized who it was coming in. Harlen stopped and brought up his hands. I glanced over to Nikita; she was still sleeping from the meds.

Doc had told me that she had been poisoned. The only one that I could think of that would do something like that would be her old Alpha. But I didn't notice him near her. His mate was and if she was in on this too, I would kill her as well.

"How is Luna Nikita doing?"

"She's sleeping right now. Doc says she will be fine. But we haven't figured out what the poison is. I do think I know who did it. We are no longer allied with the Shonokite pack." I glared over at my beta as he came to the other side of Nikita's bed. I finally noticed the gift that he had under his arm.

"That is fine by me. But Bella has made the Luna this, and I was told not to come back with it." Harlen placed the blanket over the other blanket she was under. The crest of our pack and Luna stitched into it.

"We both know when Bella says something you do it." I laughed as the expression on Harlen's face gave me 'the don't I know it' look.

"Has everyone been questioned and searched? Who all is left?" I glanced back at Nikita as I waited for Harlen's answer.

"No one that was still at the pack house had poison on them and they were all questioned. A few are pissed but the others were fine. They understood." Harlen answered me. I knew some would have a problem but I didn't care. I was going to find out who did this.

"Okay, thanks Harlen. I'm going to be here with Nikita until she wakes up." I glanced back over to him just as he stood. I walked him to the door and opened it.

Harlen nodded and then left me with Nikita. He and Bella had kept the other wolves away from this room. We had decided not to tell the pack anything until she was awake. Just in case something went wrong.

Nikita tossed and turned on the bed. I went back over to her and took her hand. She stilled as soon as my hand slid into hers. Bringing it up to my lips, I placed a kiss on each finger before ending at the back of her hand.

She is calm in her mind when we hold her hand. Aloysius chimed in. For him to be this calm himself made me think she would make it.

I know. I just wish Doc would stop giving her whatever is keeping her asleep. I need to see those eyes.

She needs to heal. Her wolf is also needing to heal. Aloysius answered me. *By the way, do you think you could eat something? I mean, if I'm starving, I know you are.*

I chuckled at him. It had only been twelve hours since Nikita had been brought to the hospital. But if food was going to keep him off my back. Then food is what I would get him. I kiss Nikita's forehead and head out the door to find Doc.

Doc stood beside the nurse counter as I came up to him. The she-wolf that sat in front of him glanced up at me and then bowed her head. Doc turned and inclined his head before speaking to me, "Alpha, is everything okay?"

"Everything is fine. I was just going to get something to eat. Can you mindlink me if Nikita wakes?"

"Of course Alpha. We can get you something to eat if you want to stay with her. But I'm sure the rest of the pack would like to see you as well."

I had thought about it. The pack had been worried about us. Their worry laced the packlink like a black cloud. It would be good for me to join them tonight. To hopefully put it to rest even though she still had yet to wake.

"I'll go get my own food. Thank you for the offer, but the worry from the rest of the pack through the packlink is something I need to address." I placed a hand on his shoulder before walking down the white hall. It hurt to leave her because I wanted to be there when she woke. But I also needed to but this worry to rest.

As I strolled out of the sliding glass doors of the hospital, I spotted most of the pack on the steps. Candles in their hands. My heart clinched at the sight of all the wolves either standing or sitting here with me. I hadn't even thought of what to say to them. Considering that, I thought I had more time to think everything out.

"Dolostone. It is late, you should go home and rest. Luna Nikita is resting. Doc is sure that she will be fine."

"That is a relief, Alpha. But what are we going to do about whoever did this? We can't let them get away with this." Bailey's voice rang out over the rumble that followed. He had been in the pack since I was a young pup. He was a badass warrior and didn't mind showing the younger ones he still had it.

"This is true. And I have a hunch about who did it, but I'm not yet sure if it was. We will have to be on guard. I will not put it past them to send warriors to our borders." I answered him as I swept over the crowd. Each one nodded as they sat their candles on the steps to the side.

Two warrior wolves stayed on the steps. Their heads bowed, but their chests were out. I knew that stance. "Blake, Conner, what are you doing?"

"We will stand here to guard the hospital in your stead, Alpha." Their unison voices answered me.

This was the reason I appreciated my pack. These guys right here.

CHAPTER TWENTY-NINE

NIKITA

The pain that had raced through my system was unbearable, even for me. Only the comfort of my mate allowed the pain to go away. I had been poisoned before with this type, but it had been smaller doses. That was probably why I was able to stay up for as long as I had.

But that also meant that I knew who the person was that had poisoned me. Once I was up and moving around, I was going to rip them limb from limb. They will feel my wrath.

Yes, any wolf that has helped with this. Will meet the Moon Goddess sooner rather than later! Enyo growled weakly in my mind. But her eyes glowed with the ferocity that I knew that she had.

I felt Fin's presence leave, and the pain didn't shoot through my system. Whatever they were pushing through my veins was working. It made me sad that Fin left but he would only have done that if it was something important. He still had a pack to run and just because I was sick didn't change that.

You know he won't leave you for too long. He went years without you; I doubt he will be more than a few minutes.

Someone's hand, calloused yet soft, slipped into mine. But it wasn't Fin's because I was under whatever meds that Doc was giving me. I couldn't tell who it was. It didn't calm me as much as Fin's touch did, but it helped.

I could start to hear the soft humming. The sound was like what my mother used to sing to me when I was just a pup. Did every mother know this song? The squeak of the door was louder than the woman humming. Could I be getting my hearing back?

"Bella, what are you doing?" It was Fin! I would know that deep baritone anywhere.

"I came to keep her company while you grabbed something to eat." Bella's voice came from my left side. Oh, how I missed her sweet voice.

"Thank you. Has anything changed since I was gone?" Fin's hand slipped into mine and I felt the sparks race up my arm. Goddess, I love when his skin touches mine.

"No, Luna is still sleeping."

Fin sighed and placed his lips on the back of my hand. I needed to wake up. The sadness in his aura made me uncomfortable. He wasn't supposed to be like this.

"Fin, Luna Nikita is a fighter. I don't think anything could bring her down. As small as she is, she has a heart of an Alpha."

Bella really did like me! When I first got here, I thought she was just being cordial. But she had never spoken ill to me or changed her demeanor toward me. After Jade had said what she said.

"Did you see the candles the pack left on the steps of the hospital?"

"Yes, Alpha. You know the pack would never want to see you lose your fated. She has changed you in a way, and she has made you stronger. Along with this pack." The squeaking of the chair sounded up to me.

I tried to move my fingers, but they wouldn't budge. How long was this going to take to get everything back? This made me vulnerable, and I didn't like it. It wasn't that I didn't think Fin could protect me. But what about when he would go get something to eat?

"Did you station Blake and Conner at her door?" Bella asked with concern in her voice.

"No, they volunteered. I'm hoping that I can find the right person who did this to her. Aloysius has been wanting to go to that pack and trash it. But it's her home pack and I don't want to make her hurt more." Fin rubbed my hand over his cheek. I just wanted to reach out with my fingers and touch him. To let him know that I was okay.

"They are great boys."

Enyo, I need you to help me. Can you not talk with Aloysius?

I can. But only sometimes.

Okay, well, I need you to help me move my fingers.

I pushed my mind to make my fingers move. Fin now had my palm on his face. All I had to do was to move my pointer finger along his cheekbone. Why did this have to be so hard? What was the reason to keep me under?

Because they don't know that you are immune to small doses of poison. That's why.

You make my head hurt sometimes.

I sighed and resigned to wait out the meds to be stopped. At least I could hear the people around me now. Maybe soon I will get more of my senses.

I knew it was night because the warmth from the sun which came from the window was no longer beating down on my body. Fin wasn't with me, but I could hear his voice somewhere far enough away that his voice was muffled as he talked with Doc.

It was so much cooler in the room and I wondered if someone had turned the A/C on or if it was just because it was nighttime. The door slammed before a mumbled, "Fuck." Came from Fin.

"My feisty Luna, I need you to wake up. Doc is weaning you off the meds. He thinks that most of the poison is out of your system. But not only that, I need to know that I wasn't too late." I had never heard him like this. Which made my heart hurt.

Sometime when I had fallen asleep I had started to be able to smell. The scent of the saline bag and the other meds that were in the other bag excited me. Because that meant I was coming out of this sleep.

Fin's breath fanned the back of my hand. Which caused goose bumps to race up my arm. What I wouldn't give to touch him. I could feel his hand underneath mine and in my mind, I gripped his hand.

"Nikita! Are you awake? Squeeze my hand if you can hear me!" I could feel his excitement through our bond and it made me excited because he was.

I gripped his hand again but couldn't hold on to it long. It was like I didn't have the strength.

"Doc, get in here! She's waking up!"

The door to my room swung open and Doc was at my other side, checking vitals and opening my eyelids. When he did open my eyes I could see Doc and Fin, but like with my hand, I couldn't hold them open.

"She's reacting to the light. But it seems like her body can't move at the moment. I'll stop the coma inducing meds right now and we will see if that will help speed this movement for her now." Doc continued to speak to Fin and checking me out. "It's okay Luna. We are going to get you out of this bed."

Doc squeezed my shoulder and left my side. Fin continued to kiss the back of my hand. The sparks erupted with each kiss. I loved it because I wanted to be with him again.

I had been awake for the last couple of hours. Fin was again sleeping at the side of my bed. His head laying next to my head. It was amazing to be able to see him again. As much as I wanted to be selfish, I let him sleep. I didn't want him to lose any sleep, even though he probably already did.

My door slowly opened and Bella locked eyes with me and stifled her gasp when I brought my finger to my lips. Bella smiled and nodded before sitting down on the other side of me. She grabbed my hand and silently sobbed.

I haven't told him yet.

He is going to be ecstatic and I don't think I want to be in here when you wake him up.

I smiled and nodded. Bella stood up and left the room. Her silhouette in the door's window. Knowing her, she was talking to Harlen, letting him know I was awake and not to come in at the moment. I turned my attention to Fin, who was still asleep.

Slowly, I turned on my side and ran my fingers through Fin's hair. It was coarse, like he hadn't been showering regularly. Which was not like him to do. He stirred under my hand and when his eyes met mine Fin stilled.

Hey. I used my mindlink to talk with him since I was unsure if I could actually talk since I had been asleep for so long.

Are you okay? Do you need some water?

Yes, please. I'm not sure how my voice will sound.

Fin stood and pulled me to a sitting position before he crashed his lips to mine. I wrapped my arms around his neck and pushed my tongue into his. He moaned as he pulled me flush against him. I missed this. When Fin pulled away, the whimper that left me made him chuckle.

"Nikita. Let me get you some water. I'm going to get Doc and have him check you out again."

Okay. Don't take too long. I need you.

"Don't worry. I'm not going to leave you now." Fin chuckled again and kissed the top of my head. He let me go and went out the door leaving it ajar.

I sat here waiting for them to get back. When Bella came back in the room she grinned at me as she sat down. Bella patted my hand as we waited for Fin to return with Doc.

"So, he is very excited that you are awake."

Yes, he is. Can you tell me how long I've been out?

"Three days. It's been hell trying to keep Fin and Harlen from going to war with your old pack. The warriors were not helping matters. They were hyping them both up." She shook her head as both Harlen and Fin came in along with Doc.

"Good morning Luna. How are you feeling?" Doc's gruff but friendly voice asked me as he took out his stethoscope.

Fin came up to the side that Bella was on and handed me the cup of water. I gulped it down, even though they had been giving me fluids while I was in the medically induced coma. This helped with the parched feeling that I had.

"I'm good. Ready to get out of this bed." I told them all. My voice was not my normal tone at all and I felt like I could drink a lake and still not get the parched feeling gone.

A nurse came in with a pitcher and then refilled my glass. I gulped it down too before I turned my gaze back to Doc.

"Do you happen to know who it was that poisoned you, Luna?"

Everyone waited for me to answer. Could my delta have actually poisoned me? I mean if the Alpha told him to then he wouldn't have had a choice. So, that meant the one I wanted was my old Alpha.

"I have a hunch on who it was. But I don't know if they did it willingly or if they were made to do it." I answered the Doc. My gaze went to Fin and I could see along with feel his anger in his eyes. He wanted blood as much as I did. But we needed answers before we started a war. "I know what you are feeling and I want it too. But we have to be sure what they want."

"And when we find out. That whole pack will be no more." The blue of Aloysius' eyes glowed like I had never seen before. And I knew that in my mind he was telling me and the people in this room the truth. One hundred percent.

CHAPTER THIRTY

Fin

It has been a couple of weeks since the poisoning. Nikita has been taking it slow but has been on edge. I had more warriors on patrol than I had ever had before. There was no way that Alpha Roy would just let this go. He wanted me dead and now that I had completed my mate bond with Nikita, he would have to kill her now, too.

I watched as she fought with one of our biggest males. He wasn't too keen on fighting with his Luna, but she insisted he train with her. Telling me I was too busy with pack things to train with her. Hank was pulling his punches, and she was getting frustrated. I could tell by the way she kept pushing him. She hated that even though she was able to fight with the best of them. They thought because of her size that they would hurt her.

"Just go on Hank." She sighed as she placed her hands on her hips as she shook her head. Nikita's head bowed while she took deep breaths.

You know I wouldn't pull my punches.

Nikita's head snapped up to me on the hill, and she shook her head. A few of the wolves that were around the fighting ring noticed I was there. I had changed into only shorts, knowing that I was going to shift and make her fight me. This was going to be the only way that they would treat her like me when we trained. They needed to know that she could take as much as she gave.

You would cause Aloysius wouldn't let you hurt me. She snapped back at me through our mate link. Aloysius shook his but he was in on my game.

If you are so sure, then shift and we will train our wolves.

You're on. She shifted and everyone around her gasped. Most of them hadn't seen her beautiful wolf before.

I took off running and jumped the fence, along with a few of the other warriors. Shifting into my solid white wolf in the air. Enyo had her ears against her head and teeth bared, but Aloysius held his cool. We rounded each other in the fighting area. Enyo jumped in and pulled a tuft of hair from my shoulder. It hurt like a bitch and lunged at her.

Enyo jumped away just as my teeth closed and I came away with some of her brownish red hair in my mouth. I crashed into her and Nikita slid into some of the warriors. A few of the males and females growled their displeasure.

Good they should get mad when something happens to their Luna. Aloysius snickered as he laid his ears against his head. Baring his teeth at the closest ones. The wolves bowed their heads even though they still showed their displeasure.

Nikita stood and raced back toward me. I hadn't realized that she was as fast as she was until it was too late to move. She crashed into me with her shoulder and sent me into the other warriors on the other side of the ring. Fuck, she was strong. I believed that I was going to bruise later after this fight.

Sometimes I couldn't help but think that maybe she had alpha blood in her lineage. Which would be the reason why she was bigger than most other females in their wolf form. Her strength was another reason why I thought that she had alpha in her. I mean, it could happen. Packs have been lost and alphas had went rogue. So there was always a chance.

We continued to fight; she grabbed hold of my ear and tugged. Wolves on the side lines cheered her on. They had never seen her actually fight with someone like me. I wish they could've seen her fighting the big wolf in her pack. She was fucking spectacular. It made me hard just thinking about her fucking up that wolf.

Jumping away from her she continued to lunge at me. I was trying to tire her out, so that she didn't think about what had happened the morning after her Luna ceremony. When I found out who did it, they would lose their life. I had waited too long to find my mate to just lose her to someone trying to get revenge.

If it was Alpha Roy, I would enjoy tearing him limb from limb. The only thing I didn't like was the fact that he was mated and she would feel his life leave her. May the Goddess allow her the strength to pull through that pain. Because there had been talk that when a mate died, it normally took the other too if they weren't strong enough.

You are keeping to your word. I haven't had this much fun since we last fucked. Nikita's voice resonated in my head as I circled her again. She had latched onto my leg at one point and caused it to bleed.

Yeah? We can have fun again. Once we finish this. Or we can finish this early and we can meet in the bedroom. I'd love to fill you with my cum. I had never spoken to a female like this, but she had started it. Besides she seemed to like the way I was talking to her.

Are you horny? I was only out for three days. I guess when you get used to getting pussy everyday you start to miss it sooner. She cocked her head with her ears facing me as she wagged her tail.

Well, you seem to be horny too. Care to take a wager on who can make the other one cum first?

Nikita snorted and flicked her tongue over her canines. Her eyes flickering between her human and her wolf's eyes. Yeah, I was getting under skin and she was emitting her need. All I needed was for her to own up to needing a release as much as I did.

Well, yeah. Who wouldn't want to fuck you? You are the perfect specimen of an alpha. No wonder all the females in my pack were drooling.

I couldn't care less what those females wanted. Because I'm yours and you need to use this perfect body that you claim it as like it's going out of style.

There was no way that she wasn't going to take that. We needed each other right now and hell; I wanted to make sure that she would be carrying my pup soon. I was surprised that she wasn't already carrying with as many times as we had fucked when she had went into heat.

But it could just mean that it wasn't our time yet.

Or you could be getting too old. I mean, in canine years, you are pushing six hundred years already. Aloysius chucked in my head.

I'm in my prime asshole. I snarled. *Fucking prick.*

Nikita came up to me and I made sure to watch her. She was cunning, this feisty wolf of mine. I wouldn't put it past her to attack me while she thought she had me distracted. Nikita came up to me and rubbed her head underneath my jaw. I could smell her calling me with her scent.

The crowd had started to leave when she began to nuzzle me. They didn't want to witness anything that might come next. The females that had brought pups over to watch as me and Nikita fought left with them wanting to know who won. I licked Nikita's face and then her ears before nipping her shoulder, making her race after me. Nikita never missed a beat as she and I shifted and went into the packhouse.

I grabbed her up and took the back stairs two at a time as Nikita ran her hands through my hair and between my shoulder blades. The way her fingers made sparks race to catch up with them. Excited every nerve in my body.

"Nikita, I need to know how you are feeling. I don't want to be rough with you if you are not feeling up to that." I nuzzled into her neck. The great thing about going up the back stairs was that the younger wolves were never back here. Since it only went to our suite and no other wolves would be on this side of the house. So being naked and roaming my hands over my feisty mate was nothing.

"I'm ready for whatever you have planned for me. I wish everyone would quit treating me like I'm fragile." Nikita nipped my ear lobe as I pushed open our door to our suite and walked with her down the hall. Getting to the bedroom door I shouldered it open.

If she didn't want to be treated like she was fragile, I was going to rock her world. Hell, I needed to be inside this woman right now, but there were people still in the front part of the packhouse and I didn't want them to hear her scream.

Kicking the door closed, I pressed her against the wall. I was so hard there was already pre-cum leaking. Nikita pulled my lips to hers and snaked her tongue into my mouth. Fuck, I loved this woman. She moaned into my mouth as I adjusted her to one arm and rubbed the head of my cock through her slit before plummeting inside of her.

"Fuck, Nikita." I groaned as her pussy sheathed me to the hilt.

"Fin. I need you harder!" Nikita moaned out her words while I pulled out and then slammed back into her. Her nails bit into the base of my hair and her pussy tightened around me as I found my rhythm.

I pulled her from the wall and took her further into our suite. Lifting her off my hard cock, I turned her around with her back facing me. I bent her over the armchair and stood behind her. Nikita stared at me over her shoulder as I pulled both her legs up and between my legs. I entered her again before taking both her ankles and holding them in the air.

"Right there Fin!" She screamed as I hit her cervix over and over. Nikita's and my flesh slapping against each other while I pushed her into the couch. Her moans spurred me on and I let go of her ankles, taking hold of her hips, bringing her harder into me.

Nikita's mouth hung open as I continued my assault on her pussy. Her hair was a mess around her face, tendrils of the dark color covering her hunter green eyes. That watered each time I made contact with her cervix. Leaning over her, I grabbed a hand full of her dark brown locks and pulled her up flush against my body.

"Fin, I love feeling you beat my cervix with your cock." Nikita's hand snaked around the back of my neck as I forced my tongue inside her mouth.

"I love when you talk to me like this." I pulled out of her and then turned her back to face me. Lifting her I slung her over my shoulder and walked her to our bed.

Dropping her on the bed I crawled over her, taking a nipple between my teeth and popping off of it I heard a hiss come from her lips. I covered her and plunged into her while I crashed my mouth onto hers. Keeping her from moaning out loud since the balcony doors where wide open.

I broke the kiss and removed myself from inside of her. Nikita whimpered at the loss of my cock.

The grin that spread on my lips as her hands ran over her breasts and then dipped into her folds had her moaning for me again. "On your hands and knees feisty wolf. Show me that beautiful ass in the air."

Nikita quickly turned on her belly and lifted her ass into the air her chest and face in the mattress as she turned her eyes to stare back at me. She licked her lips and wiggled her ass taunting me as I stood there stroking my cock that was leaking and aching to be inside her once more. I wanted her pussy filled to the brim with my seed.

The animal part of me wanted to put a pup inside of her but the rational side of me told me that it wasn't time yet since I still had to deal with the coward of an alpha that she used to be under. Kneeling on the bed I rubbed her ass before bringing back my hand and giving her a quick but hard slap.

"Yes Fin! More!" Damn it. I found a kink that she liked. She was going to give me a run for my money with her being younger than me.

I caressed the other cheek before bringing down my hand on it causing her to groan and whimper at the same time. Entering her again I seated myself balls deep inside of her. I pulled her tighter into me and reached down to play with her clit. My other hand's thumb playing with her puckering asshole.

"Scream my name again, feisty wolf." I groaned as I began to thrust in and out of her. Even without her being in heat. I could feel myself swelling inside of her.

"Ah! Goddess Fin I'm coming!" My brain was mush as my thumb went inside her tight hole and I unloaded everything I had inside of her.

CHAPTER THIRTY-ONE

Nikita

Fin ran beside me in his wolf form in the early mornings. He decided that since we had trained that previous afternoon that we would run in the mornings. I didn't mind. It was refreshing to be able to have this moment of togetherness as the sun rose over the mountains.

When we rounded the next corner I spotted something in the middle of the trail. At first I thought it was a log. But then when we got closer it was my old delta from my pack. I shifted and ran up to him with Fin at my side.

"Nikita be careful."

Kneeling down beside my old pack mate I searched his body for any type of wound. When I didn't find one I realized that he had been poisoned like I had. I couldn't understand why he would be here on my pack and why was he poisoned? Did he know what had happened at my Luna Ceremony?

I glanced over my shoulder to Fin who stared back at me. This wasn't good. If people found out that we had a wolf from another pack dead on our land. Alpha Roy would attack because he now had reason to. He could claim that we killed him.

"Fin we need Doc out here. He needs to run tests on him." Fin glanced over to me, his eyes frosting over as he reached out to Doc.

"Doc says that he's on his way. He's bringing things to go ahead and draw blood from him. So, that way we won't lose it."

I nodded and stood. It blew my mind that he would do that to a delta that had a mate. I hoped that she was strong enough to keep her life. But then again, would she want to after her fated mate was killed? I know I wouldn't want to live. Then again, I'd want to live until I avenged my mate. That way I would know that whoever did kill him knew I had the upper hand.

"Doc is almost here why don't you shift?" I smiled at him and shifted. He didn't like any male to see me naked. The only time I think that he would, would be if I was actually having his pup but even that might be unlikely.

Doc came around the corner and stopped as he stared between me in my wolf form and then back over to my very naked mate. He kneeled to my fallen ex pack mate and started to pull vial after vial of blood from him. It was crazy seeing him lying there when I had seen him the morning of my Luna ceremony.

A few more wolves came to get him. Placing him on the gurney and covering him so that no one saw him. It made me wonder how he got here. Did he run all this way?

What are we going to do? Are you going to call Alpha Roy?

Yes. I'm going to call him and let him know that one of his wolves are here. And that he needs to come get him. I don't know what he is planning, but he won't get whatever he's looking for. Fin's voice spoke to me in my head so that the other wolves here wouldn't know what we were talking about.

Okay. Be careful because he may try to spin this on you.

We will be ready for the pack. I won't let him hurt you again. Fin growled in my head. He was just as upset as I was about the poisoning.

You know that I can take care of myself. I'm not like most females. I chuckled in my head and wagged my tail. I didn't understand why he continued to try to treat me the way he did. I had a guess but I wasn't like her and his uncle was gone. The only alpha that wanted me dead was Alpha Roy and I knew I could take him because he wasn't as strong as he let on.

I know you aren't but it is my duty to protect you as much as I can. He sighed in my head as he shook his head. Doc had come up to him. Whispering something to him so that the other wolves didn't hear him.

I lopped up to Fin's side rubbed my head against his arm. He reached up and rubbed my ears. I don't know why but having my ears scratched as a wolf just felt so damn good. It made it feel even better with the sparks chasing his hands.

"Okay Doc, just run what you can on his blood. I'll handle the rest." Fin turned to me and then shifted his massive white wolf just as tall as I was.

The size difference between us always astonished me since I was just a warrior wolf. I had never seen another female the same height as her alpha.

They had said that a female born alpha was almost the same size but since I had never seen one that was shifted I couldn't say if that was true or not.

He nipped me and raced ahead of me. I caught up with him just as we jumped the river that ran in the territory. The tip of my tail dipped into the water when my back paws hit on the other side of the bank. We continued into the middle of the town and pups ran with us until they couldn't anymore.

We got to the packhouse and spotted Harlen with another wolf that I didn't recognize. I nuzzled Fin as we came to a trot. He licked my muzzle as we headed up to the front steps. The older man turned as Fin shifted and a wolf brought him some shorts.

"Olli it's been awhile. How's everything been going?" I stayed in my wolf form and noticed that the man named Olli continued to stare at me.

Part of me thought I had seen him before but then again I couldn't have since I rarely left my previous pack. And the only way to see other wolves was to go to other packs. No one at my pack ever let me leave so when I came to this pack it was so surreal.

"Yes, it has. How about we go and talk in your office?" Olli took one more glance at me and then followed Fin and Harlen inside the packhouse.

Bella came up to me with a large shirt. I shifted and pulled the shirt over my head. It was Fin's I could smell his scent.

"Who was that Olli wolf?" I asked as we headed in. Part of me wanted to follow them to the office but then I didn't know if Fin would want me in there with them. He might have business that I didn't need to be in there for.

"He's a wolf that was with Fin when they were looking for Alpha Nolen. He stops by sometimes to check in. Olli is a good friend." Bella smiled at me as she explained who he was.

So he was one of the rogues that he sometimes talked about. I wonder why he didn't talk about him as much. I mean he seemed to be a big part of Fin's life. Following Bella down the other hall I started hearing pups cry.

"Luna I don't believe you've been to the nursery yet. I know that Fin has been keeping you occupied for a while. But I figure now would be a good time to show you." She opened the door and I stepped in with her. "A few of the she-wolves have had their pups. I didn't know if you had one at your pack."

"We didn't have one. Alpha Roy didn't like the idea of having pups in the pack house that didn't need to be. He hated the crying. So a lot of the females had to bring their pups with them to do their chores." I walked around the room and the pups seemed to quieten. This pack was so different than what I had come from.

"Well, sounds like he needs to be a little easier on the she-wolves. It takes a pack to raise pups. Not individuals." Bella's eyes hardened as she glanced over at me and then at the little ones sleeping in the cribs.

"I'm glad that we are not like that." I told her while I stared at a pup that had dark hair like Fin. What would our pup look like? Would he or she look more like him or me? Since he was an alpha I figured his genes would come out more dominate.

We headed back out of the nursery to allow the pups to sleep. Three females sat on couches watching them and nodded as we left. The way packs differed so much was crazy. You would think since we were wolves that we would all value our packmates. But it seemed that some didn't have that natural protective instinct.

"I never thought you'd say we."

"Why? This is my pack now too, right?" I stopped, bringing Bella to a stop too.

"Yes, you are and I'm glad that you are. You have brought a breath of fresh air to this pack." Bella caressed my cheek before turning and heading up the hall.

At the end of the hall, I turned up the stairs. I needed to change into something that wouldn't have Fin going crazy if an unmated male saw me. As big as this shirt was it was still not something that could be bent over in. Reaching the door to the alpha suite I pushed it open and shut it back with my foot.

The first day that I came into this room would still be etched in my memories. I had never seen a room so big and the way it was decorated screamed bachelor. But it had its charms. Over the last few months, I had added a few things of me.

Heading over to our bedroom I jerked the shirt off and left it in the living room on the couch. I hoped that Fin wouldn't be too long with Harlen and Olli. Even being out of my heat now I still wanted him. But I can control my urges now.

I went into the bathroom and started the bath. After the run this morning, my body felt heavy and tired. I turned the water on and waited for the bath to be filled. Standing in the shower didn't appeal to me, so I stepped into the water. I couldn't help but moan as the hot water started to work out the tension in my muscles.

My hair and face submerged in the bath. I laid there for a while as the steam from the hot water fogged the mirrors of the bathroom. It was such a beautiful room. The soft white tones mixed with grey and blue. A claw foot tub stood in the middle of the ceramic tiled floor. Pulling in the beauty.

Goddess this was something I didn't ever think I could get used to but being here made me think that I was meant to be here. I couldn't ever think that this was my destiny, but I would walk through this life just to be by Fin's side. He sometimes wanted to be big bad but most of the time he was a big pup.

Sometimes it's good to allow someone to take care of you. That is what mates are for. They protect one another. Enyo spoke up while I leaned my head back against the edge of the tub.

That's true but can I allow him to?

Enyo shook her head and laid it on her front paws. She was my one and only friend since I was a pup. I had never been alone my entire life even though it seemed like I had been.

CHAPTER THIRTY-TWO

FIN

I sat at my desk as Harlen and Olli sat in front of me in the high back chairs. This room had been completely renovated from what my uncle had done to it. Harlen had saved a few of the alpha books that had been passed down from alpha to alpha. Along with things that my mother had.

New bookshelves and furniture had been purchased. It had been stripped to the bones and new walls were put up. When the entire house had been stripped, I slept outside in my wolf form. A few of the wolves had offered me a room at their house but I was still so used to sleeping outside.

Everything had worked itself out and the packhouse had come back to its grandeur. The way a packhouse should look and the way a pack should look as a whole.

"So Olli, what brings you all the way out here?"

"Just letting you know the school is being built and is almost finished. We should be able to start admitting students next year. It will be small the first year but I feel that it will grow. How has the alliances been going?" Olli stared at me. I could tell he had a question about something but he wasn't ready to ask.

I had noticed that he was staring at Nikita a lot and I wondered if he knew anything about her and her pack. If anyone knew anything it would be Olli. He was just as wise as an elder. Maybe even more so.

"It's going. I only have one pack that has become an issue. My Luna's birth pack's alpha is upset that she went against his orders and allowed me to mark her. She then told me that he wanted her to kill me since I had taken a chosen. That chosen was his cousin." I sat up and rested my hands on the new desk that graced my office.

"I thought her birth pack was killed by your uncle?" Olli questioned me.

"No, she came from Shonkinite pack."

"Fin. Did you not ever see the Obsidian pack's alphas? They were the only wolves that looked like her. Beta Harlen can you get me the alpha books?" Olli turned to my beta and watched him as he went to the book shelves and brought him the two books.

It had been a long time since I had skimmed through those. My father had made me "read" them when I was in training but I didn't really. I just turned the pages because I wasn't interested in the history of the packs. Now Olli had piqued my interest in them. Was the Shonkinite pack not Nikita's birth pack and if it wasn't, was it the Obsidian? Because that was Kalila's.

"Ah here it is." Olli stood and handed me the first book of the histories of the packs. My eyes followed his finger to the description of the pack and then the picture of the two alphas in wolf form.

They both looked like Nikita. Fuck was she an alpha? And why the fuck was she raised as a warrior in the Shonkinite pack? I glanced up at Olli and he nodded.

"So, she is the last surviving heir of the Obsidian pack?" Harlen asked before I could. If I remember correctly. The first night of the party only the male beta came because the Luna of his pack had gone into labor.

If the pup that was born to them that night was Nikita then she would've been a lot younger than she is. I continued to read the book. This was the first alpha of this pack so this would be her descendants. Damn she was an alpha by birth. No wonder she was so strong and her wolf was just as big as mine.

I had only ever seen one other female born alpha and that was Nolen's Luna. Glancing up to Olli and Harlen I stood with the book and continued to read about the Obsidian pack.

"So, that would mean that the pup that was being born during the party was her sibling." Harlen's voice floated into my consciousness.

"It would seem so. But there was another pup. A pup that was told to the pack had died during birth. What was suspicious was that they didn't hold a funeral pyre for her. So the pack wondered what really happened to her." Olli made me turn. Only a wolf part of the pack could know about that.

"Olli, was Obsidian your pack?" I stared at him and he held my gaze.

"Yes, I was the elder of that pack."

"So, what really happened to her? You have to know. The fucking elder in our pack knows everything going on here." I snapped the book shut and rounded my desk to stand in front of the man that I had ran with for six years.

"That's all I know. The Alpha and Luna didn't tell me what happened to her. But apparently they gave her to the Shonkinite pack. For what reasons I have no idea. We would have to interrogate the alpha to find out." Olli never flinched as I continued to stand in front of him. No wonder he never had any issues with dealing with us.

"Alpha Roy is an idiot. He wouldn't know anything about this. His dad might, but I don't know if he is still alive. Because I don't think he would let his son act the way he has been." I told him as I sat back on the desk. Placing the book down beside me I crossed my arms over my chest.

Damn I couldn't believe that my mate was a alpha born female and that two had been born so close together. I did read the book how Selene the Moon Goddess created us and that the first alphas were born alphas but as our lines crossed fewer and fewer alpha born females were birthed.

"Obsidian was a very small pack as you know. I did know that the Shonkinite pack had come to make an alliance but we didn't have anything to offer them." Olli bowed his head as he sat back down in the chair.

"It doesn't matter now. All that matters is that we protect Nikita more than ever. If Alpha Roy finds out she is an alpha born female then we will for certain have a war." I glanced between the two men in the room with me.

You know Nikita hates when you try to protect her. Maybe you should tell her about her past? I mean she thinks that she is a warrior. She has been putting her life on the line for that dipshit as long as she has been with that pack. Aloysius commented in my mind.

He was right so I was going to have to do this so that she wouldn't know and when the time is right I would let her know about her pack. I had claimed the territory after I had gone to see it. From what Olli was saying, Nikita had never known what her pack had looked like before she was taken. Because she was said to have been dead at birth.

You don't need to wait till the time is right for you. She is going to need to know soon and you know this. You always hated when your mom and dad kept things from you. Are you going to make your Luna resent you?

Goddess damn wolf always having to be right. But how do I tell her about a pack I know nothing about and I'm sure she will have questions on how she came to be in the Shonkinite pack. Olli could tell her about the pack, but we would still need to find out about what had happened all those years ago.

"Well Olli, would you mind helping me to tell Nikita about her birth pack? I'm sure you could tell her about her parents."

"I can do that. But I think it would be wise to let her come to me. I'll be here for a few months and let her get used to me. I can tell that she is curious about me." Olli chuckled. It would be nice to have him here with me.

"I'll have an omega get you a room ready and you can stay in the pack-house." Harlen stood and walked out with Olli on his heels.

It was something to learn that my mate was from the same pack as my chosen. Fuck I should have asked Olli about Roy being related to Kalila! I slammed my hand down on the desk and went to the door to my office. I needed to get to Nikita and make sure that she was okay.

She had been silent since I had been in this meeting with Olli and Harlen. It was nice getting to see him again but the information that he told me. Still blew my mind. I headed up the stairs following Nikita's scent to our floor. Opening the door I spotted my shirt that Bella had given to Nikita on the arm of the couch.

I could feel the grin on my face widening as I pushed open the bedroom door and smelled the bath salts. She was relaxing in the bath. I did have her running hard. But now that I knew that she was an alpha. I'd be pushing her harder than ever. She wants to protect herself well. She was going to go through Alpha training just like I had when I was younger.

The training that she had as a pup was nothing compared to what an alpha would have and I doubt that Alpha Christian would train her as such. Which was the reason Alpha Roy wouldn't make her delta. They had to keep her under their thumb as long as they could and why would he promote her? It would be better to let her stay a grunt than become a delta.

I entered the bathroom and spotted her in the clawfoot tube. She had it sweltering in here like a sauna. Padding to her I knelt and took hold of her hair, pulling her head back and kissed her. Her hands wrapped around the back of my head.

Breaking the kiss I stood and removed my clothes before stepping in the tub with her. Nikita's eyes were flashing between her wolf's and her human's.

"Come here feisty Luna. I want to hold you." I reached out to her and she filled my arms. Nikita turned her back to me and allowed me to run my hands down her body in the bath.

Her skin was pruning at her fingertips, and I brought one hand up and sucked on them. Nikita's lips parted as she stared at me. Watching me play with her finger in my mouth with my tongue. She spread her legs and her other hand dipped below the water and grabbed my cock that was already hard when her scent assaulted my nose.

"Fin..." The whimper from her had me pulling her finger from my mouth and crushing my lips to hers. My tongue found hers and they fought as Nikita tried to keep the upper hand. Her hand caressing and playing with my shaft and balls under the water.

My Luna you are going to make me explode in this bath and if you do that then I won't be able to see my cum drip out of that beautiful pussy of yours.

I love the way you talk to me. If you beg I might just let you have your way. Otherwise, I'll make you come and see all those potential heirs go down the drain.

I growled and turned her to face me. Nikita cocked her head as she stretched over the head of my cock. Her head thrown back as she pulled my face into her chest. I grabbed a nipple and nipped it just as Nikita sheathed me fully.

CHAPTER THIRTY-THREE

NIKITA

"So I learned something crazy today."

I sat there with my fork and knife in my hand in the process of cutting my steak. When I stopped and stared at him.

"Yeah? And what did you learn today?" I cocked my head and then continued to cut into my food. I was starving even though I had snacked before deciding to get into the tub.

"Yeah, Olli told me that your birth pack isn't Shonkinite." Fin scooped up his veggies and popped them into his mouth as he stared at me. When I slid over him in the hot water I couldn't help the loud moan that exited from me caused him to thrust into me. While he pulled me down on top of him crashing into my cervix. As much as it hurt it felt amazing as well. Fin's mouth on my nipples as he continued to thrust harder inside of me.

Water splashed over the sides of the tub as we rocked in sync with each other. Each time we were together it felt like the first time. It never got boring the way he made me feel even without intimacy that he loved me. Most of the affection was the mate bond but I couldn't help but think that it was more for him. Since Fin and I had waited so long to have this bond of ours.

"Fin."

"Yes, feisty Luna. What can I do to make you feel even better?" The huskiness in his voice when he was inside of me made me shiver.

"Bite me..." I moaned, threading my fingers in his hair.

As you wish my Luna.

Fin bit down so hard that the orgasm that was on the edge of spilling over came crashing through my system. I loved when he nipped and bit me. It was exhilarating. None of the other males had ever been as rough with me. They always thought I was fragile and I hated that they did.

"Yes! Goddess yes!"

Fin slipped his canines from the bite and sealed the wound with a lick.

I sat in the kitchen with Fin at the stove. We had missed dinner so instead of making the kitchen staff work overtime, Fin decided to cook for me. This wasn't the first time that he had cooked for me, but it was the first time that he had made dinner.

It wasn't that bad to wait either as he was in his birthday suit and I could stare at his ass the whole time. I could tell that something was not being said as he moved around the kitchen. My eyes were being very naughty as I stared at my mate. For being in his thirties Fin was gorgeous.

"Is there something wrong, Fin? You know you can't hide anything from me anymore." I tilted my head, trying to get him to look at me.

"I know. I'm not hiding anything from you. What I have to tell you can be discussed when we sit down to eat." Fin glanced over his shoulder and smiled.

Shaking my head I continued to sip my drink. I didn't know what he was planning on telling me but it better be good. I stood and went to the cabinets pulling out plates and setting them down beside Fin. He started to plate them with the steak, au gratin potatoes, corn, and green beans. I picked them up and took them to the table in the suite.

Fin walked up with champagne flutes and a bottle. I had never had any alcohol since I wasn't a top ranked wolf. So I didn't know how I would act with drinking it. Fin sat them down and then poured a hefty amount in my glass and then his before he sat down.

Shonkinite wasn't my birth pack? I mean I didn't resemble my parents at all but genes were crazy and then when I shifted for the first time. Alpha Christian made sure that I didn't shift in front of strangers for a long time. Not until Alpha Roy took over and even then it was with wolves that he knew.

Most of them wanted to buy me and I couldn't understand why. Sure I was a strong fighter but they didn't mention anything til they had seen me shift. Sometimes I thought that they wanted me for breeding which a lot of the packs did. Find strong females and then breed them.

"What do you mean? Of course Shonkinite is my birth pack. What other pack would it be?" I was confused and I think that whoever this wolf is that was telling him this. Was giving him false information.

Fin stood and went into the living room and came back with a book. He opened it and then laid it down in front of me. I stared at the page, at the two people in the black and white picture and then the picture of their wolves. Their markings were the same as mine. I glanced up to Fin who shoveled more food into his mouth as I returned my gaze back to the pictures.

"Where did you get this?"

"That book there is in every alpha's office. It shows us the lineage of the alphas. It also shows us where the packs came from. Those two wolves there started the Obsidian pack many years ago." Fin sat there in front of me as I read the information. My line, if these were my grandparents, was one of the oldest packs.

"So you knew about my line all this time?"

"No, I didn't know. When my father was teaching me about the packs I didn't really pay attention since it bored me. Why did I need to know about the packs of the past? They were in the past." Fin shook his head while he sat back in his chair. "I didn't know about the Obsidian alphas until Olli came and saw you. You are a rare wolf Nikita. And you are an alpha born female."

"This can't be true. Why would my parents give me to another pack? If I was an alpha born female? It just doesn't make sense." I stood leaving my untouched food on the table and went to the windows. So many questions ran through my head. Most of them were why? I turned back to Fin who sat there and stared at me. "I want to see the pack lands that Obsidian controlled. I want to talk to them and find out why."

"Well I can take you to your pack. But you won't be able to ask anyone there anything. They are gone, my uncle killed them all. Well other than you and Olli that is."

"So I'm the last?"

Fin stood and came up to me, pulling me flush against him. I would never know my parents, my real parents. No wonder the man and woman I called mom and dad didn't give me as much attention. I'm not saying that they were lousy parents, but it was more of a chore. That was until they were killed by rogues. I then stayed in the pack house and began my training.

"Yes. I won't let anything happen to you. I promise." Fin whispered in my ear before he pulled away from me and caressed my face. "Now come eat and tomorrow you can talk to Olli."

I sat in Fin's office waiting for the wolf who was going to let me know about my actual birth pack. The Obsidian pack. A pack that didn't make it through the tyrant that Alpha Christian was keeping us hidden from. If there was one thing about the previous alpha of the Shonkinite pack he protected his pack. Unlike Alpha Roy, all he cared about was the fame of it. He wanted the thrill but not the responsibility. Which was why if he was the one I know who poisoned me, the Shonkinite pack was about to no longer exist.

The door opened and Fin came in with the older wolf. He was greying on the sides of his hair. But no one could say he was balding he had a head full of hair. The way his eyes started to water had my heart clenching in my chest. What did he see? Who did he see?

"Luna Nikita. It is a pleasure to finally meet you. My name is Olli." The old wolf stuck out his hand and I slipped mine in his big one. Olli kissed the back of my hand before he kneeled in front of me. My hand on his forehead. Just like an elder would do meeting a ranked wolf.

"Please stand." I pull him up to his feet and glance over to Fin and he nodded. "Fin said you know things about my real birth pack."

"I do Luna." His striking green eyes held my own. "Why don't we sit down. Fin you can sit with us."

"I'm not going to leave my Luna all by herself with you. You know that Olli." Fin laughed as he came around to sit beside me. His hand on my thigh.

"You alphas are all the same. I'm not going to mess with your mate Fin. You know me well enough." Olli chuckled as he sat down on the other couch facing us.

"So, what do you know? How do you know things about the Obsidian pack?" I asked him as I sat on pins and needles.

"There's a lot to say about the pack that you and I were born into. I'm years older than you but I knew your parents and your grandparents. They were good alphas until Alpha Christian came to make an alliance. That's when things changed. Your mother lost her first born at birth. But I couldn't understand why we didn't hold a funeral for her." Olli hung his head before he pulled it back up to gaze at me. "I didn't understand until I saw you yesterday. The only reason they would change was the alliance that they had made. Because they were never like what they were before the alliance."

"So they traded me for an alliance?" My hand went to Fin's who's had tightened on my thigh.

"That is what I'm thinking, Luna. Your mother was so happy to find out that you were a girl. You were the only second female born alpha in the land. Quartzite had the first." Olli's eyes glazed over and I thought that he looked like he was remembering something a long time ago.

I stood and walked over to the windows of Fin's office. There had to be a reason they didn't tell the elder the truth about them giving me up. Did they really do it to save their own skin? Would I ever know why? I turned back to the male wolves that were staring at me. "Did you find out why?"

"No, I left after they started to do things I wasn't comfortable with. Your father's parents, I'm sure, were wanting to tear him limb from limb. Because they raised him to be a good alpha with morals." Olli held my gaze before I glanced over to Fin.

"I want to see the pack lands. I want to see what has been done with it." I crossed my arms over my chest.

Fin stood and came up to me. His hands rested on my arms. "Whatever you want, feisty Luna. We can leave today if you want."

I nodded before he kissed my temple and pulled me into a hug.

CHAPTER THIRTY-FOUR

Nikita

When we arrived at the edge of the territory. All I could see was trees and buildings that were either destroyed or covered in vines. Some even had trees growing inside of them. While I walked up the paved road that was littered with tree roots and upended stones my eyes continued to take in everything on either side of me. What would this place look like if the pack was still here?

Fin and Olli didn't say anything to me as I continued on through the ruins of the Obsidian pack. Everything was overgrown, my heart sped up as I spotted the packhouse. I was never much of a sentimental person but the thought of growing up here in this house and the friends I possibly would have made, made it a little hard to think.

I walked between the hanging and broken doors. The place inside looked just as run down as the rest of the pack territory. Walls had fire marks racing up to the ceiling and some of the floor was missing in certain areas. Why did that tyrant take this small pack? What would it give him?

Continuing down the halls I came to a room, its doors no longer on its hinges and laying on the floor. I could tell that this was the alpha's office. But everything in it was either gone or burnt. Did they take the stuff or...? Everything was a question. But nothing gave me information.

"I searched this place along with my pack. I didn't find anything." Fin's voice startled me. I had been so consumed with my thoughts that I didn't even know that he was behind me.

"So why did you leave the buildings? Why not just demo them?" I turned to him and I could see the sorrow in his eyes. Was it for me or her? The thought of his chosen being from here made me wonder if he kept it like it was since it reminded him of her.

"I don't know why. But I did and then I pushed this place to the back of my mind." Fin stayed in the doorway as I continued to roam the room while keeping an eye on the floor.

I nodded before stopping and staring at the wall I tilted my head as I tried to figure out why the candlestick sat untouched on the burnt bookshelf. Everything in this office was in ruins but that simple item was there sparkling in the sunlight. My feet moved first to the silver candlestick, my hand reached out on its own and touched the cold metal with my fingertips.

Glancing over my shoulder I noticed Fin's eyes widened before I gripped it and pulled. The sound like an airlock escaped as the bookshelf opened and ground across the floor. I peeked in before Fin's hand gripped my shoulder and held me in place.

"I don't think so feisty Luna. I go first." Fin opened it more just as Olli came in and stopped.

Fin disappeared behind the door and I followed him in and what I saw made me stop where I was. Everything that was supposed to be in the office and possibly the alpha bedroom was untouched in this safe room. Pictures of the previous alphas and books were stacked along the walls. I went up to a table that held what looked like a journal.

My hand caressed the teal leather, the designs on the front were worn from years of use. It looked like it used to have a ribbon to hold it together. Frayed silver ribbon hung from the journal. I picked up the book and opened it to the front page.

Beautiful script handwriting graced the antique paper. The name *Katona* was fading on the page. I glanced up to Fin and Olli from the journal. They both stared at me, Olli looked from the journal to me as I closed it and pulled it to my chest.

"I never would've thought there was a secret door in this room."

"Alpha Cain was always doing something to the packhouse. Especially since the first child was lost." Olli answered as he looked around the room.

"So you didn't know that this room was here?"

"No. I think it needs to remain our secret. It could be used to keep people that don't know about it away from a certain Luna."

I glared at Fin and Olli. If they thought I was going to run and hide they were sorely mistaken. Resting one hand on my hip I pointed the journal to them both. "I don't know what you think you two are planning but I will not hide when I can help protect my pack."

"Nikita, if you are pregnant or get pregnant you won't be able to shift. I know you are a strong wolf and we both know that you are an alpha by blood. But you will need to be protected. I can't lose you or any unborn pup." Fin's eyes were watery as he held my gaze.

Would it be so bad to heed his wishes? You know that he has experienced a loss like that before and I feel like it would break any alpha. If it didn't then he has no heart. Enyo popped up in my head. I sighed.

"Fine, *IF* I'm pregnant then I will come here and stay. BUT if I'm not I will be on the front lines with you protecting *our* pack."

"I can work with that, my feisty Luna." Fin came up to me and pulled me into a hug. He always made me not so mad at him when he did this. "But in the meantime I will try to put a pup in you to keep you safe."

"You are one hundred percent a male." I huffed as I pushed him away from me to head further in the room that had old things that the previous alpha had collected. Fin chuckled and followed me around the room.

Pictures of the previous alpha and luna sat in a box. Detailing their life. I found one where she was pregnant and I wondered if that was me or the sibling that I will never get to meet. They looked happy that she was with pup. So why did they use me as a bargaining chip to Alpha Christian?

I hoped to the Goddess that the journal in my arms would let me get to know my biological mom and dad. Fingering the photo of them I grabbed it as well and placed it in my arms. Everything else in this safe room was just random things that didn't hold too much interest to me.

"I think I want to go home." I turned to Fin and he nodded.

Leading both Fin and Olli out of the room, Fin shut the door behind us and the scraping across the floor wasn't so loud as it was when it opened. The candlestick gleamed in the fading light from the sun. I hadn't realized that we had been here for most of the afternoon.

After dinner I stood at my side of the bed staring at the young wolves in the photo along with the journal. I wanted to sit down and see what her life was like through her words. At the same time I didn't want to find out why she gave me up.

"You keep staring at it, you won't ever know if that thing will answer any of your questions."

I didn't turn to Fin and I picked up the old journal. Taking in a deep breath I plopped down on the bed and crossed my legs. I glanced up to Fin and the small grin spurred me to open it.

"I've never been so undecided about things, Fin. What if what's in this journal makes things even worse than not knowing?"

Fin came up to me and sat down beside me. His arm wrapped around my shoulder and pulled me close to him. "But what if it tells you why and it makes sense?"

My eyes came up to his and I nodded. Fin kissed my forehead before pulling me closer and then standing up. He held my hand and brought it to his lips and softly kissed each of my knuckles. "And know that whatever it says I will be here with you to make your future better than your past."

Leaning back against the headboard I opened the journal and read her name again. Katona, it was a beautiful name. I turned the page and began to read.

Today is my fourteenth birthday and Mom gave me this journal to write down what happens in my life. I really don't know what to write since this is the first time that I have had one of these.

I guess I could start out by introducing myself. Not like someone would be reading this. These are supposed to be private, right?

Well, I'm Katona and I'm the second daughter to the high-ranking Deltas of the Obsidian pack. Everyone ignores me since my sister is the pretty one. She turns eighteen next month. So she will be able to find her mate. A lot of the pack thinks that she will be the alpha's son's mate. They have been dating for years. So the pack thinks they make the perfect pair.

Britona is the perfect daughter, she is a strong fighter along with being gorgeous. I mean who wouldn't want to be my sister? Yes, I'm jealous. Is it bad that I don't want her to be fated to the alpha's son? That way it would take away her perfection.

I'm a good fighter too. We both were taught at an early age on the fundamentals and how to protect ourselves. But she was still better than me and I hated it.

The alpha's son Cain will be turning eighteen next month too. Which is another reason the pack thinks that they will be mated. I mean what would seal their bond more than to be born in the same month.

All the females in the pack fawn over him and the beta's son, Mark. They both are the same age other than Mark turning eighteen today with me. I'm glad the pack hasn't thought that we would be mates. Don't get me wrong he's hot but he's a douche as well. He would probably be nice to his mate but I hated him.

Anyway, I think that will be it for now. All I've written about are others and nothing about me. Maybe next time I can give you a little more insight about me.

Ciao!(I'm not even French hehehe)

Well, she had a sister. So did she find her mate in the pack or was he in another pack? I guess I will read a couple of entries a night. She was interesting to say the least. Wonder what had happened when her sister turned eighteen and my father wasn't her mate. Did she try to find him? Or did she live alone until he came to her? All these questions and so few answers so far.

The door to the bathroom opened and Fin walked out in a towel. My eyes traveled down his body, watching the droplets race down the perfect pecs and abs and down the 'v' that told me just where his cock rested.

I don't think that I could ever get used to seeing him naked or half naked. He was just too gorgeous. My gaze went to his face and I caught him grinning at me. I smirked back at him and licked my lips. The journal laid on my chest as he used the other towel to dry his hair and face. I shook my head and glanced back at the journal. Part of me wanted to skip to the end and find out what was going through her head when she gave me up. But then the other part of me rationalized that if I didn't learn about her before she became Luna then I wouldn't understand.

Grabbing a bookmark, I placed it in the journal to mark the next entry I needed to start with.

CHAPTER THIRTY-FIVE

FIN

Nikita continued to read through her mother's journal and helping me deal with what Alpha Roy was throwing at our pack. Ever since the phone call I had with him about his Delta Kyle he has blamed us for his death. I wasn't surprised that he would and neither was Nikita because that was who he was.

We had more wolves in our dungeons than we ever had since I was a pup. I wasn't too sure if he had any pack left or if he was doing this on purpose to get as many wolves in my pack and then have them break out. So, I made sure to double the guards inside and out. We had also upgraded the cells and doors getting down to the cells.

Now only Dolostone wolves could open the dungeon.

"Alpha we have reports that more wolves from Shonkinite are coming to the pack. What do you want to do? Troops are along the border waiting for instructions."

My gaze went from the Delta to Nikita her eyes held mine before she placed the book on my desk and turned to the Delta.

"We will be there. Go ahead and wait for us to get there. If they attack, defend yourselves."

"Yes, Luna."

Nikita turned to me and placed her hands on the desk. Her gaze holding mine with her emerald orbs. "Are you ready to see what I can do?"

I smirked and stood from my seat. We both headed out the door and went out the pack front doors. Jumping from the top step we both shifted and ran to the edge of the territory. I didn't slow my speed and she continued to be beside me. It was good to know that I didn't have to slow down for her.

Nikita what are you thinking about? I asked her as we ran through the underbrush.

When the wolves get here we will show force. She snipped through our link.

We have been showing force. I bumped her a little to get her to look at me. Nikita nipped my shoulder and then sped up to get in front of me.

Then I will fight the strongest one. Once I win they will either leave or submit. Nikita had been itching for a fight and she wasn't too interested in our training since she got her mother's journal. Which I understood because if I didn't know my mother I would try my best to find anything to help me learn what she was like. And I wasn't going to keep her from being able to do that.

Nikita, we need to be strategic about this. We don't need to rush into this; we still don't know what Alpha Roy is planning. I cautioned her as we slowed and pressed through the crowd of warriors that were holding the line at the territory border. Wolves parted for us to get to the front as they bowed their heads.

Nikita growled low in our link. I didn't understand why she was being so moody. She wasn't due to have her heat for another month. And I didn't sense that she was pregnant. I wonder if she read something in her mother's book that she didn't like.

Alpha, Luna, they should be getting here shortly. I've been informed that Alpha Roy is with them this time.

Thank you Hank. The wolf nodded and backed into the group of wolves behind us.

Nikita, don't fight Alpha Roy. We don't have enough information from the informant right now. I nuzzled into her neck with my muzzle.

But if I kill him now we can have the informant return home and increase our pack at the same time. Nikita snarled in my head. The alpha part of her was starting to rise the more that Olli taught her. Each of her lessons she was surpassing like she had always known the shit he was showing her.

I'm not going to tell you again but I'm telling you now. You let me handle Alpha Roy. He is here for a reason and I'm not going to let you get yourself hurt because you want to rush in there without knowing. I growled back at her. *We don't need him to know that you are an alpha if he doesn't already.*

Nikita gave me a side eye before she snorted and backed up. Her head in line with my shoulder. I was glad that she decided to yield. I didn't know if I would be able to correct her in front of most of the pack.

The sounds of heavy feet came through the brush before Alpha Roy emerged. His Beta and Gamma flanking him with more wolves behind them. I glanced over mine, *No one attacks unless he starts it.*

Yes Alpha! Their voices as one inside my head.

I turned back to the wolves that were coming towards me and my pack. Shifting so that I could speak to everyone involved. I waited for Alpha Roy to shift as well. When he didn't and his Beta did I glanced over at Nikita. If he tried anything to harm her I would shift in a blink of an eye and tear him limb from limb. Fuck what I told Nikita.

"Alpha Fin, we would like to come to a truce and would like to talk about getting our wolves back from you as well."

"The only way I will make a truce is to know who poisoned my Luna and then a public apology for blaming our pack for Delta Kyle's death." I growled not being able to hold my anger back from the memory of the poison.

"Alpha Fin, I don't know who poisoned your Luna but you need to look into some of the other packs that were there." The Beta was treating this like he was talking to a child that was having a tantrum.

"I've already interrogated them and have found them telling me the truth. The only one that left before things started to happen was you and your Alpha."

The Gamma beside him snarled at me showing his teeth. He didn't faze me, he didn't have the skill set to even come close to beating me. I held Alpha Roy's gaze as the Beta glanced over at his alpha to give him more information.

"We are not at fault, Alpha Fin. I am more than happy to be interrogated as long as the wolves starving in your dungeons can come home." He spread open his arms in a sign of submission.

They took the wrong intel. I was hoping that the informant would be able to get something in so that I knew what I could and couldn't tell them. Smirking, I took a step forward and Nikita came with me. I held out my hand stopping her. Her tongue came out and ran across my palm.

"I think you are. Because I don't know who you are getting your intel from but we are not like a normal pack. We don't starve the wolves in the cells. They get three meals a day, the only thing they don't get is yard play. Can't have them running back to you right?" I widened my stance and crossed my arms. I had it in good faith that our informant never showed them who he was. But used another one of the pack to pass on the information.

The Beta glanced over at Nikita before he turned his gaze to his alpha again. He was getting nervous and I had a feeling that he wasn't in on anything that his alpha was. I had noticed that the Luna of their pack had hugged her. But there were no punctures. Staring at the alpha from Shonkinite, I realized that the reason he didn't shift to talk to me himself, was that he knew I would be able to tell he was lying if I could see his face.

"If you can't do what is asked for this truce you can make your way back to your pack. I'd hate to have your Luna hurt when I took your life."

Alpha Roy snarled and showed his fangs, his ears plastered on his head. The Beta came in front of us to hold his alpha back. He knew that I would win. I had the experience and strength.

"Fine we will leave and will be back to make a truce." He shifted and pushed his alpha back to keep him from attacking me. By the way he acted he was the person trying to keep the peace, which made him the smart one because even though we didn't have as many wolves we still could take them.

As fast as they had appeared they left. I had thought that they would want to try to fight and it could've come down to that. But we will see if they actually want a truce and if they will tell me the truth. I turned to my pack and dispersed them. Nikita still had her eyes focused on the brush.

I shifted back to my wolf and nudged Nikita.

Come my feisty Luna. They are long gone.

I don't like that they came all this way and didn't attack. The tone of her voice would've put me on edge if I didn't know for sure that they were gone.

They were probably trying to find out how many wolves we have here. Which was why I didn't have all of our warriors come to the border.

I knew you weren't all brawn. Nikita chuckled as she turned with me and ran to the center of the pack. I needed to make sure that we were prepared for whatever that Alpha Roy thought of next. Besides, she didn't know how smart I actually was. Even though I was the bulkiest wolf on this territory.

We both shifted and Nikita pulled a shirt over her while I pulled some shorts off the line. Pulling them up we went back to my office. Nikita went straight for the journal and sat down with it beside my desk. I sat down in my seat and continued what I had been doing before Alpha Roy wanted to make his appearance.

"So, are you going to tell me what you have learned so far?"

Nikita looked up and then came over to me and sat on the desk beside my laptop. She turned the book around and pointed to a spot that she was reading. "She was a delta's daughter. In this entry here she goes on about the alpha's son not finding his mate when he turned eighteen. Along with her sister finding her mate in a different pack but he was an alpha."

"Well, she wouldn't be luna anymore. From the timeline you are giving me. She's nineteen years older than me."

"Yeah, I would love to talk with her. To find out what my mother was like. Maybe she would be excited to see me?"

"Nikita, why don't you get through the journal and find out if this woman even knew her sister had a pup. We don't want to find out that they never talked after she left." I rubbed her leg when I noticed the name of the sister. Britona... where had I heard of that name. "Once you find out if they continued to talk, I will help you search for your aunt and we will see if she will talk with you."

"Okay, as long as you come with me."

I chuckled and brought her hand up to my lips. The shiver that ran through her arm amused me. She always reacted to me and I was glad that she did. Nikita was made for me just like I was made for her and I didn't forget my promise to her that I would make it my goal to have her with pup so that she would have to go to the Obsidian pack's safe room.

CHAPTER THIRTY-SIX

NIKITA

This journal of my mother's had become an obsession to me. I want to know what she was like and this journal only gave me a glimpse of her. My mother rambled a lot in this thing but it also told me about life in the Obsidian pack. She was a fighter like me and tried to show her parents and her pack how strong she really was. But it seemed like they always favored her older sister.

It was crazy how obsessed this was for me. Before now I thought I was just a warrior wolf but then I learned that I was one of two female born alphas. Which would explain why I was so strong and most of the wolves in my old pack gave me a wide berth.

Today I was sitting on the balcony reading through the journal...

Today is my eighteenth birthday. My sister and her alpha mate are here to see me shift for the first time and find my mate. All the pack will be there including the Alpha and Beta sons. I'm nervous. What if I don't find my mate? Or what if he rejects me? That would be embarrassing to go through that in front of everyone. I just want to run away and never return. I've never seen someone rejected but I've heard talk about it.

What do I do? As much as I keep all my emotions from everyone around me. This is something I don't think I could keep from anyone. My mother and father are excited to see me shift. My heart is hammering as I write. I really don't think that I will be able to do this.

Most of my friends have already turned eighteen and found their mates. So it has been a little lonely around here. As they say sometimes you just have to let them leave. Now it's just me and you.

This morning I woke up to my sister in my room. I'm surprised that she isn't pregnant yet. They were hanging all over each other when they arrived last night. The alpha of our pack gave them a room on the top floor of the pack house. Since they were now alpha and luna. My parents didn't care that they didn't stay with us at our home.

Why should they? They were ranked higher than us.

I should be grateful that I'm getting a party. Most wolves don't get a big one at the pack house but since my sister is now the luna of another pack, my alpha is allowing her to throw a party for me. Which is again why I'm so nervous.

Well, I guess tomorrow I'll let you know how it goes.

Ciao

Flipping the fragile page I noticed the date was there but no words graced the pages. My heart raced. What happened to her? I turned the pages two more times until I found another entry.

So.... I found my mate. And it's someone I never would have thought it would be. It's the alpha heir of our pack. I think that he is embarrassed that he is mated to me. When our eyes connected he turned away and ran off. So I've been in my bedroom sitting here waiting for him to come and reject me. Because that is the only reason he could be taking this long to come to me. He is wanting to put as much distance between us as possible.

I knew that something like this would happen because why would he want someone like me? He has been with so many of the she-wolves that are here. I'm just his ex-girlfriend's kid sister. Why did this have to happen? Why couldn't I have just not found my mate and then went on with my life? This is a short entry I'm going to lay down and close my eyes. I don't believe that this is a dream since it has been weeks since my birthday. I just wish that he would come so we could reject each other.

Wow my father was a dick. Why did he not claim her as his? I will never know now since they were both dead. I mean he didn't reject her but why did he run from her? Was he scared? I had to know if he actually came and told her why he left her at her party. I turned the page again and found the next entry.

So he came back and apologized that he had run from me on my birthday. Cain has made these last few days bliss. The pack seemed to have accepted me as they have with any luna before me. And my sister is happy that I had found my mate and that he didn't reject me.

Now that Cain has decided to claim me as his mate and luna. I can finally take in the excitement of when our eyes locked. His smell was what brought my eyes to him in the first place and then when I noticed that his eyes had changed to his wolf's color. I knew that he was my mate.

When our bond snapped into place I couldn't see anyone else but him until he turned away from me and ran. I had glanced over to my alpha and luna before turning my eyes to my sister who was growling at the man who was running away from me.

She had kept me company until she had to return to her pack. Her mate had already gone after the party. I had never known her to be the way she was that day when she was in my room. But it had been nice to know that part of her existed.

My Luna ceremony will be held in the next few days and on the same night Cain and I will be named Alpha and Luna of the Obsidian pack. I've never been a leader and I don't know how good of a Luna I will be. But I will try to be a fair and just one.

Well I will let you know more later.

Ciao

I wonder if she was a fair and just Luna? Sitting the journal down I got up from the balcony chair and stretched. My mother never once mentioned who the alpha was that her sister was mated to. I hoped that in the other entries that she would tell me who the alpha was so that I could hopefully talk with her sister if she was still alive.

The air was changing as well as the season. So most of the wolves were putting firewood and other things away for storage in one of the storage buildings. Grain along with extra canned goods went in as well. We would be able to hunt but for the growing pups and she-wolves that were with pup needed more so that they would have the best outcome at birth.

"Feisty Luna, why is it that I always find you on a balcony staring out into the abyss?" Fins' hands ran down my arms and then landed on my hips.

"It's so calming up here and the view is always changing with each of the seasons." I turned in his arms as the wind picked up.

"It is very calming. I think that is why my mother gave me this room as a child. It always calmed me to look out over the pack and at the mountains. They are gorgeous when the snow settles on the top of them." His breath fanned over my face as I held his gaze. "You know we can forgo dinner tonight and just feast on each other."

Fin grabbed me by the back of my neck as he plunged his tongue deep into my mouth. The moan that escaped me wasn't lost on Fin as he ran his other hand up my shirt and kneaded my breast. I wrapped my arms around his neck as he continued to kiss me breathless.

Breaking the kiss I heard the groan come from deep in Fin's chest. "I think that I have been holed up in this room all day and the pack needs to know that their Alpha and Luna are okay."

"Fine but afterward I intend to make you scream at the top of your lungs. I want to be buried inside your pussy until you come all over it again and again."

I lifted my eyebrow with a smirk. As I pushed off the railing on the balcony and forced Fin inside our room. "Really now? And what has sparked this manner of speaking to me?"

"I told you my feisty wolf that I intend to put a pup in your belly. And if breeding you more than once a day will help me achieve that then I will."

Fin wasn't playing when he told me that he was going to put a pup inside of me. I wasn't opposed to having his pup, but I wanted to be able to help when the time came. Not to be stuck in that safe room while others defended the pack and myself.

"You've told me this before. But you also told me that if I didn't then I would be at your side protecting our land and pack together."

"I did. Which is why I'm making sure that you are with pup. Because I will not allow you to be in harm's way." His hands came up and cupped my face. I loved when he touched my face. It was probably the wolf part of me. Since we used our heads to show affection.

"Let's go to dinner. I'm starving as it is." I chuckled while bringing my hands up to Fin's and pulling them down.

"Fine, but I still plan on having you afterward."

I shook my head and led us down to the dining room.

We sat at our normal seats. Harlen and Bella are sitting beside me with Tobey running around the room. Once all this was settled and over with I would have a pup or pups running around this room and territory. Possibly even going to the school that Olli would be at.

I glanced over to Fin who was sitting there watching the wolves in the room having a good time. He was calm as he sat there and he was at his most handsome.

The door burst open and two wolves from the patrol came in and kneeled before Fin and I. I didn't like the way their emotions came through the packbond. My hand went to Fin's on the table.

"Zac, Henry, what is going on?" Fin's voice rang out through the room. Wolves closest to us turned to us at the head table.

Alpha, Luna forgive us for interrupting your meal. But we have another wolf on the territory. Zac answered us. His eyes flickering between Fin's and mine.

Bring her here. Fin's voice answered in the link that Zac had started.

She is in the morgue, Alpha. The sorrow in his voice unnerved me.

Who is it? Curiosity got the better of me. I needed to know who this person was.

The Luna of Shonkinite. I gasped out loud. Bringing Harlen and Bella's attention to us. Why would he kill his own Luna and mate? What was he playing at?

I glanced over to Fin whose face had become stoic. He must have been trying to figure out why Alpha Roy would do it to Luna as well. He knew what the Moon Goddess would do to him. If not now but later. That is if Fin or I didn't get to him first. She didn't have to die.

CHAPTER THIRTY-SEVEN

NIKITA

Staring at Luna Adia I couldn't help but want to kill Alpha Roy. She had always been a wonderful person and probably the only one that didn't mind me being so brutal. We had trained together and then when she found out she was mated to Alpha Roy she balanced him out. She was a great Luna and I wonder what the pack was doing now that their Luna wasn't there. Did they know? Or did they think that she had left to go do something?

The balance that she held on Alpha Roy shattered when Fin's tyrant uncle had come into power. He started to change then. I had never seen him come to our pack. But his tyranny was felt even in our pack. I didn't even know that he wasn't the actual alpha until I met Fin.

"Doc what happened to her?" Fin's voice brought me out of my thoughts and my gaze went to Doc. His eyes held a sorrow I felt within myself.

"Poison. Same kind as the others that have been put on our territory." Doc covered her face and then pushed her in the cooler and shut the door. Which was good in my case because the longer I stared at her the more I wanted Alpha Roy's head on a pike.

I shook my head. Was Alpha Roy losing his mind? Why did he do this? My hand went to Fin's arm as I tried to continue to wrap my head around the craziness about this. Fin's hand covered mine as we stood in front of Doc.

"Have we found out what type of poison? Wolfsbane?" Fin questioned as Doc went over to the computers.

"We have found that this is a hybrid poisoning. It does have wolfsbane in it but the more lethal poison is from the plant called Oleander, or its kingdom name **Nerium oleander**. I found some in each of the ones that have been poisoned along with Luna Nikita." Doc's eyes went to me.

"I've been poisoned before. They gave the poison to warrior wolves to get them to be intolerant to the poison. They never told us what was in it."

"They must have been doing that to keep other packs from poisoning their warriors. No wonder you were able to survive. Small doses build immunity which would then help you recover. But whoever is doing this must have been giving more than what their bodies are used to." Doc's hand wrapped around his jaw as he sat there at the computer.

"When you find something out, let me know."

Doc stood and walked us out of the morgue and into the hallway of the pack hospital. Fin and I continued in silence as we stepped into the elevator to get back to the first floor.

"Fin what is going on here? Have you heard from the informant?"

"No, not in some time. He might have been found. I need to find someone to go find out."

I nodded to him while we strolled through the pack at night. It was nice out tonight even though it was getting closer to winter. We had never walked the pack like this before. The silence between us allowed me to gaze around at the stars and woods.

Eyes from the wolves that were patrolling the woods shone in the dark making it look like the stars had fallen and now shown in between the trees. Other than the rocky start, this pack has been more home than Shonkinite ever was.

Fin and I headed into the packhouse and up the stairs. Dinner was coming to an end but I wasn't hungry anymore since seeing Adia.

"Are you going to continue to read your mother's journal?" I glanced up to Fin and he gave me a small smile.

"Yeah, I'm closer to her Luna ceremony and I'm hoping that she will mention who her sister's mate is. I'm also hoping she tells me what happened before my birth."

Fin's hands slid over my cheeks and into my hair. "You learn as much as you need to feisty wolf. I'm going to go take a shower and think of a way to tell this alpha that his luna is on a table in my morgue."

"I don't think we need to tell him. There is something wrong with him and I think we need to find out what that is before we cause a war. Because that right there will." My fingers slid along his forearms as he pulled me into a kiss. The feel of his muscles as they tighten under his skin made my core pulse.

"Fine. We will wait and I'll see what has happened to the informant." Fin kissed me once more before heading into the bedroom.

I went to the balcony and grabbed my mother's journal. Making my way into the bedroom I placed it on the table next to my side of the bed and stripped naked. I hopped in while grabbing the journal and snuggled in under the covers. The luna ceremony was like any other ceremony, nothing crazy or special during that day. She did mention that her sister didn't get to make it to it.

I skipped a few entries to land on one that caught my eye.

Today my nephew was born. He is such a wonderful boy and he looks just like his father. Blue eyes and black hair. They named him Archer after our father. I was fortunate that I was here visiting after my loss. It had hit hard on both me and Cain. My parents think that something is wrong with me since this is the second time that I have lost my pup. But I have never been perfect in their eyes. That was always my sister.

They are here as well and they are ever so excited. I wonder if they would ever be that way with my pup. Cooing and babbling to the pup. If I continue to lose them I would never know.

Being twenty-four and mated along multiple heats, Cain is starting to get upset and I feel like he will end up leaving me to find another female that would be able to give him an heir. Would the Moon Goddess be that cruel to me? I'm so afraid that he will and it's eating at me, hence why I'm here with my sister and her mate. It's beautiful here and everyone is nice.

Well another short entry. I have to go to bed soon. I have to travel back to Obsidian.

Ciao

So, my grandfather's name was Archer. It's so crazy to know that my real family was just a few days away from the Shonkinite pack. But if she was having an issue getting and staying pregnant then why would she give me away? I'm still so confused. I skipped through the book to the entry a year later.

I found out today that I'm pregnant again. I haven't told Cain yet but I'm sure he will be able to tell soon. That is if he would take the time to be near me. I don't want to disappoint him again. I can't think about the baby this time. If I do and get further along and then lose it, it will be devastating. I will just pretend that I don't know about it. And if some asks I'll just deny it. Like that will work. Right? We are wolves. We have great noses. uh....

We also were visited by Alpha Christian of the Shonkinite pack. They are looking to combine our packs but he is wanting us to step aside. Cain told him no but I feel that since we are a much smaller pack that he would be able to destroy us in one wave. Cain is supposed to go to Dolostone and see if they would be willing to be allies.

I can only hope that the alpha will help us. If not we will be in trouble. My sister's pack is only allies with us because my sister is Luna and for them to help us we would have to tell them what had happened. But Cain doesn't want to go to my sister's pack. I still think that he still loves my sister and going to her would make him feel weak.

Anyway this Luna is tired.

Ciao

I sat there in the bed trying to figure out what had gone on with all of this. This still didn't tell me what had gone on. Why was Alpha Christian there and why did he want a pack that was on the other side of one of the largest packs. Did he really think that with his pack and Obsidian that he would be able to make that work. I swear male brains didn't always make sense.

The bed moved beside me and I turned my gaze to Fin. I had been so focused on the journal that I didn't hear him come out of the shower. Fin sat there a moment before he turned to me and kissed my cheek. "You looked deep in thought, what have you found now?"

"Here look at this. I can't quite understand why another alpha would want another's pack with a large pack between them." I leaned over and pointed to the lines in my mother's journal.

Fin was silent as he read over the words that I had read. "I think I remember Alpha Cain coming to meet with my father. I was just a young pup then but I remember my father being out that day and my uncle turning him away. There was always something about my uncle that didn't sit right with me and I didn't notice it until I became alpha."

"So, my father came?"

"I believe so. But the only one that would really know is Harlen. Are you still talking with Olli?" Fin glanced over to me as I sighed and stared at my mother's book.

In two months from this date I will be born. That same night or day I would be in the hands of Alpha Christian and would never see my mother and father again. Everyone in the pack would think I was dead but really I would be living with another family in another pack.

"Yes, I plan on meeting with him tomorrow. But I wanted to get through to the birth. I had thought about skipping but learning this I think I need to see what was said? Do you think that my father would've told my mother?" I skimmed over the two entries and reread the name Archer again. "Hey, Fin, do you remember a male named Archer?"

"No, I've never heard of him."

"Okay, I don't understand why she doesn't say who the alpha is that my aunt is mated to. You would think that it would be something she would know." I sighed as I placed the book on my table and snuggled into Fin's side.

"Well, maybe she was trying to keep her safe. If anyone would have gotten that book they would know how to manipulate her sister to get whatever they were looking for." Fin answered me as he pulled me closer to him.

I stared into the dark as I played with his chest. What would things be like if I had grown up in the Obsidian pack? Would I have met Fin sooner? Would he have allied with the Obsidian pack? Or would I have seen him kiss and grow with his chosen and their children?

"You're overthinking again." Fin's sleep-filled voice pierced the darkness and his arm pulled me tighter to him.

I sighed and closed my eyes. Trying my hardest to get my wandering mind to stop so that I could sleep.

CHAPTER THIRTY-EIGHT

FIN

I sat in my office as Olli and Harlen spoke with Nikita. She had learned a lot in the book that she found in the safe room. I worried that she would become heartbroken from what she would learn in that book. But I wasn't going to stop her from learning what she wanted.

"I know Olli but my father went to the Dolostone pack a few days later. What happened there?" Nikita paced the room as I worked on pack things. She had insisted that I needed to be there.

"He did go to Dolostone. But the Alpha turned him away."

"No alpha came to Dolostone. Alpha Fin's father never met with the Alpha of Obsidian." Harlen glanced over to Olli and then to me before landing on Nikita. "I should know because. I'm always in the room with him when he meets with them. The only other Alpha that has been on these lands before Fin came back was the previous Alpha of Rhyolite and his eldest son."

"I thought I saw him come to the pack? I remember that I was going to the candy shop. You mean the Rhyolite pack came after my uncle took over?" I was curious now. I had previously tried to ally with them and the Quartzite pack. I knew my uncle would send them away. But I could have sworn I saw the other alpha.

"If he did, we didn't see him. So I don't know who would have turned him away. Unless it was your uncle. Yes, and what your uncle did next infuriated me. It took everything in me to continue to be his Beta. He sent out some of the rogues that he made pack members out to kill the Alpha and his son. I stood by and did nothing." Harlen's eyes glowed with his wolf's color. He hated not being able to stop my uncle. But that wasn't the reason I left him here to continue as his beta. I wanted him to protect the pack from too much damage from my uncle's rule. After I came back I would handle everything else.

"Harlen, if you would have said something you wouldn't be here right now. You did what you had to, to protect this pack and yourself. I hate that Nolen had to lose his brother." I shook my head and glanced over to Nikita.

"You mean Alpha Nolen the prophesied alpha had an older brother?"

"Well yeah. That's why he was the one prophesied. Have you never read the prophecy?" I asked her and she shook her head. Standing I went to the shelf and pulled the book that held all the prophecies and handed it to her. "I'm pretty sure it's chapter sixteen."

Nikita read over the small chapter and then glanced up at me. She placed it on the desk before sitting down in one of the chairs. "I think I'm related to Alpha Nolen."

"What do you mean?"

"Have you not read the full prophecy?" Nikita glanced over to me and she slid the book across the desk to me.

Opening it I went to the chapter and read through it. She was right it mentioned two sisters and one would give birth to the prophesied alpha. If Nolen's mother gave birth to him then there was a good chance that she was Nikita's aunt. "Well, the only way to know is to go and ask her."

"Or you could ask the elder that is here in this room with you." My gaze went to Olli along with Nikita's.

Fuck, why didn't I realize that Olli would know who her aunt was? "Okay, well all knowing elder why don't you tell us if she is Nikita's aunt?"

"She is. And I'm sure she would like to meet you." Olli smiled widely at Nikita.

"Do you think? I mean she thinks I'm dead." I could hear the sorrow in her voice.

"I'm sure of it. She was very distraught when she found out her sister was murdered. I'm sure she would like to connect to her last living relative." Olli bowed his head to her. "I think I'm going to get us something to eat."

"I can send for someone to bring us something." I glanced up at the aging wolf.

"It's okay. It gives these old bones something to do." He bowed his head and left out the door.

"So has Alpha Roy tried to contact you about his missing Luna?" Nikita turned to me as I sat back down to work on my computer.

"Alpha Roy's Luna is here? Why haven't I seen her?" Harlen got up and came to the desk staring at the both of us.

"The wolves that came to the dinner. They told us she was found dead on our territory. She has been in our morgue. Doc has determined that all the wolves that have been sent to our territory have been poisoned by the same thing." I answered him.

The shock that graced his face told me the same thing that we had been thinking. Harlen dropped down in the other high-backed chair. His hand went to his jaw as he continued to stare off into space.

"So Alpha Roy doesn't know that she is here? Or are you thinking that he is the one that killed her and put her on our territory?" Harlen's gaze refocused as he questioned me.

"I don't know. But I don't think it is him bringing the bodies here and dropping them off. My scouts are not picking up his scent. But that doesn't mean that he isn't using someone else to do it." I answered him. Sighing, I turned off the computer. I wasn't getting much done with the three of them in here.

The doors to my office opened and Olli came in along with two omegas. They each had a tray with food and drinks on them. My stomach growled at the pleasant smell of the food that had been brought in. Nikita turned and I could see her nostrils flaring as she took in the smell.

"I figured everyone was hungry. So I brought different things." Olli had the omegas sit everything on the table and thanked them as they headed out of the room.

"Thanks Olli." Nikita went to the table and started in on the food. Olli grabbed him something from the table along with Harlen.

I came around the desk and found what the smell was that had my stomach rumbling and basically cursing at me for waiting this long to feed it. Sitting beside Nikita I dug in the food. Everything was silent as we all ate the food that Olli had gone to get.

"I think we need to call Alpha Nolen and see if his mother would speak with us." Olli sat back taking a sip of his drink as we all stuffed our faces.

"I would like that, Olli. But I really want to finish the book before we contact her. I want to make sure she was on good terms with her sister before I start bugging her." Nikita was always weary when it came to things like this.

"Of course Luna. I wouldn't want to put you in anything awkward." Olli bowed his head and placed his glass down on the tray.

Nikita and Olli stayed in the office talking about what she had learned in the book. I had to get out of the stuffy room before I burst. Harlen walked with me to the inner part of the territory where the shops were. It had been a while since I had last come down here.

"So, Fin what are you thinking about these happenings?" Harlen was all for keeping the pack safe and I felt like he didn't like that I hadn't contacted Alpha Roy yet. But Nikita had asked me not to until we figured out what was going on.

I still hadn't heard from my informant that was at the Shonkinite pack which unnerved me. Part of me was hopeful that the wolf was fine and heading back here. But then it would be hard for them to get back here if they were trying to keep their pack safe. I hoped that they weren't in a dungeon or dead.

I think mind linking would be safer. I don't know what to do because I can't wrap my head around killing my own mate. And if he didn't, who did?

Yes, it is very odd especially since they are already marked and mated.

Harlen, how crazy did this part of the territory get while I was gone?

We won't talk about that. Your uncle made this place a looney bin, that was for sure. I worried a lot about the pups those ten years. I tried to get the mothers to go to Bella's pack but they didn't want to leave their mates.

Things wolves do for their mates. I would kill someone if they tried to hurt Nikita.

I don't think you have too much to worry about. Nikita could take care of herself, but I wouldn't put it past some of the warriors to stand beside her as well.

I chuckled. That was true. Most of the warriors that had been watching her train with me would love to fight with her in battle. She was the most amazing thing to watch as she sent blow after blow into her opponent. Hell, I had to start deflecting her punches.

We need to find out what is going on over at that pack otherwise we are going to have a war that shouldn't have ever been started.

Harlen nodded his head as I went into the ice cream shop. I had figured out that Nikita, for all her boldness, loved vanilla bean ice cream.

"Harlen, I think we need to go back to the old Obsidian pack and see if there is anything that we have missed. I can't believe that the alpha there would allow everything in that pack to burn without putting what was needed in that safe room." The bell for the shop rang alerting everyone in the small room that someone else had entered. I went up to the counter to the greying red-headed woman and looked at all the other flavors. "Joan, can you get me a half-gallon of the vanilla bean and then another half-gallon of the peanut butter chocolate?"

"Of course alpha." She smiled and turned to grab her needed items. I was so ready to have this thing in my stomach.

"When are you wanting to go?" Harlen ordered a pint of Tobey's favorite flavor as he waited with me in the store.

"I think we need to go soon. I do believe that Nikita will have that book read by the end of this week if not sooner. But I do believe we need to handle the other thing as well." I nodded to Joan and smiled as she gave me my purchase and Harlen grabbed his.

"Yes, are you wanting to send another wolf there to see if we can find the other?"

"No, I was thinking of doing some recon myself. It's about time that I do something useful in this pack other than shouting out orders." I chuckled with Harlen as we headed back up to the packhouse. The wind was biting cold as we traversed the sidewalk. Trying to stay out of the wind as much as we could.

When I went to the pack what was I thinking about getting into these things when I had others to do this type of work? Another thing was what was I going to tell Nikita about my absence?

She wasn't just like any other female. She was an alpha born female. Last living heir to the Obsidian pack that was no more. I just hoped that with everything going she would be able to keep her cool and wits about her.

CHAPTER THIRTY-NINE

FIN

I had left early this morning to get to the Shonkinite pack before anyone was up. Nikita would probably be pissed at me for leaving her in bed but I was sure that her scent was changing and I wasn't going to have her shifting with me to come on this. When I knew that things could go wrong and that she could get hurt.

Aloysius ran silently despite his massive size. It had snowed this morning so it camouflaged me better than in the summer. I was hoping that getting closer to the pack that I would be able to find my informant. Along with the other scent that was bringing the poisoned bodies into my pack.

Slowing down at the edge of my territory I brought my nose up as the wind brought the scent of the other pack to me. Since I had been here last it had changed. But it could also be that the smell that made this pack appealing was now sleeping or cursing my name.

The sound of disappearing paws told me that I had just missed the patrol wolves. If they had been mine they wouldn't be running side by side. That way they would be able to catch something that would be trying to sneak in. Which bothered me with how many bodies had gotten through unnoticed.

Was one of my pack members part of this?

I went forward onto the territory slowly making my way further into the middle of the pack. I couldn't bring myself to think that one of my own was trying to betray me. Because if they did then that would mean that they had always been loyal to someone other than me. My uncle? Possible. Could they be trying to start a war that would almost decimate the pack?

We will need to talk with the patrols. Something is fishy about bodies getting on to our land. Aloysius commented as I made our way even further in the pack.

Yes, Someone is in on this. Maybe I shouldn't have left Nikita by herself.

Our feisty Luna will be fine. She is of Alpha blood. He was right, but with her scent changing I wonder if she even knew that she was pregnant.

A scent caught my attention. One that had been detected on my territory. I had never been one to not remember a smell. This wolf had to be the one coming onto my territory and bringing the dead. Loping through the brush I made my way to the smell. I needed to know who it was that was doing this to my pack.

While I followed the scent a sharp snap brought my attention to my left. I jumped in time to keep the brown wolf from tossing me into a tree. Turning on the wolf snarling and baring my teeth. I can't let him tell the others that I'm here. If he does then Alpha Roy will either kill me and take my pack or put me in a dungeon.

The wolf lunged at me. We met in the middle, my teeth sinking into the wolf's shoulder and took a chunk of it's muscle with me as I tore it away from the bone. The scream from the wolf excited me. It had been a long time since I fought with another wolf. Actually fought. Falling to the ground it continued to scream, I lunged forward resting my fangs in his throat.

Silencing him forever.

Hundreds of paws thundered behind me and I stood facing them. Alpha Roy standing in the front his murderous gaze on me. Maybe I shouldn't have fought with the brown wolf. I should have known that he would have mind linked his alpha. Now he is going to think that I was the one that was killing his pack mates.

Glancing around me I realized that I was surrounded. Well this was going to be hell to get out of. One behind me thought it would be a good decision to snap at my tail. I turned my back on Alpha Roy and took hold of the silver wolf and killed him in an instant.

I turned back to Alpha Roy. Waiting for him to attack me. He stood there before he shifted, his grey pallor told me that he knew that his Luna and mate was gone. Standing there in front of me he looked horrible. If I was to ever lose Nikita, I hoped that I would leave this world with her.

"What have you done with my Luna!" His face reddened as he yelled at me. "Shift and tell me what you have done to my Luna!"

I shifted not because he commanded me but so that I could talk with him. He needed to know that I didn't have anything to do with her passing.

What I found funny was that he thought I killed her just like he thought I had killed the others. So who was the one actually killing them?

Whoever it was. Was the person's scent that I had picked up before the brown wolf got to me. And they were able to get in and out of both packs without trouble. Now who could that be? If not Alpha Roy? Is someone from his pack killing them and then bringing them to mine? Did I also have a traitor?

"I've done nothing to your Luna. But she is in my pack in my morgue. Someone is playing us both."

"You lie! Take him to the dungeons! And let him rot!"

"You will bring the whole of Dolostone on you if you do not allow me to leave." I answered him sternly but calmly. This alpha needed to be spoken easy to. Even as his wolves grabbed hold of me. He had gone mad with grief and I didn't blame him. I would probably be the same way.

"That's what you think. But who is going to send them this way? Dungeons!"

Well isn't this a good thing. Back in a dungeon. Alyosius snapped in my head. He paced as if he was in a cell as well.

Can you just shut up? Dolostone will come for us. Besides, there's always a way to get out of here. I answered him as I sat there. My wounds from the fight with the brown wolf were already starting to heal. I doubt they would scar since I didn't get them before I had my wolf.

A male wolf had brought me some shorts a few hours after they had thrown me in here. Which was more than what my own uncle gave me. He was going to allow me to be naked as a jaybird when he killed me. If not for Harlen coming to get me out.

Did you even tell Harlen when to actually come if something was to happen? Aloysius taunted me. He sat down to stare at me in my head. I swear sometimes I worry that he never came out of his puppy stage.

You sure are worried that our pack would leave us in this cell. I mocked him. While I sat against the cold damp brick. The cells were smaller than the ones at Dolostone and I didn't think that they had been used in some time. By the smell of them I could bet my pack on it.

Well aren't you?

Harlen would never leave me here. Nikita wouldn't either. I answered him just as the squeal of a door alerted me someone was coming down.

By his smell I knew that it was Alpha Roy. Along with his beta. The way his face held so much misery when he came into view. Could only mean that more of their pack was gone.

"Why are you on my territory? Haven't you done enough damage!" Alpha Roy snarled into my cell. Claws were slicing through to his palms as he held onto the cell bars.

"I've not killed anyone but the brown wolf that attacked me. I was here trying to find out who was behind your attacks. Because apparently they are trying to frame me." I stayed calm. If I didn't then Alpha Roy would become even more hostile.

"You're a liar! You were coming to get another wolf!" His eyes blazed as he tried to get to me. I kept to the wall. Knowing that whoever kept the key to my cell away from him was my saving grace. Because if Alpha Roy had it we would already be fighting and there wouldn't be a wolf in this pack to keep me from actually killing him.

"You have lost your mind. I have no reason to hurt your pack. If anyone should be mad it should be me at you. You wanted me dead because of something my uncle had done to Kalila. I tried to save her but he already had her in his grasp. So tell me, why would I want to hurt another the same way I was hurt?" I had planned on killing him since I thought that he was the one who had poisoned Nikita. But there was no way that an alpha was going to kill his fated mate to try to frame me.

Alpha Roy took a step back like I had slapped him. Whoever was doing this was wanting revenge on my pack and Alpha Roy's and they weren't going to stop until both packs laid in ruin. As much as I still wanted to believe that he had something to do with Nikita's poisoning. Something inside me didn't think he did now.

Roy pushed past his beta and back the way he came. The beta came forward to me. His green eyes holding my dark ones. "Did you find the wolf that has been taking our pack members?"

"I'm pretty sure I was tracking them before the brown wolf attacked me." I answered him back. I didn't know what he was wanting to know but I would answer anything to be able to get out of this cell and go back to Nikita. She didn't need to be here with the state that Alpha Roy was in.

"I've been noticing a different scent hanging around the pack since your luna's ceremony. Since Luna Adia's death I have enacted a curfew. I'm afraid that pups will be next." His head dropped onto the bars as he hung on them to keep him standing up right.

"First thing you need to do is stop allowing your patrols to run side by side. That's how whoever it is, is getting through. I'm sure he has been scouting the pack before I even came into the picture." I was up front with him. There's no reason to let his pups get hurt if they could be protected.

"I'll make note to let them know. Is that how you got in?"

"Yes," I answered him as I continued to watch him. This whole pack was a mess if their leaders couldn't get their act together. "We need to work together here Beta. Otherwise we will lose both our packs in this process."

"I don't think Alpha Roy will. After he lost her he lost his mind. He has always been a little shit even when we were younger but he hasn't ever been this bad. I will see what I can do about getting you out of here. But I don't think I will be able to." He steps away from the cell and I stand.

"Then you need to get a message over to my Beta. You cannot allow my Luna to come to this pack. He will kill her."

"I will make a call to Harlen. He has been a good man." He nodded his head and left me in the cell. I could only hope that Harlen could convince her not to come to save me. Nikita would be in trouble if she came here.

Not only from Alpha Roy but whoever was attacking this pack. If anything we needed to be finding out who it was and fast.

CHAPTER FORTY

Nikita

You could only imagine how pissed I was when I found out that Fin had left me here to go and see who was behind the attacks. I paced the entire morning trying to get someone to tell me why he had to do this himself. If his ass got killed I would pray to the moon goddess to bring him back just so I could send him back to her.

Olli was sitting in our living room scanning through the book that held all the prophecies. Why was it my family that this had to happen to? Not that I would wish this on anyone else. But did there have to be a prophecy at all.

I could have grown up with my parents and possibly a sibling. This whole thing made me mad. I stomped over to the couch and picked up my mother's journal. This was the only thing I had left other than an aunt that didn't even know I was alive and an alpha cousin that didn't even know we were related.

"Olli, why did you go rogue?"

"Your father started to do things I couldn't get behind. So I rejected the pack and left." Olli glanced up from the book and stared at me.

"What did he do?" I needed to know. Why would someone as loyal as Olli just leave and never look back?

"I'd rather you read your mother's journal. If she put it in there I'd rather you learn it from her than me." He shook his head and started to read again in the book.

Sighing I opened the journal to the entry I had left off.

I went to the pack doctor today for my checkup. I'm getting closer to delivering this pup. She has made it through all the ups and downs during these past two months. She is my fighter. When they told me that she was a girl I just knew that Cain would be upset. If the only child I could give him was a boy then that's what I wanted to give him.

But this little girl. She is something special. I can't wait to watch her grow into the wolf and leader I know her to be. The doctor says that she is growing well and that she is growing at a normal rate. She is healthy and strong.

The only thing that has me sad is that Alpha Christian is still wanting to take over our pack. But now he wants my little victor. He wants to take her for his son. He is sure that they will be fated mates. He wants to bring her up in his pack to teach her their ways so that way it is easier for her to become luna.

I have begged Cain to go back to the Dolostone alpha for help. From what has been told he has always been a fair alpha and he could help us. If I was to barter my daughter to any alpha it would be to his son. I have told Cain that I would go if he would let me. But he shot that down. I can't understand why he would want to give our daughter away like this.

Somedays I want to call my sister and have her help us. I know that she and her mate would. But Cain has commanded me to not say a thing about this to her.

Next time I hope I have better news.

Ciao

Damn alpha males and their egos. Why couldn't he just go back to the Dolostone alpha. Did he not know that the male that he talked to was a fraud? I shook my head. If I ever have a son I will make sure he never lets his ego get in the way of protecting the pack or his mate.

I continued on in the book but it was the same thing over and over again about her trying to get my father to go to one of the alphas. But he continued to tell her no. If Fin ever tried that with me I would do it anyway.

Fin couldn't command you anyway Nikita. We are alpha born. Enyo said she had been quiet for some time but she was excited about learning what our mother was like. I figured she was sitting back and reading with me. If wolves could read that is. *Watch it! If you can read I can read.*

I chuckled as I continued to read through. My father allowed his pride to get in the way. I just can't understand as to why. Turning my gaze to the window I realized that it was getting to be evening and I hadn't heard from Fin.

Damn him and leaving me here. I told him unless I was pregnant I wanted to be able to protect our pack with him. But I was in my room waiting for him to come back. When I had woken up I figured he had gone out for a run which was his normal but then when he didn't come home at his normal time I went to find Harlen.

It took some time getting it out of him but he finally caved and told me that he had gone to the Shonkinite pack to find out who was killing over there and bringing the bodies over to our pack. I was so pissed that he had left me that it was getting harder to read my mother's journal now that I was to a part that my father was making a decision while my mother pleaded with him.

I had given Harlen the cold shoulder ever since he also left me in the dark. How could they. Yes I wanted to learn about my mother and why I was given to Alpha Christian in the first place but I still was capable of helping him run this pack.

Slamming the book down on the table I startled Olli and got up without apologizing. I mean why should I? The door opened and Bella came in with a tray of food. She smiled at me and I gave her a weak one back. Bella rounded the table sitting the food down and went to the kitchen to grab three drinks.

"It will be okay Luna. Fin is a big boy he can take care of himself. Besides, he would never put your life or a pup's in danger by taking you with him." She motioned for me to sit beside her as she put my plate beside my mother's journal.

"I understand Bella but I'm not pregnant."

"Still he is being cautious. Eat dear." She pushed my plate further in front of me and I grabbed it with the fork. "Olli here. You both have been in this room with your noses in books. Food is good for the mind as well."

I laughed at her. Bella always knew just what to say to get people to do what she wanted.

The sky was darkening and I was starting to worry about Fin. It shouldn't have taken him this long to get the information that we needed and then get back. Olli had headed to bed and Bella was making sure Tobey was in bed as well.

Wolves in the pack were heading to their homes for the night with their families.

He's still alive. If he wasn't then we would know that he had passed on. Enyo whimpered. She didn't like that he was late getting home.

Sighing I paced the balcony as we waited for him to come home. An SUV had pulled up and Harlen met them with Doc and a gurney. The back door opened and Fin's scent came up to me with the wind. Two other wolves took the gurney to the back of the black vehicle and loaded up the body that laid on it.

If I wasn't mistaken the other scent that was with Fin was my old beta. Fin came into the light and I noticed that he was holding his arm. What did they do to him? They must be trading my mate for Luna Adia. It hurt that I didn't know who had killed her.

As much as I wanted to run down there. I was still pissed off that he had left without me this morning and then was captured because that would be the only way that we would be trading. Fin and Harlen shook hands with my former beta and he entered the SUV. They left as My mate and Harlen came into the packhouse.

I went to the foyer of our suite, arms crossed and waited for them to come up. It didn't take them long to get up here. When the door opened Harlen was the first in, followed by Doc and his medical supplies and then the culprit himself.

He glanced up at me and gave me a sheepish smile as he came up to me. I could see the other wounds that were healing on his upper body and other arm. Which pissed me off even more.

"So, you decided to go find out information and didn't let me tag along."

"Now, now feisty wolf. There's no need to be mad. I took care of myself." Fin chuckled but he stopped when he realized that I wasn't smiling. "Nikita, I didn't want you to get hurt. It's one thing for me to fight them but they used to be your pack. Besides, if I had run into the person killing off loved ones then I didn't want you to be there to entice him."

"You still didn't give me a choice and then your choice got you locked up in the dungeons. For however long you were down there." I snapped. It wasn't like me to be this way but he had not only pissed me off but hurt me that he didn't trust I could take care of myself and him.

"How do you know I was in a dungeon? I didn't tell you anything about anything yet." His left brow rose and he gave me that alpha look.

"You do realize before you came and took me back here I was a warrior and I put plenty of people in that dungeon. So I became well acquainted with the smell."

"Then yes I was in the dungeon. But if I wasn't I would have had to fight Alpha Roy and I wasn't about to fight someone who was overcome with grief." He shrugged his shoulders and then kissed my cheek before he went to Doc to get looked over.

I walked over and watched as Doc listened and poked and prodded my mate to make sure that he was healing well. Whoever got a hold of Fin did it quickly. Because there was no way that he would allow someone to get him otherwise. Harlen sat on the couch across from him watching as well. Fin never learned that I probably could have gotten in him without being seen and then back out.

"So, Luna, when are you going to come see me for your exam?" Doc's voice snapped me out of my thoughts as he put everything back into his bag. Fin's and Harlen's eyes darted back over to me and I didn't miss the flare of Fin's nostrils.

"What would I be going to get checked Doc?" I inquired as he came up to me. The way he looked at me had me curious.

"I would think that you would know along with Alpha Fin." Doc dropped the bag and pulled his stethoscope out again to listen to my heart and then he placed it on my belly. He had to be kidding. There was no way. "Luna you are with pup and I advise you to come to my office in the hospital to get an ultrasound. You might be further along than you think."

CHAPTER FORTY-ONE

Nikita

There was no way that I was pregnant. I would know, right?

I glanced around the room and my hands went to my stomach. Fin came up to me and made me look up at him. This couldn't be happening, I needed to be able to help keep the pack safe. How was I going to do that if I was pregnant? Fin's eyes were soft as he held mine.

"It's okay, feisty wolf. War with Shonkinite is not going to happen. We just need to keep you safe right now." The way he spoke to me like I was going to break.

I mean, I very well could break. This was something I didn't think would happen because I had been in heat for so long. But then again with as much as we were fucking I shouldn't be surprised. "Fin we still don't know who has been killing the pack and then bringing them to our territory."

"We will find whoever it is. I won't let them anywhere near you or the pup." Fin's voice was laced with his wolf's.

There was never any doubt that he would protect me. But I still felt like I was going to be useless and I hated that feeling. I had told myself I would never be useless or feel like that ever again. Now that pledge was out of the water. I shook my head and then went into our room.

This was all so much and I needed to get away from it all. Why did the Moon Goddess decide that it was a good time to allow me to be pregnant. What was her plan? I stood in the middle of the room trying to figure out the plan. While I had been okay with getting pregnant before I got poisoned, now with everything up in the air about the person or people that were killing the Shonkinite pack. I didn't think it was a good idea.

"Nikita,"

I turned and realized that Fin was standing in the doorway watching me. He made his way carefully to me like I would go off at any moment.

"I told you when you were in heat that this could happen. You didn't care." Fin's hand came up to my check and I nuzzled into his palm.

"I didn't care then. We didn't have anything to worry about but Roy. But now we don't know what is happening." Fin searched my eyes before he pulled me in close to him.

"It will be okay Nikita. We won't tell anyone until we have to. But I do want you to go to that secret room at Obsidian. I can't lose you." His arms tightened around me. I felt the sorrow and grief through our bond.

This was the reason I didn't want something like this to happen after all this happened. I couldn't defend myself in my wolf form but I would make sure that I would be able to in my human form. "Fin we need to have someone take some weapons to the safe room. I don't want to be there without anything to protect me."

"Okay, just because if I tell you no you will hurt me." Fin chuckled as he pulled away and crashed his lips to mine. The love and passion that he put into that kiss had me wet.

I pulled away from him and took a step back to take a breath. "Fin we need to be practical about this. We don't need to have anyone with me so that the safe room stays between me, you and Olli."

"I have to veto that. You need to have at least someone in there with you. I'll give you weapons but you will also get another body with you in that room. But I won't leave you in there by yourself."

Deciding to let him have his way this time.

Doc had me on the table with my shirt up and waiting for the ultrasound to be done. Fin was sitting beside me watching him move the wand around on my flat stomach. The gel was warm at least. I continued to stare at the black and white monitor trying to figure out what Doc was trying to find.

The sound of a heartbeat filled the room and my heart started to race with it.

"Ah! There it is! The pup was hiding."

It didn't look like any blob that I had seen before. The pup looked more developed than what I had expected. Was Doc right about me being further along? I glanced over to Doc and the grin on his face allowed me to calm my heart. My attention went to Fin and I realized that he had tears in his eyes.

My hand went to his face bringing his eyes to me. Fin smiled at me before placing a kiss on my forehead. This pup made him happy as he returned his gaze to the screen. Losing them all those years ago really messed with him. Did he get to see his other child before his uncle killed his chosen?

"Doc, is it old enough to find out what the pup is?" Fin's voice held a certain longing.

"It's not quite time yet to know the gender of the pup alpha. But this one is strong. It has a nice strong heartbeat and the way it is moving around in there it's going to be healthy." Doc printed out a few ultrasound pictures and then took the wand off my stomach. He wiped my stomach with a warm wet cloth and then handed me a dry one with a smile.

"Doc, with everything going on we need this to remain between the three of us. Until this is over." Fin's hands fisted on the sheets under me.

"I understand Alpha but the other wolves will find out sooner rather than later. It might be a good idea to let some of them know. Ones that you are sure are loyal to you." Doc answered him. I had never known another wolf other than Harlen and Bella to tell him what he didn't want to hear.

Fin nodded and helped me up. It wasn't that I needed the help, it was just letting Fin do something with himself. I pulled my shirt down and stood from the bed. Fin continued to stare at the black and white picture of our pup. He glanced up at me and the corner of his lip lifted and Fin held out his hand to me.

Taking his hand he pulled me in close as Doc left the room to give us a moment together. I wrapped my arms around him as he squeezed me to him. He made me feel so much better about this than I was. I didn't know if I would be a good mom but with him here I would be anything that I needed for this pup.

"Nikita, I swear on my soul that I will not let anything happen to you. If it was your life versus my own I would lay down mine so that you could live." His hard whisper tingled my neck as he held me.

"Fin, I will need you to be here with me. You can't leave me here to raise this pup by myself." Fin pulled me to arm's length and nodded.

"I will do whatever you want me to do, my feisty wolf."

"Then don't die. Because if you did I don't think I would be able to survive the bond breaking." His eyes searched mine as we stood there and then he crashed his lips to mine.

"Bella is sure to want to talk with you. I think we will have a small dinner with them and Tobey. What do you think?"

"I think that is a wonderful plan. I think this pup is hungry." I rubbed my stomach bringing Fin's eyes down further than my flat belly.

"Well if his mother gets hungry for something later tonight than I'm sure daddy can help her." His hand went into my hand and softly pulled my hair to bring my head back.

"Fin... I think that hunger is what made our pup. Besides, why do you think the pup will be a boy? You don't think you will have a girl?" The corner of my lips pulled up as he gripped my hair tighter.

"The pup could be a boy or a girl. I could not care. All I care about is that he or she is healthy along with its mother." Fin brushed his lips over my neck as his right hand roamed my body.

"Fin, we are still in the room. We can't... They will hear and smell." The way my words came out as moans excited him. I could feel his cock pressing against my stomach.

"Come on, I need to feed that pup and then feed you afterward." His husky voice made me not want to eat yet. To have him inside of me filling me with his cum.

"We will have to make this dinner short." I chuckled as he released my hair and grabbed my hand.

We exited the room and strolled past the wolves that worked in the pack hospital. Each one bowed their heads as we went by. Just knowing that they could smell the arousal between us both had me on edge. I wasn't embarrassed to say the truth. I didn't want them to think something happened in there.

By the time we made it to the packhouse the kitchen staff were running around the lower level. They didn't normally do that unless they were having to make two different meals. I glanced over to Fin but he seemed to not notice them.

"Fin, I thought we were going to have a small dinner. Like one that we make on our floor." I questioned him and the corner of his lip lifted in that sexy half smile that said he was up to no good.

"We were but I want to get dinner over quickly so that we can have our time together." Fin pressed his hand against my lower back. The warmth that it radiated there made me warm all over.

Fin you need to watch what you say. There are pups running around here! I scolded him as we continued up to our floor.

Oh feisty wolf. The time for mind links like this is over. The pack knows what was happening last month. So they won't be offended by the way I talk to you. But if you feel better with me talking to you in mindlink than I will. He chuckled out loud which startled a couple of omegas cleaning the floor we were passing. *If I talk to you like I want to it will let everyone near you know what you are thinking, my feisty Luna.*

I rolled my eyes. I swear he couldn't act more his age at all. You would never believe that he was thirty-five almost thirty-six. And the fact that we were having a pup I didn't know how he would even act around it.

Fin can I ask you a question? I didn't know if he would answer it since he always seemed to be distraught speaking of her and their pup.

Of course what is it? He was so lighthearted right now I didn't really want to bring him down. But I needed to know, no I wanted to know if he had found out what his pup before me was before the murder.

It's about your chosen and your pup. Did you know the gender of it?

Fin froze for a moment and then sighed. *No I didn't. She was killed before I was even able to see it on the ultrasound machine. I've been wondering what it would have looked like.*

He turned to me as we reached the door to our suite and pulled me close to him. This was the reason I didn't want to ask him but curiosity always won.

I'm sorry Fin I shouldn't have asked.

You're fine Nikita. One of these days it won't be like this.

CHAPTER FORTY-TWO

Nikita

It has been a couple weeks since we went to see the pup on the ultrasound. Later today we were going to see what the gender was. I had never been as excited about something like this. This wasn't something I ever thought would happen to me. I sat in the living room this morning reading my mother's journal.

I was getting closer to my birth. Come to think about it, I didn't really know when I was born. No one could actually tell me when the day was. So we just celebrated it during the month. But it started to make me wonder why my parents at the Shonkinite pack didn't know the day. Which now I know why. They weren't really related to me.

It's getting closer to my due date and I can feel our little warrior moving in my stomach. The pains are getting closer together. So I'm sure that it might be tonight when I have her. Cain has been gone for a few weeks. He told me that when he left that he would be back by the time our girl was born.

Alpha Christian has been here multiple times to get us to conform with his plan to blend the packs. I've been trying to keep my contractions a secret. I'm sure that he has someone here in our pack watching. I can't be parted with my girl.

Well, my water just broke. I'm going to leave this entry right here and lock myself in the bathroom.

Ciao.

It has been a week since my little warrior has come into the world with her bright green eyes and dark black hair. She was beautiful. No one knew that she was here. I had kept the other pack wolves away from our floor. Cain was keeping them away too.

He was finally happy. Every time that he came to us he would pick her up and carry her around. She loved him. My little warrior was strong. The only thing that worried me was when Alpha Christian came to the pack again. And I knew he would be here. I'm surprised that he hasn't been here sooner.

Well she is crying.

Ciao.

I worried about reading further. Part of me didn't want to know what happened. Who was the one that was telling the other pack what was going on? As much as I didn't want to find out I needed to. I needed to know why I was given away.

They took her! It has been too long since I held her. Alpha Christian told Cain that if we gave her to him that we could keep the pack. I was begging Cain not to take it. I would rather live as a rogue with my baby and her father than to give up my girl.

But gave her away like it was nothing. Like he didn't love the fact that she was his. I didn't want anything to do with him.

He would try to get me to talk to him but I can't. Cain told the pack I had lost another child but this one was a still born. I hated him for giving her away. She needed me. Who in that pack was going to love her like I would be able to? No one that is who.

Anyway, I'm going to go lay down for a while. This has to be the worst days of my life.

So Alpha Christian had given my father an ultimatum. Me for his pack, I can't believe that he would allow me to be taken. Just so he could keep his pack. I didn't blame my mother for not wanting to have anything to do with him. If he wasn't already dead, I'd kill him myself.

The door to our suite opened and Fin came in. I glanced up to the clock on the wall and realized that it was almost time for my ultrasound. Placing the book down on the coffee table, I waited for Fin to come to me. He had been up before the sun and coming home after dark.

Harlen and some of the Deltas had been chasing after a scent that they had picked up after Adia had been put on our territory. Fin had been very adamant that I wasn't to leave the pack house. Not like I could shift now. Enyo was enjoying the fact that her mate was being controlling.

I, on the other hand, didn't really like it. But now I wasn't just thinking about myself but a pup that would be our heir to not only Dolostone but Obsidian. Fin plopped down beside me and laid his head in my lap as he snuggled my growing belly.

"Fin, it's about time to go to the doctor." His lips brushed over my stomach and our little one kicked out like the pup needed more room.

"I know. I just want to lay here with you both. It's been awhile since I got to be with you both." He sighed as he stood from his position and held out his hand to me.

I chuckled and slid my hand in his. Fin pulled me to my feet and grabbed hold of a handful of my hair. The moan that escaped me couldn't even be kept inside. As much as I loved that he wanted to protect me, him being gone all day had me horny. We won't even talk about the damn hormones that plagued me. I know for a fact that he could smell the room and my arousal that was all over the bed.

"Nikita, I'm going to have to fuck you tonight. I can't keep smelling you and not sinking deep inside you." Fin's breath fanned over my ear as he pulled the lobe into his mouth.

"Fin, you are going to make us late if you keep touching me and talking to me like this." I moan into his ear.

"Fine, I'll just have to find a place in the woods beside the pack and take you. Because there is no way that I will be able to wait until we get to our room." Fin released my hair and brought my hand up to his mouth. Kissing each knuckle on the back of my hand sending sparks up my arm.

I shook my head and brushed past him. His quick steps told me that he was right behind me as I opened the door. Fin's arm wrapped around my waist while we made our way down the staircase. Like I said he never let me out of his sight much less away from his side.

The wolves that we passed bowed their heads. I was just starting to actually show. Pack members were making things for the pup. Some made sure that they made things neutral while others were making either blue or pink things for the pup. I liked that they were excited about the pup growing in my stomach.

At first I was worried about it. Because my mother had lost a lot of babies before me. I was still making my way through the book. It made me sad that she had to go through all of this. Mostly by herself.

Fin was nothing like my father. He had stayed by my side even though he was working all day everyday. I never felt like I was unloved. Unlike how I felt while reading that journal of my mother's. When I could, I wanted to go to the Rhyolite pack and talk to her sister. To find out what my mother was like not just through the vintage pages of her book.

We quietly strolled through the pack to the hospital. Everyone that we passed bowed their head and smiled. I smiled back at them as we went our separate ways. If you would have asked me a few months ago what my life was going to be like. I'd have told you that it would have been the same, fighting my way through the warrior ranks of Shonkinite pack.

I would never have thought that I was what I was because of what happened when I was born. The thought of a mate was even low on my chart of things to find. If anything I didn't think that he would be an Alpha.

The pup moved around in my stomach and my hand instinctively went to the place it was last at. Like every new mother I was scared of what was going to happen and if I was going to be the mother that this pup needed to become the best that it could be. I knew that female born alphas were rare but I hoped that it would be female.

"Your mind is wandering, Nikita. Tell me," Fin's voice forced its way through my thoughts.

I glanced up to my mate, his eyes looked with mine as he opened the door to the hospital to allow me in.

"Just thinking about what our little pup is and how I'm going to be as a mother." I told him as his hand went to the small of my back. Being this far into our territory I didn't think it was really necessary that he be so close. "What do you hope the pup is? Boy or girl?"

"You are going to be a fantastic mother. As far as wanting one over the other. Either will be fine. Because I know if we have a girl that she will have the same fiery attitude as her mother. But that won't keep me from wanting to protect her like I try to do with her mother." Fin smiled and winked at me before he turned his attention to the wolf at the desk. "Doc around? We have an appt with him today."

"Of course Alpha. I will get him right away." The male stood and went to the back.

Doc always made us a priority unless he was in surgery. Which was understandable, I'd never want him to come out of surgery for either one of us. The male wasn't gone but a few minutes when he came back with a smiling Doc.

"Well, well, we have grown. Let's go see if we can get this pup to cooperate this time." Doc chuckled as he motioned for us to follow him.

Last time it was still a little too soon to tell the gender but Doc had wanted to see if he could take a peek. Our little one was obviously shy because it kept everything hidden. I had laughed at Fin and Doc, which made me think that maybe the pup was female.

Today though we would find out. Hopefully otherwise the pup's gender would be a surprise and we would find out when it was born. I didn't mind either way but I was sure that the pack would love to know what the heir was going to be. Walking down the familiar hall had my heart starting to beat fast in my chest.

We went into the ultrasound room like normal. This has become our current situation, come in the room, lay down, warm gel on my stomach and then see the pup. It was something I was looking forward to every two weeks. As Doc began to spread the gel over my stomach I could hear the pup's heartbeat. Now that it was bigger it was easier to find and hear the heartbeat. It always made me tear up.

"Growing well Luna. You must be giving the pup what he wants to eat." Doc laughed as he pushed the wand into my stomach to try to get the pup to move. The pup finally moved around so that Doc could hopefully see what we were having. "Well I'll be. Looks like we are going to have an alpha in the next week or two."

There in all his glory was my son.

CHAPTER FORTY-THREE

FIN

I couldn't get Nikita out of that room fast enough. When I told her that I was going to take her in the woods that was exactly what I was going to do. I bid Doc goodbye and then hurried her out of the building. The fact that she could feel what I was feeling in our bond made it even more urgent to get her undressed and wrapped around my cock.

Bringing her a little further beyond the tree line. The wind blew toward us and into the woods, keeping our scent from the rest of the pack. I gently pressed her against the tree. As much as I wanted to ravage her. I couldn't hurt the pup inside her belly.

"Fin... I've never seen you lose this much of your control. Even when I was in heat." Nikita moaned near my lips.

The soft vibration of her words against the soft tissue had my cock twitching in my pants. My hands went into her hair before I crushed my lips to hers. Nikita's skin shivered under my touch while her hand found my shoulders. I never should have waited this long to take her again. But the natural wolf instincts to protect my mate were too strong. I had to make sure she was going to be safe.

"Nikita, I need you. Badly, I have to make sure I'm not rough with you." I didn't even recognize the tone in my voice. There can never be another long break without being with her.

"Then take me Fin, because I need you too."

"I'll be gentle, I promise." I lifted her and sandwiched her between me and the tree. The dress that she had on was convenient with my plan to take her after the appointment.

Pulling her panties to the side I unzipped my pants and pulled out my already hard cock. I pressed it against her already wet core. It was easy to slip in, no resistance as I held her thighs and made sure her bottom half was a little bit away from the tree.

Nikita held onto the tree as I continued my assault on her pussy. Her moans and whimpers egged me on as I sunk into her. Moving her over to a rock that was sitting very close to where we were, I laid her on it with her legs resting on my shoulders. Taking the pressure from her lower back.

"Fin... Right there! Don't stop! Fuck don't stop!" Nikita's hands ran through her hair, fisting and unfisting it as her pussy clamped around my cock. The swelling that started in the base thickened to where I didn't know if it was just me or it was her as well. But it got to a point where I couldn't even move inside her.

My eyes connected to hers and the color of her wolf's shone through. I gripped her hips as my balls tightened and released the cum inside her. Not that I needed to get her pregnant, when she was already with pup. It just felt amazing to be inside her, coating her insides with my seed.

Once we found out what our pup was going to be. I couldn't keep anything contained. As much as I was hoping for a girl having a boy to pass down the reins to was exciting. All the things that he will learn from me and his mother.

At the moment though I was sitting in yet another meeting about this wolf that no one seemed to be able to find. I had my best trackers on this and now that Nikita was getting closer to having our boy we had to find him fast. There was nothing that I was going to do other than protect what was mine and that meant my pack, my Luna and my heir.

"Alpha, it may be wise to send the Luna to the safe house. That way if the wolf we are tracking even gets close to the packhouse they won't be able to get to her."

I glanced up at the newly recruited delta. He was old enough to remember the tyranny that my uncle ensued on this pack and others. He wouldn't know that I had done just that with my chosen and it didn't end well. Harlen cleared his throat beside me and spoke for me, "We are glad that you are able to give us advice on this matter Kit but that will not be where the Luna will go. We have another place for her."

The delta nodded his head and sat back. Even though it had been so long ago I still couldn't get over the fact that I had failed to protect mine that time. But this time, I would lay down my life before anyone touched a hair on Nikita's head.

"I will go out tonight with you. We need to find and do away with this wolf that has been pitting us against the Shonkinite pack. Ready more of our patrol wolves and have a couple extras around the packhouse." I needed to find this wolf before they try something else.

"Yes Alpha." The four deltas that now sat at my table stood and went out to relay the message.

I glanced over to Harlen and sighed.

" I don't know who to send with Nikita to the Obsidian pack room. I don't want too many people knowing about it but I can't leave her and the pup in there by themselves."

"We can send Bella and a warrior. Bella has been a midwife to many wolves when Doc had things come up. Plus she can help keep Nikita calm. You know that there are two warriors that would give their lives for the Luna." Harlen answered me.

I didn't want to put Bella in danger but if I sent either Blake or Conner with them then they would be safer. Blake and Conner had been with me since I first became alpha. I trusted them with my life. I was going to need to figure out something soon because she would have to go quickly if a fight started.

"Fine, we will send Blake or Conner with Bella and Nikita. But no one needs to know other than those three. We keep this between us." I glanced up at my old mentor and friend. He was one that I wouldn't ever not take his advice.

"You know that we will. Do you want to bring them in? Talk to them now?"

I took a deep breath and nodded. This needed to be done now and not later. There was no way to know if this wolf was already on the territory or had a way to take more from us. I can't let anything go one more day. "Tell them to meet me in my office."

Harlen nodded while I stood making my way to my office. As much as I liked the sun from this room. I loved the view from my office even better. It made talking about things like this a lot easier. Not that I had to worry about these two warriors not doing what I needed from them. They always made sure that they were early to training and even volunteered for extra patrols if someone needed off.

Stepping in the room, I made my way to my desk as Harlen sat on one of the couches. My ass made contact with the seat of my leather chair just as they knocked on the door. It didn't take them too long to make it to me. Like I said they were always very prompt.

"Come in,"

They both stepped in the office and shut the door. When I returned back I made sure when they renovated this office that they made the doors automatically shut and they were soundproof. If I learned anything as an alpha while my uncle was here was to keep your enemies as close as you can get them.

"Alpha you summoned us?"

I was glad that they didn't kneel like my father had made them do before I came into power. As much as I was their leader I wasn't someone they needed to kneel to.

"Yes, I have an important task for the two of you." Conner and Blake didn't even bat an eye or glance at each other. "If things turn to a fight I need you both to take your Luna and Beta Female to a secret location. You are not to tell anyone. This is to stay here between the four of us."

"Of course Alpha!" They both answered me.

"Take a seat, this will be a very lengthy conversation." I motioned to the high-backed chairs in front of me and they took the seats.

By the time I finished filling Blake and Conner in it was already dinner time. They left before I got up and watched the night patrols leave to the edge of the territory. I had to find that wolf if I didn't. He was going to continue to be a threat to Nikita and my pup. Along with my pack.

I will have to get something quick and head out.

"Let's go Harlen. I have patrol tonight."

"Have you let the Luna know?" Harlen asked as he followed me out of the office and to the dining hall.

"No but I will let her know at the table. She will understand. It's coming down to the wire and we still don't know who this wolf is and why he is doing this between the packs."

Harlen stayed silent behind me as we entered the large room. Nikita was up at the big table with Bella and Blake and Conner stood at the ends of the table. Heading over to Nikita I kissed her temple and then grabbed some of the food that was on the plate.

"Are you not eating tonight?" Her eyes went from the chicken leg in my hand to my face.

"I'm running patrols tonight. I will see you in the morning okay?" I could tell that she was upset that I hadn't forewarned her but she kept her cool in front of the pack that was sitting in the dining room.

"Well stay safe, I don't want to wake up a widow."

I chuckled and kissed her lips this time. Causing some of the younger male wolves to wolf whistle. They were being boys and the girls weren't quiet either. Their sighs told me they were on the same page as the boys.

Quickly heading out the door I pulled my shirt off as I stuffed the rest of the leg in my mouth. Shifting into Aloysius I bounded out to the edge of the territory. Tonight I was going to find this wolf and I was going to bring him down if it was the last thing I did.

I ran all night and nothing showed. No smell, no sight of this wolf, no nothing. It was getting to be morning as I continued down the path that had been worn into the ground. It would be the one night that I was on patrol that they wouldn't show up.

Just means he's a coward.

And how do you know that the wolf is a he?

I don't I was merely stating that the wolf was a coward. I mean any true wolf with any dignity would show themselves and fight us. Aloysius came back at me.

I started to make a comeback to him when I smelled it. The wolf was here! Quickening my steps I raced after him. My belly brushed the grass and dirt as I sailed over it to find this wolf that was causing my pack trouble. Just as I was gaining on the wolf I lost him and now I knew that it was a male. I couldn't refute the smell of another male wolf that I didn't know on my territory.

Following him to the other edge of my territory I realized that he had gone over to the Shonkinite packs territory. That's okay I will be waiting for him.

Alpha! The wolf is on the territory!

Capture him!

Blake, Conner take Luna and Beta Bella to the secret room.

Yes Alpha!

This wolf was mine now.

CHAPTER FORTY-FOUR

NIKITA

I was sitting eating the rest of my food when Blake came over and grabbed my elbow. He made me stand and I noticed that Conner had went to Bella and pushed her over to the other side. A few of the other wolves were grabbing pups of all ages and taking them to the safe room.

Fin! What's happening?

Just go with Blake and Conner. They are going to take you to the secret room with Bella. She is going to be there to help with anything that could happen.

Is it the wolf?

Yes, now move your pregnant ass.

This time only I would allow him to talk to me like this. Blake shifted once he was out of the pack house. I climbed up on his back and held onto his hackles as the other two shifted. The fact that I couldn't shift and help out my mate and pack really made me mad but then Enyo didn't feel that way.

"You better make sure you don't hurt me. If you do, Fin will not be happy."

The dark brown wolf under me snorted before shaking his head. He took off and the others followed behind us. I had never been on another wolf's back before since I could always shift for myself. Fin had to be okay with this because if not he was going to have a coronary.

We made it quickly to the old Obsidian pack house and Blake let me down. Bella and Conner had shifted and got dressed. Blake stayed as a wolf and held me out of the building until Conner made sure that our path was fine. Conner came back out of the doors and motioned for us to follow.

Blake turned and sat on the top of the steps. He was so still if you weren't looking carefully enough he looked like a statue. I just hoped that Fin was careful out there. If he died I would have the Moon Goddess bring him back just so that I could kill him myself. I made my way back to the office and couldn't help but notice that there were paw prints in the dust that hadn't been there before.

I mean it had been a couple months since we had been here and any of the patrolling wolves could have been in here to investigate. As I made it to the office Conner and Bella were behind me. I pulled the candlestick and the door opened.

Glancing around the room I then understood why there were paw prints here. Fin had someone move things around and bring things in to sustain us for a little bit. Bella came in along with Conner and he shut the door. My son moved around like he knew that we were in my birth pack.

"It's okay little one. We are safe."

"Is he moving around?" Bella came over to me and placed her hand on my stomach. Which made him kick and move faster.

"He has been moving like crazy these past few days." I smiled back at her.

"Yeah, they do that until it gets time then they go still. It will make you worry but it just means that he is coming."

I nodded and sat down on the couch. This better not be long. I'm not in the mood to have this go on for days. I couldn't even read my mother's journal because I didn't have it with me at dinner. Whoever had been in here had pushed most of the stuff to the side and made the room look more like a sitting room. Only without a Tv or anything to do.

There was no telling how long we had been here. The secret room didn't have any windows to look out. Which was a good thing since we were hiding. Bella had fallen asleep and I was thinking about doing just the same.

Conner sat with his back against the door that let us in. I have to say they were good at their jobs. They were the ones that were standing outside the hospital and they weren't even told to. Conner stood up quickly and turned to the door. I stood from my seat and moved to the back of the room.

Blake had to have told him something. Something is wrong. I glanced over to Bella who had gotten up and moved in front of me.

"Conner, what's wrong?"

"Don't worry Luna, I have you. Blake is keeping the wolf at bay until Alpha Fin and the others get here. I won't let anything happen to you." Conner answered me as we waited for more information.

The house shook as snarls and growls become louder than my racing heart. Someone was fighting with Blake. I didn't know if it was the wolf that we were looking for or if it was someone else. All I could hope was that Fin could make it here in time.

I didn't like that the person that was doing all this to these two packs was this close to me and my family. The other thing I didn't like was that I couldn't protect myself or the others around me.

The sounds outside went quiet and I glanced over to Conner. He didn't move from his stance beside the door. Padding of paws came through the door and all I could do was hope that it was Blake or even Fin coming to get me.

My heart hammered as the door opened and a man stood in the opening. A man that I hadn't ever met before. I'd met everyone in the pack. This man wasn't part of my pack or Shonkinite pack. His eyes flashed green. They were the same green that were mine. Who was this man?

Conner shifted and attacked the man in the doorway. Pushing him back out of the secret room. The snarls were explosive and I didn't know if it would be okay to go forward to shut the door. Even though the man apparently knew how to get in. Conner yelped and everything went quiet. Bella pulled me closer to her and farther into the corner of the room.

The man came back in the doorway and laughed. "I knew you'd find your way back here. But not with a Dolostone member. We are going to have to fix that. They are nothing but cowards. They will never help when you need it." He paused to bare his teeth at Bella before bringing his gaze back to me. "Haven't you figured it out yet? I'm your father."

The man that claimed that he was my father had tied up Bella in one of the chairs in the room. Conner was outside the room not moving. The massive wolf had changed back to his human form a few hours ago. I could only hope that he was still alive along with Blake. Because if this man was telling me the truth then he was an alpha and they wouldn't have stood a chance.

If he had noticed that I was pregnant he didn't make it known. His hair was greying and his body was leaner than Fin's was. As I studied his features I could tell that I had some of his. What I couldn't understand was why he was still alive and if he was why wasn't my mother. This was the reason I was trying to find out what was going on in her journal. What happened to my mother?

"What are you wanting from me?"

The man stood up and came over to me. Bella growled in the corner as he approached me. She didn't like that he was so close to me. He reached out his hand for mine. I was never one to be afraid of things but at this moment I didn't know what he would do if he noticed that I was pregnant.

"My daughter, with you still alive we can make Obsidian into a pack again. With a mate of my choosing it will become the strongest. You are a female born alpha. We will find you someone strong to rule beside you. Your pups will be strong as well." The way he talked it seemed like he didn't understand that I was already mated.

"But how will I rule if there are no pack members? And if you haven't noticed already, I'm mated and he is one of the strongest males in the territory." I stood in front of him and his eyes went from my face to the mate mark that rested at the base of my neck.

This shift from calm to anger in his eyes pushed a tiny bit of fear through my system. But he wasn't the first man to try to bring me to heel. I could tell that he was trying to keep calm but the fact that I was already mated. It threw a wrench in his plans, I just had to keep him from realizing that I was with pup.

"Who is this mate?" His voice was calm but the fire in his eyes told me he was pissed.

"He's the Alpha of Dolostone. I'm the Luna and if they find me here with my Beta female tied up they will kill you. As you know a pack protects their Luna and Beta female." I answered him with my arms over my chest. If he wanted to act like he was big and bad I can show him big and bad.

"Then I will kill him first. He denied me help when I needed it. I will take his head for taking you as a chosen!"

"He didn't take me as a chosen. Alpha Fin is my fated mate." I growled out. As much as he said that he was my father he definitely didn't act like one.

"You allowed a Dolostone alpha to take you as his? After what his father did to us?"

"Alpha Fin is not the one in the wrong. If you're talking about the time you came there seeking help you talked to the wrong brother. You didn't actually talk to the alpha. If you would have gone back when mother told you, you would have been able to get the help that you needed! But no! You let your ego take over and you did this to your family!" I pressed my finger into his chest. Pushing him into the wall. "You chose to let Alpha Christian take me to keep your pack. You rolled over and let him take me.

Instead of going back and asking for help or going to mother's sister's pack for help. You bowed down! You are no alpha!"

"Your mother told me the same and I should have listened to her. But I was a younger alpha and didn't want to tell other alphas that I was weak. But I made up for that. I've taken down the Shonkinite pack. Their alpha is no longer able to lead. I'm the one that has done this." The manic laughter that escaped him showed me just how much he had gone mad. I didn't see it before when he was calm but I did now.

I had heard of this with mates. That if one dies that they lose a part of themselves if they are bonded strongly. From what my mother had written in her journal they were, which was the reason that it hurt her so badly when he let me go.

"A few years later we had another pup, a boy this time. He would have been your sibling." His eyes changed again, to hold sorrow that was so deep that nothing anyone would say would take that away. "The alpha that you say wasn't the real alpha that I met with that day. Came to Obsidian pack and tore us apart. He killed your mother as I tried to hide her and my son. That alpha took my world from me. He almost took my life but my beta saved me and I was able to get away."

The sound of the door opening caught my attention and his. I turned to see Fin with Harlen behind him. The man that called himself my father grabbed me by the neck with a claw stretching out to my jugular.

CHAPTER FORTY-FIVE

Fin

I couldn't help the deja vu that came over me when I saw the male, that I had been hunting, grab hold of my mate and the single claw that inched its way to her jugular. With my heart racing I never took my eyes off Nikita. Why was my life so cruel that it put my mate in danger?

"You take one step closer and I will end her life!"

Aloysuis was boiling inside of me. Harlen's hand went to my shoulder and I realized that I was subtly shifting to my massive white wolf.

Alpha, we need to be careful. We don't want to make him kill her. He has Bella tied up. Harlen's voice kept me grounded as I stared at my mate.

My gaze went to the man's eyes and I noticed that his was the same color as hers. She looked like him a tiny bit. If I hadn't been with Nikita for as long as I had, I would have missed it. Could they be related? If so, who was he to her? Everyone from this pack other than Olli and Nikita was killed.

"Why don't we talk this through. Let Nikita and my Beta female go and we will talk about what you want." I spoke to the enraged man that held my mate tightly to him. Making no move to go forward or leave the room.

"There's nothing to talk about. Just go away!"

"Look, let me take my Beta and then me and you can discuss this. You don't want to kill the woman in your arms." I had to get him to let her go. Otherwise if she died I'd surely lose my mind and I didn't need that I had a pack to run.

The male's nostrils flared and his eyes hardened. His canines started to crest his lips as he stared back at me. His grip tightening on Nikita's throat as he realized that I was her mate. "You are the Dolostone alpha. Your father was the one that took my family away from me!"

"Why would he do that? I think that you need to know which brother you were talking to..."

"You think that I would believe you? Your father turned me away!" He snarled at me while tightening his hand even tighter around Nikita's throat. She was turning blue. I had to get him to let her go and soon.

"Look we can argue about this but you need to loosen your grip on her or you won't have anyone to hide behind."

Fin, look if anything happens to me. Don't blame yourself please.

Nikita, you know that I won't be able to do that. This right here is too close for comfort as it is and a hell of a memory that I don't want to remember right now.

The look in her eyes as her wolf started to take over worried me. Even with her being an alpha I couldn't let her shift. She was pregnant. I had to think of how to get them both out of here safe. Nikita then did something I didn't even see her do. She took her elbow and slammed it deep into his hip bone causing his grip to loosen and she stumbled away to Bella.

I shifted and grabbed the man by his arm and pulled him out of the room. Harlen went in to help untie Bella before shielding them both from anything that might harm them. The male before me began to shift as I pulled him out of the rundown packhouse.

When he completely shifted I realized who he was to her. He had to be her father. His line was the only one that had those types of markings. From what Olli told me the night before he talked with Nikita. He started doing unethical things in the pack. Which was the reason Olli left to go rogue.

This had to be Alpha Cain that Ollie was talking about and in wolf form he looked exactly like my mate. Part of me wanted to kill him because the craze in his eyes like he was rapid could only mean that the broken bond had been getting to him. The only way to cure that and that would be to end his life.

The only good thing about this, it wasn't rabies and I wouldn't ever get this unless someone took Nikita away from me. Which wouldn't happen, and I was going to make sure that it didn't. Alpha Cain moved left while I jumped in front of him. I didn't know if he was trying to get back in the room with Nikita or if he was trying to circle me. Either way I wasn't going to let him do it. I growled before lunging at him.

His claws raked down my shoulder before I grabbed hold of the tuft of hair in his mane. Slinging him away from the pack house. I didn't want him to be anywhere near there as Harlen brought Nikita and Bella out of the house. It was no longer safe in that room for them. If I would have known that the old alpha was still around then I would have put Blake and Conner to guard them in our suite.

Cain came at me, canines bared and drool streaming down his jowls. He was really wanting to kill me, he really thought that who he talked to was my father. At this point I didn't know if I should try to drug him and take him back to a cell in Dolostone to set him straight or give him mercy and take his life.

Nikita needed closure too. So I decided that I was going to try to set him straight. As he lunged I lunged with him and clamped my jaws around his neck. To put him to sleep. Cain struggled and then finally slumped on the ground at my feet.

Harlen came out with Bella and Nikita. Blake limped over as the patrol that I brought with me came up. I had made it here before them trying my best to catch up with the wolf that had kept me at bay.

Roco, James grab him and bring him back to Dolostone and put him in a cell. We will deal with him in the morning. Make sure to put him in the alpha one.

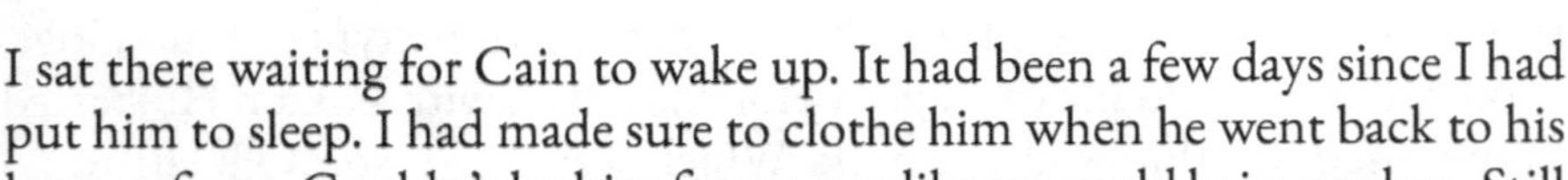

I sat there waiting for Cain to wake up. It had been a few days since I had put him to sleep. I had made sure to clothe him when he went back to his human form. Couldn't let him freeze, not like we could being wolves. Still I wouldn't be like my uncle and let someone stay naked.

Cain began to stir as I sat there watching him. Shaking his head as he sat up against the wall. When he realized where he was. He stood and came over to the bars and growled. "Let me out! You cannot keep me from my daughter!"

"You and I need to have a talk. Since you are in that cell it looks like you will have plenty of time." His eyes flashed to his wolf's while he stood there facing me.

"You are just like your father. Thinking of no one but yourself."

"I think of a lot more people other than myself. My pack and my Luna will always come first." I crossed my arms over my chest and widened my stance. This was going to take a while. He was just like Roy there wasn't much I could do.

"Ha! You will cause her death."

"No, I won't. If anyone dies it will be me. I will not let her or my pup go the way my chosen went. When you had her like you did, all I could think about was that day that my uncle had Kalila..."

"Kalila? Beta Mark's Daughter? You took her as a chosen! You son of a bitch! Why would you take away her fated! You see all you care about is yourself!" The bars shook in front of me as I continued to stare at him. He didn't know what sacrifices I had made. "And now she will never know that love. You then took MY daughter!"

"I chose her because one of the wolves in your pack rejected her. So if anyone was going to lose out on a fated it would have been me. I would have lost out in the end, not her." I answered him before I thought about what I had said, because it would have affected Nikita as well. "It doesn't matter now. The Moon Goddess has already punished me. I don't intend to piss her off again."

"Ah yes the Moon Goddess, the one that didn't bat an eye when your father tore my pack apart." He snarled back at me. I can relate to that emotion. When she took Kalila but now I knew why and that was because Nikita was my destiny and had always been.

"My father was dead when your pack was taken from you. My uncle had taken my pack from me and killed my parents. I then went rogue to figure out how I was going to get my pack back. But as time went on I didn't feel that my pack needed me anymore because I didn't think they would want me." I made sure to hold his gaze. He needed to know that I was telling the truth. "My uncle did a lot of evil things when he had hold of the Dolostone pack. But he has been dead for almost a year now. He will never do the things that he did ever again."

It was a quick moment but I was sure that I noticed the realization before his anger showed through again. If he lost his mate all those years ago and made it this long then he was in the end stages now anyway. There was no coming back from this for him and I hated that for him and Nikita. She needed to know her family but not like this. "How long have you been alone?"

"A little over ten and a half years."

"I'm sorry for what my uncle has done to you and your pack. But know that your legacy will live on through Nikita. Our pup will be the strongest wolf born since he will be from a female born alpha." Cain glanced up at me when I mentioned Nikita and the pup that would be born soon.

"My daughter is with pup?" I nodded and Cain backed away from the cell bars and slid down the brick.

"Cain, were you the one killing the Shonkinite pack?"

Cain nodded as the sob crossed his lips. I didn't know why he was crying now but I had him mostly calm. I needed to find out the answers. "Why were you punishing the Shonkinite pack?"

"Their previous alpha took my pup from me and then his son found his mate. He was to have his son choose Nikita. Because he wanted a strong heir but when the Dolostone alpha came he didn't even come to help us. He turned me away when I came to him for help when I was all alone."

Hearing him talk like this. Made my heart hurt for him, to ask someone for help and nothing. No wonder he was killing people off in that pack. But the fact that he put them on my pack was unnerving. The other question was did he poison his own daughter? "Cain, did you poison Nikita at her Luna ceremony?"

"No! I'd never do that to my own daughter. I overheard the other alpha and another wolf talking about it before she had her ceremony. I wanted to keep her from getting hurt but they did it anyway. I didn't know if she was going to live. So I began poisoning his pack."

CHAPTER FORTY-SIX

Nikita

I stood there on the stairs as Fin led my father to his death. My father was already too far gone to help him. He had been without his mate and family for a long time. I didn't know exactly how Fin was going to dispatch him, but I couldn't just sit in our room. This was going to be the last time I saw my father. I didn't know if I was relieved or sad.

As I watched him and the warriors take him toward the pack hospital, I realized that he was going to let him go easily. Shonkinite pack's beta was meeting with us later, since they no longer had an alpha or an heir. There were two ways to do this: they could make their beta alpha or they could merge into our pack but still live where they are at. Then again, they could also move into the pack town on our territory and we demolish those on the other territory so that we can use that one for something different.

But that would be decided later. Now we were handling the issue of my dad. I didn't even get to know him, to learn from him like any other pup would from their father. It's crazy how my life would have been different if he had just returned to the Dolostone pack or even went to my mother's sister's pack. The sound of footsteps brought my attention to behind me.

Bella came up to my side and pulled me close to her. She had been the closest thing to a mother I had ever experienced. Tobey and Sydnie were lucky to have that type of mother. I mean I had a mother but she didn't give me as much attention as I thought a pup should have. I mean hell once I started to get older and started my training she wasn't any more attentive than she was when I was younger. Which was probably the reason I pushed myself to become the best.

"I know that you didn't have many people as far as family. But we are here for you and Dolostone is your family now. And was supposed to be when you got your wolf." Bella held my gaze, while we stood there.

"I know and thank you for making me feel like I belong." I smiled at her as the warriors and my mate disappeared with my father.

"Let us go inside and prepare for the Shonkinite wolves to get here. I know it's going to be hard for them to decide on what to do." I nodded and turned on my heel with Bella and headed into the packhouse. This wasn't a time to think about the pending death of him. The man that thought that he was doing what was right. When he was most definitely doing the wrong thing.

Other wolves were already cleaning and getting things ready. The only reason we were here was to make sure that it all went the right way. Not like I didn't trust them because I trusted these wolves with my life.

"Bella, other than my father have you seen someone that did this?" I stopped us just inside the foyer. My pup inside of me was flipping and rolling around in my stomach. The happiness that he brought me was something I couldn't deny.

"Only one other time but he was already evil and it didn't mess with him like it did with your father. He was also able to keep it hidden for a very long time. Until he took this pack from Fin." Bella answered me.

Of course it was him. Fin's uncle. I never would have thought that he had a mate. But the Moon Goddess wouldn't keep a mate from someone. Everyone was equal in her eyes. Some just had to wait longer than others. Like Fin and I. "Fin's uncle is the wolf that you are talking about."

"Yes, Harlen told me that he saw it more, the madness, after he took over here. Which was why he didn't think about the wolves here or the packs he conquered. Harlen was trying to keep as many of the wolves from dying but it didn't always work."

"I can't believe this. Does Fin know?" I glanced over to her. There was no way that he knew that his uncle was like this.

"No, but I'm sure Harlen will tell him. It's been known that mates will do that. But it's so rare." She shook her head as one of the omegas that had been running with the towels tripped. Bella headed over and helped her pick them up.

Maybe that's why Fin didn't go through that when he lost his chosen. I wonder if the reason my father was so insane was because he had literally lost his entire family. He didn't know that I was alive and okay. So he could only assume that I was gone as well. This man watched another alpha take his mate and his heir from him in a blink of an eye.

Fin sat at the head of the table with my chair beside him. Harlen sat to his right and two Deltas sat to his left. My old beta sat at the other end with two of their warriors. The beta looked tired so I didn't blame him. It was hard running a pack. I didn't know how Fin had done it for as long as he had.

But I guess when you are trained to lead a pack from a young age. You can handle almost anything and Fin was most definitely able to handle it.

"Beta Nathaniel, what have you decided?" Fin's question brought Nathaniel's eyes to him they looked dim.

"Alpha Fin I believe that it would be better for my pack to integrate them into yours. I know that you have a beta and if I have to go rogue I will." He was resigned to do what he needed to ensure that the Shonkinite pack had a place to be.

Fin sat forward and stared at the beta before him and he rapped his fingers on the wooden table. My heart was breaking for my former pack. Even though they were not my birth pack as I originally thought, they still were the ones I grew up with. "You do not have to go rogue. I'd be happy if you accepted the position of Gamma."

"Of course I would gladly take the position." Beta Nathaniel didn't even hesitate to take it.

Fin nodded and sat back in his chair. I didn't think that this would be settled this easily but with the way Nathaniel looked and acted it seemed like he was ready to hand over the reins. I couldn't blame him. Even only helping with some pack things with Fin I knew what it was like.

"Good, we will start making preparations with the move. I'll go over to the territory with you in a couple of weeks to give them time to pack up everything. We will bring trucks over to bring their stuff over to this part. There will be homes available to them. Any unmated wolves that are old enough can move in with the others here that are unmated. Patrol is not an option and since we are expanding the size there will be more of need for wolves to patrol." Fin stood from his chair and glanced between Nathaniel and the two warriors. They both nodded and Nathaniel bowed his head. He had always been one to heed what his superiors have told him. "You and the warriors are welcome to stay the night and head back in the morning. Since you would be taking over the Gamma position you will be over the Deltas and warriors."

"Of course Alpha Fin. Thank you again. I'm sorry Luna Nikita for what had happened to your real family." Nathaniel glanced over to me and I nodded my head. I didn't need him to apologize for something he didn't have anything to do with.

"Harlen, can you show them where they can stay please?" Harlen stood up and motioned for the three male wolves to follow him.

I watched as the four wolves went out the door and our deltas followed them out. Leaving only me and Fin in the room. Since arriving here I had never been in this room. It was a beautiful room even if the most important decisions and discussions were made in this room.

"How's our little boy today?" Fin turned to me and pulled me close.

"He's been moving like crazy all morning. Now he's not moving as much." I rubbed my hand over my swollen belly, brushing it along his as I did.

"He's tired himself out."

"Maybe, but Bella says that when they stop moving as much it's almost time." I chuckled as Fin's hands came up to cup my face.

"Then he will be here soon. You are going to be a wonderful mother." The deep and husky tone in Fin's voice caused goosebumps to race down my body.

"You don't know that. I've never had a family that really treated me like their own. What do I know about parenting?" I sighed as Fin continued to hold my gaze. He was always so confident about things. I was too but not this. This was something I couldn't figure out.

"You have me here to help you. Bella and the rest of the pack are here too. We won't let you fail, I promise you that."

My heart clenched at his words. How could he be like this after everything that he had been through? My mate had a heart of gold even if he didn't always show it to others. But he loved his pack there was no doubt about that.

"Thank you. I never thought I'd have anything like this."

"Well you will always have it now."

I woke up to the most goddess awful pain. Fin's side of the bed had already gotten cold letting me know that he was already out and about in the pack. Enyo was laying down with her head on her paws, her tail slowly sweeping back and forth.

Getting up I went to the bathroom since the pup was on my bladder. At one point I didn't think I would make it. Between getting up and waddling over to the toilet the pain became worse. I sat on the cold porcelain seat and let go.

The gush that came after startled me and the pain after that got worse. *FIN!*

Nikita, are you okay? The worry that laced Fin's tone brough it through the bond. He was scared.

No, I need you here! Like now! I begged him through another bout of pain, I needed him with me now. I needed his calm exterior to ground me.

I'm on my way. Bella will be there in a few moments. There was nothing more that I could do but wait on them. I didn't know how far he was away from the packhouse.

When the door burst open and Bella was staring at me I felt relieved. I wasn't going to be alone with this. That's when the next crumpling pain hit. I didn't know how much longer I was going to be able to handle this.

"Nikita, I know that you are hurting right now. And I can help you until Fin gets here but I need you to get up from that toilet. We need to get on the bed." Bella moved forward and helped me to a standing position.

My knees felt like jelly and I didn't know if I was going to be able to stay on my feet long. Bella wrapped her arm around my waist and then put mine over her shoulder. She guided me to the bed. Fuck why did this have to hurt so bad? I normally was able to handle any pain I was dealt. But this made me feel like I was weak.

"Lay back, Fin will be here soon and I believe Doc will be here too."

CHAPTER FORTY-SEVEN

FIN

I made it to the pack house in record time from the edge of the territory. Something was wrong with Nikita and when she called me like that through the mate link. All I could think about was when Kalila did the same thing.

The first person I mindlinked after talking with Nikita was Bella. She was already in the packhouse and she would be able to get to her quickly. Doc was next on my list because it was close to her having our pup and I wanted him there. I had never heard the anguish in her voice like that.

Not bothering to shift back to my human form, I burst through the main door of the packhouse. Causing screams from the omegas that were in the foyer and making some of the guards come out of the kitchen that were heading to bed. When they realized that it was me they backed down.

Doc was taking the stairs two at a time and I ran up to him grabbing him by the shirt. Jumping the rest of the landings to get to the fourth floor. I placed Doc down at the door and he opened it while I shifted back to my human form. The ones in this room had seen me plenty of times in the nude. Besides we were a wolf pack it was normal.

I followed Doc into my bedroom and could hear Nikita groaning just before Doc threw open the doors. Bella was at her side holding her hand and wiping her forehead. Doc sat everything down beside Bella and she looked up at me.

She's in labor and it's progressing fast. Bella's tone in our mindlink was hurried and out of breath.

How close is she? I questioned her as I stood there trying to get my bearings.

Very. Her voice had turned stern as she stared back at me.

I went over to the other side of the bed and sat next to Nikita. She opened her eyes and glanced over to me. That's when I realized that I could feel her contractions and that was what was happening this morning while I was out running. They were not too painful which was probably the reason she had stayed asleep until a few minutes ago.

"I'm right here my feisty Luna. Let's get this pup out." I whispered to her and she nodded. Kissing her forehead she barred down as Doc moved to the end of the bed.

"Okay Luna when you feel the next contraction I need you to push down."

Two hours later Nikita was sitting up on the bed feeding our pup. She had done amazing through everything. There for a few moments I thought that it was going to be bad. The pain that she had gone through almost toppled me. But she fought through it and brought the most beautiful boy into this world.

Nurses had come in and weighed him and made sure everything was good. They even cleaned up anything that was soiled during the birth. I had moved over to the large balcony doors to give everyone room to do what they needed to do. Still standing here I couldn't bring myself to bother her as she sat there with him in her arms.

When he opened his eyes they were her color. Which didn't bother me at all. Nikita had beautiful eyes. Mine were dull in comparison to theirs. Doc was impressed with how he started to eat as soon as he was out and lying on her chest. The boy sure could eat.

I couldn't take my eyes off of them. Nikita was doing great as a mother just like I thought that she would be. I never had a doubt in my mind that she would be the best at this along with being the Luna that my pack needed. And now the two on that bed would show the pack just how much this pack would grow.

"Why are you staring at me?" Nikita never looked up to me as she kept her eyes on our boy.

"Just looking at the two most important people in my life." I moved from my spot by the window over to them and sat down beside them.

I very carefully ran the back of my finger over my son's small chubby cheek. The soft mewl that came from him made the grin on my face more of a smile. His skin was soft against my aged finger. Turning my attention to Nikita, I pulled her to me as we sat there staring at the little pup that we made. The little pup snuggled in closer before he popped off her nipple. His little sigh while he relaxed in her arms made me happy. "I think we need another."

Nikita socked me in the arm, it wasn't too hard but she made sure to put a little strength into it. Rubbing where she socked me. She shook her head and giggled. "We can have another later. But right now he is all we need."

Over the next few days the pack had brought in the things that they had made for the pup. We had finally decided on a name for the pup. Grayson was already alert and active. Just like any wolf pup. The entire pack was overjoyed and the doors were constantly opening to allow others in to come see the new alpha pup. Nikita had been near to pick him up and get him away from the many gathered wolves there giving him their gifts.

I stood in the corner watching as they all presented my son with the things that they had brought him. Harlen and Nathaniel stood by the door. Once he brought the rest of his pack over he found his mate in Jade, here in the Dolostone pack. He had quickly become part of the pack. Which was why I loved this pack so much they were normally very pleasant. Well, besides Jade giving Nikita an issue.

Since we had found the culprit and dealt with him. It was hard to put down a man who had gone mad from losing his mate. If I ever lost Nikita it would probably do me the same way but I'd probably off myself. Because I couldn't live without her.

Alpha, Rhyolite Alpha is here. With his mother.

Thanks, Hank make sure they are brought here to the packhouse.

Of course Alpha.

I had spoken to Nolen a couple of days ago to see if he would come and bring his mother with him. He had told me that he would come. I didn't tell him about the journal or that Nikita just might be his cousin. That was something that I wanted her to be able to tell them.

They arrived a few minutes after Hank mindlinked me. Making my way over to the door, I reached out my hand to Nolen and he took my hand.

"Thanks for coming. How was the trip over?"

"Good, just a little confused about why I needed to bring my mother." Nolen chuckled as his mother came up beside him. It was the first time I had seen this woman but I could tell that she was related to my Luna. Nolen didn't look a damn thing like his mother, he was his father's clone.

"We need to talk about something and it involves both of you."

"Really? Now, and why am I just now finding out?" Nolen glanced over to his mother. Who was staring at something over my shoulder.

"I would really like to meet that female over there with her pup." His mother's voice sounded in awe as slipped her arm from her son's and headed over to my mate.

"Come with me and have your mother meet us in my office. I'll get my mate." Nolen nodded and I went over to my mate.

Nolen took hold of his mother's arm and led her behind us to my office. I know that Nikita was nervous but they needed to talk. She needed to know her aunt and hopefully she would be able to tell her about her mother. Nikita had brought her mother's journal to the office. She was hoping that Nolen's mother would be able to tell her about the woman she had never gotten to meet.

Opening the door, I stepped aside and allowed Nikita to go in and then Nolen and his mother. I closed the door and headed to my desk. Taking in each of their faces. Nolen's mother continued to stare at Nikita like she recognized her. Which made me wonder if she looked like her mother.

"So I brought you both here to first meet my boy but also to talk about some other things that may or may not bring us some insight." I told them. Nolen nodded and then sat back on the couch that he was lounging on.

"Who are your parents?" Nolen's mother's question brought my gaze to her as she continued to stare at Nikita.

Nikita rose from her seat with our son in her arms and grabbed her mother's journal from my desk. She took it over to Nolen's mother and then stood there. The dark-haired woman looked from the book to my mate before she opened it to the first page.

The hitch of her breath confirmed that she was my mate's aunt and the tears that pooled in her eyes as she read through the first entry made it concrete. She stood from her seat and moved the hair from my mate's face as she continued to study her features.

"But how? She told me that you had died. In her letter to me you were stillborn."

"This here tells why. If you want to read it." Nikita pointed to the book in her aunt's hand. "She says why. I met my father, he told me what happened to her and my brother. He had gone insane. It all started after Wade took her from him."

"I thought all my family had been lost that day. But you have been alive all this time? Where?" The way she held my mate's face was just like any mother would to their child.

"I grew up in the Shonkinite pack. They trained me to be a warrior."

Nolen's mother dropped the journal and brought her other hand up to Nikita's face and pulled her to her. Before letting her go. "I started asking questions and didn't tell you my name. My name is Britona. I'm sure that you gave your opponents hell."

"That she did. The first time I saw her. She was beating the shit out of a wolf ten times bigger than she was." I chuckled as Britona turned her gaze to mine and then back to Nikita's.

"I'm sure you did. Because you have your mother's strength. And are an alpha born female. This little boy along with his cousins are the only ones that are born of two alphas. These three will be the strongest of them all."

Nolen stood from the couch and pulled my mate into a hug. I didn't have an issue with that. He was her family after all and I was glad that he and his mother were allowing her to be a part of that. This is what she was supposed to have. A family that was her blood, one that would forever be with her.

I continued to stand at my desk allowing them to bond. Her aunt finally reached out to hold Grayson. Britonia is right, he and his two sister cousins will be the strongest ones in the land. There is no doubt about that.

DID YOU LOVE THE FALLEN ALPHA?

I hope that you loved reading Fin and Nikita's journey as much I did writing this book. Most of you have read The Second Alpha Heir and had requested to know more about the other wolves that helped out Nolen. So I started with Fin.
Wherever you are most comfortable, please consider leaving a review on Amazon, Goodreads, or social media. Your honest review means the world to an indie author like me!
Love,
C. L. Ledford

Also by C.L. Ledford

ABOUT C. L. LEDFORD

C. L. Ledford was born in the city of Chattanooga, TN. Where she was raised by her grandparents, to be a strong and independent person. She became an avid reader at the age of eleven, when her fifth grade teacher gifted her the book, The Black Stallion. With this book her love of books grew.

In middle school she began to write what would be one of many books swirling around in her head. Silver Moon Kiss came to life with two chapters and multiple scenes before it was packed away and not thought of until after she had become an adult. C. L. Ledford writes in Paranormal Romance and Contemporary Romance. Her first published book The Second Alpha Heir released on June 14, 20 22.

By this time she had moved to a little town called Ringgold, GA and married her husband where they raise their three children and five German Shorthair dogs. Along with her love of writing and reading, she also enjoys hunting behind her dogs.